A TASTE OF PASSION

"Come now, I would like to see the face of the woman that I'm about to bed—or had you planned to take the initiative?"

"Why do you think I'm here?" she taunted. Minna reached out and placed her hand on his bare chest. He was smooth, warm, and velvety to her touch, yet she was acutely aware of the steely muscles underneath. There was nothing to stop him from overpowering her and taking her. Daringly, she dragged her fingertips along his hard flesh. "You're adorable, Lord Whitecliffe."

He tilted his head back and laughed. "The game begins. Let me be by fire touched." He drew her up and held her closer. "The fire of your ardor."

CAPTURE THE GLOW OF
ZEBRA'S *HEARTFIRES!*

MARIA GREENE

MINE FOREVERMORE

To Amber,
Good luck with
your writing!!
Maria Greene
1993

ZEBRA BOOKS
KENSINGTON PUBLISHING CORP.

ZEBRA BOOKS are published by

Kensington Publishing Corp.
475 Park Avenue South
New York, NY 10016

First Printing: August, 1993

Printed in the United States of America

Dedicated in loving memory to my grandmother, Signe Grannas, who, despite her hardships, was the strongest woman I've ever known.

Special thanks to the ophthalmologist Philip Lempert who explained the various types of glaucoma to me.

Prologue

Minna Smith never dreamed it would be so difficult to commit suicide. Always neat, she disliked the idea of an untidy death by drowning, but she could see no other way out but to jump into the river. In her mind she pictured herself floating lifeless in the water, hair clinging to her face, and mouth grotesquely open. And what about the eyes . . . would they give the person who found her body nightmares for the rest of his life? Ugh, she thought. Could she die with that offense on her conscience?

She shivered with dread as she stared at the murky Thames flowing under the bridge. The water looked awfully cold, but the air seemed colder still. Freezing drizzle soaked her cloak and dreary shades of gray surrounded her—London in the January gloom, looking just as listless and drab as she felt inside. Her legs were leaden weights as she dragged herself toward the middle of the bridge. She would jump at the deepest point of the river so that she would sink fast, and her heavy cloak would prevent her from rising to the surface.

Recoiling at the thought, she wished she had chosen a more ladylike way to die. But she had to act before she changed her mind. She could already imagine the frigid water closing around her, and she sobbed in desperation.

"God, what is there left? Nothing," she said to herself. "Less than nothing. After years of toil, all I have is a bad name." Other than Ellie, no one cared whether she lived or died, and she was tired of the gnawing hunger, tired of struggling to survive, of returning every evening from a grueling day at the workshop to her rat-infested attic room. She was simply *too tired*. Her back always ached, and her eyes stung from working day after day on minute embroidery in the weak light of smoky candles. Perhaps she could have lived with those conditions; she could have gone on dreaming of a better life, but now everything had changed. First she'd lost her beloved parents, then her home, and today, her employment.

Accused of stealing one of the spools of gold thread that was used to embroider leaf patterns and birds on sumptuous gowns, she had been kicked out without a reference. This prevented her from finding another job in London. At least Mrs. Hawkins, the owner of the shop, had let her go without calling in the law, but what did it matter now?

Minna sighed. She was an excellent seamstress, but who would hire a thief? Not that she had stolen the thread, another seamstress had, a schemer who had Mrs. Hawkins's ear. *I was so careful not to antagonize anyone, but it didn't help,* Minna thought. *That woman wanted my job; it paid slightly better than monogramming handkerchiefs by the dozen.*

Even though she'd been at the point of starving since her parents died, she had never stooped to stealing.

She dragged her icy hand across her eyes, but tears kept blinding her and clogging her throat. Besides reading and writing, she had acquired no other skills but sewing since there hadn't been time to learn anything else. Mother had taught her everything she knew, then had died quietly one morning, slumping over in her chair during breakfast.

"Why go on living this poverty-ridden, useless life?" Minna said to the empty night as the drizzle soaked through a threadbare place on her shoulder.

A fire bell clanged in the distance. Sounds of hurried footsteps echoed in the darkness, anonymous shadows flitted past her, but no one took any notice of her. She wiped her tears on the damp sleeve. Her eyes burned from the soot-laden fog, and a noxious fume rose from the river. "It must end."

Coward! a voice remarkably like that of her father said in her head, and Minna shrunk against the railing. Her worn-out boot dislodged a pebble and it fell into the black river with a plop. Yes, her father, the gentle curate, would have called her a coward. He had always had a firm belief that people were put on this earth for a purpose; to fulfill one's allotted destiny without complaint. "Life is nothing but hardships," he used to say, "but we are here to learn, to conquer our weaknesses. You must rely on the Heavenly Father to guide you."

His voice rang so clearly in her mind that she thought he was standing next to her. She stared into the water, almost feeling it pull her toward the glacial depths below as though slippery, wet fingers were reaching up and beckoning her. It would be a relief to die — it would be easy. The struggle would be over.

"Papa, I have no fight left in me. I want to join you and Mother on the other side," she whispered.

9

Coward! the voice in her head shouted once again.

She closed her mind to that insistent voice and hitched up her patched, gray skirt high enough to swing one leg over the rail. The cold air touching her bare skin made her tremble, and sorrow tightened further in her chest.

Just the other leg, then a push against the railing, and she would be free. Her heartbeat pounded in her ears, crowding out all other sounds. A fear like nothing she'd ever felt before overcame her. She was cold, so cold.

The other leg was easier than the first, just a swing and she was balancing on her backside on the top rail.

One small push. . . . She wanted to pray for help, but nothing came to her except more fear—paralyzing terror. A drumming sound penetrated her thoughts, and, dazed though she was, she recognized the clatter of galloping horses on the bridge. Or was it the sound of her racing heart?

Fool! the voice came again, jolting her out of her trance. She laced her fingers in desperate prayer. "Heavenly Father, save me from myself . . . please forgive me . . . forgive me." Her lips were stiff and cold as she formed the word *help*.

Then she gripped the railing with both hands and prepared to push away. She emptied her mind and jabbed her toes against the wood. Taking a deep breath—

"Stop right there! What are you about to do?" someone barked behind her.

She turned her head, registering a stately man with snow-white hair under a tall beaver hat, sloping shoulders, and a swinging black cape. When he came closer, she saw that he was only middle-aged, despite his silver hair. His face was hard as stone, and wrathful. A shiver of unease traveled up her spine.

He gripped both her arms and dragged her from the railing before she could protest. Automatically, she noticed his black, bushy eyebrows and small, penetrating eyes. She sensed no kindness in him and tried to pull away, but his grip was too strong to break.

"What folly were you about to commit?" he demanded, shaking her. "Suicide, by Gad!"

"I don't really want to," she whispered. "But I have no choice."

He shook her until her teeth rattled. "There's always a choice," he said. "Give me one reason why death would be preferable to life, and I'll let you jump."

"I've lost everything."

He snorted. "We all lose something or someone important in life. Do you think you're an exception?"

Minna shook her head in anguish. "I can't carry the burden of my misery any longer. It gets worse every day."

"Miss, only weaklings choose the easy way out."

She couldn't reply, but she knew that he was right. "I'm sorry," she whispered, as if she'd wronged him in some way.

"I came just in time," he said and dropped his hands from her arms with a heavy sigh. "You must promise not to do anything so foolish ever again."

Tears scalded her eyes, and she couldn't speak. *It had happened!* Her prayer had been answered, after all. She couldn't stop shaking, and she was unable to stop her teeth from chattering.

He pressed a flask to her lips, and brandy burned her throat as she swallowed. "I'm glad I arrived in time," he said. "Is life really so bad that you have to consider suicide?"

"Today was the last straw." Her voice sounded childish and complaining to her own ears. She looked at him for his reaction, but his face showed nothing. She could barely make out his features in the murky light from a lantern at the end of the bridge. Judging by his proper speech, she guessed that he was a gentleman. He was wearing a silk cloak, black evening attire, and a faultlessly starched neckcloth. He was a distinguished man who wore his years with grace, yet not a man to inspire confidence. Minna's uneasy feeling increased as she watched his hard face, but she pushed it away. After all, hadn't he stopped her from killing herself?

"I, too, tried to end it all once," he said, his voice lowering an octave. "I was stupid. If someone hadn't stopped me like I stopped you, I wouldn't have had a chance to discover that life truly can change for the better."

"Change? Never!" Minna said with conviction. "I lost my parents six months ago, and ever since, I've struggled to survive." She paused. "Life is not the same without them, and as far as poverty—"

He thrust the brandy flask toward her. "Drink some more. It will take away the chill."

She obeyed, willing to listen to anything he had to say, but he said nothing more, only stared at her as she sipped from the flask.

She felt as if she'd been outside of herself, floating about in a thousand fragments. The brandy slowly made all the pieces come together again, and she could breathe more easily.

"You know," he said. "I would like to help you, Miss . . . ?"

"Minna . . . Minerva Smith," she offered. "You've

12

helped me already. I know I was feeble-minded to think that I could end it all. The madness has left me. I just wish I had something to live for."

"What would you like to do if you had the wherewithal?" He seemed to hold his breath as he waited for her answer.

She dashed her fingers along the dripping brim of her soggy straw bonnet, and pulled her cloak closer around her. "I would like to have my own dressmaker shop," she said without hesitation. "I'm capable of doing much better work than I did at Mrs. Hawkins's. She only did outwork from the affluent modistes in Bond Street."

"Hmmm, a very tall dream, m'dear." He tapped his chin with the knob of his cane as if deep in thought. "Tailoring is becoming more exclusive every year, y'know. A difficult trade indeed."

"My designs would be first class. I'd hire as many starving needleworkers, cutters, finishers, and shop girls as I could." Her voice tightened with concern. "I hate to see the pale, despairing faces of poverty every day."

He didn't seem to hear her. "I'm a rich man now," he said. "I wasn't always, but my import business has been highly successful." He reached into his pocket and pulled out a heavy leather purse. "I'm going to challenge you to do something with your life. You shall have this for a start, and then I shall let you have a draft of two hundred pounds on my bank."

She gasped. Two hundred pounds! A fortune. Never had she owned so much money, let alone *seen* it. "No, I can't accept that. I wouldn't know what to do with it."

He flung the purse at her brusquely, and she had to catch it against her chest. Without a word, he turned on his heel. "It's a challenge, Miss Smith. I

13

shall visit you in one year to see what you have done with my money."

"*Who* are you?" she cried after him. The purse weighed her hands down.

"My secretary shall find you wherever you are and forward the two hundred pounds. You must put the money to good use."

Too confused to figure out how the secretary could learn her whereabouts in the slums of the East End, she stared after him in silence. She never thought of returning the money. She sought the light of the lantern at the end of the bridge and pulled the drawstring apart. Gold sovereigns glittered in the faint light. There must be at least fifty of them—*fifty pounds!* She had to pinch herself to make sure that she was awake.

She couldn't take this much money from a stranger, but how would she find him and return the purse? He probably lived in Mayfair among other affluent Londoners. No doubt about it, he was a rich man, and she didn't even know his name.

Once again she weighed the pouch in her hands, then hid it deep in the pocket of her cloak. While her heart had been heavy with despair only a few minutes earlier, a warm hope now glowed in her chest. Again she pinched herself to make sure she was awake. The encounter with the stranger hadn't been a dream. She had been given a chance to leave her dreary existence behind and start anew. If ever they met again, he wouldn't be disappointed in her, she vowed with a smile. She hurried toward the nearest church where she planned to give thanks for the answered prayer.

At the end of the bridge, she ran into her only friend at the workshop, Ellie Nichols.

"Blind me, but I was 'fraid for you," Ellie said. "I

had an awful feelin' in me stomach that something bad had happened to you, Minna."

Minna placed her arm around the shorter woman's shoulders. They were as frail as a bird's wings. "It almost did. But now I'm rich, Ellie. You must help me to start my own business. You shall be head seamstress there, and you shall have enough food to eat every day, and the workrooms shall be warm and filled with light."

Ellie looked at her with huge, doe-like eyes. "Lawks, limitless food? You're a barmy one, an' that's a fact, Minna. Hunger has addled your brain. Where we goin'?"

"First, we're going to pray at St. Bride's, then we'll have a supper fit for royalty. After that we'll spend all night planning our future, and what a future it'll be!"

Chapter One

Five years later

Minna's knees were cradled by the soft, gray carpet in the fitting room as she pinned up the hem of the last customer of the day. The oil lamps with their frosted globes gave out a muted, expensive light, and the walls, painted a pale rose, were flattering to the patrons' complexions. The very air was hushed as if knowing that a viscountess was on the premises.

"That's the last fitting, Lady Minton-Brown," Minna said with pleasure. She viewed the dark blue evening gown critically. Every pleat, every stitch was faultless, the simple lines complimenting the viscountess's matronly figure.

The august customer made some comments in her modulated voice as Minna helped her fasten her old gown. On her way out she nodded so that the plumes in her straw bonnet swayed and said, "I'm very pleased with the dress, Madame LaForge. I shall refer my friends to you."

Minna locked the door, pulled the gray velvet curtains across the windows, and took a dance step across the floor. She admired the ornate mirrors on the walls of the oval showroom, and caressed the gilded chair rail along the wall. Even though she'd done it numerous times before, she tested the springs of the soft armchairs upholstered in the same gray velvet as the curtains. She tossed a pink silk pillow into the air and hummed a tune. She longed to embrace the whole shop and hug all the loyal seamstresses that worked upstairs.

She had succeeded, just like the stranger, whom she now knew as Mr. Thurlow Wylie, had predicted. The gentry had discovered her shop. The pain of all the back-breaking hours she'd worked to achieve her goal paled in this moment of ultimate triumph. With her own two hands, and Ellie's help, she had built a wall against poverty. Inside the tall, narrow house on Clifford Street, they were safe against the brutalities of London. A more intense satisfaction could not be found, she thought. She valued her employees' friendly smiles more than she valued the chime of coins when customers paid their bills. A gratitude so intense came over her that she had to jump up and twirl around the room. Where was Ellie? Her friend and partner ought to share this moment of bliss.

Fondly, Ellie Nichols studied Minna—now Madame La Forge, fashionable modiste at Clifford Street just off the busy Bond Street. According to Minna, La Forge meant "smithy" in French. Ellie shook her head in wonder as she, from the doorway, watched Minna dance in the showroom. Her friend was so clever, knowing all those foreign words. Minna called the elegant salon a smithy—a place where fashion was "wrought," just like iron was bent into different shapes at the blacksmith's. Minna was full of good ideas, and changing her name had

18

made her sound more important. She had even tried to borrow a French accent, but in the middle of a phrase spattered with French words, she often broke into laughter and ruined the effect. The customers adored Minna's sense of humor, and her judgment of their wardrobe. They trusted her sense of style, and anyone wearing a La Forge creation was an instant success. *Blind me, but she works day an' night, harder than anyone,* thought Ellie.

Ellie's back ached, but it was an ache of contentment. She didn't regret any of the grueling days of labor that had brought them to this rewarding time.

Minna's full-throated laugh sounded across the room, reminding Ellie of such a burst of mirth earlier in the day. Minna had been pinning a sky-blue bodice and skirt together on their best customer, Mrs. Davina "Divine" Shield, rich widow and fashionable hostess. Mrs. Shield was one of the loveliest ladies in London, but next to Minna, Ellie thought, her golden hair looked brassy, and her eyes pale in comparison.

Minna's hair was so light in color that it was like spun silver. Now it hung in a heavy coil at the nape of her neck and was covered with a golden net, but Ellie had seen it spread out. It reached almost to Minna's waist, and had a sheen like silk. Her features were so delicately molded, and her skin so pale and translucent that she looked like a fine porcelain figurine. Mrs. Shield's flawless milk-and-roses complexion looked blotchy in comparison. Minna's wide eyes were gray, sometimes a stormy, rainy gray, and sometimes like diamond chips when laughter or anger twinkled in her irises.

"Unfair," Ellie said and touched her own coarse, black hair, wishing she had been born with such patrician beauty. No, she had to be content with compliments about her brown, pansy-like eyes, and her narrow waist. *Gawd, at least I have forms,* she thought, and pulled down her bodice tight over her rounded breasts. Minna was like a rail. Her wrists were so thin they looked as if they would snap if someone squeezed too hard, but a person didn't notice the bony parts. Oh no, not on lovely, laughing Minna. Her hands were long and graceful, and she always spoke with them — lively expressions of movement. *The customers were always charmed by Minna's grace and her bubblin' laughter,* Ellie thought with a sigh. She had one flaw, though, a dark, crescent-shaped mole on her left cheek. Usually, she wore a round velvet patch over it, but it looked like the Creator had made a slip when he created Minna's flawless skin. Somehow it made her look less angelic — more human and Ellie considered it a blessing.

"Ellie, are you skulking in the shadows?" Minna asked as she stopped dancing. She came across the room, and Ellie admired her smooth, graceful walk. Minna glided like the angels in the church paintings at St. Bride's. *Life was far from fair,* she thought with a grimace.

They were standing by a shelf laden with bolts of shimmering silks and satins. "Aye, I was wool-gathering, thinkin' how fast the shop has grown in five years."

" 'Tis a miracle." Minna placed her hand on Ellie's arm. "Thanks to you, the gowns are perfect down to the last stitch."

"Without you we wouldn't be here in Clifford Street, would we now? You've a good head for business."

"Luck and hard work is all it is," Minna said with one of her winsome smiles. "When Madame Monette was moving back to France, I had to take the chance to get this shop. I don't regret it. And

20

when Mr. Wylie let us have the pick of the latest fabrics from France and India at his warehouses, why, that was the day when our fortune was made. Don't you agree?"

Ellie nodded. "New customers arrive every day."

"Divine Davina brought the first really influential customer to our shop," Minna said. "The viscountess."

"You know 'xactly what suits her and what doesn't, Minna. 'Tisn't just luck. You have the *eye*. All you have to do is to take a step back and *see* the costumes on them even before you have the material in your hand. Such a knack is hard to come by."

"And you know exactly what trim goes with every type of cloth. Oh, Ellie," Minna chuckled and tossed her head, "we are a superior pair of seamstresses, don't you think? The greatest! Let's have some tea."

Laughing, they walked arm in arm among the rows of shelves that were laden with tartan wools, kerseymere as soft as cat's fur, velvets, taffetas, twilled sarsenets, muslins, and French cambrics. Every color of the rainbow was represented in the bolts, every trim and button available in neat labeled drawers. The fashion whims of the aristocracy could be fulfilled at a moment's notice, and there were more fabrics to choose from than the gentry could possibly need.

Minna's heart contracted with pride, and she gave her partner's shoulders a soft squeeze. "Ell, you're my best friend, you know that." She shared a small apartment above the shop with Ellie. Their six embroidery girls, two pattern cutters, four needleworkers, and the rest of the work force lived in the annex that formed an L at the back of the shop. If the weather was favorable, like today, she would share a late tea with Ellie at the round table under the elm

21

tree that stood in the middle of the paved courtyard. In the winter they sat in front of a cozy fire in their minuscule sitting room upstairs.

Mrs. Collins, combined cook and char, was talking to a filthy woman outside, and Minna noticed the poor beggar's deformed face in the slit of moth-eaten shawls. Minna had told her staff never to turn away the hungry, and every day Mrs. Collins fed someone on the back steps.

The old cook glanced at Minna and motioned across the yard with her elbow.

Minna saw that Mrs. Collins had covered the table under the elm with a white tablecloth and the best china. To her surprise, Mr. Thurlow Wylie, the man who had given her the money pouch that had started her business, was seated in one of the chairs.

He looked pinched and old, shoulders bony under the fine material of his gray jacket. His already rigid face looked harder, and she wished he would soften sometimes. They had known each other for five years now, and he never unbent enough to smile. Fortune had not brought him happiness. He was always proper and precise in his business dealings with her, and she appreciated the support from his vast warehouses by the docks. He would always try to find the items that she sought and sell them to her at a fair price.

His shoes were — as always — polished to a shine, and he was now constantly using a cane to support his weak left leg. The faint limp lent more distinction to an already unique man. His thin white hair fluttered in the breeze. He stood and gave them a stiff bow, his lips stretching into a parody of a smile.

"Mr. Wylie! What a lovely surprise," Minna said, knowing he set store by polite expressions. "I'm so

22

glad you could come to tea."

The pot was already on the table, its fragrant steam reminding Minna how hungry she was. Golden omelets and baked ham drew her gaze. Newly baked scones gave out a mouth-watering aroma, and pots of marmalade and jams were spots of color against the white tablecloth.

"Do sit down. No need to stand on ceremony," she said brightly, and spread her mauve silk gown around her on a chair. She nervously fingered the amethyst brooch at her throat, suddenly wondering if her dress was immaculate. Somehow, Thurlow Wylie always made her uncomfortable, made her wonder if she was good enough at her work. Perhaps it was his penetrating, cold eyes, or his almost imperceptible sneer that made her uneasy. She had always sensed that the real man hid behind that fastidious exterior, and he would never give any hints as to his past—or his current life, for that matter. She knew nothing about him, other than what her business dealings with him had taught her. She suspected that his private life had branded him with deep bitterness.

Ellie refused to look at him, and two red spots on her cheeks gave away her alarm. She had never liked Mr. Wylie, and she was always clumsy in his presence.

"I saw Viscountess Minton-Brown come out of the shop," he said as Minna poured the tea. "How often is she here?"

"Oh, this was the first time, but Mrs. Davina Shield, our best customer, comes once or twice a week," Minna said and watched him put one exactly level teaspoon of sugar into his cup, then arrange his spoon meticulously on the saucer. "She spends money as if her coffers are bottomless."

He nodded. "As long as you keep pleasing her,

23

she'll bring new customers. Still, you're doing very well, just like I knew you would since that first night we met."

This was the only time he'd mentioned the night on the bridge, and Minna shivered at the dark memory. Her life had almost ended that night, and she still felt ashamed of her intention to commit suicide. She gave him a curious glance, wondering why he'd mentioned the incident. She sensed that he had something special on his mind. He looked more secretive than ever, and she noticed a new tension in his face that she hadn't been aware of before.

Ellie spilled her tea, and the cup fell to the ground, shattering. "Aw Lawks! What a widgeon I am." Without another glance at Mr. Wylie, she brushed off her skirts with her napkin and hurried into the house. Minna knew that Ellie wouldn't join them again. Her gaze followed her friend across the yard, and for a brief moment she looked into the penetrating eyes of the beggar woman who was slumped on the bottom step eating a chunk of bread. A flurry of unease went through Minna as she viewed that misshapen face before it disappeared behind a shawl.

She returned her attention to her benefactor and steeled herself for one of Mr. Wylie's lectures on "pinching pennies." Successful enough to wear pretty dresses and eat aplenty, she didn't want to turn every penny before she spent it. He always complained about her various charities, and her kindness to her staff, but today he seemed to be different. He looked angry, and his silence was icy.

The late afternoon sun didn't feel as warm as it had five minutes ago. "Is there something you want to say, Mr. Wylie?" She braced herself and wished her voice hadn't trembled on the last syllable.

He cleared his throat. "Yes . . . well, you have

done very well for yourself, Minna. Better than I thought possible in such a short time."

She nodded, and touched the calluses that would always remain on her index finger from all the friction of pins and needles. Sometimes her hands were so cramped from sewing that she could barely straighten her fingers. "I can never thank you enough for what you've done, Mr. Wylie. It's because of you that I'm in this position."

He nodded sagely. He set down his cup carefully, rearranged the spoon, then gave Minna the full force of his dark gaze. "Seeing that I have in some way assisted in your success, I would like you to do me a small favor in return."

Minna stiffened further, wondering why she was so worried. He had never showed the least amorous interest in her, so why was she nervous? But what else would he want from her? She had nothing else to offer. Would he demand that she become his mistress after all these years?

No, she sensed that he had other thoughts on his mind. This type of man was the dry, sexless kind who cared more for his business than about ladies.

"I would like you to seduce a young man, a man who is my bitter enemy," he said without preamble. "Can you do that for me?"

She stared in shock, then stuttered, "But—but, how can I?" She couldn't make herself explain that she was a virgin. Would he believe that a young girl who had lived in the slums would still be untouched?

"I'm sure you won't have any difficulty with any fellow you choose to pursue."

"But why?" Bewildered, she stared at him as if to read the answer in his eyes.

"You don't need to know the reason. Just do it, and as soon as possible. Mrs. Shield, who is the man's aunt, will contrive to give you an introduction." He made a move as if to stand up.

"Who is this gentleman?" she asked, wanting to clutch his arm and hold him back.

"Roarke Harding, the Earl of Whitecliffe."

He looked down at her. "I expect you to fulfill this little wish of mine. As you well know, you still need my support in this precarious business venture of yours. You know that the tastes of the rich are fickle."

She stood, too, her back rigid with anger. "Are you blackmailing me, Mr. Wylie?"

He shrugged. "It pains me that you would use such a vulgar expression. As I see it, 'tis naught but an exchange of favors."

"I have to give my *body* to a stranger?"

"Surely, Miss Smith, it isn't too great a price to pay for this elegant niche on Clifford Street." His eyebrows rose a notch. "Well, will you do it?"

What could she say? What could she do? Ellie, Mrs. Collins—so many people depended on her for their livelihood. Without her, poverty would enter the Clifford Street shop. She nodded tightly.

"Perhaps—if I must." She would have to think about this, then find out why he demanded such an outrageous favor in exchange for her success.

"I know nothing about this man."

His lips lifted at the corners. "You shall soon find out more about him."

A cold shiver rolled down Minna's spine as he got up, towered stiffly over her for a moment, then left the table without another word.

Chapter Two

Roarke Harding, the seventh Earl of Whitecliffe, closed the book in front of him on the desk with a snap and folded his steel-rimmed spectacles on top. The gritty feeling in his eyes and the pounding headache told him it was time to stop. He traced the fingers over the embossed title on the leather tooling. THE SECRET OF LIFE, A STUDY. The author was some obscure professor whom he'd never heard of before.

Secret, bah! he thought. No one knew what they were talking about, and neither did he. He wished he could solve the riddle of *life.* One thing he knew for sure, life wasn't a heap of dusty boring words so closely spaced together and so laden with footnotes that he needed a magnifying glass to read them.

He looked at the stack of books on metaphysics with distaste. No one could convince him that he'd lived previous lives, or that there were other dimensions that humans couldn't see — except a few "chosen" ones. He didn't believe in the existence of guiding spirits and guardian angels, or "voices." *Balderdash! Nothing but a lot of excuses to make fools believe that man was immortal,* he thought with a snort. In the history of man, many had tried to solve the puzzle of life, but it evidently eluded everyone, including the most celebrated of scientists and archbishops.

Roarke touched another stack of books on the opposite side of the desk, these explaining the major religions of the world. They were beautifully written he had to admit, yet full of riddles that made his head spin. Perhaps he ought to travel to the Orient and pursue one of the holy men who claimed they knew the Secret.

He yawned and pulled his hands through his hair. The tall pendulum clock in the foyer clanged twelve. The mournful sound wound through the house. After that, silence was complete, quieter than a tomb. He viewed the familiar study with its leather furniture, dusty potted plants, and books by the thousands in glass-fronted oak cases. The closest he'd ever come to the Orient was to walk on the many Oriental carpets in this house, he thought with a grudging smile.

Thinking that it was time for bed, he toyed with a stack of yellow documents that dealt with excavations of the pyramids of Egypt. Perhaps the old Egyptians had known the Truth. He doubted it. The more he read the more he doubted.

Clumsy footsteps sounded in the corridor outside, and he glanced toward the door. After the briefest of knocks, the door opened, and Zach entered. Zach Gordon, the restless soul, couldn't sleep.

"Ah, there you are, coz," Zach said as he heaved himself across the floor on his crutches.

"How's your leg today?" Roarke viewed the handsome dark-haired man in front of him, the perfect symmetry of a body hardened by sports. Lovesick ladies had written odes to those lazy blue eyes, he recalled with a chuckle.

"Damned painful if you must know the truth." Zach stopped in front of the desk and viewed the clutter of books. He jabbed the top one in the stack of religions and it fell to the floor. "Soon you'll be writing your own study to add to the confusion of mankind," he said derisively.

"Studying never hurt anyone," Roarke rejoined. "You could use some broadening of your shallow mind."

If not curtailed by his crutches, Zach would have gestured in protest, Roarke knew, but he only said, "Heaven forbid. Those years at Oxford almost killed me." He hobbled to the closest chair, and sat down with an audible sigh.

"What I don't understand is why you've suddenly buried yourself in the books. You used to be great company in the past. What became of that wild buck who liked gambling, wine, and women?"

Roarke sighed and leaned back in his chair. "There are other things to life besides drinking and gambling."

Zach shook his head. "I don't understand you."

Though he could barely see Zach's face in the shadows, Roarke calmly met his cousin's scrutinizing gaze across the desk. "I've changed, that's all. Something might happen to change you as well."

"Yes, the King might make me a Knight. God knows I deserve it after working so hard to prevent this town from dying of boredom."

Roarke laughed. "Your view of London is remarkable. The city is surely falling into a state of gloom what with you laid up with that broken leg."

Zach gave an airy wave of his hand. "Before long, I shall yet again dance in the streets. No, it's you I'm worried about."

"Spare your energy for more important worries," Roarke said and loosened the knot of his neckcloth.

He unbuttoned the top buttons of his waistcoat, and said, "It's time for bed."

"I can't sleep. Oh, what wouldn't I do for the sweet company of a courtesan—and a bottle."

"Grandmother would turn in her grave if she heard you talk like that," Roarke said, and stood. "I'm going up. You can sit here and brood, and while you do so, you might as well read a few books."

Zach gave a derisive laugh. "Of course. Well, I came here to tell you that Divine Shield and I have plans for the seventh of May, and the plans include you."

"My birthday? What's going on?" Holding on to the armrests of the chair Roarke leaned over his cousin. "What are you plotting with fair Aunt Davina? You know that I abhor to be the center of a gathering."

Zach shrugged with indifference. "It's about time you get out of this mausoleum. You've grieved long enough for Thomas."

Anger slowly rose in Roarke, and he longed to shake the irreverent man before him. "I'll never forget Thomas, and nothing you'll do will change that fact."

"It's noble to grieve, coz, but two years? You must learn to forget."

Roarke grimaced. "Drown my sorrows in alcohol and bed every wench in Whitechapel, is that your solution?"

Zach shook his head, and Roarke cringed under the earnest gaze. "I'm your friend, Roarke. I've known you all my life, and I recognize the signs. You're becoming a recluse, and all your studies won't explain the mystery of life or the puzzle of your son's death." He smiled. "I've come to save you from yourself, and you ought to give thanks to the powers that look after you. Namely me."

Roarke could not stop from smiling. "You have more gall than anyone I know in London."

Zach's face contorted into a mask of mock sadness. "No one appreciates my sterling qualities. Least of all you—or the fair Aurora Bishop."

"Are you still running after her—or rather hobbling?"

Zach shook his head. "I did until her dragon of an aunt whisked her off to the country. Aurora is as elusive as a butterfly." He pursed his lips in thought. "Truly, I believe they're keeping her prisoner. She never goes anywhere without two attendants. Deuced difficult to get a moment alone with her."

"But when you do, you make the best of it, don't you, Zach?"

Zach's eyes grew dreamy. "Her lips taste like the sweetest of nectar, her skin feels like the finest satin."

Roarke slapped his hand to his forehead. "Spare me! I'm going to bed."

As he left the room, Zach called after him, "Don't plan anything for your birthday, coz."

Mr. Wylie returned two days later to demand Minna's answer. She felt confused and angry at his request, violated somehow. However, it hadn't been difficult to decide. If she wanted to keep the shop and feed her employees, she had to accept his demand. A shop she might be able to start anew, though she doubted it would succeed if Mr. Wylie ruined her reputation. The workers relied on her for their livelihood. They trusted her and she could never abandon them.

Mr. Wylie, her mentor—her adversary—as it turned out, was sitting stiff-necked in her little office at the back of the shop. She asked him the question that he had refused to answer before. "Why Lord Whitecliffe? Why me, Mr. Wylie?"

His shoulders lifted a fraction. "You're beautiful and ladylike. You are perfect for this plan. Róarke Harding doesn't know your true identity, and he won't be able to find out since you don't move in his circles." Mr. Wylie paused. "I suppose if he really started looking for you later on, he might—"

Minna's hands tightened around the armrests of her chair. "I have to seduce this man. What else?"

"It's more than that. You must make him fall in love with you, get him to propose marriage. Then you must abandon him." He held up his hands when she started to protest. "I know it sounds strange, Miss Smith," he said, "but hear me out."

He looked older and seemed to shrink in his chair, and Minna knew she was about to discover something important about him. Never before had he shared any personal secrets.

"Once I had a young daughter, Isobel. Ten years ago, she was just on the threshold of womanhood, and as lovely as a newly opened rose." His voice started to tremble, and Minna was aghast to see tears clouding his eyes.

"I wanted to marry Isobel off to a young partner that I'd taken on, an honest hard-working man. However, Isobel spent one summer month at Brighton with my sister. I had rented a cottage for the season. My sister is wholly reliable, but somehow Isobel got entangled with Roarke Harding and his set of reprobates. I don't know how it happened, and now I'll never find out. Isobel isn't alive to tell me." He took a deep breath.

"She fell in love with Harding, and I saw no objection should they marry. After all, Harding was a peer and a wealthy man, and a match with him would have been brilliant. Then she came to me,

32

teary-eyed one morning and told me that she was—er, *enceinte*. I was shocked, of course, and tried to make Harding marry her then and there by special license. 'I wouldn't marry a Cit,' he said, and gave a cruel laugh and told me the brat wasn't his."

Mr. Wylie pulled a handkerchief from his coat pocket and mopped his brow. Two red spots glowed on his cheeks, and his hands trembled. "Then he said he would never consider marrying Isobel when she was trying to foist another man's bastard on him."

"How awful," Minna whispered.

"We left Brighton in a hurry, and I took her to my country home in Sussex. She fell into a deep depression, and when she had the child, a son, she rejected him. While at the estate—" his voice grew so hoarse that he could barely speak "—she drowned herself in the pond." He looked straight at Minna. "I would have given anything to save her."

"As you saved me."

He nodded. "Yes, like that. It wasn't the child that drove her to such a desperate end, but her broken heart. She loved Harding more than her own life, and he—the cad—just stepped on her heart and ground his heel in it. After that, I almost took my own life in that same pond that claimed Isobel. I couldn't live—" His voice cracked, and he buried his face in the handkerchief.

Minna felt a sudden surge of anger toward the heartless man who was responsible for such heartache.

"I've made it my business to discover everything I can about this . . . this *beast*. He lives a reclusive life here in London, and there's little gossip about him. Evidently, he's deep into some type of studies."

"He isn't married?"

"No. He's almost thirty, but this is clearly a man

33

who doesn't want to marry and set up his nursery."

"In other words, a stuffy curmudgeon before his age?" Minna shivered at the thought of trying to make such a man fall in love with her. Seducing him might prove difficult.

"That he is, but he didn't use to be. I know he was a ladies' man and a gambler. He's changed in every way. He's not over-indulgent with drink and card play like so many of his class. He's slim and hard as a whip with an arrogant face and a cold heart. He carries his aristocratic title well."

"I don't see how I can impress him." She didn't want to go near the man!

"Oh, he won't be able to resist you. You see, I've heard that he used to be partial to blondes. My Isobel had the loveliest blond hair. Anyway, by now he must be ripe to the allure of a lovely woman. Any normal man has his . . . ah, well—appetites." He shoved the handkerchief back into his pocket, then stood, leaning heavily on his cane.

"One more question, Mr. Wylie," she said. "Why wait all these years? Why didn't you put the bargain to me when you found me on the bridge?"

"Well, Harding was with Wellington during the campaigns until '15. Then he traveled frequently abroad scouting for Arabian stallions. He breeds thoroughbreds at the Whitecliffe Towers in Kent. Besides, I was curious to see what you could do with yourself if you had the wherewithal to rise above the gutter. I saw you as a wilted flower that only needed light and water to revive. You were sort of an experiment—sort of a lost daughter, I suppose. I'm glad I waited."

"Harding could have married in those years."

"No . . . he'll never marry. I'll see to that!"

Minna sensed that the old man knew something about Lord Whitecliffe that he wouldn't tell her.

"Davina Shield will be your entry into the aristocracy, Minna. You already have the poise and the careful speech that sets you above the workers in the East End."

"My father was a curate, and he taught me to read and write, and speak properly."

"With the right grooming, you'll blend in splendidly."

Minna knew he was right. If she put it to the Divine Davina that she wanted to seduce the Earl of Whitecliffe, Davina would be thrilled to help her. Anything that smelled of illicit love and masquerade drew Davina like a bee to nectar.

Mr. Wylie gave her a pale smile, one of the few he had ever given her over the years. "I knew I could count on you, Miss Smith. Just remember that you're doing this in the name of Isobel Wylie. That devil's spawn Harding needs a lesson he'll never forget."

Minna nodded and went with Mr. Wylie to the door. When he'd left, she sank down on her chair, strangely exhausted. It was the tension. Every time she spoke with Mr. Wylie it was as if all her nerves tautened into strings, tying her inside a panicky shell.

"I must do it," she murmured, hoping that the heavy feeling inside would go away, but it didn't. She glanced at the crescent-shaped window and noticed that it was raining outside. A length of lemon-yellow silk hung like a bright banner on the wall, and beside it, she had tacked numerous sketches of her own designs.

She couldn't lose this life. It was unthinkable. She had to tell Ellie to inform her when Davina Shield came next. Then she would have a long talk with the Divine Davina, perhaps over a tea tray in the sitting room above.

35

* * *

Two days later she was pinning a yard of Point de France lace on a bodice in the workshop when Ellie came in. Her face was red with excitement.

"What is it, Ellie?"

"We have a new customer, perhaps *many* new customers," Ellie said, rubbing her hands.

"That is good and well," Minna said, "however, I have to finish this trim today. Who is she?"

"Blind me, but 'tis a *he,*" Ellie explained with a conspiratorial grin. "He's with the Divine Davina to judge her new wardrobe. If he likes it, there's no tellin' who he'll refer to the shop in the future. Davina says he has the most expert eye for style and color." Ellie rolled her eyes. "I doubt he can beat you on that score."

"My, what a paragon."

Ellie laughed and held the door for Minna. "You must come and meet him. He's the most handsome fellow I've ever seen," she whispered. *"Gentry,* you know."

A warning bell sounded in Minna's mind, and she didn't know why she slowed her steps. "Who is he?"

Ellie's whisper rasped as she launched her next announcement. "The Earl of Whitecliffe. He said he'd heard from the Divine Davina that you're the most fashionable modiste in London."

Minna's heart started to pound, and her legs weakened. Why had he come? It was almost as if he knew about her and Mr. Wylie's conspiracy against him. She stopped and inhaled deeply. He mustn't see her, or he would remember her later.

"Ellie," she said. "Why, this is your chance. He shall be your special customer, and I know he will be pleased with you. I don't need to wait on all the important patrons."

Ellie paled, but Minna pushed her into the shop

36

area. The darkness of the rainy day outside sent long shadows into the shop. Still, the silk-upholstered walls with their rose sheen, and the gold woodwork gave the room an intimate air. The scent of fresh flowers filled the air, and the thick carpet silenced Ellie's steps as she hurried across the room. She looked crisp and neat in her black gown and smooth chignon, and her face lit up as the customers stood.

Minna flinched when the earl turned his head toward her. From the shelter of the door, she watched him move. He had a smooth walk, the grace of a lazy sensual tiger, tall and lean and whip-like, as Mr. Wylie had described him. He truly was the most handsome man she had ever seen. Ellie had not exaggerated. His hair was wavy and dark blond, so dark it could almost be called brown. She noticed golden streaks among the brown in the light from the chandelier above him. She studied his face, a face that wasn't as much regular as it was interesting. He exuded a magnetic quality that gave him an air of mystery. His nose was too sharp, and his jaw too angular, the eyes deepset and seemed to hide secrets. She couldn't tell their color from across the room, but she guessed they were blue. His features had the patina of arrogance and self-confidence. He was a member of the privileged class all the way to the tips of his gleaming boots. *Intimidating* was the word that came to mind, yet she sensed a deep sadness in the downward tilt of his lips and the tired lines around his eyes.

Minna's fingers ached after clutching the door frame too hard. Her senses reeled. How would she begin to seduce this man who could have anyone for the asking? The ladies must be falling down at his feet, and she resented the sensual power that he exuded.

37

She felt like a moth drawn to a flame that might burn her badly. Her mind screamed that she ought to reject Mr. Wylie's deal, and her senses were already in wild confusion after just one long look at the "target."

Her cheeks burned as she hastened into her office and closed the door behind her. Walking up and down the room in agitation, she thought of ways to get out of the agreement with Mr. Wylie, but she could think of no valid excuse. Mr. Wylie was a businessman with little compassion beyond his ventures. She was one of his business undertakings, and if he wanted to, he could close the shop at the flick of his wrist. It would only take rumors about her background, her disreputable discharge from the workshop, to make her customers flee. Reputation was everything in this city.

She sat down and massaged her temples with her trembling hands. Never had she felt more lonely. She wished her father had been alive; she had always been able to confide in him. Her memory of her mother was more vague. Mother had been a taciturn, exacting woman who had drummed into her that she must always behave properly and do her duty. Somehow, Minna had been unable to form a close relationship with her. Every time she had tried to share intimate thoughts, Mother had pushed her away with the words, "Not now, dear. Let the Bible give you guidance."

Minna fingered the key on its silver chain that she always wore next to her skin. Mother had given it to her on her sixteenth birthday, and it fitted into the lock of a extravagant, brocade-covered box that held few things of value, only a comb and a brooch that had belonged to the strict Mrs. Smith. Minna carried it because it was the only frivolous thing she had ever received from her mother, besides articles necessary for survival, like food and clothes. Mother had been a fair woman, but Minna wished that she hadn't been so strict.

Father had been kind and gentle, always setting aside time to speak with her and educate her. He'd never managed to get a vicariate, and they had lived in near poverty in damp stone cottages in parishes all over Sussex and Hampshire. But Minna still remembered those golden days with her father. It was as if the very air had glowed around him, and he had always tried to ease the burdens of people less fortunate then himself.

Minna smiled at her recollection of him. He had given her an old illustrated Bible, and she kept it in a drawer in her bedroom. Sometimes when she felt lonelier than usual, she would open the Bible and trace the notes and comments that Father had written in the margins. The ink was fading, but she could clearly picture him dipping his quill in the ink and writing his clever comments. God, how she missed him!

Minna clasped the armrests and thought hard. If she could fulfill this one wish for Mr. Wylie, she would be free. She would insist that he put her freedom in writing. Then the shop and all she had worked for could not be threatened further. Her staff — her family — would be safe, and so would she. She pushed her chair back and stood abruptly. She would stop agonizing and just do the job. The sooner she started, the sooner it would be over.

Chapter Three

"Oh, Minna, you are a naughty lady!" the Divine Davina exclaimed on the following day as Minna was pinning up a sleeve embroidered with silver vines on Davina's latest ball gown. "Roarke will crush your poor heart. He has no *feelings* any longer. He's a changed man since his son's death. The man is aloof—colder than ice sometimes. Still, I love him dearly; I know he's hurting inside, that's what's made him cold." Pouting, she studied the sleeve critically. "I've known him since we were children, y'know. To think that I married one of his uncles! It seems eons ago."

"He can't be that unreachable. He must have some weak spot like everyone else." Minna stood back and viewed her handiwork. The sleeve puffed nicely around Davina's shapely arm. Just another tuck on the bodice, and the gown would be finished. "I would love to go to your masquerade, Mrs. Shield, and try my luck with this gentleman."

"Hmm. How come you're interested in him of all people? Where did you meet him?"

"I saw him one day and decided he would be the perfect gentleman to expel my loneliness." Minna thought about Mr. Wylie and cursed the deal he'd forced upon her. "I might as well set my sights high."

Davina's eyes widened. "What a daring girl you are! I'd never thought . . . well, you must come to the masked ball, of course. I can't wait to see the outcome of this charade. Poor Roarke, the masquerade is his birthday celebration, and I've invited all his friends. He hates crowds, but he needs to get out of his house. He needs to be *seduced,* by a lovely young woman, so I'm happy to help you."

Giving Minna a wink, Davina took two dance steps in front of the mirror. The tiers of watered, sapphire blue silk crackled around her. A hint of lace showed below the hem. "It's very elegant, Minna. I will be the best dressed woman at the ball." She laughed. "I can see the banner of the society column now—'Hostess Outshone Them All.' I'm thrilled." She took Minna's hand and squeezed it. "And now back to you. You must not eclipse me on Wednesday night, Minna, or I must take my business elsewhere."

Minna's lips turned down, but she couldn't hide the laughter in her voice. "I have the loveliest creation in mind. Yours will pale in comparison."

The Divine Davina glared. "Hmm, mayhap I'd better cancel that invitation."

Minna shook her head. "No, Mrs. Shield, remember that I must make an impression on the cold Lord Whitecliffe."

Davina's laughter filled the fitting room. "Indeed you must! How thoughtless of me. He promised he would attend since the party is in his honor, but Zach, my cousin twice removed, had to literally bludgeon him into accepting the invitation. It's Roarke's thirtieth birthday." She tilted her head sideways as if preoccupied with deep thoughts, then said, "I shall introduce you as my dearest friend's cousin from abroad. Your father could have been some diplomat." She snapped her fingers. "In India!"

"But I don't know the first thing about India. What if the guests start asking me questions?" Davina furrowed her brow. "What then? What parts of the world do you know?"

"Only England. Could I be a cousin fresh up from the country? That would explain any awkwardness on my part."

Davina squealed with excitement. "Of course! You have a tyrannical grandmother who always wanted you to become a nun. You have finally broken down her resistance, and now you're visiting the fleshpot that is London for the first time. You threatened to stop caring for her as she grows older if you can't have a season in London."

Minna laughed and smoothed out the material at the back of the gown. "That sounds easy enough to remember. Now, please let me help you undress. You must try on your new walking ensemble."

"I can't wait to play this little romantic game," Davina said, and smiled at Minna. "You will be the mystery lady who disappears in the middle of the ball, and every male will be clamoring to know more about you." Davina held her finger to her lips. "I won't say a word, of course. The *haute monde* will be agog with curiosity."

"That's a good idea. The earl won't be able to resist a mystery, and I will soon snare him."

Davina patted her cheek, not too kindly. "I never thought you had such lofty aspirations. I say! Mistress to a gentleman, an earl, no less. You're a bold young woman, Minna Smith."

"Madame LaForge, don't forget that. But I can't use that name on Wednesday, can I? I shall be Miss Minerva . . . hmm, Sargent. That will be an easy name to remember."

"Very well," Davina said with a pout, "Miss Sargent, you have a lot of gall."

Minna didn't think she could go through with the charade, but here she was, at number 10 Green Street in Mayfair, Mrs. Shield's residence. The room was stifling hot and filled with guests in glittering dresses and sparkling jewels. Minna didn't recognize anyone; not even her own customers since they were wearing half masks and elaborate headdresses. She had come to the ball dressed as a Grecian goddess in a softly draping chiton with a band of gold cloth around her waist, and a himation held with two gilded brooches at her shoulders. Ellie had fashioned her hair into a cluster of ringlets surrounded by a circlet of gold braid. A mask covered most of her face, but she worried that someone might still recognize her. Not everyone in London had her pale hair, and her customers had often admired it at the shop. She jumped with fright when someone touched her arm.

"*I* would recognize that hair anywhere," Davina whispered. "I thought you would cover it."

"No, I've heard that the earl likes blondes. I will seduce him with my hair."

Davina giggled. "You're so devious! Anyway, I'm the most daring hostess in London. Who would dare to invite their modiste to a ball at their own house and pass her off as a friend's cousin?"

"Only you, Mrs. Shield," Minna said. Her gaze strayed to the people milling about the oval foyer

43

below the half-circle of stairs where she was standing. "Your guests dazzle me with their affluence. Everything they wear is expensive and elegant. Their very *skins* seem gilded somehow."

"I've never thought of that. The look comes from never knowing hardships." She pulled Minna with her to introduce her charge to the guests as they entered the door to the ballroom.

Minna's legs trembled, and she felt strangely weak as marquesses and viscounts bent over her outstretched begloved hand. Imagine that, aristocrats kissing her fingers! Minna's stomach turned over with excitement, and she patted her perspiring forehead discreetly. The room was getting hotter with the many burning candles and the increasing crush of people. "Who is this ravishing creature?" a tall man asked as Davina introduced her. He reminded Minna of a slightly older, stouter, version of the Earl of Whitecliffe, and her heartbeat escalated. "By jingo, where have you been hiding her all this time, Davina?"

Davina's eyes glittered with mischief. "Melchior, dear, my friend's cousin was on her way to the Order of . . . hmm, the Sixteen Sisters in . . . er, Scotland," she invented, "but jumped out of the moving carriage and took refuge here with me. I was appalled to learn that her grandmother wanted to shut such a beauty behind the heavy door of a convent."

Minna nudged her distinguished hostess in the ribs. *Be careful,* she wanted to say, but she only pulled her lips into a tight smile and nodded every time Davina opened her mouth.

"It would have been a sad loss to the world indeed," said the stranger who beamed at Minna. "I must write my name on your dance card, my dear."

44

Davina introduced him as Melchior Harding, Roarke's cousin from Kent. He grabbed the card dangling from a golden cord around her wrist and scrawled his name across two lines. " 'Til later," he murmured with an elegant bow.

"You're a success, my dear," said Davina. "I will be fighting off irate gentlemen when you disappear tonight."

Unease squeezed Minna's heart. "I hope this charade won't cause too much trouble for you."

Davina flung out her arms. "Oh, no, I love every moment of it. You have enlivened a dull gathering. I will be invited everywhere so that the ladies can interrogate me about you." She laughed. "I will be the center of attention for weeks to come."

Minna listened with only half an ear. "Where is he? Are you sure he's coming tonight?"

"He will, but he usually arrives late. Dashed insolent, if you ask me. The cream on his birthday cake will go sour in this heat."

"Perhaps . . ." Minna waited as her nerves tightened more every minute. She viewed the colorful flower arrangements that exuded a lovely, sweet fragrance. The jewel-toned carpets were so soft they drenched her footfalls, and the chandeliers glittered with a thousand prisms. Every new impression dazzled Minna, and she thought she had entered a magical grotto that held nothing but beautiful things. The ballroom was filled with roses, and at one end stood a dais where the musicians were tuning their instruments. Bewigged footmen in black cut-away coats carried heavy trays with wine glasses on their shoulders.

The violins' fragile tunes wafted through the air. Minna gasped as if jolted out of a dream. This was real! The gentlemen would claim her for the dances, and she didn't know the first thing about dancing.

"I don't know how to dance," she whispered urgently to Davina. "I will make a complete fool of myself."

Davina stared at her speculatively. "I never thought of that. Hmm, nevertheless, you shall prevail. Just follow the others, and if you're a bit clumsy, you can always pretend to be dizzy and sit out the rest of the dance with the gentleman, then return here to me." She clucked her tongue. "The ladies will gossip about you of course, wonder why you haven't been introduced. But we'll worry about that later—besides, this isn't really your social debut."

Minna tensed, fearing the ordeal ahead. A rivulet of perspiration coursed along her spine, and she opened her fan (borrowed from the shop) and fanned herself.

"He's here," Davina whispered and pointed over the balustrade.

Minna's gaze darted to the door below, and her heartbeat accelerated when she viewed the tall man. His hair gleamed golden in the candlelight. He wasn't wearing a costume, just the fashionable black tailcoat, starched neckcloth, and white waistcoat that was favored evening dress among the gentlemen.

The white linen contrasted sharply with his sundarkened skin. He was so handsome and so remote that she felt a sudden ache inside. How would she ever engage this man's interest?

"He's here alone," Davina murmured, "which means that he doesn't have to dance attendance on some simpering mistress. Not that he's had one for many years."

"He looks . . ." Minna sought the right word, "dangerous."

"He is. Roarke is a man who never does anything in half measures. I've never met a more purposeful man, nor a more interesting man. He's been hurt in the past, and I think you'll find it difficult to impress him, but he'll be unable to resist you in the end."

Minna was confused. What kind of person was the earl? In what way was he hurt? She remembered Mr. Wylie's words. If a man could cast off a pregnant woman without as much as a flicker of conscience, he was indeed a beast. Her resolve hardened as the Earl of Whitecliffe leisurely handed his gloves and hat to one of the flunkies by the door.

"I shall conquer him. Every man has his weakness." She tightened her lips and patted her hair.

"You look lovely, Minna. You're bound to intrigue him. Like you said before, he used to be partial to lovely blondes, but now he's forever buried in his books, and thinks of nothing else. Be careful, he might hurt you."

A cold shiver went through Minna. She didn't tell Davina that her thoughts had traveled much the same route. Any woman would be intrigued by such a handsome and magnetic man, so why would he be interested in her? She must remain strong. He sauntered across the floor and started climbing the stairs. In a few moments, she would stand eye to eye with him.

Then he was there, bending over Davina and pecking her cheek. "Aunt Davina, I hope this gathering won't be as boring as your last one," he teased. "My birthday isn't something to remember; I don't know why you bothered."

47

Davina slapped him over the wrist with her fan. "Bah! That's gratitude for you!" She laughed as he gave the parody of a humble bow.

"You must meet my friend . . . Eliza's cousin, fresh from the country, Miss Minerva Sargent."

He seemed to be taken aback as Davina introduced her, but almost instantly his smile, that never reached those veiled eyes, returned to his lips. His eyes were a deep blue-green, not blue, as she had imagined in the shop on Clifford Street. Her legs felt like water, and her throat, papery dry. His grip was assured as he held her fingertips.

"Delighted," he murmured. His gaze raked over her face, probing, as if he was searching for a clue of recognition. "Why haven't we met before? I would have noticed you."

"Like I told you, Roarke, Miss Sargent has never been to London," Davina said. "And where would you have met her? You never go out. She is a beautiful rose, don't you think? I especially wanted to introduce her to you," she added with a twinkle; "but you must be careful with such innocence."

His eyes flashed with fire. "I'm the most cautious gentleman in London. She has nothing to fear from me."

Davina chuckled. "I had hoped she might be in slight danger with you. Isn't it about time you started enjoying life, Roarke?"

He gave Minna an enigmatic smile that made her stomach somersault with alarm. "Mayhap a leopard can change his spots, after all. Especially when faced with such a heady challenge." His eyes raked over Minna. "Country miss, you say? Are you sure about that?"

"Don't be silly, Roarke!" Davina hit his arm with her fan anew, and Minna blushed. She cringed under his scrutiny, and she sensed that he wanted nothing better than to take off her mask and study her face. She found his inspection unusually thorough, but perhaps he treated all ladies to the same intimate survey. There was something about his eyes—as if he saw everything but nothing at all.

With a leisurely movement, he lifted her dance card and studied the names narrowly. Startled by his closeness, she took a small step back, but he only gave her a chiding smile. "You must allow me one of the waltzes, my dear."

"No . . . eh, well . . ." Minna stuttered.

"Of course you must dance with her, Roarke. I would be mortally offended if you ignored her."

"Well, I can't risk that, can I?" he chided, with that flat smile that only reached his lips.

"No need—" Minna started, but lost her voice.

He frowned, then gave her a quick glance. "I perceive you're worried, Miss Sargent. And you should be. Everyone tells me I'm an awful bore."

"I don't especially like to dance," she said lamely, wishing that her father's education had taught her some measure of sophisticated repartee.

His eyebrows lifted a fraction. "How unusual. Well, I will scrawl my name on your card, and we shall sit and talk for the duration of the waltz." His fingers brushed her wrist as he wrote his signature, and she flinched. Everything about him made her nerve ends come to life, and she was overcome by a wave of confusion. Mr. Wylie must be sorely mistaken to believe that she could make this controlled aristocrat fall in love with her. She swallowed hard, and he seemed to sense her discomfort.

A wicked gleam came into his eyes. He leaned close to her ear and whispered, "I don't bite." He laughed as her blush deepened. " 'Til later." He sauntered to the edge of the dance floor and started a heated conversation — an argument almost — with his cousin Melchior.

"I couldn't believe —" Minna began, pressing her hands to her burning cheeks.

"Outrageous," Davina muttered behind her fan. "He says the most unexpected things. I was delighted to see how taken he is with you."

Minna struggled to find her composure. "Are you sure? Perhaps this is a hideous mistake. I was in error to think —"

"Nonsense, my dear. You shall wind him around your little finger. There's nothing more pleasant than a dalliance with a handsome man." She smiled, and Minna felt better. Possibly he wouldn't be so difficult to deal with. She would have to keep her wits about her. She had to keep remembering Mr. Wylie's ultimatum.

Damned Mr. Wylie for forcing me into this farce, she thought as her first dancing partner claimed her.

Her chiton was too long and she kept tripping on it. As the couples lined up for a cotillion, Minna didn't know where to turn. The uncertainty, and the many mistakes during the dances made her hot and edgy. Her partners had sympathy for her plight and assured her that a season in London would make her an expert dancer. She did notice, however, that the female guests had no such compassion as they stared at her with contempt. It wouldn't be long before someone wormed the truth out of Davina.

If she failed . . . the thought was unthinkable. She couldn't lose everything that she'd worked so hard for. All she had to do . . . She fanned herself by an open window and longed for a glass of refreshment. The exertion on the dance floor had made her very thirsty. A long cloth-covered table held bowls of punch and other beverages at one end of the enormous room. Stone-faced waiters served the guests, and Minna decided to make her way to the table.

"My wilting beauty," a male voice said behind her.

She jumped with fright, instantly recognizing Lord Whitecliffe's deep voice. She whirled to face him, only to find that he was only inches from her side. Her elbow bumped his arm. Instinctively, she stepped away as if he would singe any part of her that came into contact with him.

"Skittish, by God," he said, in the last moment saving the champagne glass in his hand from a shattering fate. With a mocking bow, he handed her the wine. "The corners of your lips were drooping most sadly. I thought a little of this would restore your spirits."

She accepted the glass. "Thank you." She looked uncertainly at him, wondering how she could have been so foolish to comply with Mr. Wylie's demands. This man seemed so in control, and she knew that he would control her if she let him.

The music started again, and he said, "I believe this is my dance. But since you look as if you've had enough, we might as well go out on the balcony and enjoy some fresh air." He took her elbow and led her through the open French doors. A balcony with a marble balustrade marched the length of the house. Whispers and subdued laughter hinted that they were not alone outside. Huge flower urns concealed the other couples from view.

She leaned against the wall and inhaled deeply. He stood shockingly close, bracing one hand against the wall just beside her head. She tried to adopt an indifferent stance, but she knew he could see through her, even read her every thought. She gulped down some champagne to calm her chaotic nerves.

"Tell me the truth, who are you?" he asked calmly.

"I . . . Davina introduced us I believe."

He laughed dryly. "Don't think you can fool me. The first thing a properly brought up country miss learns is how to dance. *You* don't know the first dance step."

Minna took a deep, steadying breath. "Perhaps I wasn't properly brought up," she said weakly. "Or perhaps I don't have any sense of rhythm."

"Excuses, excuses," he said with an exaggerated sigh. "What is Davina up to, I wonder? Why did she introduce us?"

To her surprise he took out an eyeglass case from his pocket and proceeded to put on a pair of wire-rim glasses. He studied her closely. "Such perfection," he said. "Such radiance. The power that created you loved beauty." He moved his arm and scraped his knuckles against an urn. Wincing with pain, he cupped the head of a lily among the flower arrangement. "You're just as perfect as this blossom."

Amazed by his unusual comment, she could only stare at him. He peered nearsightedly at the center of the bloom. "Just look at it."

She had to bend over and study the flower at close range, and she had to agree that nothing man-made ever reached such flawlessness. "It's magnificent."

She couldn't meet his searching glance, so she stared into the night which was balmy, the sky studded with stars. The sweet aroma of the flowers was overpowering. He touched the loose ringlets of her hair, and she realized it would be all too easy to let him seduce *her,* not the other way around. But she knew that if she succeeded in this part of the plan, he would drop her after a night of passion, and every effort to make him fall in love with her would be futile. She would have to create a mystery about herself, and make him fall in love with that enigma. However, she remembered Mr. Wylie's story and doubted that the earl could actually fall in love with anyone besides himself. She shrunk against the wall.

He kept toying with her hair. "I wish I could read your thoughts, but . . . I wonder if they are as wicked as mine."

Minna collected her scattered wits, forcing herself to remember that she was here to entice him, to enflame his passion. Even though her insides quivered with apprehension, she gave him a dazzling smile. "That's highly likely. The night is very seductive," she leaned closer to him, "and so are you."

He held his breath, then murmured in her ear, "By God, I believe you are a siren. You are as eager for my company as I am for yours."

She patted his cheek playfully. "You're very sure of yourself, Lord Whitecliffe." She swallowed the rest of her champagne, and it went straight to her head. The night took on a soft glow, and her nerves settled—but not entirely. He was too provocative to let her nerves rest, especially when he was standing so close that she could smell the spicy fragrance of his shaving soap. *He* smelled so good, not just his clean-shaven jaw. He smelled of man, a scent of danger and excitement, something exotic. At her shop she was used to the odor of ladies' perfumes and powders, and this new experience tantalized her senses until she felt weak and soft all over.

"I believe the champagne has dissolved your fears, sweet one." He moved slowly, ever so slowly closer to her, then cupped her face between his hands. "I shall kiss any residue of apprehension away," he whispered.

With a whimper, she turned her face away from him, and he pressed a string of light kisses along her jaw bone, and moved down the column of her throat. His arm snaked around her waist, holding her firmly.

"My . . . lord," she whispered, and wound her arms around his neck. "You are so forceful." Her heart slammed against her ribs in anguish, but she made herself pliable and seductive.

He gave a purring laugh. "I'm beginning to truly enjoy myself, and I think you are too." Without a moment's hesitation, he brought their mouths together. His was cruel and tender at the same time, and his tongue fought through the barrier of her teeth. His kiss stripped away any shred of composure that she still had.

A sweet, intoxicating sensation ran from the top of her head to her soles, and she was melting, her very bones disintegrating in a radiant glow of rapture. His body pressing her up against the wall was the only thing preventing her from falling. He demanded her response, and she didn't know the exact moment when she pushed herself against him, or when her tongue began to caress his mouth. It was the most natural, the most silky, arousing kiss she had ever experienced. When it stopped, she felt bereft.

His breath was coming in short, hard gasps against her ear, and he was still molding himself against her as if there was no letting go. Startled by her passionate response to his seduction, she pushed her hands against his chest.

"My God, but you are beautiful," he said hoarsely. "I'm thrilled and delighted. Davina and Zach outdid themselves when choosing my birthday present. I knew right away that you were their gift to me, because Davina has no cousin Eliza in the country." One of his fingers probed at the back of her neck to undo the knot of her mask. When it didn't work, he tried to pull the mask down. "I want to see your face."

He was playing into her hands, she thought, believing that she had been bought to bring him pleasure. She stilled his hands on her face. "Don't," she admonished, and managed to wiggle free of him. "I like to remain a stranger. So much more intriguing, don't you think?" She had lowered her voice to a seductive purr, and she hated herself for the deception. It went against her grain to play on a gentleman's emotions. Her father had taught her to be forthright and honest. She slid away from him as he tried to pull her once again into his arms.

"Not so fast, my lord. Let's savor every moment to the fullest."

"I'm beguiled," he said, "but surely . . . we can't end our dalliance here. There's so much more to enjoy."

He gripped her arm, hauling her toward him. She wondered what to do next. She had to keep him intrigued, to spin a web of mystery around herself.

"I like to go slowly so that, at the time of the *culmination,* no step has been rushed, no part of the intricate dance of wooing, neglected." She blushed at her bold words, and sensed that he'd noticed her discomfort. She moved away from him.

He chuckled and crossed his arms over his chest. "Why, is that rose petals I see on your cheeks?"

"You're deluded, my lord. The heat has brought the bloom to my cheeks."

"I didn't think courtesans could blush, but it's a pleasant surprise nevertheless." He followed her to the balustrade and caught her in his arms. He held her tight, mesmerizing her with his gaze. "Surely, Miss Sargent, I have done nothing to make you blush." He sighed. "I like a mystery just as much as the next man, but how will I stand the agony of waiting?"

"Is there a hint of derision in your voice? Are you laughing at me behind those wicked eyes?"

"Wicked? Surely not. I'm spellbound by you, Miss Sargent, and that's the truth." He caught her mouth with his as she was about to protest, but she managed to untangle herself from his embrace. "Don't pressure me, my lord. Everything comes to he who waits."

He surrendered with a sigh and sat down on the railing, slowly folding his glasses back into their case. "Well, well, Zach and Davina are eager to see me come out of my seclusion. They knew you would enchant me." He gave her a lopsided grin. "I'm not sure I'm ready for your wiles, my dear."

"That's why we're taking only one delicious step at a time." Minna held her breath. Did he sense her confusion, her subterfuge? She had never played coy before, but she fluttered her fan languidly, as if seduction was part of her everyday

56

life. "Shall we say tomorrow night at Davina's gazebo?"

"Hmm, yes, Davina has a most delightful marble belvedere at the far back of these grounds, among the loveliest of climbing roses. There won't be any danger of interruption there. But my birthday is today, not tomorrow." He waited for her answer with an expectant lift of his eyebrows. How would she find the way to this gentleman's heart, if he had one . . .

"I'm sorry, but I can't—"

"A pity." His lips curled sarcastically. "I shall complain to Davina that her birthday present is a day late, but then again, anticipation will add spice to our encounter."

He bowed before her, a wholly arrogant tilt of that proud head. " 'Til tomorrow. I will wait in longing agony."

Minna had the unsettling feeling that he was reluctant to see her again despite his suave words. She had sensed a subtle barrier that she'd been unable to penetrate. Any gentleman would be interested in a romantic tryst, but how would she make sure he wouldn't forget her as soon as he turned his back?

She touched her lips in wonder. His imprint still clung to her, as did his scent, and her cheek was tender in one spot where the slight stubble on his chin had raked over her skin. She had never dreamed his kiss would be so tantalizing, so consuming that she felt as if part of her had left with him. Confused, she tried to gather her thoughts. She would have to come up with a plan that would make him fall head over heels in love with her, and she hadn't the least idea of how to go about it.

Chapter Four

Roarke Harding considered his aristocratic heritage a heavy burden that night, as one of the footmen held the door open for him at the mansion in Berkley Square. He was born to distinction, but it was his prison as well. The Whitecliffes were a powerful family, and had always been prosperous—until the times of his grandfather, the fifth earl. The clan had never seen such a spendthrift, and now it was left to Roarke to repair the sagging Whitecliffe finances.

Roarke wished his father had had a better head for business, but all he'd done was to marry their neighbor in Kent, a wealthy widow, to boost the Whitecliffe fortune. The widow, Portia Wayland Seager, had brought the neighboring Meadow Hill estate to the union, except the most valuable grazing land in the area. They had always belonged to her brother-in-law, Aloisius Wayland Seager, and the Whitecliffes had leased the acres until Aloisius's death, then managed to rent the land until the solicitors could find Aloisius's heir.

Roarke sighed as he thought about the land. If

he lost the acres, he would lose his horse breeding business.

With all the worries, Roarke found it difficult to enjoy life; it was as simple as that. Except for the brief moment he'd held the delicate courtesan in his arms, his birthday celebration had been a bore. Thirty years had past. Life was running between his fingers and he hadn't accomplished anything of true value.

It seemed that dark clouds had gathered around him, haunting recollections from the past, from times when he'd been a wild young blade ready for any lark. Mistakes always returned to haunt you, and by God, they had for him. He'd walked a thin line of sanity these last two years. Life had been hell since Thomas died. He remembered every detail of his son burning up in a fever. Roarke sighed. He had been helpless to prevent the quick death; Thomas had been snuffed out like a candle. That familiar catch in his throat, and that ache in his stomach returned as he thought of his dead son. *How could I love another human being that much? So much it almost snuffed out my own life when he went,* he thought.

Blast and damn, he said to himself as he handed his hat and gloves to the servant. He had to push away the thoughts of his son.

As he walked across the vast foyer, he thought about Zach and Davina's trick to pair him with a courtesan. Did they hope to change him? Nothing could be changed, but Davina never accepted that. He wished he knew why he'd found Minerva Sargent, or whoever she was, so intriguing.

He had no time for dalliance, for love—not yet, perhaps not ever. He certainly would not marry, not with the taint that the Harding family carried.

59

Sighing heavily, he brushed his hand across his eyes, knowing that every day brought him closer to total blindness.

It had started insidiously enough, slowly shrinking his world. He hadn't even noticed it until he failed to see obstacles at the edges of his vision and walked straight into them. That happened more and more frequently, and he did not wish to pass on the Harding "curse." Not ever. He'd better stay away from the lure of tantalizing female curves. But the memories haunted him.

He shouldn't have kissed her, but he'd found her full, vulnerable lips irresistible. The kiss had stirred his dormant passion, and it disturbed him. These past two years all women he'd met reminded him of his dead son. He rejected them all, and what they stood for—motherhood. A woman could give him another son, but he shuddered at the thought. He didn't want another son, he wanted Thomas back.

"There you are, old fellow," said Zach Gordon as Roarke entered the study and closed the door behind him with a slam.

"I thought you'd never return." Zach propped his splinted and bandaged leg higher on the mountain of pillows before him. At his elbow he had a carafe of port, and in his hand he held a book.

"Well, coz," greeted Roarke. "By your merry twinkle, I'd say you're deep into the bottle." He went to stand by the fireplace where a small fire was dying in the grate. It was pleasantly warm in the room, and the musty smell of books and old leather was welcoming this evening, *safe* somehow.

"Any port left?" Roarke didn't wait for an answer, serving himself a glass from the tray on the floor. He sat down on the carpet next to his cousin and leaned against the worn leather wing chair that had belonged to his father and grandfather before him. He patted Zach's leg. "This will stop you from any foolhardy neck-or-nothing rides, at least for the time being."

Zach laughed, an unruly black curl falling over his eye. The devil was too handsome for his own good, Roarke thought, viewing the friendly open face of the younger man. What Zach needed was to fall in love with a sober, practical widow who knew how to keep hotheads under control.

"I never dreamed that someone would try to shoot me off Aladdin when I returned from Scotland."

"I'm telling you, Zach, some poacher missed his mark. He wasn't shooting at you, nor at the horse! I'm certainly relieved that you only got a broken leg when Aladdin threw you. It could have been worse."

"It almost was the end of that expensive Arabian of yours."

"Aladdin got away with a mere skin burn, and I'm grateful for that."

"No one found that poacher. I'm telling you—"

Roarke heaved a deep sigh. "Let's not get into all that again. Sinister plots, bah!"

Zach's chin jutted aggressively. "Mark my words, someone doesn't want you to succeed with your horse breeding program. Aladdin is a champion, and he endangers old Mel's success with Tokayer. Mel is very aware of that, and I'm sure he wouldn't hesitate to have Aladdin put down."

"Your imagination is running away with you as usual. Mel is too lazy to scheme the failure of my enterprise." Roarke glanced at the portraits hanging in a row on the wall by the door. There was his

61

cousin Melchior Harding whose stables rivaled his own in Kent. Mel's mare Tokayer was first-class blood, and he had a few promising colts. Roarke was acutely aware that Mel viewed his stables askance and accused him of trying to ruin Mel's business. Mel was poor, but so was he—what with the constant upkeep of the estates. He looked at his father, Dennison Harding's stern face next to that of Mel's on the wall. Twelve years had passed since his death, and it was only this last couple of years that the finances had started to recover.

Not enough, Roarke thought, and rubbed his chin. Only hard work and success with Aladdin at the races and in consequent breeding would redeem the precarious Whitecliffe wealth.

"Don't say I didn't warn you about Mel," Zach grumbled and pounded one of the pillows. "I'm certain that someone wants Aladdin dead."

Dead. The word echoed in Roarke's mind and he felt old. A death always brought changes to a person. That ache, that debilitating sorrow, returned to his stomach, and he tried to soothe it with port. It didn't help much.

Every morning was a struggle to get up, to dress, to keep up the pretense of normality with the servants, when all he wanted was to sit in a dark room, doing nothing, seeing no one. Besides his failing vision, there must be something wrong with him. He hated his inability to push away those dark clouds that smothered him every waking hour of the day. He didn't have the strength to push them away. It was as simple as that.

"Day-dreaming again, Roarke? You're quite unreachable sometimes." Zach punched him in the ribs. "You mustn't stand outside your life and watch it go by. You have to come back to the living. By the devil, Roarke, I miss you!" He crashed his wine glass against Roarke's, and Roarke had to laugh.

"I know you're right. I ruminate too much — truly a waste of time." He stared at the painting shrouded in shadows above the mantelpiece. He knew every line and nuance of that portrait. Lawrence had painted it when Thomas was six, and the artist had captured the very essence of the boy, the blond tousled hair, the brown eyes, that roguish grin that had gone down through the ages from great-great-great-grandfather Cromwell Adolphus Harding, Justice of the Peace.

"It was a damned pity that he died, but," Zach said as he nudged Roarke's arm, "the boy did his fair share of pranks, so don't make him into a saint."

"Afflicted with blindness, Thomas wasn't as wild as some, but *you* still are, coz," Roarke said. He sighed. "But you're right, of course. Thomas was no saint."

"Thomas is gone. Let's talk about something else. Did you meet any lovely debutantes at the Divine Davina's house?" Zach asked guilelessly. "Sorry I couldn't attend the dance, but I would have tripped everybody with my crutches."

"Don't play the innocent with me, Zach. I know you plotted with Davina to pair me with this heavenly apparition with hair as blond as silver, and blessed with such a graceful body that I thought Aphrodite had come down from Olympus. However, the goddess had a Roman name, Minerva."

"Hmm, it sounds like you actually took notice of a member of the fair sex."

Roarke inhaled deeply. "I'm not sure I'm ready

for romantic trysts, but if it'll make you happy to know it, I made a real fool of myself."

"It's a start anyway. You've been celibate for much too long."

Roarke blushed. "Not exactly . . . celibate, but I'd rather pay—"

"Say no more. You don't want to take the risk of another heartbreak like the one you went through at Thomas's death. No marriage, no more children for you, and I don't blame you for feeling that way."

Zach sipped his port. "But you can't stop living, turning yourself into a recluse. 'Tisn't right."

Roarke felt a stab of guilt. "Don't you ever give up on me, Zach? Well, I suppose hope springs eternal in the human breast—in yours anyway. You know I can't marry."

"What you need is to fall in love. Then you might change your mind about marriage. Besides, it'll help you out of your depression."

Roarke changed the position of his back uneasily. "What *exactly* do you have in mind?"

"You could always begin by cultivating the lady you met tonight." Zach held up his hands. "I swear I didn't have a clue about Davina's plans for the evening. I didn't hire a courtesan for you. It must have been Davina's idea."

Roarke studied his cousin narrowly. Zach's words had the ring of authenticity. "I don't know what to believe, Zach. My common sense tells me never to believe anything you say."

"I'm telling the truth! Rest assured, Davina has your best interest at heart," Zach chortled. "A monk lives a more sinful life than you do."

Roarke swatted Zach's head. "Don't try my patience! Like I said, I pay for my pleasures."

"Don't we all?" Zach's eyes glittered wickedly. "Except the ones we can get for free." Another paroxysm of laughter shook him, and Roarke thought the evening would have been more entertaining if he'd just stayed at home drinking port with Zach.

"Even with your leg up in the air, you perpetrate more mischief than the average blade, coz."

"I can't abide boredom. I would marry if only I could catch a certain lady's interest."

Roarke grumbled into his port. "I take it you're alluding to the fair Aurora."

"I'm telling you, her dragon of an aunt, Lady Herrington, is keeping her a prisoner."

Zach was silent, brooding, and Roarke recognized the unspoken anguish. "When did you last see her?"

"At a ball for her cousin in the Dales. The aunt whisked Aurora away right from my arms on the dance floor." Zach cleared his throat. "Aurora had tears in her eyes, and she looked as if she hadn't slept for days. As far as I know, she never had a coming out ball. Her dress was outmoded and threadbare. I must discover what's really going on."

"I don't blame the aunt for keeping the fair Aurora from you, old boy," Roarke said dryly.

Zach patted him on the shoulder. "Never could resist a challenge, you know that. But to return to you—one day you'll meet the lady who shall help you break through your sorrow." Zach closed his eyes, raised his chin, and spread out both his arms as if he were in a trance. "She will be as lovely as sin, as fair as snow, as warm as the sun, and as sprightly as an imp. You shall fall like a stone to the bottom of her heart, never to resurface."

"Damn you, Zach," Roarke said good-naturedly

and pushed down his cousin's arms. "You're never serious."

Zach reached over and made the sign of the cross on Roarke's forehead. "What has been said here tonight, shall become true." A warm grin spread over his face. "You'll see, my furious bear, my prediction shall be fulfilled."

Roarke gave a dry laugh. "Indeed. Meanwhile, I shall go up to bed."

"She'll be as lovely as Portia Harding," Zach continued, and pointed at the portraits.

Roarke viewed the two wives of his father. Juliet Harding had been his mother, a tall, narrow-featured woman whom he'd never known. She'd died at his birth. According to those who had known her, he had her blue-green eyes and dark blond hair. Lovely Portia Harding, Father's second wife, had been young and lonely when Father married her. Portia had been a soft, compassionate woman, and had treated him as her own son. Roarke had loved her like a mother, and he knew that she had suffered at the hands of his father, who had turned more and more bitter as the blindness shrunk his world. Father had been a man of violent, unpredictable temper, and Roarke well remembered the beatings he'd received as a child. Portia had always tried to shield him against his father. She had been desperately unhappy in the loveless marriage. He'd gone off to Oxford, and she died at Christmas that year. If he ever married, he wished his wife would be like Portia, loving and kind.

"Zach, I don't trust your predictions. Not many ladies would be as good as Portia. They are more like Lady Barton, my vitriolic aunt." Lady Edna Barton was his mother, Juliet's, younger sister — a busybody who never failed to point out his short-

66

comings. She disapproved of everything he did, and as her other sister was married to Melchior's father, she always sided with Mel.

Zach emptied his glass. "You're a killjoy."

"And you're a trickster. It wouldn't be above you to pay someone to seduce me. Good night." As he climbed the stairs, he thought about the intriguing woman he'd met at Davina's house. Against his will, she had touched him more deeply than he found comfortable.

Minna's thoughts spun in turmoil as she went back home to Clifford Street in Davina's coach. She had taken off her mask and shaken out her hair. Playing a genteel lady was more exhausting than she had anticipated. As the steel-banded wheels grated against the cobblestones, she went over every detail of her conversation with Roarke Harding. It was strange, but what she remembered most was the deep pitch of his voice, not so much the words he had spoken. And his magnetism. Just thinking about that arousing kiss that he'd forced on her made her heavy and languid inside. A deep yearning had sprung to life somewhere in the region of her stomach, and she couldn't name it. The sensation was uncomfortable and exhilarating at the same time. Never in her dreams had she pictured that the earl would be such an attractive man, so dangerous to her composure. Mr. Wylie hadn't warned her about that aspect of the deal.

She fidgeted with the tight gold-cloth belt around her waist. In this costume she didn't feel like Minna Smith, but like some exotic creature that belonged to the night. She wished she had already accomplished her part of the bargain. The thought of what lay ahead made her cold with anxiety.

Bond Street was deserted at this time of night. She glanced out the window and saw that they were almost home. Gas lamps glowed at intervals, shredding the gloom of the overcast night.

The horses stopped in front of the shop with a jingle of harnesses. The groom at the back jumped down and opened the door for her. She climbed down and pressed a coin into his hand.

"Thank you," she said.

He looked puzzled but pleased, and Minna realized that he wasn't used to gestures of gratitude. "What's your name?"

"Knobby, ma'am."

To her surprise, he lifted his powdered wig and bowed. Then he placed the coin on top of his head and covered it with the wig. She couldn't help but laugh.

The short, monkey-like fellow patted his head. "No thieves would think o' lookin' for money under me flash."

"How clever." As Minna moved to go inside, a sound reached her ears. It was coming from the far side of the adjoining building, the boot-maker's shop.

She stopped, listened, and noticed that Knobby had tensed as he closed the coach door.

"What was that? A dog in pain?" she asked.

The sound came again, louder this time.

"A human moan, if I'm not mistaken," Minna said. "Come along, Knobby, we must investigate."

Knobby seemed reluctant to obey, but he followed her as she went down the street toward the lantern at the end.

Minna heard the woman crying before she reached her. The sound was so plaintive that it filled Minna with a chill. The crying came from a bundle of rags propped against the wall.

"Look, Knobby," Minna said. "What happened here, do you think?"

"Dunno, ma'am. Most likely a gang attack. Doesn't look like she 'ad much to give 'em."

Minna bent over the form, then, repulsed, took a step back as she saw the disfigured face. In the weak light, she noticed the swellings and bruises, but it was something deeper than that which disturbed her. Half of one ear was gone, and half of the face seemed too smooth and lifeless, and somehow askew. One eyelid drooped uncannily. Sudden recognition darted through her. She'd seen this woman speaking with Mrs. Collins some time ago.

"Help me," the woman wailed in a surprisingly clear voice. "I was beaten. They took my purse."

Knobby helped the woman to stand up, and Minna noticed that her clothes had been torn. "Miss, did they, er . . . violate your person?"

"No . . . just stole my money." The woman hiccupped with fright and clutched her middle. She swayed on her feet as Knobby let go of her.

Minna took her hand, finding it icy cold. "You must come to my house and have some tea. We ought to send someone for the police."

"What can some decrepit old watchman do to help now?" the woman said with a snort of contempt. "Crime is everywhere."

"Nevertheless, it should be reported."

The woman mumbled something as she shuffled along, leaning heavily on Knobby. "They won't do anything. I will never see my money again."

Minna noticed that the woman limped badly. One hip seemed higher up than the other. "Did they kick your leg as well?"

69

"No . . . my hip was ruined in an accident years ago." The woman was crying softly, and Minna's heart squeezed with compassion. She remembered that dark rainy night when she had almost jumped off a bridge. This woman was in the same state of destitution that she'd been in that night.

"You can stay with us until you feel better," she said kindly. "What's your name?"

"Rosie Long. I used to be a housekeeper in the household of a rich merchant, but they emigrated to America without taking me along." She sobbed quietly into a handkerchief. "At least they left me a letter of reference." She paused, blowing her nose. "No one wants to hire a cripple, let alone an *ugly* cripple. I've been looking for employment for weeks."

They reached the back entrance, and Minna unlocked the door. Knobby helped the woman downstairs to the kitchen, and Minna followed. A fire still glowed in the hearth, and Minna pulled up a stool close to it. "Here, have a seat, Miss Long."

The woman muttered her thanks. Her face was pale with shock, and a faint sheen of perspiration covered her forehead. Knobby looked uncomfortable as he stared at the disfigured face.

Minna realized that Rosie wasn't old, perhaps twenty-eight or thirty years of age. "Thank you, Knobby, I can manage from here."

He was jerking his head sideways as if eager to speak with her in private. Minna went with him to the door.

"Are you sure—?"

Minna nodded. "I'm not afraid of her. You have done more than enough, Knobby. Good-night."

"Just be careful. There are people in this town—"

70

"She doesn't look like a criminal. I feel it is my duty to help her any way I can."

Knobby said nothing else, only bowed and left the house. Minna returned to the woman named Rosie and found that the kettle on the trivet still held hot water. "I shall make us some tea, and then you can tell me your whole story."

"There isn't much to tell. I've only served in one household, and before that I was in an orphanage. My mother was a governess, but she died when I was ten."

"Governess, eh? That's why you speak so well."

"I suppose," Rosie said. She seemed to shrink on the stool as Minna gave her a cup of tea and a slice of marble cake that Mrs. Collins had baked that morning. Rosie reminded Minna of a sick vulture with her head sunk deeply between her shoulderblades. The image filled Minna with unease, but Rosie couldn't help that she looked revolting.

Minna sat down on another stool and made herself study the strange face. She figured that Rosie Long had once been a handsome woman. Now a few scraggly blond strands of hair hung from under the mobcap on her head. Rosie had a direct stare, dark, sorrow-filled eyes, and Minna steeled herself so as not to show the horror she felt.

"The family I worked for got used to my face," Rosie muttered.

"You'd like employment here?"

Rosie nodded, showing some animation at last. "Yes. Yes! I can sew, clean, cook, just about anything in a household. I'll be the lowliest scullery maid if only you'll give me work." Her hands trembled visibly around the cup, and Minna's compassion rose again.

"Very well. I'll give you a trial period of two months to start with. First we must bathe your bruises, then give you some clean clothes. Tonight you may sleep down here in front of the fire, and tomorrow, Mrs. Collins, my housekeeper, shall give you a room in the attic."

Rosie fell to her knees and clasped Minna's hands with both her own. Minna found that they were still icy. "Thank you. You shan't regret it." She delved into the pocket of her filthy skirt and pulled out a folded paper. "My recommendation letter."

Minna scanned the glowing reference and nodded. "Well then, I'm pleased that I found you, Rosie. Mrs. Collins is getting old and needs some help."

Rosie clasped Minna's hands anew. "It must be Higher Guidance that brought me here." Tears of gratefulness rolled from under that strangely drooping eyelid in a most disconcerting way, Minna thought. It made her heart light to know she was putting some happiness into the life of an outcast. She worked for the less fortunate, and they worked for her. She never wanted to change that, and Mr. Wylie would have no power over her just as soon as she'd fulfilled her part of the bargain.

Chapter Five

Thank goodness it was a warm night, calm and spiced with the scent of roses, Minna thought on the following evening as she sat down to wait for the Earl of Whitecliffe in Davina's marble gazebo. "I will surely fall to pieces before he arrives," she whispered and adjusted the broad sash of her corn-flower-blue silk gown. She smiled wryly as she smoothed the straight, narrow skirt. Not too long ago she had made the finishing touches on this dress, never suspecting that tonight she would borrow it from Davina. The bodice fit too tightly across her shoulders, and the skirt was too short for her, but it was better than anything that Minna herself owned. Though she had lovely clothes, she didn't bestow the same luxuries on herself as she lavished on her customers.

"Where is he?" she said, listening for footsteps. He would probably arrive through the gate at the mews. She kept glancing toward the path, but saw no movement.

A twig dropped to the ground from the beech tree beside the belvedere and Minna jumped with fright. "Silly girl," she said and rubbed her bare arms. "He is fashionably late." She gave a silent moan. She would be at the mercy of a man she knew practically nothing about, except that he'd ruined Mr. Wylie's daughter. She had to find a way to control him before he controlled her. . . . *Be calm my heart.*

A clock somewhere inside Davina's house chimed twelve. He's very late, she thought. Her anguish grew, and she strained her eyes to penetrate the darkness. Perhaps he was arrogant enough not to bother to come.

A cold wind started blowing with a ghost-like rustling of leaves. She pulled her gray, silk-lined cloak closer around her. Feeling edgy and unhappy, she moved away from the soft cushions that lined the benches to look outside. Sighing, she stared at the sky where heavy clouds had started to obscure the stars. Before long, it would rain.

Leaning over the rail, she emitted a muffled sob. Dashed tears! There was no need to cry; no need to worry. She could handle the situation. With an angry gesture, she wiped her face and adjusted the half-mask.

A soft step fell on the floor behind her. She whirled around and saw the earl silhouetted in the door opening. His arms folded over his chest, he leaned against the frame. She couldn't see his smile, but she sensed it. His voice holding a teasing note he said,

"It isn't the first time a lady sheds tears over me, but I didn't realize you were that desperate to see me."

"These are tears of anger, Lord Whitecliffe," she said, trembling with nerves. "I was pondering whether I was foolish to trust that you would come tonight. Are you always this late? 'Tis very thoughtless."

His silent arrival had taken her by surprise and she momentarily forgot her anxiety. She noticed his slow smile.

"My, you *are* impatient, my sweet. I'm flattered that you are so eager to see me again. I, however, was in two minds about coming here tonight, but my curiosity got the better of me."

Minna tilted her head to one side and slowly unfurled her fan. Cringing at her own duplicity, she spoke in a come-hither tone of voice. "I'm charmed that you could not stay away."

He slowly rubbed his cheek, and she smelled the spicy, seductive fragrance of his shaving soap. "Miss Sargent, to tell you the truth, I'm reluctant to embark on an *affaire de coeur,* no matter how much you intrigue me."

She moved toward him swinging her hips provocatively. "I never mentioned an involvement of the hearts. There are numerous other ways to enjoy ourselves." She stood very close and fluttered her fan in front of her face, wondering if her smile was suggestive enough to melt his resistance. She had to keep him intrigued. "You *did* come here, after all . . ." Her voice trailed off tantalizingly.

He sighed, still not making a move toward her. "I have to adjust to the idea of involving myself with a dangerous lady like yourself."

"Dangerous? Surely not." Minna sensed his inner struggle, and tapped his arm with her fan. "I suspect I might have competition. Who is the lady fortunate enough to be your mistress?"

His eyes narrowed thoughtfully as he kept staring at her. "Mistress? What gives you the idea that I'm already engaged in an affair? It would be rather unkind of me to retain two ladies at the same time."

"Some gentlemen have a great appetite for love-making." Minna flinched, feeling vulgar and false. This was a mad game, but she had to progress on the chosen path.

He chuckled. "Again I'm flattered, but no, I don't have insatiable appetites." He pulled the tip of his forefinger along her jawbone. "Do you, Miss Sargent?"

Minna blushed to the roots of her hair and was grateful that the darkness did not reveal her acute embarrassment. She had to keep playing her role. "Sometimes," she said. "Especially when I've discovered a gentleman who I know would excite me beyond my wildest dreams."

"You have a honeyed tongue," he said with a purr in his voice. He tickled her chin, and she felt his longing.

"I invite you to taste it." She lifted her face to his as if to offer her mouth to him. He inhaled sharply, and she noticed that he'd stiffened, staring as if mesmerized at her lips. She pouted, wondering if he could hear her pounding heartbeat.

With a sudden movement and a groan, he turned away from her, and she suspected that her daring move had repelled him.

"I look at your innocent face and marvel at your brazen offer," he murmured. "I cannot conciliate myself to such contrast. Tell me, how does such a sweet face hide such cunning calculation? Are you so corrupt that you're willing to go to any length to snare me?" He took a step away from her. "Are you hoping to lay your hands on my leather purse?" He delved into his pocket and pulled it out. "I thought Davina had already purchased your favors for my pleasure."

"Why so suspicious?" Minna asked, sensing failure. "I harbor no plans beyond a pleasant time shared. Be it one night, be it a fortnight, or longer. It matters not. My eyes are not on monetary gains."

Feeling inadequate to the task of soothing his suspicion and engaging his interest anew, she stepped toward him. Her smile felt forced and shallow.

Evidently, he sensed her duplicity. "I can't help but think that you're trying to trap me, Miss Sargent. Is your game to become the Countess of Whitecliffe, or are you only seeking the protection of a gentleman?"

"It's always a courtesan's goal to find a powerful protector. Does it make a difference?"

"To me it does." He stared hard at her, and when she didn't continue, he turned as if to leave and his arm brushed the marble pillar that flanked the steps. "I'm sorry, Miss Sargent, but I've changed my mind. I don't want to get involved with you. Therefore, good-night. Concentrate your charms on the young men just down from Oxford. They will be thrilled to share the dance of love with you." He moved hesitantly down the steps and along the brick path, his walking stick swinging back and forth in front of him.

Confused by the turn of events, she ran after him. "You can't leave like this," she cried. "I'm at your disposal." *Help! This isn't the right way to handle this,* she said to herself in agitation. She was pushing him away instead of attracting him. "I thought you were as delighted to see me as I was to see you."

He stopped. "Perhaps I was. But I'm cautious by nature. I'm not about to do something I'll regret later."

77

"I've never met a gentleman who would turn down my offer. Are you afraid of pleasure?" She reached his side, and he suddenly grabbed a handful of her hair that was hanging loose down her back.

"I don't deny that you're lovely," he growled and yanked her so close that she could feel the contours of his hard body against hers. "You're *too* lovely, my sweet stranger." He kissed her hair and she heard him inhale its fragrance. "I don't trust beautiful women," he said and dropped his hand. "Never did. I certainly won't start now. Especially not you. You'll ruin me."

"It's cowardly of you," she whispered, not knowing where she found the courage to taunt him. "Why not enjoy what's freely offered to you?"

His eyes sizzled with suppressed emotions, but his face looked stiff in the bleak light of the emerging moon. Minna wondered if she'd provoked his anger, but he remained motionless.

"Your taunts can't hurt me," he said, and turned on his heel abruptly. "You just don't like my rejection." He moved again with his hesitant, slow gait. In a flash of insight, she realized that he couldn't see very well.

She ran after him in desperation, searching for a way to hold him back. "Why did you come if you weren't planning to fulfill our bargain?"

He stopped and faced her. "Our decision to meet was made in haste. Right now I just want you to understand my position. I simply don't want to be involved. Now, let's not argue any longer." They reached the back gate. "We shall part here."

"No, wait!" Her thoughts racing, she ran after him. "Listen, you were right, perhaps I've been too hasty. Surely, we could while away an hour, talking?"

He laughed. "You're very persistent, but I suspect that discussing the latest news would bore you."

"I resent your condescending attitude," Minna said, stung to the quick.

"I would return home if I were you," he said, marching along with his cane. "The streets aren't safe for a female on her own. Tell Davina her scheme didn't work out, but I appreciate her effort."

"I'm in no danger; I know the streets."

"Of course you do," he said sarcastically, "but even courtesans might have their throats cut. You're by no means exempt."

Minna placed a hand on his sleeve. She had to persuade him to spend time with her so that she could discover his weak points. "Please, Lord Whitecliffe, let's end this arguing and return to the gazebo?"

He shook his head and gave her a quick glance. "No, I've told you, I've lost interest. I don't like to play games, and I fear whatever you tell me won't be the truth. Good-night."

"Very well, as you please." Filling with anxiety, she slowed down. She wasn't using the right tactics, and she had no idea what to do next. Working hard over the years to create her shop, she had neglected friendships with the opposite sex.

"Botheration!" She waited until he'd turned the corner of the street. She would have to find a way to his heart, an endeavor that seemed doomed before it started.

She knew he lived in Berkley Square, but she wanted to view the mansion with her own eyes.

Perhaps if she saw him in his own setting it might give her an idea on how to proceed. She began to follow him. *This is folly!* she thought, furious with Mr. Wylie for putting her in a position of such humiliation.

He'd slowed down, touching his cane to the pavement in front of him. His evening cloak billowed behind him, and it helped her to distinguish his form in the darkness.

Tense with worry, she almost cried out as a cat streaked past her leg. Knowing there were dangers lurking in dark alleys and courtyards, she made sure not to lose sight of the earl. Apprehensive, she passed a group of night revelers. She pulled the hood of her cloak deeper over her face, hoping that they could not distinguish her from the surrounding shadows. To her relief, they didn't.

The earl went around the enclosed park in Grosvenor Square, and all was quiet. She followed him as he turned down Charles Street and she had no difficulty keeping up with him. Just as she passed the entrance to Adams Mews, someone slid up beside her, falling in with her pace, slowing her down with a hand on her arm.

"Wot's a fine lady like yersel' walkin' alone at night? Ye don't 'aveta be lonely."

Minna cringed as the large man in a worn coat and a stocking cap squeezed her arm. "Let me go," she said, more afraid that the earl would discover her presence than for her own safety.

But the man's grip didn't lessen. He laughed gleefully. "A right li'l filly ye are," he crooned. "A right li'l lovey."

Minna wanted to scream, but it wasn't the first time she had been attacked in the streets. She knew some tricks from living in the East End. Ellie had

80

taught them to her when it was unsafe to walk home from the workshop after nightfall.

She forced herself to keep her stride and tore her arm from his grip.

Her assailant chuckled. "A bit o' fire, eh? I niver tire o' a filly with a bit o' fire."

Minna sensed his next move, the one where he would lift her off the ground and carry her away into some dark nook. She forced herself to stay calm, and when he made the sudden lunge for her, she stuck out her foot and hooked his leg. As he tripped, she punched his face with her fist. Reeling from the blow, he crashed to the ground. Minna took off running, but the man was soon in hot pursuit.

Minna saw the earl turn the corner of Mount Street with its clutter of townhouses. She couldn't afford to lose her view of him, and her attacker was almost upon her.

Her heartbeat raced with fear as she turned around abruptly, then jumped aside as the man came up to her. Hoping to trip him, she held out her foot. However, this time he knew to avoid her trick, and he fell heavily against her. As she cried out with terror and tumbled to the ground with him, she knew she might have relied too heavily on her own skills. However, she wasn't beaten yet. He sprawled across her middle, trying to ease himself up and over her without giving her leverage.

She could not knee him in the groin, which usually was a great defense, but she grabbed his hand and bit him hard.

"Ahhoo," he moaned, and his weight lessened momentarily. She wriggled away, still holding on to his hand. Due to his bulk, he was slow in rising, and she had already managed to reach her knees

81

when he lunged for her with his other hand. She quickly pulled his index finger back, and pressed it down with all her might. He screamed and convulsed in agony. Like some grotesque beast, he gyrated from the pain.

Dry in the mouth with fear, Minna got up on trembling legs, still twisting his finger with both her hands. It almost met the back of his hand, but it wouldn't break. As he struggled to get up, she finally jabbed her knee under his chin. His head snapped back, and he fell on the ground. Then she ran and ran until she couldn't run any longer. A stitch burned in her side, and she leaned against the iron fence of a townhouse and breathed deeply.

There was no sign of her assailant, but neither was there any sign of the earl. "Blast!" she swore, clutching her aching side. She touched her hair with her other hand, and found that it was tangled and matted with dust. So much for seducing Lord Whitecliffe, she thought with a sigh. Her cloak looked a mess, too, she saw in the weak light from the windows of the townhouse.

Smoothing out the rumpled cloak, she steadied her marrowless legs and walked toward Berkley Square. Every part of her body trembled with fatigue, and her mind was filled with fear and doubt. *What had I hoped to gain by following the earl?* she asked herself.

As she was about to run the last stretch to the square, someone came up behind her on quiet feet. She whirled, expecting her assailant, but this was a different man, tall and strong with a hat brim brought level with his eyes. She sensed danger and cringed. Behind him came another ruffian, and her previous attacker.

"You li'l bitch. 'Arvey said 'e could 'andle ye

82

alone, but ye were a tough one." The tall man gripped Minna's arm and snatched her up against him.

Fear made her blood into ice water. "What do you want with me?" She knew she could not fight off three men. Making a valiant effort, she kicked the first man in the leg, but he only laughed.

"A bit of fun, that's all. If ye give it to us fer free, we might let ye go, despite what ye did to 'Arvey. 'Is finger is swellin' summat terrible."

She was surrounded, and her captor laughed. " 'Arvey wanted ye for 'imself, but 'e wasn't man enough to take ye. I am."

Minna hadn't given it a thought that Harvey was part of a gang. "I don't have any money."

"We don't want yer money," the man holding her said. "We want *you,* then we want yer 'air. Should fetch a godly sum at the wig makers'." He dragged his hand through her tangled tresses, and laughed. "Aye, but first—"

He planted his wet lips against her neck, and she screamed. She struggled to get away, but he only clutched her tighter. The others egged him on, and a roaring started in her ears. This time there was no way out. "Let me go," she pleaded, but the answer she got was evil-sounding mirth.

Her captor stopped abruptly as a rock hit his head. He reeled back, losing his grip on Minna.

She whirled and recognized the earl in the gloom. Weak with relief, she held out her hand toward him, but two thugs stood between them.

Although half paralyzed with fear, Minna took the initiative by kicking the man called Harvey. Then she brought up her knee with full force in his groin. His hands that had closed around her shoulders moments before, slackened, and he collapsed with a groan of pure agony.

The earl had engaged the other two in fisticuffs, and soon one of the toughs was reeling sideways clutching the lower part of his face. A broken jaw perhaps, Minna thought as her heartbeat pounded in her ears. Her attention didn't linger on him as she flew onto the back of the third man. His movements thus hampered, he could only watch in terror as the earl drew his fist back and delivered a crushing blow to his chin. With a moan, he staggered and lost his foothold. Minna jumped away from him as he fell.

"Thank you," she said breathlessly. "If it hadn't been for you—"

The earl's eyes blazed with anger. "What the hell are you doing here?" he snapped and pulled her unceremoniously along the street. "I have a mind to let those rowdies finish what they set out to do."

"You don't mean that," Minna said, losing her breath completely. The stitch in her side had begun to ache again as his pace increased. She tried to pull her arm away, but he held her too tightly. "I'm truly grateful that you came to my rescue," she continued. "You can't be entirely heartless, after all."

"Don't count on it," he barked. "If it pleases me, I can leave you here." Contrary to his words, his hand tightened further around hers. "Your foolishness angers me beyond belief." He stumbled momentarily on a cobblestone and had to slow down.

She could not prevent the taunt on her lips. "I thought that you couldn't be touched by anything I say, or do."

"I'm not touched, I'm angry."

Minna drew a sigh of relief as he stopped in

front of a stately house that had two Corinthian pillars flanking the door. The earl's imposing home was white-washed and consisted of three stories with multi-paned windows that stared darkly at the night.

"You'd better come in while I rouse the coachman to take you back home." He pulled her casually up the steps. " 'Tis fortunate that it's dark, or London would be agog with gossip by breakfast. "It's unthinkable to bring one's light-o'-love to one's home." He snorted. "Not that a courtesan with class would fight like a street urchin." He pulled the hood over her head just as a footman opened the door. "Your hair is very distinctive."

Minna blushed, wishing she had some witty remark to deliver, but she could find nothing at all to say. If anything, this latest event had sorely diminished her chances to ever crush the earl's heart—let alone discover a way into it. He despised her now.

He pulled her inside. "Good-evening, John," he said to the footman. "Show the lady to my study, then see that my coach is ready in half an hour."

The footman nodded and ogled Minna. "Yessir. This instant, my lord."

The earl left her there without another word, and with downbent head, she followed the footman to a door at the other end of the hallway. Her steps echoed in the majestic ceiling above. The sound made her feel small and insignificant. The man she was trying to seduce wasn't some jack from the London docks; he was wealthy and powerful, and he cared nothing for her. Who was she fooling? Shrinking more every minute, she entered the dark room. The footman lighted the oil lamps on each side of the fireplace, then left.

Minna had never felt so small and so lonely. Gone was all the confidence her successful shop had given her. Clifford Street seemed to have disappeared to another world, another time. Here, among old, gleaming furniture, costly carpets, and Chinese vases that looked centuries old, she was nothing but the modest curate's daughter who had known nothing but simple things all her life.

She went to the fireplace where a long-dead fire still gave off some warmth. "Hopefully I don't have to see *him* again tonight," she murmured. "I must go home and lick my wounds."

Her gaze strayed to the portrait above the mantelpiece. The golden boy stared down at her in triumph, she thought. This young fellow knew nothing about starvation. He'd probably never seen the East End, nor had he entered the dark, vermin-infested shacks that were the living quarters of the poor. Sometimes when she took a bath, she wondered if she'd ever be able to clean off the stench of those years in poverty. She never felt completely purged, no matter how often she bathed. Ellie laughed at her and said she would scrub off her skin if she kept soaking in tubs every week.

The room was hushed, the air dignified. She wished to be elsewhere, but she was drawn toward the dim light from an oil lamp on the desk. Here was the heart of the house, she could sense it, and she could also sense the earl's presence even though he wasn't there. That faint male aroma that she connected with him was in the air, and she could picture him move the papers and the books around on the desk. Her fingertips traced a stack of untidy papers. *His* hands had touched these, she was sure of it, and a delicious thrill traveled up her spine. She grew quite breathless as a strange glow filled her. Viewing the spines of some books, she read titles like *Hinduism: The Upanishads; The Wisdom of Lao; The Bhagavad Gita; Confucius: A Chinese Philosopher.* Intrigued, she wanted to leaf through them, but a sound alerted her.

The door opened behind her, and she glanced toward it. The glow inside her intensified when she saw that it was the earl and not a servant. He had taken off his cloak and coat, and was wearing a burgundy brocade dressing gown over his shirt. His sun-bronzed face looked forbidding, but she was only aware of that elusive part of him, the male magnetism, the spicy fragrance of his cologne. He was wearing his eyeglasses and they gave him a dignified air.

"The coachman won't be a minute," he said tonelessly. He crossed his arms over his chest and studied her. Then his gaze went to his desk. "Are you spying?"

Anger pushed the sensual impact of him from her mind. "Yes, as a matter of fact I was. But you have nothing in here that interests me, milord," she said, lying.

"A pity. I quite like my books, but I can hardly expect someone like you to share my pleasure."

"Someone like me? You're the most inconsiderate and rude man I've ever met!" Minna said, tossing her head so that the hood fell back. "I hope you fall flat on your face someday and break your nose."

He laughed. "You don't intimidate me, young lady. What you wish or don't wish is beyond my interest." He stepped up to the desk and Minna expected him to sit down and pretend that she didn't exist. Instead, he poured two glasses of wine from a decanter on a tray.

"You must be exhausted after your ordeal," he said, and handed her the glass. "This is sherry."

She eyed him icily. "If you're about to deliver another lesson about my foolishness, forget it. And I don't drink with enemies."

He shrugged and set the wine glasses down. "Suits me fine. I don't especially want to drink with you."

Minna's lips trembled, and she took a step back as he came to stand at her side of the desk. His words wounded her more than she could have imagined.

"Poor, dejected creature," he chided, and his eyes lit up unexpectedly. "You can't always have what you desire."

She moved farther away from him and her hand dislodged a slim volume on the desk. She recognized the titles of Shakespeare's plays. It lay open on the carpet. The earl bent to retrieve the book, and read. "O mistress mine, where are you roaming? O, stay and hear; your true love's coming . . ." The earl gave her a teasing smile.

Her cheeks blazing, Minna tried to snatch the volume from his hand, but he held it high and read from his memory. "Journeys end in lovers meeting, every wise man's son doth know." He flipped to another page. "What is love? 'Tis not hereafter. What's to come is still unsure. Then come kiss me, sweet and twenty; youth's stuff will not endure."

The earl chuckled, and Minna lashed out. "Stop teasing me!"

"You wanted romance, didn't you, Miss Mysterious? No one could twist the words like Shakespeare; the fellow certainly knew about love." He turned the page. "Shall I read more?"

"No!

He laughed. "I didn't know you were partial to Shakespeare."

Minna squared her shoulders and glared at him. "You want me to deny it, but the truth is, I've always liked the bard." She swallowed her ire and recited a verse from *King Lear*.

He clucked his tongue, and folded his arms over his chest. "I'm impressed. Courtesans usually don't have anything but love on their minds."

"What a generalization. It shows you know nothing about them—us—*me,*" she said, stumbling on every word.

"You know, to accomplish your goal, you shouldn't be so blatantly obvious. A little more subtlety would go a long way. Remember, a gentleman likes to pretend he's the one initiating the seduction."

"I don't see why that should be the rule."

He seemed to see right through her. He reached out and held her jaw in a hard grip. "Wonderful gray eyes behind that ridiculous mask." He dropped his hand with a sigh. "Miss Sargent, you confuse me. A real courtesan would not go about seduction the way you do. You lack sadly in sophistication, and I find that highly suspicious." He sat down on the edge of the desk, dangling his leg. "How much is Davina paying you? I'll offer you the same just to end this farce. Tell me." He reached for her hand, but she pulled away.

"Don't," she warned. The light from the oil lamp glinted in his dark blond hair, and created shadows over his face, but Minna could feel that probing glance even if she couldn't see it. "I only ended up here because I wanted to take some night air," she lied. "I wasn't really following you."

"And I'm the Prince of Wales," he said with a snort. He took a step closer, and just like that first time she'd seen him, he reminded her of a lazy tiger. Dangerous, and with eyes so deep she couldn't read his thoughts. She wasn't safe in the room alone with him — but then again, wasn't that her goal? This moment it seemed that the chase had turned against her. His suddenly wicked grin said that he could devour her in one bite.

She backed away, and he came forward. Her breath clogged in her throat, and she felt as if she was moving through a languorous sea of golden warmth. She had difficulty walking as if the very atmosphere — charged with his presence — was drugging her.

"Your chin is dirty," he whispered, breaking the spell. Only then did she see the handkerchief in his hand. "I was going to wipe it clean with this."

"Don't bother," she snapped and turned away from him. Her heart was beating rapidly, and she hated herself for being attracted to his virility. He was a selfish, arrogant man, not worthy of adoring attention.

Her thoughts shattered as his arms came around her waist from the back. Again that drugged lassitude came over her, and she had no power to push him away.

"I admire a woman of purpose, even though I would've appreciated a bit more finesse."

An angry sob caught in her throat. She turned around, dislodging his arms. "You say the most wounding things. I regret the moment —"

He silenced her with a kiss that was as long as eternity. Her focus centered on the velvet, yet demanding taste of him, the slick seduction of his tongue against hers. Her whole body weakened at his touch, her nostrils filling with the scent of him, a scent she had already learned to love. If he held her any longer, treating her to the exquisite torture of his kiss, she would dissolve and never come together into one piece again. The tip of his tongue traced her bottom lip, and made her shiver with longing. Champagne, not blood, flowed in her veins, and her head spun giddily.

He pulled away a fraction, and the wave falling over his forehead tickled her nose. "This is what you wanted isn't it . . . and this?" He gently parted her cloak, then enclosed one of her breasts with his hand. The touch burned through the thin silk of her gown, and the dizziness returned to her head. A sensation so sweetly agonizing seeped through her as he massaged her nipple through the fabric until it was painfully hard. At this point she was no longer Minna, she was a muddle of luscious sensations that she couldn't even begin to unravel. She didn't want to; she wanted to stay like this forever. But when she tried to curl her arms around him, he dropped his hands and stepped back.

"No!" he said. The color on his cheeks had deepened, and his eyes sparkled with something that she couldn't read. Anger? Frustration? Lust?

"I don't want you to imagine that you've won," he chided. "I still have my senses under control. You'd better go home now, and tell Davina that I'll pay you more than she ever will." He turned away from her. "Please inform her that I don't like her choice of birthday present. I don't like to be tricked into a situation I don't desire."

Minna gasped at his cold words. "You're cruel!" Anger and disappointment churned through her. She itched to clout him over the head, but she chose to compose herself and pull the cloak closer around her. Somehow, she'd won something from him even though she didn't know what it was. But she could feel it. Only a cool head would bring about the next step in this seduction.

"Boring old curmudgeon," she retaliated and left the room, her head held high.

Highly disturbed, Roarke watched her leave. He had gone to the gazebo only to tell her that he didn't accept her bold offer even though Davina probably had paid for his seduction. He'd been reluctant to go, but something had pulled him to the belvedere, and he'd actually sent away his carriage so that no rumors could be started about his new "paramour." Damned nuisance, he thought, and pulled a hand through his hair. He sat down at his desk and moved his books without looking at them. However much he loathed the idea, the lovely blonde intrigued him. Who was this courtesan who mixed innocence with knowledge of street violence, who tasted like the finest old cognac? Who was she? God, that kiss had intoxicated him more than cognac could; it was as if he'd kissed her very soul, and given her part of his. Afterwards it had left a weakness in his heart, a new pain, a sweetness that could not be denied.

He slapped his hand against the blotter on his desk. Damn and double damn, why had Davina embroiled him in this scheme? He didn't need a courtesan and the aggravation she brought. Blast the mystery!

A small nagging voice inside told him that he had to see her again.

Chapter Six

Zach met Roarke at the top of the curving staircase. He was thumping along on his crutches, but the grin across his face said that he'd seen Minerva leave.

"*Who* was the cloaked lady? No one that I know," he drawled and jabbed Roarke with one of his crutches. "You sly dog, bringing ladies here secretly!"

"She has no part of my life. I only saved her from a gang of ruffians outside, then let her wait here until Riggby could drive her home."

"Not part of your life, indeed," Zach chided and shook his head. "I've heard that bland voice of yours before — when you're trying to hide something. You can't fool your old childhood friend and cousin. In fact, I believe I know you better than I know myself."

"Then you ought to know when to shut up!" Roarke snapped and stalked to his bedchamber. Since Minerva Sargent's departure, the house looked cold and uninviting, especially this room. With its huge bed topped with a pleated canopy of green silk, and its massive dark furniture, the room was too vast and lifeless. More acutely than ever before he felt that the house needed talk and laughter to fill it with life, and he couldn't very well chat with himself.

He flung off his dressing gown and pulled the shirt from the waistband of his breeches. Thomas had once given life to this hollow tomb, and it had been doubly quiet since the boy's death.

Roarke buried his head in his hands and sank down on the bed. He had to forget Thomas. To his surprise, tonight it wasn't as difficult as other nights; after his meeting with Minerva, his pulse still beat erratically, and he felt as if every inch of him had been touched by fire. A longing so profound, a need so urgent that he wanted to moan out loud had caught him the moment his lips tasted those warm, soft, sensuous lips of hers. His blood had turned to honey, and the barrier he'd erected against the fair sex had tumbled about him in a silent protest. He'd been so careful not to let treacherous desire break him, but he'd met Minerva at an unguarded moment.

He tore off his shirt and his breeches, and when his valet knocked softly on the door, Roarke yelled, "Go away, Harris, I don't need you." What he needed was to sink into the softness of some woman to kill the longing for the mysterious Minerva. He could always go to a house of assignment. . . . *No!* He could control his urges.

"Blast and damn!" He tossed aside the cover and lay down, folding his hands under his head on the pillow. Weak moonlight slanted through the opening in the drapes covering the French doors that led to his private balcony. Moonlight. He could almost picture her standing there, her hair streaming behind her like the softest silvery light. He wanted to touch her, wanted to bring her to his bed and quiet the desire that still churned inside him. Never in his life had he been that overcome by a simple kiss. He almost laughed out loud in disbelief. If someone had told him that something like this was possible, he would have snorted with derision.

He punched one of the pillows to ease his frustration, but he couldn't forget her, or the fire in his blood. Something very significant had happened to him, something wonderful and exhilarating. But it was also a threat that might bring him more heartache than he'd ever experienced before.

Minna closed her eyes after a long luxurious bath. She had shut them many times during her ablutions and after, and every time she did, she saw *his* face. The hard, almost cruel smile, the penetrating eyes. Every fiber of her remembered each nuance of that spellbinding kiss, the contours of his lips, the texture of his skin, and his tongue that brought havoc to her entire body with its insinuating caress. Just thinking about him made her feel heavy and languid, filled with a golden glow that threatened to consume her completely. She knew she could go on dreaming about him forever, but she also knew that she had to see him again. She *had* to, for her own sake, but also to complete her bargain with Mr. Wylie.

Somehow the deal didn't seem so repugnant any longer. She had set out on this road of seduction, and now she was eager to explore what would come next. Who knows, she might learn something about love. There was a whole different dimension to life that she needed to discover, with *him*. The only question was: did he want to discover it with her, or had he already walked this road many times? Perhaps to him an *affaire* would mean nothing, perhaps he'd never loved anyone, and never would. If he had, surely he would have married.

She grimaced and parted her braided hair. According to Davina he had no interest in love, and Davina had urged her to pull him out of his shell. Perhaps he was only bored, but he hadn't seemed bored when he kissed her. No . . . he hadn't. The kiss had caught them both in a web of enchantment.

Excitement spread through her at the thought, and after drying herself and pulling on her long nightgown, she burrowed under the covers of her narrow bed. She would go on with the next step, but first she would have to invent the best plan to go about it. This time, she would make no mistakes.

During the following week, her business received less of her attention, but Ellie knew perfectly well how to take care of the customers' every whim. Minna spent every waking hour brooding over the situation with the Earl of Whitecliffe, except that there was no situation to speak of. She'd only met him twice, and even if their two kisses had been earth-shaking, it didn't mean that she could make it happen again.

Minna sighed as she sat in her office one morning. She would have to find a way to see him, right away. The memory of Mr. Wylie's visit last evening preyed on her mind.

"I have yet to see any results, Miss Smith," he'd said in his stiff, precise voice, and pinned her with an icy stare. "My patience is not limitless."

"Please Mr. Wylie, you must give me more time," she'd replied. "I believe you won't be disappointed when I'm finished." She doubted that she would find a way to make the earl fall in love with her, but she could not voice such doubts to Mr. Wylie.

"Your time is running out," he'd said and went to the door. "I'm serious in my threats. You'll lose everything. Remember that."

"I understand that. However, I've made considerable progress," she'd lied as he left, but he wasn't listening.

Today, her stomach was a tight knot of worry. She hadn't gotten very far, *not far enough!* A fear that she would never fulfill her part of the bargain made her stomach tense even further. A dull headache added to her discomfort. Massaging her temples, she knew she would have to get out of the shop before she suffocated with self-doubt.

There was a knock on the door and Rosie came in. She was wearing a mobcap trimmed with a profusion of lace that both concealed and softened her strange, repulsive face. Minna had grown used to her, and Mrs. Collins delivered glowing accounts about Rosie's willingness to work, and her deferential manner toward everyone. Rosie bobbed a curtsy by the door.

"Do you want a cup of tea, Madam LaForge?" Rosie always called her by her business title, and Minna was always touched by her soft voice.

"No, Rosie, I'm going out. Do you want to come with me for a walk? You work too much in the house. You don't get enough fresh air."

"I don't mind, ma'am. I'm so grateful to have a roof over my head." Rosie lowered her disconcerting eyes, and hid her hands under the enormous white apron that Mrs. Collins had given her.

"Nevertheless, you must come with me."

Rosie curtsied again. "Very well, ma'am, just let me fetch my cloak."

Fifteen minutes later the two women headed up Bond Street. They drifted from one shop to the next, but Minna couldn't concentrate on ribbons and posies at the milliners, nor could perfumes or sweetmeats entice her.

"Pardon me, ma'am," Rosie said, bobbing a curtsy, "I think that you're worried."

Minna glanced at her and Rosie instantly averted her gaze. *That girl perceives more than I realized,* Minna thought. "I am disturbed, yes."

Rosie twined her fingers together in an agitated manner. "Can I be of any help?" She blushed fiercely, and Minna sensed how shy Rosie was.

Minna smiled. "I don't know. Perhaps." She stopped by the wall and watched a handsome carriage drawn by four horses stop at one of the shops. A gentleman got out and helped his female companion down. Minna tilted her head in their direction. "Do you see that handsome gentleman?"

Rosie nodded. "Yes . . ?" She gave Minna a questioning glance.

"What if I'm interested in such a man, a gentleman who cares nothing for me. How do I snare his affection?" Minna didn't expect an answer from Rosie, but the maid spoke after a few moments of silence.

"Why, you must apply yourself with heart and soul," she said passionately. "Not let one day go by without an effort to tempt him."

Minna laughed. "You sound like you're speaking from vast experience."

Rosie's expression was hidden behind the lace of her mobcap. "I wasn't always . . . er, ugly. I had my share of romance." She suddenly gripped Minna's arm, taking Minna by surprise. "Tomorrow might be too late, ma'am. Tomorrow you might look like me, and then no gentleman will admire you." A sob escaped her. "Your lovely hair might fall out, and then you'll have to hide your head with a cap all the time." A tear rolled down her cheek, and Minna's heart constricted with compassion.

"I'm sorry," Rosie whispered, and turned abruptly. Before Minna could stop her, the maid had run halfway home. A dog barked shrilly after her, and a coachman swore at her as she darted in front of a horse.

Minna stared after her in silence. It was true. Tomorrow might be too late. It was a chilling thought, and she pulled her cloak tighter around her even though the day was sunny and warm.

Filled with frustration, Minna watched the people in the street. She glanced into a display window and wiped a tear from the corner of her eye. Was she fooling herself thinking she could make someone as assured, and *wealthy* as the Earl of Whitecliffe fall in love with her? Anyhow, love was not a consideration in the upper classes. Love was *never* an issue it seemed—the marriages of all classes were based on transactions of estate and monetary gains. It pained Minna to realize that she'd never known love, not the dizzying, abandoned feeling that the poets described. Except . . . just for one moment in the earl's arms, his mouth against hers, and his hard body molding her soft curves. If she fell in love with the earl, she would be hurt, and yet, what choice did she have? Mr. Wylie was serious in his threat, and he would never give up his desire for revenge.

No closer to the solution of her problems, Minna headed back to her shop on Clifford Street.

She went into her office, took off her cloak, and

smoothed her black bombazine dress that she often wore as Madame LaForge.

As she stepped into the showroom, Davina Shield accosted her instantly. "*There* you are, Minna. I thought you had abandoned ship."

Minna shook her head and smiled. "No, I have no intention of leaving this—my dream." She viewed the mauve and purple fabric that Davina was holding up to her face. "Let me show you something more flattering," she said. "Let me show you some blue gauze shot with gold threads that arrived yesterday." She went into the storage room at the back and pulled out a bolt that was still wrapped in paper. The material shimmered in her hands as she extracted it, the gauze as light as gossamer.

Davina inhaled sharply when she laid eyes on the fabric. "Divine!" she breathed, then glanced at the other customers surreptitiously to see if they had noticed the coveted bolt. She grasped Minna's arm, and pulled her toward the fitting rooms. "Let's discuss this in private."

Ellie, who was waiting on other patrons gave Minna a knowing glance and a smile. They had ordered the fabric especially for Davina, and she loved it. Minna felt a glow of pleasure inside, knowing that her good instincts—and Ellie's—had brought this shop to its present success. None of these wealthy ladies knew the satisfaction of prosperity through hard work. They had always had everything handed to them. Perhaps they would never discover if they had any talents, Minna thought as she followed Davina. In a sense, they were poorer than she, and as she visualized that thought, she knew she had gained real wealth through her accomplishment.

Davina flung the gauze over one shoulder and draped it across her curvaceous figure. "Absolutely perfect! You must make me a gown, lace inset on the bodice and across the shoulders — and puffy sleeves. I shall wear it to a rout at Richmond this coming Saturday." She shot Minna a glance. "I — we — have been invited to supper with Viscount Marsdon and his wife. Dear friends of mine, if a bit stuffy. Marsdon was an old crony of my father, so I view him as my uncle." She held up a rope of gold braiding. "This will be perfect around the hem, don't you think?"

Minna nodded automatically. "We, you said?"

Davina nodded and wagged her finger under Minna's nose. "You haven't seduced Lord White-cliffe, have you?. I thought you would 'retire' after that masked ball — the affair, er, unconsummated. People have been talking about you."

Minna blushed. "How did you know that I . . . er, failed in my pursuit?"

"I know *everything* that transpires in Roarke's house." She patted Minna's arm. "I care about him, I want what's best for him. What he needs is the warmth of a woman to pull him out of his doldrums. We must keep up the charade until you succeed."

"But how? The earl is not the least interested in me. He's suspicious of my motives."

Davina pursed her lips and toyed with a box of buttons on Minna's desk. "Hmmm, I'm sure he'll come around if you're persistent enough. I have yet to meet a man who could resist the charms of a lovely woman."

Minna pinned a swag of contrasting gauze to Davina's neckline for effect. "He believes *I* was your birthday present to him." She didn't divulge the fact that she'd told the earl that she was a courtesan.

Davina laughed in delight. "Birthday gift? How droll. I shall berate him for his lack of gratitude when I see him next."

"I'd rather you not talk about me."

Davina turned in front of the mirror. "He would love to seduce you, Minna, but as you pointed out, he might be leery of your eagerness."

Minna sighed. "But I don't know how to go on from here. He believes that you're paying for my 'services.' He has rejected me most firmly."

Davina patted her arm. "Oh, you truly are innocent! There are so many ways to reach a gentleman's heart." She gave Minna a hard stare. "How old are you anyway? You must have turned down plenty of offers."

Minna shook her head. "No, I haven't had time for romance. The shop occupied my every thought, day and night, until this last year."

Davina gasped. "You've missed so much. Come, come, you must have some romance before your skin starts sagging and the luster goes out of your hair."

"You make me sound like an ancient crone," Minna said with a hollow laugh.

"I'm not surprised that you've fallen for the most enigmatic man in London, but I must warn you, Roarke's like an impenetrable fortress. He belongs to no one but himself." She sighed. "I do so wish to see him happy."

Minna shuddered, thinking about the possible loss of this shop and everything in it. "If I change him," she murmured, "you will be the first to know, Davina."

Davina squealed with excitement. "I like your determination. In fact, if you order a tea tray to be brought to your office, I shall stay and help you plan your strategy."

Minna's heartbeat escalated. "Yes." It was almost as if she sensed him right there with them. In her mind, she could see every nuance of his face, every wicked smile, every hard glance he'd given her. "We must be very careful."

"How do we know that the earl will be at the rout?"

Davina said, "I'll ask Marsdon to invite him."

"But . . . but the earl might confront you about my presence."

"You can go as Leverett Epcott's escort. The baronet is dotty about me, he'll do anything I ask him, and if he sees a chance to ogle me all evening, he won't mind escorting you. We shall endeavor to dress you so that the earl won't recognize you—at first." She clapped her hands together and laughed. "He'll be titillated. You must make a surprise rendezvous with him in the garden. I shall steer him outside, and lead him to the folly where you shall join him." She touched the neat bun of hair at Minna's neck. "We must of course emphasize this striking mane, and dress you in something so provocative that the earl is bound to take notice." She went toward the door. "I have items that will conceal the most ravishing beauty—or accentuate it." She winked and closed the door. Minna heard her laughter as she walked along the corridor. Perhaps it was a joke to Davina, but her own life hung in the balance.

Minna found that her hands shook as she placed the teacups on the tray.

Chapter Seven

Leverett Epcott had eyes for no one but Davina
Shield. Minna was grateful that he didn't try to seduce her. She adjusted her cloak as they waited in
the coach for their turn to enter the wide open
double doors of the Marsdon mansion in Richmond. Upon Davina's suggestion, she had dressed
in a midnight-blue gown that concealed everything
and nothing. The fine silk molded every curve of
her body, and a froth of lace around the deep
neckline and a red sash added to the drama.
Davina had brushed her hair into a crown of curls.
Silk flowers nestled among the curls, and tendrils
brushed her shoulders. Minna felt transformed into
an older, more experienced woman, and it gave her
new confidence. Tonight, she was a lady who took
what she wanted, but also offered herself. The
question was: would Roarke be tempted to take
her?

"I say Davina, you look divine, as always," Eve
Epcott said with a profound sigh, breaking Minna's
reverie.

But Davina frowned and shook her head. "Not

now Leverett," she said and removed his hand from her knee.

"It's lovely here," Minna said to Mr. Epcott as she viewed the formal garden in the lingering twilight.

"Eh?" the plump man said, staring at her as if she wasn't there. He kept turning his head repeatedly toward Davina.

"I know I'll enjoy the rout." Minna studied the guests strolling up the steps to enter the brightly lit hallway.

She dared to relax a bit. At least she wouldn't have to keep up polite conversation with a distracted escort, but it would have been a boost to her self-confidence if Leverett Epcott had shown an ounce of interest.

A waft of breeze flowed through the coach, carrying an aroma of food cooking. To her dismay, Minna saw several of her own creations move up the steps. Her fashions were gaining in popularity every week, but she wished she hadn't seen them at this particular event. One of the ladies wearing her designs might recognize her, especially since she wasn't wearing a mask.

It was finally their turn, and Minna held her breath as she entered the hallowed portals of an immensely rich family. Everything was shiny and elegant around her, not only the people, but the flowers and orange trees in tubs lining the marble foyer. The servants' buttons shone, the gilt moldings gleamed, gems sparkled, and smiles dazzled.

Minna had never seen anything like it. If only she could enjoy the evening without worrying how to best seduce the earl. Anguish skittered along her nerves at the thought of him. Davina had confirmed that he was coming. The old distinguished couple that greeted them below the curving marble staircase didn't seem to care about his tardiness, but *she* did.

Distracted, she squeezed her escort's arm, and Mr. Epcott turned bulbous blue eyes on her.

"I'm sorry," he said, inserting a finger under his tight neckcloth. "I'm neglecting you." He dragged a pale hand over his forehead. "There goes my goddess," he said as Davina joined a group of friends. "Miss Sargent, I'm in the throes of love; I can't eat, I can't sleep, I can't think."

Minna warmed toward the little man who had nothing to brag about with his enormous paunch and his balding head. Still, many a lady would have loved his wealth, and the kind glint in his eyes. Not Davina though, Minna thought. Davina had her own wealth, and her freedom to take young, handsome lovers.

Devilment came into Minna. She blamed it on the unfamiliar surroundings and the reckless mood of the evening. "I know something that might help you in your quest," she said, and smiled into the man's sad face. "Davina once told me that she can't refuse a gentlemen who discovers her secret spot."

His eyes flew wide. "Secret . . . spot?"

"Yes, right at the back of her neck, where her hairline begins. Kiss her there, and she'll be your slave forever." Minna knew Davina would gladly strangle her if she discovered that Minna had divulged her most guarded secret, but Minna felt sorry for the poor fellow.

"Do it tonight on one of the paths in the garden," she said.

The color heightened on his already ruddy cheeks. "If I can lure her away from her friends.

Davina is a difficult lady to fool. She's very worldly, y'know." He wiped the perspiration from his upper lip. "And so lovely I believe I could eat her."

Minna laughed and glanced toward Davina's group. Her smile froze on her lips as she recognized the earl. He had arrived at last. Davina wasn't the only delectable person at the rout.

He looked edible. His black evening coat molded his broad shoulders to perfection, and the starched white neckcloth was tied in faultless folds. His tightly fitting satin waistcoat added to his distinction. His hair had been brushed back, but one burnished wave kept falling over his forehead.

Minna held her breath. He had almost knocked her into a faint just by being there, so close she could almost touch him. She was appalled at her strong reaction.

She heard Mr. Epcott curse under his breath. "If only I had some of Lord Whitecliffe's devilish charm. I don't know how to make Davina notice me," he said, his face creasing into misery as Davina beamed at Whitecliffe.

"Charm isn't everything," Minna hastened to assure him. "Davina likes you."

Mr. Epcott studied Minna suspiciously. "You know a lot, it seems."

Minna wondered what Mr. Epcott would say if he discovered that he was talking to Davina's *modiste*. Perhaps he would be shocked beyond repair. Well, he isn't going to learn the truth from me, Minna thought. She had difficulty taking her eyes from the earl, and nerves fluttered in her stomach. After supper she would have to confront him. Mr. Epcott excused himself to go in search of refreshments and Minna stood alone.

Panicking, she hurried to merge with the crowd, but to her dismay she discovered that the earl had moved closer and was staring straight at her. Her cheeks suffused with warmth, and she could not avert her gaze. His blue-green eyes were like glittering chips of anger, and he saw right through her, peeling away every layer of deception.

His gaze finally came to rest on her tight bodice, and she had never felt so ashamed. This is not how she had wanted it to be. In his eyes she was a hussy, and he would never fall in love with such a woman. He gave her a mocking bow, but didn't speak to her.

Every time she saw him, she lost more ground as far as her seduction was concerned. As his eyes undressed her, she suspected that she would never find a way to his heart.

She gave Davina a frantic glance, and her friend nodded in understanding. Davina said something to the earl and pulled his arm and they went outside. Coming toward Minna, Roarke angled an insolent smile at her, and she lowered her gaze. She sensed that he knew about Davina's plan to lead him to the gazebo, and that unsettled her completely.

Davina cocked an eyebrow as she sauntered past Minna on his arm, and Minna wanted to sink through the floor. The earl gave her a mocking bow and a Machiavellian grin.

After a while, she followed them into the garden. Filled with uneasiness, she sought the path that led to the gazebo. Davina had explained the architecture of the park, so she found the right turn straight away. She had a feeling the earl would make her 'work' difficult indeed. Voices and laughter came from behind the hedge as other guests pursued the privacy of darkness. The path opened up, and Minna saw the folly in the moonlight. To her chagrin, it was empty.

"Where is he?" she whispered, knowing that Davina had had plenty of time to bring him here.

She waited another twenty minutes, but there was no sign of the earl. Knowing that he wouldn't arrive, she returned to the house and found the butler.

"Do you know the whereabouts of Lord Whitecliffe?"

The old man nodded eagerly. "Yes, ma'am. He left not fifteen minutes ago."

"And Mrs. Shield?"

"She was asking for you, then she joined a group of friends." The butler craned his neck toward the drawing room. "I believe she's playing cards with Lady Marsdon and Mr. Epcott."

Minna had failed in her strategy to corner the earl in the gazebo. She went in search of Davina, who explained—in an undertone—that she'd been unable to make Roarke stay. "I'm sorry. He kept asking me hundreds of questions about you, and I had difficulty fielding them. I believe he was quite disgusted with me when he left."

"I knew this would happen eventually," Minna said with a sigh. "I'd rather return home now— alone. I have a terrible headache."

"Oh dear, I ought to come with you."

"No! I don't want to ruin your evening."

"Take Eve's carriage, then send it back here," Davina said, and ordered her admirer to accompany Minna outside.

Mr. Epcott's town coach was one of the last. He spoke with the coachman in the darkness, and Minna clutched her cloak tightly, wishing she was already gone. It had been a mistake to come here, she thought bitterly and climbed into the carriage. The earl had seen through her scheme. The shop would surely be lost before the summer was over.

"You will manage like this?" Mr. Epcott asked as he closed the door to the coach. He scratched his head guiltily. "Can't say it's the right thing—"

"Go find Davina," Minna said, dismissing him with a pat on the cheek. "I hope you have better luck with your 'prey' than I had with mine," she whispered. He didn't hear her last words as he hastened back up the path. The coach rolled away with a jolt, but just as it gained speed, the door tore open, and a dark shape jumped inside.

Minna gasped as the person fell hard against her, then moved to the seat next to her. "Blast it! Not as sharp-eyed as I once was," said a male voice. He leaned out and pulled the door shut, and in the process banged his head against the frame. "Damnation."

Minna instantly recognized the earl's voice. "Lord Whitecliffe," she said. "What are you doing here?"

"I could ask you the same question." He sounded angry, and Minna cringed. "If you must know, I was waiting for you. I knew I wouldn't have to wait very long after you discovered that your little plan failed."

"I'm going home. There's no crime in that, surely."

"Home? I'm beginning to wonder where that home is. I wish you would tell me," he said, gripping her thigh.

Minna pulled her leg aside, but his hand still rode on her flesh. "I don't owe you any explanations. None at all."

"Since it appears that neither you nor Davina is

110

willing to divulge your address, we shall drop the subject for the time being. I won't ask any more questions."

Silence crackled between them.

"I'm grateful."

He threw his head back and inhaled deeply. "Oh, God," he said in a long-suffering voice. His hand still rested on her leg, the warmth of him seeping through her gown.

"I told you I'm a courtesan, a stranger, and that's the end of it."

He laughed mirthlessly. "Not even Davina—daring that she is—would bring a courtesan to Lord Marsdon's home."

"Well she did. You must believe it."

"Ha! You underestimated me from the start."

"You speak as if we're adversaries."

"Aren't we? I feel like a hunted fox, if you must know." He closed his arms around her, and she panicked.

"No," she cried, struggling against his tightening grip.

"Why? Don't you like it, sweeting? Wind your arms around my neck. That's what a courtesan would do," he chided. "Whisper sweet nothings into my ear."

Minna cringed and paled. He was right, but she didn't know what to say. For once she was speechless, and sensed that he saw through her charade. If she told him the truth, he would only laugh; he would never understand the depth of her devotion to her employees. People like her—the populace—meant nothing to him. Just like Isobel Wylie had meant nothing. *People like me clean his house, polish his boots, and cook his food.* Gentlemen like him never give the servants a second thought, and probably never would. There was no reason for him to help her if she told him the truth. Men like him had no compassion for the plight of lesser beings.

"It's your turn to whisper in my ear," she murmured, struggling to break his spell. His closeness made her senses swim. Her thoughts grew more incoherent the more tightly he held her. "You have robbed me of my speech."

"I don't think anything can shake you enough to make you speechless."

Perhaps some flattery would get her the results when everything else had failed. He was probably egotistical enough to absorb her adulation. "Your closeness makes me dizzy and robs me of coherent thought." This, at least, was true. Seduction would come easily enough, she mused as she inhaled his virile fragrance. How to make him fall in love with her . . . how?

He kissed her neck. "Hmmm, intriguing. Tell me more."

She pushed against him, but he only placed his leg over hers, pinning her to her seat. The carriage jolted over the cobblestones, but that didn't dislodge him. He moved against her, pressing his lips to the hollow of her throat. The tip of his tongue flicked a moist trail on her bare skin, stopping briefly at the cleft between her breasts.

She whimpered and fought to get away. An attraction so strong that she was helpless against it, came over her.

"This is what you wanted, so why struggle?" he commented in a voice muffled by the fabric of her bodice. Before she could protest, he'd bitten one nipple straight through the silk, sucking on it through the material. An exquisite wave of pleasure pulsed from that tender peak as he continued to nuzzle her. He deftly unbuttoned the buttons at the back, pulling her dress down over her arms, imprisoning her in her dress, making her a captive of his ardor. The thin silk of her shift clung wetly as he whipped his tongue around and around her hardened crest.

His hand traveled up the side of her waist, leaving a havoc of fiery sensations in its trail. He cupped her other breast, massaging it until she lost her breath. She struggled against him, only encountering rock-hard muscles everywhere. His thigh rested heavily against her, and he pulled up his knee until it touched the top of her legs. She was pinned like a butterfly to a display board.

He dragged his hand back down over her waist and her stomach, awakening feelings that she never knew existed in her body. The sheer silk of her gown and the muslin of her petticoat was hardly a barrier between them, and his devious hand probed and slid over her curves and hollows. She was trapped. Nothing would stop him from pulling up the two thin layers of material that concealed her naked skin.

"No," she whispered as he pushed the heel of his hand over the mound at the joining of her thighs. She gasped as a sunburst of sensation spread through her. "No!"

"No?" he echoed. "Some courtesan!"

As she whimpered in response, his breathing fanned her wet nipple; then he suddenly pulled his head up and stared at her in the gloom. "You have beautiful small breasts," he said hoarsely. "Did you know that I adore small breasts?"

She shook her head numbly.

He untied the sash at her waist and pulled it

113

aside. His hand warmed her skin as he cupped one breast and skimmed a thumb over its throbbing peak. Growling low in his throat, he took it between his teeth and sucked gently.

She cried out, but it wasn't from pain. A fierce jolt of pleasure shot through her, and she clung to him. His lips moved up, up, teasing her neck, then her jaw, then he nibbled on the softness of her lips. He slid his tongue against hers, a full-blown suggestion of what he would do to her in a moment of intimate union. The gesture couldn't have been more provocative, and Minna lost all reason as long as his tongue explored her mouth.

Some of the glow left as he lifted his head a fraction. His voice came in gasps as he said, "We can accomplish what you . . . set out to do . . . right now," he said. "I hope you'll be deeply satisfied."

"No," she sobbed.

He pulled the flowers from her curls and plucked out the pins. Her hair flowed over her shoulders. "Strange response from a seasoned courtesan. Very well, but then you have to tell me more about yourself."

Minna averted her face, but he held her hair trapped around his hand. "You said you wouldn't ask any more questions."

She kept silent, and he continued. "Since you won't consent to anything else, we might as well probe your secrets. How do you know Davina?"

"I . . . we have business dealings together. The fact is that I'm not a highborn lady."

"Ah-hah, the truth at last! What kind of business?"

She couldn't tell him everything, but she told the truth. "I own a shop. I met Mrs. Shield there."

"Hmm, that doesn't surprise me. Davina makes strange friends." He gazed at her for a long time as the carriage bumped along. "You seem too lady-like to be a shopkeeper."

"I'm not a guttersnipe."

"But you fight like one. On the other hand, you know Shakespeare." He laughed. "Oh, Minerva — or whatever your name is — you are entertaining."

Minna took a deep, relaxing breath and dared to smile. "So are you."

"Your hair is lovely. It's silky and sweet-smelling," he said and buried his face in her tresses. "You'd be exquisite if it weren't for that devious, conniving mind of yours."

"And I can't abide your arrogance," Minna said, dragging her fingers through the thickness of his hair.

"There are some lovely things I would like to do to you," he said. Flattening the silk against her, he slid a finger over her private secrets, and she gasped with pleasure. "There's a powerful affinity between us. Don't you feel it?"

She only nodded, embarrassed that he ignited such intense feelings inside her. The erotic tension was thick and heavy, and if he'd laid her down on the seat, she would not have protested. He seemed to sense that.

"Too powerful, if you ask me." A sudden silence came over him, a stiffness, a faraway air as if he was listening to a voice that she couldn't hear. One after the other, he slowly removed his hands from her and smoothed down her dress as if she was as frail as china. "Too dangerous."

He pulled the bodice up and dragged the sleeves back over her shoulders. Then he retied the sash and tucked the material of her skirt around her. In

115

the weak light from a house that they passed, Minna saw that he had paled, and there was a seriousness in his face that she hadn't noticed before. He had closed her out, but she still felt as if she was swimming in a pool of thick syrup, of desire, of yearning. Her arm was heavy as she touched his face, slowly tracing his hard jaw with her fingertip.

"Why the change?" She struggled to sit up normally and collect her senses. "I thought you were eager—"

"I am—damned eager, but I'm not an idiot. I don't want to start something I can't stop later."

As the carriage came to an abrupt halt, he leaned over her and kissed her cheek. "This is a madness I can't afford, yet, would you mind coming into my house for a glass of wine? We could always discuss Shakespeare. I want to know more about you."

Before she could answer, he had opened the door and jumped down. He turned back and held out his hand. "Come inside. Don't be afraid. No one will see you."

"I'm not afraid of you." Yet her legs were trembling as she climbed the steps to the front door.

Chapter Eight

Thank God he'd dismissed the servants earlier in the evening, Roarke thought as he unlocked the door. He stepped across the marble floor of the foyer and held the door to his study. "After you, Minerva." He cursed a long harangue under his breath as he watched her slender form. By God, he'd almost succumbed to his own lust. He had let himself get dragged into her web, and tonight had almost been the undoing of his control. *I want her! Help me, but I'm consumed with desire for her silky flesh.* He couldn't remember a time when he'd been more tempted to savor a woman's body. The yearning inside was so thick and hot that he thought he would burn up, or dissolve in despair.

He had saved himself at the last moment. She was his for the taking, but if he'd given in, tomorrow he'd have had to face the consequences. He didn't know who she was, but she might try to extract further favors from him, and what if he got her with child. . . . Icy fear massed inside him at the thought.

"You are a daring lady," he said as he filled two glasses with sherry. "A toast to such nerve!" He smiled and gave her a glass.

Minna tried to relax. Perhaps there was a way to his affection. "I thought daring would be the only way to win you over."

He touched his glass to hers. "You haven't won me — yet." He motioned toward a chair by the fireplace and she sat down. *And you never will,* he added silently. Not if he could help it.

"You mean I might — someday?" she asked and cocked her head to one side.

He folded his body into his grandfather's old leather chair on the opposite side of the hearth rug. "Hmm, I don't know about that. But tell me more about yourself."

Minna thought quickly. She couldn't divulge the truth, but she might make up a plausible story. This time she held his interest. "What do you want to know?"

"What kind of life do you live?"

Perhaps he would regard her with more respect if she pretended to own a business as prestigious as a jewelry shop.

"Very well. If you must know, I'm a wealthy widow — "

"And a bored one," he filled in.

She nodded. "Yes, my husband left me a lucrative gem trade, but naturally I don't run it myself."

His mind seemed to pry into hers, and she shifted uncomfortably in her seat.

"A bored lady who has too much money, too much time on her hands. A spoiled one? Hmm, the story sounds plausible." He studied the red liquid in his glass. "To relieve your tedium you play erotic games with gentlemen . . . ?"

He had a way of twisting her words so that they sounded sordid. She pushed her hair self-consciously over her shoulder. "That's not true!"

He laughed, sarcasm lacing his voice. "So this is the first time; I'm the first victim?"

"Victim? Certainly not," Minna said, her anger rising. "I find you highly . . . desirable."

Roarke didn't reply, and Minna watched as his eyes darkened. She didn't know if it was from ire or amusement. Or something else. Heat stole into her cheeks. "I'm not usually so bold."

"You want me to entertain you? Dissipate your boredom?"

"That sounds awfully crass, don't you think?"

He seemed to ponder her words at length. "The request is crass." His voice sharpened with derision. "Do you expect to ease your tedium for free?"

Minna fretted. He turned everything against her. "Have you no feeling for adventure, for daring?" she asked. "Don't you want to be reckless at times?"

He shrugged. "I get as bored as the next fellow, but I like to choose my own entertainment."

"And if that amusement is not the company of a lady, what then?"

"I enjoy the company of a fair lady as much as anyone, but you must understand that your tactics have somewhat ruined my joy. After all, you have been pursuing me. I can't shake a certain feeling of uneasiness." He lifted a book from a stack on the table beside the chair. "Literature is wonderful company. It doesn't play you false."

"I always enjoyed good poetry," she said with a smile as some of the tension eased between them. "Please read a love poem for me — or I might recite one to you," she said, searching her memory for something adequate.

His eyebrows lifted a fraction. "Love? These are the Shakespeare plays you looked at last time." He read from a page, "How silver-sweet sound lovers'

119

tongues by night, like softest music to attending ears."

Minna smiled. "Romeo said it well."

He snapped the volume shut. "I shall be well advised not to pay heed to your silver tongue, lest tomorrow I'll regret it."

Minna couldn't suppress a laugh. "You needn't worry. You circle me as if I were an adversary."

Roarke stretched out his legs and crossed them at the ankles. "If not that, what are you exactly?"

"A friend? To begin with." Minna held her breath as their eyes locked. She felt a weakening inside as his gaze touched the depths of her. Sucking in her breath as if it were the last one she would ever draw, she waited.

When he didn't reply immediately, she continued, "I had hoped—"

Roarke rose. He went to the shelves and dragged a hand along the many books. "I don't need another crony. These are my friends. As you can see, I have many."

Minna joined him, reading the titles. "Do you write?"

He shook his head, and gave a chuckle. "No, but when the mood strikes I might compose a verse."

"Love poems?"

He laughed and gave her a teasing glance. "It seems that you're fixated with love."

Minna stepped closer to him, inhaling with joy, his male fragrance. "I'm a romantic. My guess is that you're one, too." His eyes darkened as she smiled up at him. She recited, "Somewhere was written that we would meet / Somewhere words of love were engraved onto eternity as our hearts joined together."

His face softened. "By Jove, I believe I've met a poetess."

120

She took another step toward him. "Aren't you as intrigued as I am—that we're here together?"

His lips quirked upward at the corners. "Hmm, you're persistent, aren't you?" Without waiting for her answer, he continued, "I've enjoyed your company, Minerva. However, I think I must decline your offer of friendship."

Minna realized she was losing ground again. "You don't trust me?"

"I don't know. You have been known to lie to me. Still, you've intrigued me more than I can express." He gave a graceful bow. "But it must end here. I'm very flattered that you singled me out for your attention, but it won't do, you know. It won't do. I shall see you safely home."

"You don't know how to enjoy yourself, my lord. Together, we could—"

"I'll not discuss this further." Taking her by the elbow, he led her firmly toward the door. Minna had never felt more foolish.

She knew she couldn't win anything with another argument, still, with a smile, she turned toward him. "I have a feeling we'll meet again."

"If we do, I shall wave in greeting, but that's as far as it'll go." He led her smoothly into the hallway. She glanced into his eyes, and for a moment she thought she saw a struggle there, a flash of chagrin. Then the neutral expression returned to his face. "You must seduce someone else. I'll see you home—"

"No! Good-night," she said, and stood on the tip of her toes to kiss his cheek. He moved away as if stung.

As the carriage pulled away, Minna pleated the material of her gown distractedly. The earl's coolness had damaged her self-confidence badly, and she saw no way out of this latest dilemma. He wanted her, she could feel that, but at the same time, he rejected her. Only caution on his part, but why? Why would he cut off their love play without an explanation? Why was he so difficult to seduce? She had a feeling other gentlemen would not be as reluctant. Was she so undesirable? The thought frightened her, reduced her to less than nothing.

The carriage was nearing Clifford Street, and Minna saw a sleepless night looming ahead of her. Any day Mr. Wylie would return and demand to know what progress she had made with the earl.

A wave of anger poured through her. How could she let a man like Wylie dictate her life, and why did she have to humiliate herself in front of a man like Lord Whitecliffe? She detested both of them, but she would have to find a way to accomplish her part of the bargain, or her staff would be out on the streets without a roof over their heads.

As the coach stopped in front of her door, she got a flash of inspiration. The night wasn't over yet; if she gave up now, she might not get another chance.

She leaned out of the window and shouted to the coachman. "Please return to Berkley Square."

She eased back against the squabs, thinking. Desperation churned in her stomach, and she would have to devise a new strategy. At this point surprise would be most effective against the earl. If she didn't manage to seduce him soon, she would lose her chance. Perhaps he would despise her for her insistence, but he would also be intrigued. She sensed that it was now or never.

Still, there remained one unsolved problem: how to make him fall in love with her. Mr. Wylie's request was outrageous, but she understood that the earl's suffering would be greater if he loved her. How to go about that? Suffering, not seduction, was Mr. Wylie's unsavory purpose.

She hesitated as the coach halted at the earl's front door at Berkley Square. With a deep breath, she jumped down and thanked the driver.

"Will ye be all right now, miss?" the old man asked and scanned the inky black areas around the houses on the square. "Ye want me t' fetch a footman?"

A shiver of unease touched her, but she shook her head. "I'm not afraid of the dark."

The coachman shrugged and flicked the reins. Minna stood undecided in the street. The square was silent, every nobleman, every lady, and their servants sleeping behind drawn curtains. In some places lamps glowed dully beside front doors, also at the earl's residence.

Not wasting any more time, she hurried down the alley between the earl's mansion and his neighbor's at the north end of the square. She prayed that she wouldn't encounter foul Harvey and his gang. At the John Street mews, she studied the earl's house from the back. It had a closed-in garden, the brick wall perhaps six feet high. As far as she could tell, no one was awake. The windows were dark, and no sounds came from the buildings around her. The night brooded dark and silent, and she could almost forget that she was in the heart of London.

A slender tree grew close to the wall, and without hesitation, she began scaling it. Her narrow gown hampered her, so she pulled it up over her legs and knotted it around her derriere. If anyone saw her now, she thought with a grim smile, they would surely faint with surprise.

The tree trunk was rough and scraped the tender flesh on the inside of her legs, but she managed to get a good grip of the lowest branch, and swing herself up. She was glad that she had learned to scale trees as a child.

"Thank you, Charlie Muggs," she said to the night as she recalled her long-ago teacher of tree climbing techniques.

Her arms trembled with fatigue as she heaved herself on top of the spiked wall. I hope Whitecliffe doesn't have dogs, she thought. Not letting herself get discouraged by the possibility, she held onto two spikes and slid down the wall on the other side. She landed in a hedge with leathery leaves.

Catching her breath for a moment, she brushed the dirt from her legs and let down her gown. All she could see were diffused shapes of ornamental gardening. The shrubbery looked like crouching men in the gloom, and she shivered with fear.

Squaring her shoulders, she hurried up the flagstone walk to the terrace. Something rattled under the hedge that bordered the marble balustrade, and, with a gasp of dread, she hurried up the steps.

All the French doors were bolted, drapes drawn within. She saw a light coming from the library, and she tiptoed to the window. Through the crack in the drapes, she saw the earl at his desk leaning over a book. Good! Two windows were open on the second floor, and Minna figured that if she could reach one of those windows, she would get in.

Old ivy covered the wall, but as she tested it, she feared that it would not hold her weight. Perhaps if she could reach the ledge that went below the windows, she could get in. The brick facade gave little handhold, but it wasn't impossible to scale like smooth stuccowork would have been.

She inspected the lead rain gutter, and found that with some effort, she could get a toehold on each of the brackets that held the vertical pipe in place. Without thinking of what might happen if she lost her footing, or who would meet her when she got inside, she climbed the pipe, then eased herself onto the ledge. It was wider than it had looked from below.

With the aid of the ivy, she moved along the ledge until she was outside the window. She listened, but all was quiet inside. Using caution, she pulled the window open all the way, parted the drapes, and looked inside.

It was some sort of parlor, perhaps attached to a guestroom, she thought. Relieved that the chamber was empty, she flung her leg over the sill and heaved herself inside. She bumped against furniture, but soon her eyes adjusted to the deeper darkness of the house. She located the door, and opened it carefully. Thank God, it swung wide on well-oiled hinges.

She glanced into the corridor and found that candles burned in a candelabra on the table at the top of the stairs. Aided by this light, she stepped up to the next floor where the bedrooms must be located.

She opened several doors, each time holding her breath in fear, until she found the master suite behind a set of double doors at the end of the corridor.

She listened for sounds of movement, but the room was empty. Slinking inside, she drew a breath of relief. She couldn't believe her luck! Her daring had brought her this far, and she could almost smell victory. The thieves of London would have a field day if they ever decided to rob this house. Perhaps she ought to warn the earl. . . . Dismissing that thought, she lighted a set of candles and surveyed the sumptuous bedchamber.

The enormous fourposter had green bedhangings and tester, and the carpet held tones of warm rust, greens, and blues. The furniture was gilded and up-holstered in the same green silk as the bed. The elegance daunted her momentarily, but it also distressed her with its bleakness. A pall of sadness hung over the elegance, and the room seemed unused.

Her mood lightened as she viewed the disorder of the chest of drawers where the earl's shaving implements, brushes, combs, and neckcloths lay in abandon. His valet evidently didn't understand the word "order." Minna sniffed the spicy scent of the shaving soap that she had smelled on the earl's skin. The fragrance brought back the memory of the intense passion that had seethed between them in the coach. Her heartbeat escalated and she felt heavy with longing.

Every detail of his personal belongings fascinated her, and she viewed the golden hairs caught in the brush, the elegant monogrammed stack of handkerchiefs. Then she explored the dressing room behind a lacquered screen, and was startled to find a cot with rumpled bedclothes. The valet! Thank God he was not sleeping in the bed.

Minna pressed her hand to her heart in an effort to still its violent pounding. She didn't need to meet an irate servant who would immediately call in the police.

Trembling with the sudden fright, she moved away from the dressing room without exploring it further and closed the door softly behind her.

Overcome by doubt, she went across the soft carpet to the bed. This was madness. The earl would not appreciate her intrusion into his private domain. Perhaps this was the most foolish move she'd made in her short acquaintance with Roarke Harding. She would soon find out. She drew her breath sharply as she heard voices on the stairs.

Her first instinct was to flee out the window, but she pushed the thought away. Her heart raced, and she felt short of breath from fear. She pulled off her cloak and smoothed her hair.

In what she thought to be a seductive position, she reclined against the pillows on the bed. His pillows were soft and plump, and smelled of him. She longed to press her face against them, but fear trapped her in a rigid position, her eyes trained on the door. The voices were coming closer, and she could clearly recognize that of the earl. Her mouth went dry, and her fingers dug into the soft cover on his bed.

The door opened, spilling a shaft of light across the room onto her. She blinked rapidly to adjust her vision.

He stopped on the threshold, and she could feel his gaze raking over her. She cringed, fearing the anger that her presence would evoke.

The earl turned to the servant behind him. "Harris, I don't need your services tonight. Go upstairs to your room and stay there until morning. That cot in the dressing room must be deuced uncomfortable."

Minna heard some vague protest, but the earl urged the servant on his way. Then he stepped across the threshold and closed the door.

"Well, well, your perseverance astounds me, Minerva." He chuckled, and she relaxed a fraction. "I ought to be flattered," he continued, "but I must say shock is—"

"Don't say another word," Minna said, struggling to find her bravery. What had induced her to enter upon this foolish mission? The trusting faces of her employees flashed across her mind, and she knew why she was here.

"I suppose there's only one way to get rid of you for good," he said between clenched teeth. He tossed off his coat and folded his spectacles carefully. With hesitant fingers he explored a dark table before he found a tinderbox. He lighted candles on both sides of the bed. His eyes glittered wickedly as he looked at her. Was there a trace of contempt, she wondered? Cold doubt filled her anew, and she curled up in the middle of the immense bed where he couldn't reach her without climbing in himself. As she watched him pull off his shirt, she realized that he was about to join her. She had to be brave, to open up her arms for him. Petrified, she only stiffened further.

"I hadn't expected to find you here, but then again, you never do anything in an ordinary way." His laugh grated on her nerves. "It is highly entertaining. You must be desperate for my embrace to dare such an act as to seek my bed. Tell me, how did you get in?"

"Any burglar would pay me handsomely for that information. But let's just say that an *infant* could break into your house on any given day." She tried to sound defiant, but her voice faltered. A feeling of humiliation plunged her further into doubt. His mocking grin did nothing to assert her conviction that she was doing the right thing.

She could not take her eyes off the smooth, bronzed skin that molded the honed muscles of his splendid physique. A melting sensation possessed her body, and she found it difficult to think of sharp retorts. He kicked off his evening shoes, and tore off his stockings. Neckcloth and jewelry went on top of the dresser. He would soon be naked, and then what could she do? She would have to accomplish her mission. She had to, even if her teeth rattled in her head with fear.

128

With a diabolical smile, he stood by the side of the bed dressed in nothing more than his dark trousers. "I suppose I have to give up my reserve in the face of such perseverance." He stared at her expectantly. "Well, my sweet, what are we waiting for?"

Minna made herself as small as she could, a trapped animal, knowing that all her adversary had to do was to pounce. He stood there staring down at her, but without moving. The candlelight played deceptively over his face; now he was grinning, now his face was a gargoyle mask of hard shadows, now he looked bathed in pure light. Why had she ever thought she could go through with this, to make this man love her? His eyes looked distant, and for a fleeting moment, sad. The seconds passed silently, one after an other.

"Come, little frightened mouse," he crooned, and climbed into bed, kneeling beside her. "I thought you would be triumphant; after all, you have gotten me this far, and now, at last, there's nothing to hold us back." He reached out to caress her jaw, but she averted her face.

"Come now, I would like to see the face of the woman that I'm about to bed — or had you planned to take the initiative?" He shook his head. "Right now it doesn't look like you have the gumption to accomplish seduction."

"Why do you think I'm here?" she taunted. At the very moment when she was about to give in to her fear, a new strength entered her. After all, hadn't she accomplished much more difficult things in the past? This was nothing compared to establishing her own business. She had to lead him on . . . keep him off balance.

She reached out and placed her hand on his bare chest. He was smooth, warm, and velvety to her

129

touch, yet she was acutely aware of the steely muscles underneath. There was nothing to stop him from overpowering her and taking her. Daringly, she dragged her fingertips along his hard flesh. "You're adorable, Lord Whitecliffe."

He tilted his head back and laughed. "The game begins. Let me be by fire touched." He drew her up and held her closer. "The fire of your ardor."

She had expected him to be hard and demanding, but he moved slowly and deliberately, allowing her to get used to his closeness. Just as he was about to push her back against the mattress, she slid away.

He grabbed hold of her arm, but she managed to wiggle free. Standing up, she circled around him as he kneeled in bed. She trailed her hands along his broad shoulders, then bent to kiss his neck, and outline his spine with one fingertip.

He swore under his breath as she quickly stepped out of the bed. "What now?"

"We must prolong the delight, don't you think?" she teased, and hid behind one of the bedposts.

"Ha! I admire a woman with daring, albeit somewhat grudgingly. After all, I would have liked to be the one to do the hunting." He moved from the bed reluctantly, his every movement wary.

"Well, do your hunting now. But perhaps you've already seduced me in your mind and thrown me aside," she said. "You haven't."

"Perhaps we ought to stop talking. We're always arguing, and I can think of other things to do with a lovely mouth like yours." He advanced slowly, a predator on soft feet, and Minna saw that he was smiling.

"You'll have to catch me first." She took a step back, wondering where to move next. If he caught her, she would lose.

"Yes," he continued, flexing his fingers. "I think I'm beginning to enjoy myself. You made the right decision to come here." As an afterthought, he added, "but how the deuce did you get in?"

"That is my secret," she retorted, struggling against the sweet yearning of her body.

"You keep nothing but secrets," he muttered, coming closer. "I'm intrigued, but before long I'll have the whole truth out of you."

"Only when I'm willing to reveal the truth will you have it," she said with a tantalizing smile to heighten his curiosity. "You can't catch me."

To conquer him, she would have to stay level-headed and — devious.

"Well, two can play this game, but remember that I'm the stronger. You're at my mercy now, in my house, in my *bedchamber.*" He changed from tender and considerate to hard and relentless. "You came here of your own free will."

He lunged, but she was prepared. With a jump and a giggle, she took shelter behind the next bedpost. He moved forward quickly, but she leaped onto the soft mattress and scrambled to the other side.

"Damn you, Minerva! You confuse me — one moment this, one moment that. Sometimes I believe you're nothing but a mean-spirited tease. You certainly are tonight."

She hid behind the bedhanging where it soared upward to meet the tester. Dragging her gown above her knee, she lifted her leg provocatively, rotating one ankle. Laughing, she began to enjoy the game. She sensed his frustration, and realized the seduction was working better than she had hoped.

One difficult challenge remained. She had to escape before he caught her.

Chapter Nine

He circled around the bed, coming at her from the opposite direction. She quickly lowered her gown, and glanced around for her next escape route.

"You're trapped now," he said triumphantly, moving slowly forward with arms outstretched as if chasing a flapping goose.

"No, I'm not!" She darted to the side just as he plunged forward, but he got a grip on to the skirt of her gown and held fast. She heard the material rip, and he laughed in glee. He jerked her into his arms, where she wriggled and fought to get away.

"You see? I caught you!"

Minna sank her teeth into his shoulder—not very hard.

"Aaaoo," he cried out. "Why did you have to do that?"

Minna bit him again, hard enough to make him relinquish his masterful hold on her. She scrambled away from him and dashed toward the door. In passing, she snatched up her cloak, and in doing so missed valuable time. As she sprinted toward freedom, he angled in front of her, blocking her path. His wide shoulders braced against the door, and she knew she was cornered. Only trickery would aid her escape now.

"Well, this certainly is an unexpected turn of events," he chided. "You come here to seduce me in my own bed, but before that can be accomplished, you try to run away." He crossed his arms over his chest and frowned. "But you forget something, my sweet. Me. You have to pay up now."

"This is not a wager," she said, mustering a wicked smile. "There's no law that says that I have to pay—not yet, not tonight."

She dropped her cloak on the floor and went slowly to stand in front of him. "I want to intrigue you, but if you have your way with me, you won't be curious any longer," she said truthfully.

"Don't pretend guilelessness with me, witch," he said. Anger painted his cheeks red.

"Admit that you're mystified beyond endurance."

"Damn you, Minerva. I'm not intrigued at all; I'm furious!"

"Why not take the pleasure that I'm offering you?" She touched his jaw with her fingertip. "Let's enjoy the love play as long as it lasts. Soon enough, it'll be over, and you won't see me again. You make this very difficult for me."

He gripped her wrist and held her away from him. "You're unpredictable beyond endurance. If you must have an answer to my cautious behavior, it's this: I don't enjoy a night's passion with a stranger. I like to know the lady before embracing her. But you, you're full of contradictions. One night you're a courtesan, another night a street fighter, and tonight, a widow who deliberately steps into a stranger's bed, but one who is unwilling to consummate the love play. What's next I wonder? What do you really want?" His anger had left him, leaving room for bewilderment.

"Stranger? That you are no longer, are you? I know a lot about you. For one, you're stubborn and suspicious. Second, you're unreasonable and wholly without imagination."

Oh God, why did she blurt that, challenging his anger anew? "Still, I *do* fancy an adventure," she said and added in her mind, *but you must fall in love with me first.* "With you. Why won't you play it my way? We could really enjoy ourselves. Anticipation would enhance greatly the culmination of our game."

Roarke watched her in the dark room softened by candlelight. She was lovelier than he remembered, her hair a gleaming halo around her head, her bodice in sinful disarray. Something warm and unfamiliar curled around his heart, and he held his breath. He had developed a soft spot for the conniving witch! Disgusted with himself, he leaned back against the door. He drank in her beauty, her fine translucent skin that he now knew was soft as silk, her delicate bone structure that reminded him of a fragile bird. He could almost picture her in flight, hair like a banner behind her. A frightened bird trying to escape. She confused him and stirred him as he hadn't been stirred for a long time. By Gad, she'd acted like a blushing virgin, yet had come to his room as bold as brass to lie in his bed, to wait for him. No virgin would fall to such brazen conduct.

She tossed her head back, her stance defiant, her eyes smoldering. Her hair fell forward like a pale, rich mantle and he felt compelled to touch it. Damn but he desired her more every time they met. He felt sluggish with yearning, his thoughts only revolving around ways to get her back into his bed.

On impulse he pulled her into his arms, holding her tightly. She trembled, and he thought he could detect a muffled sob, but when he held her at arm's length, he noticed that she was laughing. "Damn it, you're driving me insane," he said. "I want you now, not later."

"You have to catch me first," she cried, and wrenched out of his grip. She ran across the room as he cursed her roundly. Taken by surprise, he had no choice but to follow her. He felt like spanking her for her treachery. "You trickster!"

"All is fair in love and war," she warbled as she faced him across a small table.

"You!" He lurched toward her, stumbling on a chair leg in passing. "Wait 'til I get hold of you."

As he lost his foothold, Minna rushed to the door and bent to retrieve her cloak. "Better luck next time," she sang as she dashed out the door. As she sneaked downstairs, she heard him yell, "You shall pay for this!"

The rest of the house had an air of desolation after the intimate glow of the master suite. Minna drew a shivering breath of relief. Never had she dreamed that she would play the role of a heartless coquette. She hadn't known she had it in her to do so.

She tried the front door; it was bolted, but the bolts slid aside and the key turned with ease. The door creaked faintly as she opened it, and the sound magnified in the stillness. The hallway seemed vast and bleak as she threw one last glance over her shoulder. The earl lived in a mausoleum, and she should be happy that she got away. Nevertheless, it was as if her spirit had stayed behind as she fled down the steps and across the square.

When Minerva left the bedchamber all light left with her. Somber of mood, Roarke got up from the floor, contemplating her game. She had spied on him as she'd planned this game, and by God, he would spy on her. Perhaps if he discovered her address he could see her again. . . . However much he tried to deny it, he had to hold her again.

Without wasting a second, he pulled on his boots, grabbed his shirt and coat, and flew down the stairs.

He heard the front door slam shut as he shrugged the shirt over his shoulders. On the front steps he prayed that his eyes would adjust fast enough for him to see her. It seemed to take forever before he could make out any features of the street. In the light of an oil lamp he spied a corner of her cloak flaring in a gust of wind. Pulling on his coat, he strained his eyes. She was almost gone from the square, and he would have lost her in the span of a heartbeat.

His curiosity escalated as he followed her as fast as he could. Now he would find out where she lived, that is, if he managed to keep up with her. He stifled an urge to catch up with her and beg her to stay with him. Groaning over his weakness for her, he hurried over the cobblestones only to bump into a lamp post and stumble on the edge of the pavement. This was madness, but he had to find a way to purge her from his mind.

She walked across Bond Street and onto Clifford Street and stopped abruptly in front of a shop halfway up the block. He pressed himself against a wall as she unlocked the door and disappeared into the building. The key grated in the lock on the inside, mingling with the sounds of distant hoof beats and cats fighting in an alley. This was the jewelry shop then.

He waited until a light shone in the upstairs window before venturing forward. He'd forgotten his glasses, but he could read the sign above the door—Madame LaForge. He remembered that he'd been to this establishment to judge Davina's new wardrobe once. *Wardrobe!* This was a modiste shop, not an establishment for jewelry transactions. She had lied to him again! He recalled that Davina had mentioned that Madame LaForge had the blondest hair in London. Minerva certainly did.

Seething with anger, he glanced up at the silent facade. Davina was to blame for this charade. She had introduced him to Minerva. It was Davina's fault that he was plagued by visions of a blond-haired nymph who incensed his desire until he couldn't think about anything else. Tonight's farce might have been Davina's idea of a joke. Wait until he spoke with her next . . .

One thing was certain, Minerva wasn't a highborn lady, nor was she a courtesan. Returning to Berkley Square, he pondered the tender feeling that her relentless pursuit had left in his heart. He hated her for it, just as he hated his own weakness.

Chapter Ten

Minna encouraged a stately old matron who was trying on a maroon velvet gown. "I think you look lovely in these tight sleeves, Lady Barton," she said and pinched another tuck at the back of the bodice.

"Oh, I don't know," Lady Edna Barton said. "I suppose it's fine really." She pinned Minna with cold gray eyes. "By the way, I saw a young lady at Davina Shield's masquerade who had your hair color. She spoke with my nephew, Lord Whitecliffe."

Minna stiffened and averted her gaze.

"Not only that, but her stature, her slender build could have been yours. Do you have a twin we don't know about, Madame LaForge?" The matron tittered at her own witticism.

"Of course not," said Minna, annoyed. "There must be any number of ladies who have light blond hair."

"Don't believe it," the matron said and unfastened the buttons at the base of her neck. "I know that Davina is wild about your fashions, and so are many other ladies." She sniffed. "But don't think for a moment that your work will raise you above your station in life. You may well be financially secure, but *social standing* you'll never have."

Minna almost grimaced at the self-important face,

but she couldn't afford to make enemies.

"The most disconcerting part, Madame LaForge, is that in my youth I knew a woman, Mrs. Harding, who looked a bit like you. She was Lord Whitecliffe's stepmother. The Hardings were neighbors to the west of us, at Meadow Hill, a lovely estate." She frowned as Minna stuck a pin too close to her skin.

"The Hardings?" Minna's hands grew unsteady, and her heart felt like it had lodged in her throat. "I thought the Earl of Whitecliffe lives at The Whitecliffe Towers."

"That's true. Roarke Harding inherited the title after his father—that violent man Dennison—when he died three years ago." She muttered angrily under her breath, then raised her voice, "It isn't fair. Melchior Harding would have made a much better earl than Roarke."

"I'm sure I shouldn't ask, but why is that?"

Lady Barton gave her a long stare as if calculating whether to share her opinions about the earl. "You wouldn't understand, Madam LaForge, but Roarke won't make a success of restoring the estate. After his grandfather's excesses, the funds dried up. Roarke's father had no head for business. He married Portia hoping to salvage the estate. He did temporarily, but later came the struggles. Their marriage was a farce." She lowered her voice conspiratorially. "But mark my words, Roarke won't be able to rebuild the Towers to its former wealth. If only Melchior—"

"I heard the earl breeds Arabian horses."

"Bah! Roarke knows nothing about equines. He stole the idea from Melchior, and that's a fact. Melchior is the expert. He breeds his own bloods, but Roarke's ineptitude might ruin Melchior's stables. His business flourished before Roarke opened his own stables."

Minna felt a surge of protectiveness toward Roarke. "Perhaps he's desperate to salvage the estate."

"Hrmph! He's lucky to draw off funds from Meadow Hill that came to him through his father's marriage. Besides, without the grazing lands of Meadow Hill, he

139

would be destitute. His horses would have to eat rock if they lived solely off of the Whitecliffe lands." She sighed and smoothed down the gown in front, then turned this way, that way, studying her reflection in the mirror. "Ladies are not the only ones who make advantageous marriages. I remember—"

Minna didn't listen any longer. The sound of Lady Barton's voice wafted into her mind like the distant drone of a bee. Whitecliffe . . . Harding . . . Meadow Hill. She had no idea how it came to be, but something in those words touched an obscure memory. Pieces of snatched conversation between her parents, whispered confidences when they thought she was asleep.

"Please tell me, Lady Barton, you live in Kent, don't you?"

"My country estate, Sollerlea, is there, yes, close to the village of Birchington. The Bartons have lived there for centuries. My dear sister who's been dead these many years, married Melchior's father—Dennison's younger brother."

Minna quickly pinned up the hem. Birchington? The village didn't sound familiar, but her father had been a curate on the Kentish coast when she was very young.

"I've never been to Birchington," Minna said lamely.

Lady Barton laughed. "Of course not. Native Londoners don't ever leave London, do they? They have no land to call their own, only this filthy, smelly town."

Minna considered jabbing a pin into the supercilious lady's fat calf, but she restrained her urge at the last moment.

"I believe this fitting is the last, Lady Barton. You look lovely; maroon is the perfect color for you, and the velvet looks sumptuous."

The lady pursed her mouth. "It should suit me at such an exorbitant price."

Minna drew a sigh of relief as her haughty customer left the salon. Lady Barton's parting sentence lingered in her mind. "Don't give yourself airs above your station,

Madam LaForge. I know I saw you at the masquerade."

Minna went to her office and closed the door. A letter lay on her desk, and she cringed when she recognized Mr. Wylie's handwriting. How would she explain her difficulties to snare Lord Whitecliffe? She saw no way out of her predicament, unless next time she saw the earl . . . if there would be a next time. It was possible that the game last night had put him off for all time. For once, hard work would not help her to forget her problems. A *miracle* would. It was the only thing that could bring the earl around to loving her.

She scanned the few lines of the letter. Angry that he hadn't heard word of her progress, he gave her another week to fulfill her part of the bargain. Seething with wrath, she flung the missive aside. The gall of the man! He was ordering her around like a servant, and she resented his highhanded attitude. Besides, it was a strange request, to ask her to seduce his enemy. Why not find another way to punish the earl? A bitter laugh welled up in her when she thought about the situation. Mr. Wylie was asking the impossible of her, and perhaps he knew it. Was this just a way to get rid of her? A flare of hatred burned through her as she thought about his cold face.

Minna rubbed her temples where a headache had begun to throb. She wished she could confide in someone, but Ellie would worry, and so would the others.

Suddenly, she heard a raised male voice in the passage between the showroom and the fitting rooms. Customers squealed in outrage, and Minna cursed under her breath. The man had walked into an area that was strictly female territory. She rushed to the door, and just as she was about to go out into the corridor, she heard the voice again, then Rosie's pleading one.

Minna felt a moment of surprise about Rosie's presence in the showroom, but it was the male voice that caught her attention. It filled her with dread. She would have recognized the earl's deep voice anywhere. How had he found out?

"She's here, I know it," he said, his voice laced with stubbornness. "I've seen her myself."

"I have no idea who you're talking about, sir," pleaded Rosie. "We don't have a blond woman working here. *Please,* sir, you must leave this instant. Gentlemen are not allowed back here."

Minna's hands grew damp with fear. She sprinted to the enormous wardrobe in the corner and tore out a stack of taffeta bolts. Just as she had climbed inside and pulled the door tight, he rushed inside. She held her breath, waiting. How had he discovered her address?

"I demand to see Madame LaForge." His authoritative voice would have made a lesser servant incoherent, but Rosie was undaunted.

"I told you, sir, Madame LaForge is not here. She has traveled north to attend her sister's wedding. She left yesterday."

Minna's eyes widened at such blatant lies, but she admired Rosie's command of the situation.

"Does Madame LaForge have striking blond hair?" he went on.

"That's not for me to say," Rosie said. "Now, sir, you must leave."

The earl muttered something unintelligible, and Minna sensed his great anger. Fear, and the thick air of the wardrobe suffocated her. A moment of dizziness came over her and she steadied her hand against the wall. Her gesture dislodged a spool of thread from a shelf and it clattered to the floor.

The next moment he'd torn open the door.

Astonishment, then anger played across his face. Blushing furiously, Minna stepped out of the wardrobe. She nodded to Rosie whose eyes looked enormous under the wilting lace of her mobcap.

"Thank you, Rosie, you can go now."

"But . . . but this gentleman," the maid began.

"I shall deal with him."

Rosie left and the tension escalated as Minna and

Roarke stared wordlessly at each other. "How did you find me?" she asked.

"I followed you last night. You are Madame LaForge, aren't you, Minerva?" He crossed his arms over his chest and sat on the edge of the desk. Dark clouds had gathered on his brow. "Answer me, or I might do something violent that I'll regret later."

She glanced at his tense shoulders and nodded miserably. "Yes . . . but I didn't want you to know that. A jewelry shop sounded more genteel. A widow—"

He pounded the desk so that papers and books jumped. "Damn you! Why did you lie to me?" He took a threatening step toward her. "You've played me for a fool long enough."

"I . . . never intended to mock you in any way."

He took her shoulders in a hard grip. "Don't keep on lying! Why this charade? Why didn't you tell me the truth from the start?"

Minna's knees weakened, and if he hadn't held her up, she might have sagged to the floor. All strength had run out of her, but after a moment of panic, she collected herself. Her mouth tasting like dry sawdust, she tried to explain. "I saw you in the shop with Davina in the beginning of May. From that day, I longed to know you. That's God's truth." The words fell flatly in the angry atmosphere. "I didn't think you would find a simple modiste interesting."

"There's nothing simple about you, Minerva!" He took a deep breath and gave a mirthless laugh. "Davina invited you to her masquerade. That doesn't surprise me in the least. She always liked to play tricks on unsuspecting victims. I confronted her before I came here, and she said it was about time I was seduced by a lovely modiste. Bah!"

"Well, I am a modiste, and that's the truth. It's not a crime to desire a handsome gentleman, is it?"

Minna hoped her explanation had convinced him, but he didn't look satisfied.

He studied her narrowly. "If you wanted me last night — like you implied by coming to my bed — why did you run away?"

Her thoughts whirled to find an acceptable reply. "Your ardor terrified me," she whispered, then held her breath as his gaze bored into her. Reacting instinctively, she wound her arms around his neck and pressed herself close to him. She felt his heart hammering against hers.

He pried himself loose. "Why? I'm not a dangerous man."

"I . . . I'm . . . a virgin," she blurted out. I have never known a man intimately. I was afraid."

Incredulity dawned on his face. "Another lie!" He pushed her away violently. "Do you really think I would believe that? Get away from me. Now!"

"Please believe me." Before she could draw another breath, he'd slammed out of the room. She heard squeals of outrage as he returned the same way he'd come. Minna bit her knuckles hard to suppress the despair building in her chest.

Rosie put her head around the door. "Do you need me, ma'am?"

Minna gathered her shattered wits. "No. Thank you, Rosie," she murmured.

Rosie bobbed a curtsy and gave one of her hooded, penetrating glances. "I tried to stop him, but he was very insistent."

"I have a business arrangement with him," Minna lied, feeling the maid's eyes probing her.

Rosie looked away at last. "I came down with a tray and found him in the passage."

"I'm glad *you* did, and no one else. You handled the situation very deftly."

Rosie gave half a smile. "You should have seen the ladies in the fitting rooms. They were shocked."

Minna forced a smile to her lips even though she felt dead inside. "The fox among the hens, I imagine."

Chapter Eleven

I have to do something! The thought revolved feverishly in Minna's mind during the rest of the day which passed in a flurry of fittings and discussions with customers. She was grateful for the work, but she could not calm her frazzled nerves. A sadness had lodged around her heart, and she wished she had been granted a chance to start all over with Roarke. If only she had truly been Davina's cousin . . . if only she had been a *lady*. Then he might have been impressed enough to court her. She presumed that all he felt toward her was exasperation, and perhaps contempt. Besides anger, of course. Yet, the fact that he had confronted her said that he hadn't been wholly indifferent to her. Somehow he'd cared enough to learn her address, and in some reverse logic it was a flattering thought.

When evening arrived and they had closed the portals after the last customer, Ellie and Minna sat in their favorite chairs in their sitting room above the shop and sipped cups of tea. Minna kicked off her shoes and wiggled her aching toes. Still, her anxiety barely let her relax for a moment.

Ellie tapped her fingertip against the side of her mug as she studied the room. "This is heaven, Minna. I've never lived in such luxury."

Distracted, Minna viewed the simple furniture, and the drapes of green taffeta that they had bought cheaply because they had faded streaks. The accents of flowery pillow covers and trivial knickknacks that adorned the flat surfaces did nothing to make the room elegant, nor did the many potted plants make a statement. The carpet had a hole in one corner, which they had covered with a chair. Still, compared to the rathole that had been their first home, this was paradise.

"Yes, it is ours, and if business continues to expand, we'll be able to afford even nicer rooms than this. *If!*"

"What's the matter with you, Minna? You're a thousand miles away today."

"I . . . have some minor problems with Mr. Wylie, credit and debit, you know. Nothing to worry about." She tried to smile to ease Ellie's mind.

"I heard that a man barged through th' shop today," Ellie said and slurped her tea.

"Yes, he came to see me, then left quickly." Minna's voice petered out. It hurt to think about the earl. Ellie must have sensed something because she was staring intently.

"Why did you want t' see him? Was he a dunner?"

Minna shook her head. "No . . . I believe you waited on him once, the Earl of Whitecliffe."

"Aw, him. He criticized Davina's new gowns until she was ready to kill him. I haven't seen him since. Will he be a reg'lar customer then?"

"I don't think so." Minna tried to shake off her dark mood. "In fact, I hope he won't be. It wouldn't be right to have him frighten our female customers in the fitting rooms while we fitted him with a corset."

"Ha! Give over, Minna." Ellie giggled and finished her tea. Then she yawned. "I'm so tired. I think I'll go to bed early."

Minna was too agitated to retire for the night. A strange restlessness filled her. "Tell me, Ellie, what would you do if you were interested in a gentleman, and he didn't want to see you? How would you go about meeting him against his wishes?"

Ellie's eyes were round as saucers. "Oooh, Minna! Have you fallen in love?" She clapped her hands together

146

in excitement. " 'Tis precious!"

"I have not fallen in love!" But as she said the words, Minna knew that it was true. The earl had touched a secret, yearning place in her, touched her more deeply than she thought possible. Her heart had acquired a warm glow of its own since she met the earl.

"Blind me, it's true!"

"What would you do to arrange . . . let's say, a secret tryst?"

"Minna, this gits better an' better. *You* of all people! I thought you only had eyes fer your work." Ellie jumped up and twirled around the room. "How excitin'!"

Minna blushed. "Well, what would *you* do? And don't play the innocent with me. I've seen you arm in arm with this man and that man."

"Aye, I have me little affairs, but no man is worth a lifetime o' devotion. All I'll do be scrubbin' floors an' wipe snotty noses. Faugh!"

Ellie sat down on the armrest of Minna's chair and hugged her friend. "Who is he?"

"I can't tell you about it — yet."

"You sly girl, Minna. I'm burnin' with curiosity."

"You must burn a while longer."

Ellie sat back down and tapped her lips with one callused fingertip. Her eyes glittered with mischief. "He can't refuse ye, Minna. Any normal man would be happy t' love you."

"Not this man. He pushes me away at every turn."

"Must not be a healthy man by any means," Ellie scoffed.

"He is, but every time I think that I've reached his heart, he turns away from me. And I have always bungled my part of the seduction."

"You sound like you're involved in a game o' some sort."

Mr. Wylie's harsh face flashed through Minna's mind, and she flinched. If Ellie knew that her livelihood hung in the balance of Minna's success with Roarke Harding, she

147

wouldn't be so gleeful.

"I know, Minna. You must touch him where he's vulnerable, try to reach his heart. Show him somehow that he's the only one who can help you, who can save you, who can take care o' you. Play on his male strength. Works every time."

"Oh, Ellie. I fear that this man detests me. I've thrown myself at his feet."

"How could he dislike *you?*" Ellie gave an incredulous laugh. "No man in his right mind would turn away from you. You're sweetness personified."

"Well, he has." Minna stared bleakly at the last evening sunshine slanting through the window and bathing the room with an orange glow. "I must find a way to *conquer* this man."

Ellie chortled. " 'Tain't a battle, Minna. You can win a man without fightin'."

"Not this one." She could not hide the tremble in her voice or the tears in her eyes.

Ellie gasped. "You've fallen in love in the worst way. I see the signs as clearly as I see your face." She started pacing the floor. "Where's he goin' t'night?"

"To some gathering, I believe."

"Then you must go there as well."

Minna remembered that Ellie knew nothing about her previous failures, or that she was trying to snare an earl. She stood up. "Thanks, Ellie, I think I'll turn in early after all. But I'll think about what you said."

"Aw, we just started."

Minna got up from her chair. "I'd like to rest with my legs up, and *think*."

"Lawks." With a disappointed moan, Ellie went to her door. "Don't say I didn't try to help you."

Minna entered her bedroom and lighted the candles. The cheerful room, decorated in delft blue and white, failed to comfort her. Before long, this room and all the rest might end up in Mr. Wylie's hands.

Agitated, she paced the floor. There must be a way,

there had to be! Every time she closed her eyes, she saw *him*. She brushed her hair with angry strokes. Where was it Davina was going this evening? To a ball on Upper Brook Street, or some such event. As Minna finished that thought, she knew what she had to do. He might be there, and so should she. She couldn't give up, not yet. She had probably ruined her chances with him, but the agony of inactivity made her want to try again.

Knowing that the event probably started later in the evening, she stripped off her clothes, and gave herself a refreshing sponge bath. She pulled out her best gown, a narrow chemise dress of deep green silk with lace trimmings and gold embroidered bands of matching material around the neckline and sleeves. The cut was simple, but the fabric felt sumptuous against her skin. She put up her hair into its customary chignon, and hung a strand of pearls around her neck. As darkness deepened outside, she put on her shoes and cloak, and left.

She had no real plan, and she couldn't enter the ball without an invitation. But if she were on the premises, some opportunity might turn up. Upper Brook Street wasn't far from Green Street, Davina's address, and if worse came to worst, she could always go there. Davina's butler would always let her in.

As she hailed a hackney cab on Bond Street, she felt much better, even exhilarated. At least she wasn't sitting at home bemoaning her fate.

She would have to improvise as she was stalking the Earl of Whitecliffe. *Stalking*. She blushed, hating more every day the dilemma in which Mr. Wylie had put her.

She had asked the driver to let her off at the corner of Upper Brook Street, and as she paid him, she could clearly hear the sounds of laughter and music halfway down the block.

Her heartbeat escalating alarmingly, she walked toward the sound. This was ridiculous. Not only would she not meet the earl, but she might be detected by the footmen at the door and be told to leave.

Swallowing convulsively with apprehension, she watched the guests alight from their elegant carriages. She went closer, then hid behind a pillar at the entrance next door. No one could see her in the shadows, but she would spy the earl — if he arrived.

She had never felt more ridiculous skulking like this, but she had no choice.

The night was unusually warm, and she loosened the fastening of her cloak. Perhaps this was the promise of a hot summer. Last year it had rained and rained. She inhaled the smells of London, dust and a faint odor of refuse. Compared to the East End, this part of town was relatively clean.

She waited until her feet ached abominably. She heard the faint chime of a clock inside the house whose portal shielded her from curious eyes. He wasn't coming. She had waited for three hours. Before returning home, she would pass the door that led to the ball, if only to get a glimpse of the gowns that her competitors had designed.

In the brightly lit foyer where a crystal chandelier glittered and gold leaf molding shone, she saw one of her own designs. Her spirits lifted as she admired it on the tall admiral's wife. Her gray hair and neck sparkled with jewels, setting off the rich forest green of her gown.

A carriage halted behind her, and she stepped away from the light. Feeling that her evening hadn't been a complete loss, she turned around.

Her breath caught in her throat. It was Roarke, and he'd seen her. He was so close that she could see the emotions shift on his face, surprise, disdain, then a grudging admiration. He looked achingly handsome in his black evening clothes and his unruly burnished curls. Her heartbeat thundered in her ears.

"You don't give up easily," he drawled, flinging his cloak back from his shoulders.

She shook her head. "Never."

He stood perfectly still, studying her for a long moment, closely, intimately as if he had difficulty understanding what he was seeing. She fought back her urge to flee. The horses that pulled his carriage stomped nervously behind him. Even the coachman stared at her.

"Damn you!" With a sudden movement, he scooped her up in a dizzying embrace and turned back to the carriage. "We shall go back to where it all started."

Minna did not protest. The earl said something to the driver, but Minna was only aware of his spicy fragrance and the steely muscles that held her. God, she wanted this! She liked to feel his arms around her; she liked to look into his deepset blue-green eyes. She adored his strength, his confidence, his virile magnetism. It made her deliciously weak all over, and she realized why men like the earl could have any woman they wanted. No one could resist that roguish appeal that he had. It could not be touched, or explained, only felt.

Minna cursed her own weakness, but at the same time she accepted her conviction that she was doing the right thing, the *necessary* thing.

He brought her inside the coach and closed the door. As the carriage moved, he held her against him as if he didn't want to let her go.

"Damn you, Minerva! Tonight I shall purge you from my thoughts once and for all. Get rid of you."

"Let's not talk, it will only bring back our argument." Was the dreamy voice really hers? She could not stop herself from curling her fingers through his hair. It felt soft yet springy to her touch, and she drew his head down. As if in a trance, she lifted her face to his, and he swore under his breath.

"Confound it, but you are beautiful." He closed the distance to her mouth, and Minna whimpered as he kissed her. His tongue teased the soft flesh of her mouth, sweeping away all reason.

"My God." His fingers dug into her scalp, tearing away the pins that held her hair up. It cascaded down her back, and he wound it around his hands and pulled her so close she could barely breathe.

151

"I had a wild dream about you last night," he said. "You witch! Tonight I'm going to get free of your spell. I must put an end to this madness."

Minna stiffened in his arms. His words hurt, but he was right somehow. What had started that night at Davina's ball, had to be completed. She sensed the all-consuming fire in him, and it had an equally engrossing response in her.

She held onto his wide shoulders and kissed the strong column of his neck. His starched neckcloth was in her way, and she untied it with one hand and loosened the shirtpoints.

He inhaled sharply when she planted a kiss on the tender spot just between his collar bones. His skin was smooth, and he smelled so *good*. She could stay there forever, her nose pressed to that indentation

His hands wandered over her back under her cloak, exploring the flare of her hips. An urgency moved his fingers, and he probed deeper, testing the roundness of her derrière. She longed for more, the clothes making an unacceptable obstacle between them. He had found the buttons at the back of her bodice, and deftly unbuttoned them and pulled down the sleeves over her arms. The wide lace band holding up her shift followed, and the night air caressed her bare skin.

She hardly noticed when the coach stopped and the earl lifted her down. Disoriented, she glanced at the dark street and smelled the strong scent of horse. She knew they were in the mews somewhere, and then she recognized the gate to Davina's garden.

The coach rattled off through the mews, and Minna watched as the earl vaulted the wall and unlocked the gate from inside. She was numb and trembling with a fire that only he could still.

In the rising moon, she could see the gleam of his smile as he opened the gate for her. "Like I said, we must end where we started."

Minna nodded. "This is a romantic spot. The best."

She wound her arms around his neck, and he held her tightly.

"Come," he growled and lifted her into his arms. "Help me, but what a night! It's magic." He moved tentatively up the path with her. They had an encounter with some bristly bushes that tore at Minna's cloak. It shocked her to discover that the earl had very poor eyesight. She had noticed a certain hesitation in him before, but she hadn't thought much about it. However, there was nothing wrong with him as he curled her tighter, laughing in exultation.

Shafts of silver and velvet darkness enfolded them at the gazebo. The spot held a tranquility that was hard to find in any other spot in London. The cushions were deep and soft. The earl set her down and tossed the pillows to the floor. The scent of flowering shrubbery somewhere filled the air, but Minna didn't try to figure out the name of the flower. All she wanted was to quench the pounding yearning inside her.

He came to her and moonlight touched his face. It looked curiously unguarded, the smile genuine. She couldn't read the expression in his eyes, but she sensed the warmth.

"I might live to regret this," he murmured, "but I'm weak. I must succumb to temptation. Just this once."

She almost said the words hovering on her lips, *I love you, I love you, I love you,* but nothing came out. Perhaps he didn't want to hear those words. She couldn't bear to see the sincerity in his face turn to uneasiness. Go slowly, she told herself.

He began to undress her with an urgency that was feverish, and she also fumbled with the buttons and cords of his evening clothes. She dragged the shirt from his breeches and pushed her hands under it. She felt like crying when she touched his smooth flesh, and her instinctive gesture was to press herself close to him so that every part of them touched. She wound her arms around his waist and kissed his chest, nipping one of his nipples that

153

was surrounded by a whorl of hair.

He moaned deep in his throat, and she thought he would rip the gown from her body, but he only peeled everything away and lifted it over her head, shift, petticoats, and all. Dressed only in stockings and garters she stood before him, shivering with anticipation. She slowly stripped them off, never taking her eyes from him. With another groan, he discarded his own clothes quickly revealing how he loathed even for a second to relinquish his touch on her body.

Then they met, not a thread separating them. She had never viewed a naked man before, but the sight didn't frighten her. He was the most exciting view she had ever seen—tall lean body, a narrow waist tapering to narrow hips, strong, muscled thighs, and shapely legs. From the nest of dark curls sprung the proof of his desire. She had to touch him *there*. He looked tightly knit and powerful all over, and she reached out and stroked the length of him, and he laughed with delight.

"You witch," he breathed. "You wily witch."

He pressed himself against her and the velvety length throbbed hotly against her belly. He laid her down on the pillows and explored the softness of the inside of her thighs. A rill of pleasure shot through her at his touch. When he bent over her and kissed her abdomen, she moaned. Every kiss was an exquisite torture that jolted her into ever mounting pleasure.

"I want you, Minerva, so help me," he whispered as one of his long fingers entered her softness. This might be the worst mistake of my life."

She was ready for him, he thought in exhilaration as his hand slid over the hot wetness of her. His whole body felt as if it was suspended on a taut wire, and when it snapped, he would spiral into searing mindless ecstasy. Never had anyone incensed him so, not like this siren of pure innocence and female guile. She was all soft light and shadows, her skin as smooth as the finest silk, and her secrets so tantalizing that he wanted to shout in frustration. Helplessly ensnared in her erotic response, he positioned himself between her legs, and tried the opening to paradise. Oh, she felt hot and so tight. It took all his control not to plunge himself inside. Teasing, teasing, he rotated at the entrance, and only when she arched against him in welcome, did he sink himself completely into her. At first a barrier stopped him, but it gave way almost instantly. A warning bell chimed in his head, but he was so completely intoxicated with her, and her writhing, tenuous body beneath him that he didn't pay heed. The more she moved against him, the harder it became to control the sweeping frenzy that built in his loins. He dug his fingers into her hair and pinned her down against the cushions. She whimpered, her breath gasping between half-parted lips. He ground against her, deeper and harder, until the reward was his; her body convulsed in long shuddering waves, and her tears tasted salty as he showered her face with kisses. The ecstasy built inside him until he had to let go to the rapture that raged through him, exploded in his groin, and spewed out the seed of his life. The shudders stilled, and he knew a contentment he'd never known before.

Minna was vaguely aware of his explosive release as she struggled to gain the dizzying pinnacle where she'd stood once before. Just as he cried out and drove into her in a last wave of passion, the renewed sweet torment built into a crest of molten heat within her. With a cry of ecstasy, she let herself be swept away on that wave to the shores of contentment. Happiness forced tears to her eyes.

In the trembling aftermath, she was acutely aware of the musky arousing smell of him, her lover, who she could only adore after this shared magnificence. She stroked his back and clutched his tight buttocks. Every inch of him inspired adoration, and more desire. She could already feel the seeds of it mounting in the depths of her abdomen. He'd opened a door for her, a door to a paradise she never knew existed.

Chapter Twelve

"My angel . . ." he whispered. "Fallen angel." He wiped strands of hair from her face. "I can't believe it, but you were a virgin—like you said."

She nodded and traced his jaw with the tip of her tongue. "Yes, I didn't know that love could be this exciting."

He frowned. "It didn't hurt when I—?"

"A little, but I wanted it—you." She felt vulnerable, shy, yet happy, and she hoped that the moment would last forever. But it never did; it slowly faded as he robbed her of his firm embrace and rolled away from her. Leaning on one elbow, he studied her in the faint moonlight. She curled into him, and he didn't resist her, but the incredible moment of intimacy was gone.

"Minerva, I set out to purge my desire for you once and for all." He heaved a deep sigh. "I think I failed."

He sounded so crushed that Minna had to suppress a chuckle.

"I know your true identity," he continued. "Socially, there are gulfs between us; it's no use pretending otherwise. Do you still want to be my mistress?"

"Now more than ever," she said, holding him tightly. "You made me very happy." It was true. She'd never known that such intimacy could be possible.

"I'm flattered that I could please you." He kissed the tip of her nose.

She continued. "I fancy you as many ladies must fancy you—for your splendid physique, wicked smile, and haunting eyes. Any other reason matters not." She could always tell him she loved him with all her heart, but that would perhaps make him feel trapped.

"It matters more than you think." A tightness had entered his voice. "I'm not an ogre who uses and discards mistresses once a week, you know."

She looked up at him, ruffling his hair. "Are you saying that you *care* about me?"

He was lost in a taut silence. "I care more than I like to care," he said at last, then gave a derisive snort. "Are you satisfied now?"

Minna suppressed a wild urge to cry from happiness. Perhaps he wasn't as cold-hearted and standoffish as he pretended. "More than satisfied." She pressed herself against him and caressed his chest. "I could do this many times over." She propped up her elbow and looked into his face. "They say you're a recluse, but that certainly hasn't stopped you from knowing the intricacies of making love."

He laughed hollowly. "The tattlemongers have nothing better to do than to speculate about my secret life, my past. After all, I am an eligible bachelor, and the old dowager prunes would dearly love to see me caged in a loveless marriage."

Minna curled her arm under his neck and held tight as if she never wanted to let go. "And you don't like the idea of marriage?"

He moved away from her in haste. "I'd rather be dead!" He fumbled in the darkness for his discarded clothes, leaving Minna to wallow in a sudden, painful loneliness.

"You don't have to fear anything from me," she said, though it was difficult to speak the words. "Like you pointed out, I'm not of your class, so marriage—"

"You ought to be happy about that! To belong to the peerage is incredibly restrictive." He sounded tired. With a shrug, he dropped his clothes and leaned back against the pillows. "Would you want to marry?"

The question hung heavily between them. Inches separated them, but Minna found the gap impossible to bridge. Such intense intimacy, yet such nightmarish distance. She wasn't Minna, the struggling seamstress any longer; she was a woman needy of love, particularly his love. Her dependence on him made her vulnerable. "Someday perhaps."

She twirled a strand of her hair between her fingers as a soft breeze caressed her heated body. "Tell me, why would a handsome, virile man like you shun marriage? There must be any number of eligible young ladies waiting for you."

He stiffened, and she sensed a deep turmoil inside him. "Let's just say that nothing ever lasts."

"But that doesn't mean one should never try. It's life; one has to have the courage to try, and if one fails, to go on. I know."

He looked hard at her, his eyes piercing in the semidarkness. "You sound wise for a young woman."

"Wisdom knows no age. Things happen to us, shape us, and I have had enough difficulties to see that the course of life can change when you least expect it. *They*, the difficulties, don't end either, but there are as many good things in life as there are hardships, and I wouldn't want to be without."

He took the strand of hair from her hands and kissed it. "Those were the loveliest words I've heard in a long time. Are you sure you're not a real angel?"

She chuckled. "I'm sure of it. No angels have as sinful thoughts as I do at this moment." She held out her arms to him, and he laughed.

"I wouldn't be sure of that. Surely, such delight as we just shared is not a sin, and angels don't sin — at least I don't think they do." He kissed her throat, and Minna felt the by now familiar melting weakness in her limbs.

"Roarke, please tell me the real reason that you don't want to marry."

He stiffened in her arms, then gave her a long, hard look. Sighing, he said, "Very well." He curled up against her, cradling her in his arms. "I'm going blind, and who wants to marry a blind man?" he said without preamble. The pause lay heavy and filled with sadness. Profound empathy filled Minna, and she tried to imagine the loss he was facing.

"I have glaucoma, just like many members of my family have had the last hundred years." He waited for her to respond, but she could think of nothing to say. She was sure he didn't want her pity.

He continued, "When the truth was brought home to me, I railed about it, shouted and fought. Then I learned to slowly accept it. As it is now, I revel in every day that I still can see, every sunrise a wonder." His voice trembled and petered out.

"That's why you keep mostly to yourself?" Minna caressed his hair, waiting anxiously for his reply.

"No, I've learned to accept my failing eyesight. But there's something else. In my wild youth, I fathered a child—illegitimately, by the daughter of a merchant. I took care of him from the time he was just one year old. He died two years ago when he was ten. By the age of eight, he'd lost his sight—much too quickly.

Roarke hid his face against her shoulder. "I felt it was my fault somehow, and when he died in a raging fever, I lost the one person that truly meant something to me. Thomas was the light of my life, and then he was taken away from me. I haven't . . . forgotten him . . . and I never will. I don't want another child to carry the flaw of the Hardings."

Choked up with compassion, Minna could barely speak. "I'm sure you made him happy while he lived. He must have learned to accept his disability."

Roarke shook his head. "He never did. His protests

159

were in the shape of pranks, some rather vicious. Nevertheless, I understood him very well."

Silence hung between them, then he spoke again. "I would like to know the reason why we're alive, why we have to suffer. Do you believe in a purpose of life?"

Minna thought about her father's deep faith. "My father was a curate, and he found great contentment in his religion, but the faith never touched me as profoundly."

Roarke's voice strengthened. "I've studied every possible book on the subject of religion and philosophy, and I'm no wiser."

"My theory is that life is rather simple, not a set of complicated doctrines, or rules that we're taught to honor and obey. I think that the more complicated our studies, the further we move from the real truth of life. That's why we never discover it. Still, I find the questions about life fascinating."

"If truth exists —"

"I think it's inside of us, but I don't know for sure."

"Then I must find a way to go inside. Find a book or a teacher to show me." He pushed away her hair and kissed her temple. "You're the only person who hasn't laughed at my quest. I'm serious about finding the answers. Ever since Thomas's death, I've been mulling over the futility of life, yet, with my failing vision, I appreciate every day more and more. I wish I could find the key to that puzzle."

His words touched her, and Minna brushed away a tear. "I wish I could tell you something helpful."

"You're the best thing that has happened to me since Thomas died. You're the most wonderful birthday gift that I could have wished." He laughed. "I'm surprised that Davina picked a virgin for me."

"Oh, you!" Minna tried to punch him, but he held her wrists captive as his mouth explored hers in an ever deepening kiss. In the kiss she forgot everything. Passion engulfed them anew, and Minna had never felt more fulfilled than in the reward of her ecstasy. They slept, tightly curled up together, reluctant to let an ounce of air separate them.

Minna awakened in the soft light of dawn. The time had come to leave. With a pounding heart she eased away from him. His hair was tumbled over his smooth forehead. Any lines of worry or disdain had been wiped away by the innocence of sleep. She resented leaving him, but if she was to retain his interest at its peak, she had to play elusive. It was a rotten thing to do, but she had no choice. Hating herself, she cursed Mr. Wylie under her breath. He would ruin more than he knew when Roarke found out the truth. God, she wished she could change everything, start over, but it was too late.

She dressed quietly, her heart heavy in the pure morning light. She had played a part in a deception that, when the truth was revealed, would make Roarke more bitter about life than ever. The thought was staggering. Fighting an urge to awaken him and clear her conscience, she looked down at his sleeping form. A resting god, so wonderful, so forceful and strong even in repose.

Had he, this man who could trigger her deepest feelings, ruined Mr. Wylie's daughter, made her take her life? Minna pondered the possibilities. It was hard to believe, but he had that virile magnetism that might ruin a woman to another man. If she was this deeply touched by him, couldn't he have touched any number of women before her as deeply? That was more than a possibility; it was highly likely. Her heart spoke differently. Their love was different, pure and trusting. Special.

A shiver of unease went through her, and she turned away. If she looked at him again, her resolution might falter. First and foremost, she had to think of her employees and their safety, then she would think about her own feelings. She ached terribly, but she would survive.

161

One question preyed on her mind: how much did he care for her? She was loath to destroy a man who faced blindness and who was still crawling out of the dark pit of grief, but the choice was not hers. She slipped out the gate at the back. Every step that brought her farther away from him filled her with sadness.

Later that day, Mr. Wylie appeared in her office. On trembling legs, she rose from the desk.

"Please, sit down," she said stiffly.

Giving her a hard stare, he twirled his hat between his hands. "I don't think so. I don't know if you're my friend or my enemy at this point." His voice held no compromise.

She folded her hands in front of her. "The mission is going as calculated. Before the week is out, I will have his confession of love."

A thin smile went across his face. "Well, well! I'm pleased to hear it. I was beginning to fear that you wouldn't be able to execute this plan of mine."

Minna's face grew hot with anger. "I don't go back on my promises."

"Glad to know it." He put his hat back on his head. On the threshold he added, "Oh, yes, one more thing: how will I know that you're telling the truth? I must witness—"

Minna gasped. "Oh, *no* . . . how can I—"

"You must do as I say! Part of my revenge is having the pleasure of seeing the earl suffer, just like he made my darling daughter suffer. Then your side of the deal will be completed. I'll leave you to get on with your successful life here." He swept out his arm, encompassing the comfortable office. "You have created a fine nest for yourself, and I would hate to see you lose it." He smiled in his cool, listless way.

Seething with hatred, she gave him Davina's address. "You're loathsome, Mr. Wylie!"

Her eyes challenged him, but he only hardened further. As he raised an eyebrow, defeat washed through her. "I'll leave the gate at the back unlocked, on Saturday night two weeks from now."

With a curt nod, he left, and Minna sank down in the chair behind her desk. Waves of undiluted hatred washed through her, and long minutes passed before she could gain control of her emotions.

A faintness came over her, and she had to prop up her head with her hands. Oh God, Roarke had revealed his deepest dreams . . . his fears, his sorrow. *Help me*. I will break him. I love him.

A fierce longing for him held her in its grip, robbing her of her breath. So this was love . . . this all-consuming passion, the heady feeling soaring through her every time she remembered his embrace. All she could think of was him, and she wondered if he was visualizing her just as passionately.

She feared that he would come to the shop to find her, but he didn't. All day, she waited for his footsteps in the corridor, but no. Perhaps he respected her desire for privacy, the quirky wish of a secret lover. That was what she was, his secret lover, nothing more, nothing less. She had to remember that he viewed her in that light. Love could exist in such a relationship, but it never became important. He was a peer of the Realm, and she was a simple seamstress. Oh God, why did these tumultuous emotions make her elated one moment, and depressed the next? Why did they hurt so much?

Davina arrived at the shop full of gossip about her impossible admirer, Mr. Epcott. "He found my secret spot! He walked up to me as bold as brass in the garden at the Marsdons' mansion, and simply *crushed* me with his embrace. Then he bent over and *licked*—licked, mind you, my neck." She blushed. "I've never been more intrigued. *How* did he know?" Her eyes twinkled with excitement. "Even though he resembles a toad, perhaps he's the man I've waited for all my life."

"I would say such devotion as his is difficult to find," Minna commented, holding up a bolt of blue velvet for Davina to inspect. "I would whisk him off his feet so fast he didn't know what happened."

Davina tittered. "Outrageous! You're always a fountain of advice, aren't you?" She studied Minna closely. "I must say you look peaked. You're not ill, are you?"

Minna blushed. "I . . . er, spent the night with a certain earl of your acquaintance."

Davina squealed and clapped her hands together. "I'm delighted. You wicked, *wicked* girl!"

Now that she had divulged and somehow defiled her and Roarke's secret, Minna had to plunge ahead. "I would appreciate it if we could use your gazebo for some time to come."

Davina winked conspiratorially. "Of course. I don't mind being part of delicious, clandestine romance. In fact, I shall send over the key to the gate just as soon as I return home." Her laughter filled the fitting rooms. "Thief of love, that's what you are, Minna Smith La-Forge."

Minna blushed. "Shh, Mrs. Shield, not so loud."

"Not only secret keys, but fabricated names." She stared hard at Minna. "You've never been to France, have you?"

Minna refused to look at Davina. "That doesn't mean that I don't have French relatives—"

"Pish! You don't have to lie to me. I'm sure you have some interesting secrets." She pulled a shimmering silk scarf through her hands.

Minna refused to get dragged into sharing confidences. If she told Davina the truth, the news would be flying around London the next day, and she might lose important customers. "A bit of secrecy never hurts."

Davina's eyebrows went up. "Ah! With secrets you lure the poor Earl of Whitecliffe into your bed."

"I'm sure I can't force him to go anywhere or into any bed without his consent," Minna said, blushing.

164

"After all, he's a man of the world."

Davina sighed, and placed her hand to her heart. "It's so romantic! Before you know it, he'll set you up in a cottage in St. John's Wood, and make jewels rain over your head."

That was the last thing Minna wanted, but she held her tongue. Davina left, and Minna was yet again the victim of restless and guilt-ridden thoughts about the earl. She relived the memories of the previous night and a hot flush crept over her skin. Would their next union have the fire of that first time?

Chapter Thirteen

Minna received the key to Davina's garden via a footman, and that very same night she waited in the gazebo for Roarke to arrive. He didn't. She waited until her eyelids drooped, until sadness sat like a leaden weight in her chest. Still he didn't arrive. She had been so sure that he would come even though they hadn't decided anything. She had slunk away while he was asleep. Perhaps that had angered him.

When raindrops started to fall, bringing in a damp wind from the river, she held her cloak closer around her and ran out to the street. Shivering with cold, she managed to find an empty hackney cab. She chided herself for her naivete, for believing that he shared the love she felt for him. No, perhaps he was more of a recluse at heart than she'd thought. He hadn't seemed to be when she lay in his arms, and that's when she'd mistakenly believed that she meant as much to him as he did to her. As the hackney pulled away from the corner of Green Street, she dashed the tears from her cheeks with the back of her hand. Botheration! She had been too sure of herself. What if he never returned?

Roarke watched the cab leave. He fought an urge to run after it, and he swore under his breath. The last hour he'd almost gone to the gazebo from his hiding place right inside the gate. When she had arrived, his heart had pounded with anticipation, but he had failed to make his legs carry him to the folly. Blast it, but she had ignited a flame deep inside him, and even though he'd told himself not to visit Davina's garden to see if Minerva would come, he had gone. He couldn't have stayed away.

He had stood among the trees, hiding like a coward. She could have been his this night and other nights; she *was* his. He sensed her longing, just as he felt his own. But he couldn't treat her like a trollop though she had offered herself like one. If he set her up as his mistress, her tender feelings would suffer in the long run.

The memory of Thomas's death flashed through his mind, and he knew, as he'd always known, that he couldn't continue this clandestine game with Minerva. He didn't want to hurt her, and he didn't want to impregnate her. *Perhaps you already did,* a voice said in his head, and a cold tremor rippled along his spine. He had broken his promise to himself. He had been a victim of his desire, and here he was again, panting and slavering like a mad dog. He pined for her, there was no denying that, but he also wanted more. He was surprised to find that he needed to know every detail about her life. That she lived on Clifford Street he already knew, but he'd been reluctant to confront her there. Her need for mystery intrigued him, and he suspected that she'd used it to ensnare him. Still, he didn't hold it against her. He'd made the decision to take her to bed.

Depressed, he turned homeward. The sooner he forgot about her, the better. This relationship would only lead to disaster. Why was he so weak, why was it so difficult to withstand the temptation?

Back in his study, he immersed himself deeply in his studies, a book about the travels of the soul through seven *chakras*—levels toward illumination. Supposedly the *chakras* existed within the human body. He gave a

167

derisive snort. No one but a select few knew of their existence. God, it was confusing to say the least! His head spun with all the facts, but the book fascinated him, just like the other volumes about Truth did. Could there be a liberation of the soul? Such a goal seemed completely unattainable, but every day an increasingly burning desire to *know* spurred him on to read more about the philosophers and the saints. If they had known the Truth, why was he so fog-brained that he hadn't the faintest inkling of where to start? What had given them the understanding, the *knowing—?*

His thoughts were interrupted by the door crashing against the wall. Zach hobbled inside, blood streaming down his face from a wound on his temple.

"What happened to you?" Roarke asked as his cousin came closer. When he saw the wound, he rose abruptly and led Zach to the nearest chair. "By thunder, who attacked you?" He dug a clean handkerchief from his pocket and pressed it against the cut.

"That damned Herrington butler slammed me with a candlestick when I tried to see the fair Aurora."

"You went to Lady Herrington's home?" Roarke asked incredulously. "You know that you're not welcome there."

"I . . . er, sneaked in through the servants' entrance. Aurora was pitifully pleased to see me, and I thought I would faint when I saw her in a filmy negligee." He groaned. "The fairest of apparitions—and I almost had her in my arms! Then the butler barged up the stairs brandishing a brass candlestick." Zach gave another drawn out moan. "So close, yet so far away! What I wouldn't have done to hold her in my embrace."

Zach fell into a fit of despondency, and didn't utter a word when Harris entered with a tray of bandages, lotions, and antiseptic.

"You must give up this foolish infatuation of yours," Roarke admonished. "Next time the butler won't be as considerate, mark my words."

Zach gave him a dark look. "You could use some of that infatuation yourself. That might pull you out of this gloomy study for an hour."

Roarke silently agreed, but he only pinched his lips into a disapproving line.

Minna went to the gazebo three evenings in a row, and Roarke didn't come. She contemplated going to his house in Berkley Square, but rejected the idea. What if he laughed in her face? She couldn't live with that. Every night she felt his rejection stronger, and it wounded her like nothing ever had before. Walking a thin line of hopelessness, she returned home every night. Next Saturday Mr. Wylie would know that she'd failed, and then he would ruin her business.

On the fourth night, when she had lost all hope, Roarke was suddenly standing there, on the steps of the marble folly, the moonlight outlining his powerful frame with silver. At first she lost her breath, then her heart started hammering madly.

She flew at him in anger, pummeling his chest. "You hateful man, you conniver," she sobbed, unable to control the tears pouring from her eyes. The tight knot of worry in her chest slowly dissolved as he pinned her arms down and enfolded her in his embrace.

"Shh, shh," he crooned with his lips against her ear.

"You didn't come," she wailed.

"God knows I've longed to hold you like this, Minerva. But it's wrong; every moment I'm holding you is wrong."

"No . . . this feels as right as the hugs my mother gave me when I was a child," she said into his cravat. She could not get enough of his touch, of his scent, of *him,* who had changed her life with a single kiss.

"Kiss me," she demanded, and curled her arms around his neck. She lifted her face to his, nudging him with small kisses along the hard jaw-line. She sensed his reluctance to touch her, yet he was already holding her.

"Do it. Please."

With a groan, he cradled her head between his hands and crushed her mouth with his. The ferocity of his kiss told her of his pent-up longing, and she clung to him, letting her senses catch fire under his touch. A slow, warm dizziness filled her head, and her thoughts dissolved as his tongue explored the softness of her mouth.

"Darling . . ." he muttered as he lifted his head from hers. "I couldn't stay away."

Her lips tingled, and her heart leaped when she saw the consuming passion on his face in the white moonlight. His eyes were hooded, simmering with a savage emotion.

He rapidly untied the cords that held her cloak together, then tossed it aside. Then he lifted her and laid her down on the soft pillows that were strewn over the floor. The magic that had filled her that first time they had come together was coming back, and she could barely breathe for the strong longing that engulfed her.

He unbuttoned her dress and pulled it over her head. "No expensive silk gown tonight, eh?" he chided.

"I didn't think you would come," she said breathlessly.

"I don't care what you wear. I'd rather see your silky flesh than the costliest court gown."

"Flatterer," she said with a laugh as he rolled down her stockings and kissed every inch of the inside of her legs. He gave every one of her toes a peck as if they were the most precious jewels, and every touch shot ever increasing thrills through her body. Soon she would be unable to talk, to think, to do anything but experience every moment of his lovemaking.

Roarke trembled so much he could barely contain

himself. When he had seen her waiting in the gazebo, he'd known that he was lost. He could not resist the pull of her, nor the mystery that surrounded the woman. He was drowning, and there was nothing he could do to save himself. He was damned, and he knew it.

The pearly sheen of her flesh, her soft, rounded hips, her small, high breasts, her graceful limbs, comprised a most riveting portrait. She was his to explore, to adore. The tightness in his groin made him moan, and he enfolded her slender body in an embrace, then rolled over so that she lay on top. The hard nubs of her breasts, her rapid breathing, her scent of arousal made him light-headed. He wound his hands into her silky hair and bent his head to suck on one of her nipples. The hard pebble in his mouth brought him closer to the roaring brink of no return. She intoxicated him to a point where his thoughts stopped, and all that remained was sensation.

She moved her hips against him, and spread her legs until the throbbing core of his desire pressed her most intimate parts. He closed his eyes in ecstasy when he found that she was hot and ready. Her breathing came in gasps against his neck, and he lifted her head so that he could kiss her, deeply, deeply. She squirmed against him, and he didn't force anything, but slid effortlessly into her honeyed sheath, and as it completely encompassed him, he wanted to cry.

Minna strove to quench the unbearable desire that fired every part of her body into a frenzy. His hard, smooth flesh held her in thrall, his fluid movement under her as he gripped her hips and brought her toward the brink of ecstasy. It seemed that no matter how hard she strove, she couldn't get enough of him. He rolled her onto her back and thrust into her with such force that she dissolved into fragments of rapture. As she convulsed, he crushed her derrière beneath his hands and lifted her hips, riding her with an abandon that finally brought a cry to his lips and a rapturous shudder to his body.

He collapsed against her, and she held him tightly. "I haven't thought about anything else these last few days," he murmured as the last tremors had subsided. "God, Minerva, what are you doing to me? This is pure agony! When I'm not with you, all I can think of is you—like this—naked in my arms, satiated with love."

"I think of you every waking moment of my life," she confessed truthfully.

A new awareness had sprung to life between them, and Minna held her breath. Was he going to give his confession of love? If he did, she had won. Somehow, the thought didn't make her elated, rather the opposite. Mr. Wylie's gain would be her loss. She squirmed uneasily.

"What's the matter with you, Minna?"

"Nothing . . ." *nothing,* she added silently. *Nothing but my entire future, and the future of those who work for me.* "Please touch me, hold me tighter," she whispered, feeling like a viper.

He stiffened, evidently sensing her inner turmoil. "Something is wrong." He stared at her in the milky moonlight. "I don't want you to be sad."

"I'm not," she whispered.

Silence made the air heavy. A bank of clouds covered the moon, and Minna could only make out the contours of Roarke's body. Shadows covered his expression.

He touched her face. "Are you going to tell me about your life now—bare your soul like I did that other night?"

"It's romantic with a hint of mystique, don't you agree?"

He peered closely at her face. She forced herself to remain still.

"I can't see you for the deuced clouds." He sighed. "Where are we going to meet when the summer is over?

172

This gazebo is cool even on hot summer nights—though we raise the temperature several degrees with our passion."

Minna nodded, not trusting her voice to speak. She loved this man; she had never experienced such ferocity of emotion, or such tenderness. Next week, Saturday, it would all shatter.

"You're so quiet tonight." He dragged his fingertips along the contours of her face. "Does it bother you that I'm going . . . blind?"

Minna shook her head. "I'm sorry for you, but your disability doesn't change the way I feel about you. Does it bother you?"

"No." He played with a tendril of her hair. "I would like to know about your past."

"There isn't much to tell. My parents were always poor, but I lacked for nothing. Only when they died, did my hardships begin." She squirmed. She didn't want to tell him about Mr. Wylie and the money that had helped to establish her business. "I have no brothers or sisters, or any other relatives that I know of. For some reason, my parents were never close to their relatives. Father had his Faith, and Mother her sewing. To them, work and survival was everything. They taught me that. All there is to say is: I've worked hard, and I will continue to do so."

"You must know that I respect your strength and your accomplishments. You're a remarkable woman, and I wouldn't want to change that." He fell into thought.

She listened to his silence, then caressed his lips timidly. "All I want is to touch you."

"Then do." He took her hand and guided it to his hip and farther down. She blushed as her hand enclosed the growing shaft of his manhood. "Please touch me everywhere," he said with a groan.

Their night of lovemaking was drawn out, every secret of their bodies revealed as they explored each other.

Finally exhausted, they fell into a deep slumber.

The birds awakened Minna, and as she stretched luxuriously, all the memories of the previous night returned. A warm glow remained from his loving, but in the rosy light of dawn, she was overcome with chilling unease. The proportion of her deceit was growing more monstrous every time they were together. Like a guilty thief, she rolled away from the innocently sleeping man.

This charade would break her, she thought as she struggled to get her dress over her head. Rolling up her stockings, she shoved them into her reticule. There was nothing she could do about her hair. The pins had disappeared during their wild night. Her cloak concealing her from neck to toe, she sneaked away from the gazebo, praying that he wouldn't wake up. As she slipped past the gate, she drew a heavy sigh of guilt.

She met Roarke every night at the gazebo after that, but her agitation about Saturday was taking its toll. She couldn't enjoy their lovemaking as much, and it was guilt that prevented her total abandonment into bliss. He sensed her withdrawal, but only tried to be more tender.

On Friday, she considered calling off her deal with Mr. Wylie. She entered the workshop at the top of the building that housed "Madame LaForge—Modiste". Young women's heads bent over intricate embroidery, needles flying. They all had friendly smiles for her, and Minna was torn with guilt. At a large table, the pattern maker, Mrs. Kimple, was busy cutting out expensive silks from France.

Minna admired their work, then left the room. Usually she felt enormous pride in her workshop, but today she was filled with dread. However, if she gave these excellent seamstresses glowing recommendations, they might find other positions. But would they find light and airy conditions that didn't ruin their eyesight? She doubted it. And if Mr. Wylie's anger at her for breaking the deal ruined her reputation, her letters of recommendation would be useless.

She went to her bedchamber to think. As she was pacing the floor, counting the stripes in her woven rug, Rosie knocked softly on the door. The disfigured young woman was hard-working and thoughtful, helping Mrs. Collins tirelessly with the heavy work. She had become a maid of all chores, among them, Minna's personal servant.

"I saw you go up here, so I brought you a pot of tea. Nothing like tea to pull oneself together." She slipped into the room as Minna thanked her. Her gray homespun dress looked freshly ironed, and her apron was spotless. Her face was still repulsive, but Minna noticed it less and less.

Rosie looked expectantly at Minna. "Shall I pour?"

"No," Minna said with a sigh. "I have a headache. Would you mind brushing my hair for a while?"

Rosie bobbed a curtsy. "Yes, ma'am." She took the brush from the dressing table and Minna sat down. Rosie's capable hands pulled the brush—not too hard, not too soft, through Minna's long hair, and it calmed her spinning mind.

Minna studied the maid's serious face in the mirror. The old scars glowed red on Rosie's cheek. "Are you happy here?"

"Oh, yes! Every day I wake up and I thank my Creator that I found you." She pulled half of her stiff face into the grimace that was her smile. "I think all the ladies in this establishment are grateful to you, Madame LaForge. In fact, they love you. 'Tis very difficult to find decent employment in this town."

Rosie's words echoed uncannily in Minna's mind. It was as if the maid knew what was going on, gleaned from the very air the threat hanging over the modiste shop. Minna nodded thoughtfully. As she watched her servant, she realized that Rosie had helped her to go on with her plan to ruin Roarke. She could not put all the

175

people that depended on her out in the street. The earl might suffer, but he would recover and seek some other lady to entertain. She didn't even dare to touch on her own feelings. They mattered not under the circumstances.

Rosie put down the brush. "Is your headache better now?"

"Much better, thank you."

Rosie left with another curtsy, and Minna poured herself a cup of tea. A calm had settled in her, and she knew her decision was right. Now all that remained was to give the earl his *coup de grâce* and not listen too closely to her conscience.

Chapter Fourteen

It was just like any other summer day, Minna thought, as Saturday dawned sunny and warm. Nothing ominous about it except that, tonight, her life would fall to pieces. How could she face Roarke without dying of guilt? A large bouquet of roses arrived from him, and their velvet red petals seemed to mock her.

She read the card stuck among the flowers. "Minerva, my goddess. I count the hours 'til we meet again. I love you. Whitecliffe."

Minna gasped. *I love you.* He'd written the words she had coveted since the first time they met. Her hands trembled in agitation. Those three simple words meant so much to her, meant everything. There was the risk she would never hear them again — not after tonight.

Oh, why had this happened to her? Misery swept over her, and she could barely find the strength to put the roses in water. After tonight, living would be difficult, but hadn't it always been? She had to fight through this somehow.

That night she went with a heavy heart to Davina's garden. The gate was unlocked and her heartbeat escalated with expectation, but disappointment filled her when she realized that Roarke wasn't there. If he wasn't there it meant only one thing. Mr. Wylie had arrived before her. Davina had traveled to her country seat in Kent, and all the windows of the mansion were dark.

Uneasiness made her queasy. She was alone with the man who had ruled her life these last five years. She couldn't see him even though she studied the shadows around the gazebo. She sensed his presence however, and her fingers curled hard around the railing. He would reveal himself, but only after he'd heard Roarke profess his love. Why were those words so important to him?

"Don't come, Roarke," she whispered to herself, but she knew he would. She pulled her cloak closer around her. This time would be the last, and Roarke would hate her. She didn't want to do this, every part of her protested against the plan. So what if her employees' lives were ruined? So what if she had to start over? Yet, in her heart she knew she had no choice. She couldn't start over if her reputation was destroyed.

She heard haphazard steps along the gravel path, a walking cane tapping the ground. The next moment Roarke stood tall and powerful before her, his teeth gleaming in a wide smile in the darkness.

"Darling," he said and lifted her up. Laughing, he swung her around. "I thought I would go crazy with longing."

"Thank you for the roses." Minna wondered if that small voice was really hers.

"Why so glum? Aren't you happy to see me?" He set her down and studied her face. She turned away, feeling that it would be the height of betrayal to meet his gaze. Just the promise of his love made her cringe with self-disgust.

Without looking at him, she clutched the front of his coat. "Roarke, I'm so happy to see you. I dream about you, I see your face before me every day," she whispered, but her voice had taken on a tremble that made him stiffen.

"What's wrong?" he demanded.

She threw her arms around him and held him close.

As she lifted her face to his, he bent down and kissed her, long and hard, and crushed her to him until she found it difficult to breathe.

She was acutely aware of Mr. Wylie hidden in the shrubs, watching, and it made her feel dirty. When Roarke started caressing her back, she pulled away.

"No," she said.

He gave her a puzzled frown. "I knew something was wrong." He squeezed her shoulders and stared closely at her. "Well, speak up."

Her courage waned. How could she dig out the words that would sever their romance?

"Minna, are you going to tell me, or do I have to wait until moss starts growing on my head?"

Silence stretched heavily between them, and Minna wrung her hands in despair.

He sat down on the bench and pulled her down with him. Taking both of her hands in his, he rubbed warmth into them.

"You're freezing cold, darling. Why? It's balmy tonight."

"I . . . we . . . must stop this." Minna averted her face from him.

Bewilderment tinted his voice. "Stop? This is unexpected. We've been so happy together." His breath rasped as he inhaled deeply. "Are you . . . er, with child?" he asked at last.

Minna sensed a sudden distance between them, and she feared that *he* would be the one to jilt her if he thought that she was pregnant. He didn't want any children by her, but he didn't have any scruples when it came to using her body. The unpleasant thought made it easier for her to go on with her task.

She thought she heard twigs break nearby, and she suspected that Mr. Wylie was growing impatient.

"I thought lovemaking eventually leads to childbearing," she said. "I would be proud to carry—"

He reached out and grabbed the back of her neck

179

tightly. "Don't finish that sentence! You don't know what you're talking about," he snapped.

She raised her voice. "I thought you loved me, Roarke. I thought you had made a commitment to me and accepted the possibility of creating a child."

He groaned. "I love you, Minna, like I've never loved anyone before, but all I have to offer you is a cottage in St. John's Wood—not marriage, not social standing. Even though I'm a peer, I'm not a wealthy man, nor an important man. If we married, you would be ostracized by the members of the *haute monde*. I wouldn't want that to happen to you. Really, I don't have anything to offer you except that cottage."

"With the other . . . whores?" She rose on trembling legs. She had to goad him on. Moving to stand by the railing from where she'd heard the snapping twig, she added, "Why was I so stupid to believe that you truly revered me?" She didn't need status, nor a lofty name, but she had to make him confess his love.

He came to her in two strides and whirled her around. "I can't fathom a life without you, but neither can I offer you anything but my love. I love you, dammit."

Victory was hers, but she felt no relief, no elation. Such sadness weighed her down that she could barely hold up her head. Her neck was a column filled with lead. She slumped against one of the round marble pillars that supported the roof.

"It's finished, Roarke. I don't ever want to see you again."

His face creased into a mask of disbelief, then dissolved in explosive anger. "What game is this, Minna?" He shook her. "I thought you loved me! Answer me!"

The shrubs swayed and gravel crunched outside the gazebo, and a dark shape walked slowly up the steps. Mr. Wylie looked stooped tonight, Minna noticed vaguely, as if life was a heavy burden to carry. To her it was.

"Whitecliffe, I'm sure you don't remember me, or

want to remember me, but we have met." Wylie made a mocking bow. In the ensuing pause, tension grew explosive. The older man continued, "At one point, I almost killed you, but that would have been too easy. I had to see you suffer. I've waited patiently for this day."

"Mr. Wylie?" Roarke sounded confused.

"Yes, Thurlow Wylie. If you remember, I had a daughter called Isobel, and she killed herself because of you. She sought death when she discovered that you would never love her. She carried your son, Thomas."

Roarke reeled backward, and Minna's heart bled for him.

"I did not lead Isobel to believe that I loved her; she threw herself at me. I was young, too weak to withstand the temptation of her." Roarke's voice thinned with anguish. "But I'm grateful that she gave me Thomas. I had eight years with him before a fever killed him. I loved that boy more than I've ever loved anyone. We were very close." He threw a glance full of hatred at Minna. "How are you involved in this?"

"She helped me to bring you to this point of suffering, Whitecliffe. Now perhaps you understand how my daughter felt when you jilted her so cruelly." Mr. Wylie's voice rose. "I hope you're suffering the fires of hell!" He stomped his cane into the floor, and Minna winced.

"I didn't plan to—" she began, but Roarke wasn't listening. He looked as if he was ready to strangle her.

Mr. Wylie lumbered to the spot where she was standing. "I knew Miss Smith—Madame LaForge—would find a way to help me. She's a most resourceful young woman."

"No," Minna cried out. "I didn't want to help you. You made me."

Mr. Wylie laughed. "Don't listen to her, Whitecliffe. A very shrewd and greedy lady, Miss Smith. She would do anything to keep her shop, and I knew that. I helped her and she repaid me in kind."

181

Minna clapped her hands over her ears. "Stop it! I never wished—you threatened me."

"You trollop!" Roarke roared, and Minna flinched as he lunged for her. She managed to evade his attack.

"I'm sorry, so sorry," she said. "Let it be. I'm sorry this had to happen. You'd better go now, Roarke."

"*Sorry?* Don't lie to me! You're laughing at me; you wanted to see how far you could goad me."

Mr. Wylie stepped between them. "Like I said, remember my dearest daughter, and ponder your sins, Whitecliffe. I knew that sooner or later you would pay. I've planned this for years."

Roarke braced one arm against a pillar and dashed his hand over his face. He was breathing laboriously, and Minna's heart twisted in agony. She was the reason for his suffering, and she loathed Mr. Wylie who had engineered the deception.

To her surprise, Mr. Wylie turned to her and pulled her toward the earl. "Don't you recognize this sweet face, Whitecliffe?"

Roarke stared at her murderously, but kept silent.

"Do you want to know a secret, an old secret?" continued Mr. Wylie in a silky voice.

His grip on Minna's arm was amazingly strong. Jolted by this new turn of events, she stared at him in confusion.

"What else you say can't anger me further," Roarke said.

"You must see that Miss Smith looks like someone you used to know."

Roarke nodded. "Yes . . . her hair is much like that of my stepmother, but her features—" Roarke voice silenced and his eyes widened in shock.

Minna held her breath in suspense. Somehow she knew that Wylie's next words would change her life.

"Your paramour is your stepsister, Whitecliffe."

Chapter Fifteen

"My . . . WHAT?"

"Your darling stepsister." Mr. Wylie laughed in triumph and pulled out a bundle of folded papers from his pocket. "I can prove it."

"You're lying," Minna whispered. Her head spun, and she had to sit down before she fainted.

Mr. Wylie untied the bundle and unfolded one of the papers. "I have here in part a copy of the adoption documents of a girl child named Minerva Wayland Seager who was born at the Meadow Hill estate, Kent, in 1795. The Birchington curate Horace Smith and his wife Emma adopted her. Her real father was the Honorable Justus Wayland Seager who, after being married to your stepmother, Portia Harding, for three years, died in a riding accident." He pointed at Minna. "Miss Smith is really Miss Wayland Seager, and she's the heiress of her uncle, Aloisius Wayland Seager. He owned the lands between Meadow Hill and The Towers that your horses use for grazing. Now she owns them." He snorted. "I hear you've been relying heavily on the funds from Meadow Hill to bolster the sagging finances at The Towers. The Whitecliffes always were wastrels."

Minna's senses reeled with shock.

Roarke looked like he'd received a blow to his head. "Minerva . . ." he muttered. "I heard that the child was adopted."

"The Smiths later moved away from Birchington and never returned."

Roarke stared at Mr. Wylie with hatred. "So what's the meaning of this?"

Mr. Wylie flung the papers at his feet. "I want you ruined, Whitecliffe. Financially ruined and groveling in the dust." He turned to Minna. "She at least had the courage to do something about her miserable life in hell's kitchen, and for that, and her services to me, I reward her with her birthright." He bowed to her. "Behold a lady of noble lineage, Miss Seager of Kent, landowner. My solicitors will confirm everything I've said tonight, and they have the formal papers in their care."

Minna shrunk, longing to disappear through the floor. She felt as if she'd traveled miles this night, and nothing would ever be the same.

Roarke stood in front of her, but she could not raise her face to look at him. He gripped her hair and yanked her head up.

"Aaoo," she cried, but he only stared at her intently. "My father told me once that the child had an unusual crescent-shaped birthmark on the left cheek." He flicked off the round velvet patch that she had placed over her birthmark.

"See?" Mr. Wylie said triumphantly. "I was right."

Roarke dropped his hand from her face. "So it was your game to ruin me," he said, turning to Mr. Wylie. "Not only to humiliate me?"

"I want to see you crushed. Only then will I have full satisfaction."

Roarke spread his arms in defeat. "You have succeeded so far, but I'm not beaten yet." He gave Minna a contemptuous stare. "And my hat's off to you," he spat, "you certainly held me under your spell, but I'm glad to be rid of you now." He snatched the legal documents from the floor and moved toward the stairs, his step faltering.

Minna ran after him and gripped his sleeve. "Please understand, it wasn't my choice to harm you—"

He shook her off irritably. "Be quiet, woman. Don't believe I'll ever trust you again. You might be the heiress to Aloisius Seager's acres, but my solicitors will study the matter in depth."

Mr. Wylie laughed harshly. "If you're not careful, Miss Smith, he'll find a way to take them from you. He needs the land desperately."

"Why did no one contact me before?" she asked.

"You disappeared in the bowels of London after your parents died. The Seager solicitors said it was like looking for a needle in a haystack. I had a personal interest in finding you, so I began investigating your whereabouts."

Minna was too dazed to think about Mr. Wylie's words. The inheritance meant so little now; she would think about it later. What mattered most was that Roarke's love had turned to hate. She ran after him as he marched toward the gate. His back was stiff with anger, and he slammed the gate behind him, right in her face. Pressing herself against the unyielding wood, she cried. She thought the sadness would tear her apart. Such magic with a man only came once in a lifetime.

Mr. Wylie's voice sounded right behind her. "You've done your part of the bargain, and I shan't bother you again. In the long run, you will be happier with the shop than you'd be as his mistress." He paused, patting her awkwardly on the shoulder. "Remember that. Anyway, you're a highborn lady, not the child of a humble curate."

He delved into his pocket and pulled out another set of papers. "I had two copies made, so you must study this at your leisure. The Seager solicitors will be most eager to meet with you." He tucked the thick envelope into the pocket of her cloak.

Minna wrenched away from him. She longed to slap

his face to silence him, but she couldn't find the strength. Sobbing heavily, she could only watch him in anger. "The Smiths were my parents. I knew no others, and I don't care to hear about a mother who gave up her infant child to adoption."

"She had no choice. Her husband—Whitecliffe's father—had control over her every decision. *He* was the one who forced your mother to give you up. Evidently he wasn't a very agreeable person."

She straightened, squaring her shoulders that ached with tension. "Mr. Wylie, I beg you to leave. You have ruined my life by using me shamelessly and revealing secrets that I'd rather not know. It might have been better if you'd let me jump into the river that night five years ago."

He bowed. "It would have been a waste. I knew your true identity then, and I had just found out your whereabouts. I followed you from the workshop to the bridge. When Aloisius Seager died, I learned that you were his heiress."

"You *used* me!"

"Yes, but I'm first and foremost a businessman, and I take the opportunities that come my way. In you I saw a way to destroy Whitecliffe."

"You have no heart, none whatsoever." Minna pointed to the gate. "Now go, and don't come to my shop again, or I will have you thrown out."

Mr. Wylie gave his cold smile and placed his beaver hat on his head. "Very well. Good luck to you, Minerva Seager. You made your business successful, and I admire such industriousness. And the Meadow Hill land has made you a wealthy woman."

Minna fumed in silence and watched him leave. He must be a servant of the dark powers, someone who cares naught about others, she thought.

She left shortly after him. Wiping away her tears, she walked along Green Street. Every step took her farther away from Roarke, the man she loved. Her walk took her to Grosvenor Square, and as if drawn by an inner chord, she was pulled along the path that would take her to Berkley Square. She didn't have to choose that route, but she *had* to—hoping to get another chance with Roarke. The night was unusually silent. Only the occasional rattle of coach wheels and faint human voices broke the stillness. Strains of music came from a pianoforte somewhere.

Her steps grew heavier the closer she got to his mansion. Berkley Square was deserted, and a gust of wind whipped a piece of crumpled paper along the ground. She yearned to go up the long stone steps, stand by the imposing pillars beside the front door and lift the brass knocker, then enter. Her legs would not move. She stood as if rooted to the spot, gazing, longing.

The windows were dark; the house had an air of emptiness.

As she stood there, a carriage arrived on the square, and halted in front of the mansion. Minna's heartbeat jumped, but when she saw that it wasn't the earl arriving, but a young man who limped on crutches, she sighed with disappointment.

The door opened and closed behind him, then the square was deserted once more. Minna finally dragged herself toward Clifford Street. She wasn't sure that she could face another morning.

Frozen with shock, Roarke stood in the library studying a portrait of Portia Harding, Minerva's mother. He could feel no anger toward the woman in the portrait. Portia had been a good mother to him. His fury was directed toward his father who had made this woman suffer. Portia must have grieved when she gave up Minerva. Portia had been soft-hearted and impossibly generous. Why she had fallen in love with his starchy father, Roarke would never know. Perhaps she had needed him for his commanding strength. Yet, Father had turned into a despot when the blindness took him.

Portia had been a vague, unworldly type of woman. Minerva. . . . His thoughts, which he'd held under tight rein, were circling around the name that made sour bile rise to his throat. Such a fool he'd been to let himself be seduced by her. *Minerva* or Miss Seager, like that idiot Wylie had called her, had crushed his heart.

He still reeled with the pain, the desolation that she had brought to his life. He couldn't collect his thoughts. Pressing the lids of his aching eyes, he forced himself to stop staring at the portrait that reminded him of her. God, he hated her! With a curse, he shoved a flower arrangement to the floor where the vase shattered.

Swallowing hard to ease the bitter misery, he sank down into the old leather arm chair that always made him feel at home. His grandfather had sat here pondering his problems. Had he ever experienced such heartbreak? Roarke wondered, fearing his chest would burst with all the pain. He struggled to pull deep breaths.

A knock sounded on the door, and Zach Gordon looked at him from the hallway. Light from a branch of candles spilled into the room. "Why are you sitting here in the dark, coz?"

Roarke didn't answer. He couldn't. His throat was constricted with grief.

"I say, old man. What has happened? You look like someone died," Zach said, his voice slowing with concern. He hobbled inside, and a footman followed with the candles. "Bring us some brandy," Zach ordered the servant and sat down in an armchair beside Roarke. "My God, you look positively ashen."

"Don't worry, nobody died. I've just found out that I'm the damnedest fool alive."

Zach waited, but when Roarke didn't continue, he prodded gently. "What? Did you lose a fortune at cards?"

Roarke shook his head, and gave his cousin a mirthless smile. "No . . . that would have been easier to bear than what happened tonight."

He pounded the armrest of his chair. "Blasted Minerva! I told you about her. I thought Davina and you were behind the scheme to get us together, but I was wrong." His breath rasped as he inhaled. "Brace yourself, Zach. Minerva got me in her clutches, and now I've discovered that she was *hired* to make me fall in love with her."

"What?"

"The whole cursed thing was orchestrated by *Thomas's grandfather,* Mr. Wylie. The old man accused me of provoking his daughter's death."

Zach swore softly. He started blurting a question, but fell silent as the footman returned with a carafe of brandy and two glasses on a tray. When he'd left, Zach poured two hearty measures, and placed the glass in Roarke's hand.

Roarke put it back on the tray in contempt. "I don't want to befuddle my mind with this."

"An odd fellow you are by any standards," Zach said and downed the contents of his glass.

"Dash it all, but I didn't mean to harm Isobel Wylie, and I gave Thomas everything."

"I know, coz. Now tell me all about this dastardly Minerva."

Roarke pounded his boot into the Oriental carpet underfoot. "The worst thing is that she's my stepsister."

Zach gasped. "Stepsister?"

Roarke nodded. "I know it's unbelievable, but it's true."

"How do you know?"

"The hussy looks a lot like Portia. Wayland Seager, Portia's first husband, and previous owner of Meadow Hill, was her father."

"Blast and thunder! What are you going to do?"

Roarke stared at him in anger. "What do you mean?" he spat. "I don't see that there's anything I can do — other than killing the two-faced trollop."

"I think you should plan a suitable revenge. You paid

heavily for your mistake with Miss Wylie when your son died. You gave Thomas everything; you owe the Wylies nothing." Zach fell into thought. "Are you sure Wylie hired this woman to destroy you?"

"Don't doubt it for a second! There's a possibility that Wylie coerced her into the plot, but she had a choice." Roarke rubbed his hands as they had taken a sudden chill.

"What choice?" Zach poured himself another glass of brandy.

"Between her modiste shop and me. She chose the shop."

Zach pondered his words. "Well, if that's the case, I wouldn't judge the lady too hard. She has built it from nothing, and many employees depend on her for their livelihood."

Roarke sighed. "I know, and somehow I could perhaps find a way to forgive her for that in due time, but you don't really understand." He thought for a while, remembering the precious, the pure, deep intimacy they had shared. It would forever be sullied, and nothing could alter that.

"My love for her changed my life completely. I felt like I had truly begun living again, on a level of unsurpassed happiness. She ruined it. Either she's a consummate actress or she did truly love me. If she shared my love to the greatest heights, she chose to discard it in favor of her shop. Then it wasn't *love* between us, but something else. If only she had told me about Mr. Wylie, I would have found a way to deal with him and save our love."

Zach drank some more, then wiped his upper lip. "True. However, my experience with the less fortunate is that they don't trust anyone but themselves. They have to have their wits about them to survive in hell's half-acre."

Roarke nodded thoughtfully as a red haze of anger built inside him, pushing to get out. "Yes, but she obviously didn't love me. Damn, but I'm tired of the whole debacle!" He kicked a footstool, sending it flying across the room. "God, I hate her! She's just like the rest of the whores—the ones I pay for. Nothing but a conniving mind behind the sweet smiles and the caresses. I've had enough of such schemers. I think I'll make an extended visit to The Towers."

"Like a dog licking his wounds," Zach chided. "No, you must find a way to get back at her."

Roarke dragged his hand through his hair and started pacing to ease the explosion building inside him. "Did you know that she's the heiress of Aloisius Wayland Seager, her uncle?"

Zach gasped. "He who died six years ago? He owned part of Meadow Hill!"

"Yes . . . that part of the estate is in the hands of trustees at the moment. Mostly land that lies between The Towers and Meadow Hill. Father had a long-term lease on the acres, a lease he secured before he had a falling out with Aloisius. After Aloisius's death, I managed to rent the land since the heiress could not be found. It's fortunate for my cattle that we still have the use of that land."

Zach groaned. "By God, I'd forgotten about that. You desperately need the acres, don't you?"

Roarke pounded his fist against the back of a chair in passing. "Minerva might sell. I'll look into the matter, but I fear that I won't be able to afford her price. Damn her!"

"The solicitors will handle this from now on," Zach said. "If she died, the land would be yours."

Roarke nodded, and gave a diabolical smile. "Don't I wish! Minerva is the last in the Wayland Seager line. However, I won't stoop to murder, even if I feel like her death would be a fitting revenge." He kept pacing. "No, not murder."

"No, not murder. Sit down, Roarke. We must come up with a solution to this problem. 'Twill make you feel better to have something to work for."

191

Roarke frowned, but obeyed. "You always were a stubborn one, Zach."

"Well, this time, you shall be the winner, not her, not Mr. Wylie." He snapped his fingers. "Perhaps I have the perfect solution. You must marry her."

Now you can get Heartfire Romances
right at home and save!

GET ♥ 4 FREE
HEARTFIRE NOVELS
A $17.00 VALUE!

**Home Subscription Members can enjoy
Heartfire Romances and Save $$$$$
each month.**

ENJOY ALL THE PASSION AND ROMANCE OF...

Heartfire

ROMANCES from ZEBRA

After you have read HEART-FIRE ROMANCES, we're sure you'll agree that HEARTFIRE sets new standards of excellence for historical romantic fiction. Each Zebra HEARTFIRE novel is the ultimate blend of intimate romance and grand adventure and each takes place in the kinds of historical settings you want most...the American Revolution, the Old West, Civil War and more.

SUBSCRIBERS $AVE, $AVE, $AVE!!!

As a HEARTFIRE Home Subscriber, you'll save with your HEARTFIRE Subscription. You'll receive 4 brand new Heartfire Romances to preview Free for 10 days each month. If you decide to keep them you'll pay only $3.50 each; a total of $14.00 and you'll save $3.00 each month off the cover price.

Plus, we'll send you these novels as soon as they are published each month. There is never any shipping, handling or other hidden charges; home delivery is always FREE! And there is no obligation to buy even a single book. You may return any of the books within 10 days for full credit and you can cancel your subscription at any time. No questions asked.

Zebra's HEARTFIRE ROMANCES Are The Ultimate
In Historical Romantic Fiction.
Start Enjoying Romance As You Have Never Enjoyed It Before...
With 4 FREE Books From HEARTFIRE

TO GET YOUR
4 FREE BOOKS
MAIL THE COUPON BELOW.

FREE BOOK CERTIFICATE

Heartfire Romance

GET 4 FREE BOOKS

Yes! I want to subscribe to Zebra's HEARTFIRE HOME SUBSCRIPTION SERVICE. Please send me my 4 FREE books. Then each month I'll receive the four newest Heartfire Romances as soon as they are published to preview Free for ten days. If I decide to keep them I'll pay the special discounted price of just $3.50 each; a total of $14.00. This is a savings of $3.00 off the regular publishers price. There are no shipping, handling or other hidden charges. There is no minimum number of books to buy and I may cancel this subscription at any time. In any case the 4 FREE Books are mine to keep regardless.

NAME

ADDRESS

CITY   STATE   ZIP

TELEPHONE

SIGNATURE

(If under 18 parent or guardian must sign)
Terms and prices subject to change.
Orders subject to acceptance.

ZH0893

GET 4 FREE BOOKS

HEARTFIRE HOME SUBSCRIPTION
SERVICE
120 BRIGHTON ROAD
P.O. BOX 5214
CLIFTON, NEW JERSEY 07015

Chapter Sixteen

"MARRY her? You must be out of your mind!" Roarke got up and renewed his pacing. He kicked at every chair standing in his way, and finally the wall. Flinching, he thought he'd broken his toes, but the pain didn't dilute his fury. "I don't want to see the woman again, not ever," he shouted. He stopped at Zach's chair and bent over the sitting man. "Don't you dare suggest another lunatic idea!"

"Somehow you must acquire those acres, or your cattle will have to eat gravel."

Roarke roared in anger. "After the humiliation she's given me? How can you even suggest that I contact her again?" He overturned a stand of fireplace implements and, with a furious kick, sent them clattering across the floor. "Why this? What sin have I committed to reap this kind of punishment?"

"None. Conspiracies like these happen. Remember when you inherited the Whitecliffe title? All those cousins were livid that *you* were the heir. They would have been delighted to see you die, especially Melchior. But, in my opinion, none of the other Whitecliffe relatives would have been the man to pull The Towers out of its sad state. You did it single-handedly."

"I don't care!" Roarke braced his arms against the

mantelpiece and let his head hang down. Blood pounded in his ears, and a red haze still swam under his eyelids. "I hate her!"

"Tsk, tsk. I understand that, and you shall have a fitting revenge. If she loses the Meadow Hill acres, you'll be avenged."

Roarke clenched his fists. "Once The Towers is solvent, I won't need the Meadow Hill acres. I can buy land elsewhere."

"Until then you need the acres. As things stand with the land in enemy hands, you can't continue breeding horses."

"The Arabians fetch a great price, so I don't see any reason to stop. No, I must look into buying land somewhere else in Kent. I don't want to deal with Minerva Seager."

Zach laughed. "That's understandable, but once your anger has simmered down you'll be able to see more clearly."

Roarke pounded the mantelpiece until the portraits rattled on the wall. "Shut up!"

Undaunted, Zach went on, "I'm enraged with her, too, but one of us has to keep level-headed to set up this plan."

"I don't need her blasted fields!" He paced furiously. "I must buy elsewhere."

"Dreams, only dreams, Roarke. It'll be years before you get enough funds to buy land."

Roarke rubbed his chin. "Perhaps I could find a way to dispose of Meadow Hill. I don't need the cost of its upkeep. *One* estate is difficult enough to maintain."

"Have you forgotten the clause that states that you can't sell Meadow Hill without Aloisius's acres. There's some legal technicality, and now that Aloisius is dead, you'll have to deal with Minerva Wayland Seager whether you like it or not." He leaned over and slapped Roarke's leg in passing. "Marriage is the only solution. Marriage to Miss Seager."

"I'll be dead first."

Minna spent the night crying until there were no more dry handkerchiefs in her chest of drawers. As she crumpled the last one into a ball and lobbed it across the room, she said to herself, "Tears won't change anything. You must find a way to live with this loss."

She squared her shoulders and shook herself as if trying to shed the burden of her betrayal. At least nothing had changed here at Clifford Street. Tomorrow would bring more wealthy customers, and she'd be able to hire more staff. Her business would support more starving workers, and their children would have full stomachs every day, good boots, and protection against the coming winter chill. The earl might suffer a pang of loss, but he would soon forget. Or would he?

Something in her heart spoke differently. They had shared a bond that was not of this world, something sacrosanct, something pure and beautiful. It could only be experienced, never explained, and she had ruined that. It would never come again. "Oh, God, what have I done!"

The next day, her eyes were swollen and painful after all the crying, but she had no tears left. A heaviness had settled in her heart, and no amount of cheerful chatter from Ellie, or culinary treats from Mrs. Collins and Rosie could ease her sorrow. Somehow she managed to get through the day, but she felt ill as the night came. She wondered if anyone had ever died from grieving.

That evening, she pulled out Mr. Wylie's envelope and studied the repulsive papers of her heritage. Her fingers felt sullied by the crisp parchment, but she forced herself to read. At the top Mr. Wylie had written in his precise hand that this was a copy of the original that was kept by the solicitors.

Everything he'd said was true. She was born to Justus Wayland Seager and his wife, Portia. What had they been like? Her natural mother had been more Roarke's mother than hers. He had known Portia. The parents she loved were the Smiths who had once served the village of Birchington. Not only had she lost Roarke, she had lost her identity.

She hated Portia at that moment, but she knew it was irrational. The truth was that she knew nothing about the people who were her real parents. An urge to learn more about them overcame her, but it was tempered with sadness. Whatever anyone might tell her about them, she would never know them. Perhaps one day she could travel down to Kent and unearth her past. The thought held little allure. She read the will of her uncle, but the words blurred together and she flung the paper to the floor. All the wealth in the world could not make her happy. Her shop was her wealth, and she had created it, but today, it failed to raise her spirits.

Four miserable days and nights, the knowledge that she had saved her workers' jobs carried her along, but on the fifth morning, she didn't feel like getting up. She was sick of displaying false smiles and assurances that she was fine. She knew the staff was worried about her. Finally, after Rosie had entered her bedchamber six times, Minna got up.

She needed to be alone. After dressing with haste, she left the house by the back door and walked aimlessly along the busy streets. No one noticed her, and she saw no one she knew. Wagons rumbled past, and the noise deafened her.

A carriage slowed down beside her, and the door

opened. She saw a young man with unruly dark hair and a wicked smile. He held his splinted leg stretched out in front of him, and in a flash she knew he was the man she'd seen entering the earl's mansion the last night she'd met Roarke.

"Madame LaForge?" he began pleasantly.

She nodded, studying him narrowly.

"I couldn't help but recognize you. Your lovely hair gives you away—it's already a byword in London."

"Flattery doesn't impress me. Come to the point, please."

He surveyed her leisurely, and Minna noticed the remarkable intelligence in his eyes. A dangerous man with mercurial wits and a wonderful smile, she thought. He has broken many hearts.

"I would like to choose a gown for my . . . er, sister. The loveliest of creations for her come out ball next month." He indicated the door. "Can I drive you back to your showroom? I would alight and assist you, but my leg—"

Minna was about to say no, but it might hurt her business. She viewed the interior suspiciously, as if expecting to find some kind of trap. Roarke's friend had every reason to be angry with her if he knew the truth.

She climbed inside after giving the address to the coachman. "I recognize you. I saw you at the Earl of Whitecliffe mansion," she said.

He nodded. "Yes . . . I'm staying with him while I'm incapacitated."

"I suppose you know all about . . . erm, my acquaintance with the earl." Somehow talking to this stranger gave her a renewed bond to Roarke, and she didn't feel quite so desolate.

The young man nodded. "He mentioned you." He changed the subject. "Let me introduce myself.

197

Zachary Gordon at your service. I'm Whitecliffe's cousin."

"Why should you be friendly with me, Mr. Gordon?" she asked suspiciously.

He shrugged. "As long as my cousin's quarrels don't affect me, I'm not involved."

His words didn't ring quite true, and Minna narrowed her eyes.

He held up his hands disarmingly. "I'm not about to berate you, Madam, but in all honesty, I don't see how you could jilt my cousin. A finer man I have yet to meet."

"Your view is distorted by affection, Mr. Gordon, but your loyalty does you credit. However, I can't say that I know your cousin in depth." The lie sat badly on her tongue, and she blushed. She lowered her eyes and folded her hands in her lap. "What sort of a gown—"

"I'm sorry, but it was only an excuse to meet you. I don't have a sister. I followed you from your shop."

Her gaze widened. "You only wanted to meet me?"

He nodded. "I had to see what kind of woman wrecked my cousin's life. He's miserable, you know."

Minna cringed as his words stirred up her own pain. "I had no choice."

He leaned over and stared hard at her. "Didn't you? I believe you plotted to ruin Roarke with Mr. Wylie. Roarke won't forgive you. He never wants to see you again."

Her head drooped with misery. "Mr. Wylie *forced* the choice on me. He threatened to take away my shop, and I had to save my employees. The earl will recover from his heartache in time." She sounded so cold, and she wished she could explain to this man what her loyal people meant to her. "A man like the earl will find happiness with a woman of his own

198

class."

"You know that's a lie. The man is going blind! No one wants a blind husband. Doesn't that mean anything to you? How could you be so cruel?"

"I didn't want to hurt him, truly I didn't. I believe he'll recover from his heartache. He's a strong man." She knew she was only making excuses. After what she had shared with Roarke, she should never belittle her betrayal of him. Something made her continue in a chilly tone, "Mr. Wylie had a right to be angry. He lost a daughter because of the earl's coldheartedness."

Mr. Gordon stomped his crutch on the floor. "Roarke has paid in many ways for his folly. But one thing is for sure, the earl is not coldhearted. He's a generous and thoughtful man."

Minna knew it was true, but anything she could say to this man would not bring the earl back to her. Best to leave the whole issue alone.

The carriage came to a halt in front of the shop, and Minna opened the door. The young man put a restraining hand on her sleeve. "If you don't believe me, come to his house tomorrow morning at nine, and see for yourself. I shall take you myself in this carriage. Tomorrow at the south corner of the square."

She hesitated, but her fascination with Roarke won. "Very well, perhaps you can show me a side of him that I don't know."

"Indeed I shall." Zach Gordon's smile warmed Minna's heart, and her steps were lighter as she walked away from the carriage.

The next morning she dressed in a hurry and gulped down her tea. Time couldn't go fast enough until she could see Roarke again.

Ellie gave her a hug as she emerged into their sitting room. "This is the first day in a week that I see a sparkle in your eyes. 'Tis about time."

"You must look after the shop alone this morning, Ellie," Minna said, returning the hug. "I have something to attend to."

"Is this 'something' connected to the Earl of Whitecliffe, I wonder?"

Minna grew perfectly still. "How do you know?"

"Well, rumor has it that you're romantically attached to the earl."

Minna fumed. "Has Davina been spreading this hearsay?"

"No . . . but Lady Barton whispered something about a scandal that involves you and the earl. Perhaps Davina said something to her. Lady Barton's related through marriage to the Hardings, did you know that?"

"Yes." Minna listened with only half an ear as she pulled a cape over her walking dress. Tying the satin ribbons of her straw bonnet under her chin, she said, "Lady Barton is an old busybody, but when I return you and I shall sit down and talk. I have something to explain."

Ellie stopped Minna in the doorway. "I knew there was something serious. I would like to know what's happening."

"You're right. I've been unfair. I haven't had the strength to think about anything but my problems this last week. Something momentous has happened, but I don't know how to deal with it. I will tell you everything later."

The carriage was already at the corner, waiting. Zach Gordon waved through the window. "Please enter. In five minutes, he'll be coming out. There's his town coach now."

Minna tensed up inside. She could barely breathe, and her throat felt constricted as if she had a cold.

All this turmoil because of *him*. She knew she loved him, and that she always would.

Mr. Gordon waved his hand urgently. "There he is now."

Minna leaned out and tears came to her eyes as she saw Roarke's beloved form. His hair gleamed dully in the morning light as he pulled off his hat before jumping into the carriage.

"Let's follow him," Gordon said.

Anticipation filled her, and she couldn't remain still on her seat. She craned her neck out the window and stared ahead. Roarke's coach had slowed down, but once they arrived at Piccadilly, the horses went into a trot. Mr. Gordon's vehicle weaved through the traffic, and soon Minna had a clear view of the earl's carriage. She was glad to have Mr. Gordon's protection as they crossed Leicester Square and moved into the meaner areas north of Long Acre. Just at the outskirts of Seven Dials, the earl halted on Tower Street.

Minna watched in surprise as he jumped down. "Where is he going?" What errand did he have at Tower Street where the inhabitants, who looked like walking heaps of rags with huge eyes in emaciated faces, were as different from him as the sun from the moon?

"Follow him. I'll keep an eye on you from a distance. Roarke would be furious if he found out that I brought you here. Go, m'dear."

Minna hesitated to get out. Not that she was afraid, but her good wool cape and gold-fringed handbag would draw thieves like bees to nectar.

Squaring her shoulders, she gave her escort a suspicious glance, then got down. She hid her money pouch inside her bodice. To steal it, the ruffians of Seven Dials would have to undress her, and *that* she would not allow.

Two filthy boys slid past her, probably already scouting for bulging purses and lace-trimmed silk handkerchiefs. One had his eyes on the handbag. "Be off with you," Minna demanded. It wouldn't do to show these people who looked more like walking cadavers than human beings that she was afraid. She shivered, remembering the times when she had lived in squalor. The rank smell of rotting garbage, filth, poverty, and defeat was as familiar as her own lavender soap.

More children sidled up to her with outstretched grimy hands, but she ignored them and followed the earl. He walked halfway up the street, then turned and stepped into a building that had been freshly painted. A former warehouse, Minna guessed. The earl's movements intrigued her, but she could not go inside after him. She positioned herself at an angle further down the street, then pushed a penny into the hand of an urchin who stood next to her. "Tell me about that house." It looked so proud among its gray dilapidated neighbors.

"That's th' new orphanage, miss, the ragtag and bobtail school," said the urchin. His eyes looked enormous in his pinched face. Grime darkened his pasty skin. Minna's heart stirred with pity, and she gave him another penny.

"They eat all 'ey want there," the boy said with longing. "I 'ave me mum, or I would live there now. 'Tis warm in th' winter whereas me mum's 'ouse is freezin'."

His plaintive voice touched her, and she wished she could help these little wizened boys who darted up and down the street.

The urchin watched the earl's horses with excitement. "See 'em bloods? They are th' owner's pair. 'E comes once a week, an' then they give out free food to ever'one."

More and more children, a gray swaying mass, were nearing the orphanage. Minna couldn't believe her eyes. A sea of dirty faces, rags, bony arms and feet, were moving around her.

Then the earl came out and snapped his fingers. The lackeys and the coachman began lifting hampers from the coach, perhaps as many as twenty of them. Serving girls came out of the building, and Minna noticed that their dresses were clean and their aprons white.

Her heart constricted further as she viewed the increasing mass of poor children. There were so many of them.

"Listen up," the earl suddenly shouted on the doorstep. "Anyone who learns his alphabet by the end of the summer, shall receive a guinea. You can attend classes here every morning except Sunday."

The urchin at Minna's side giggled. "I'll git me guinny, y'll see. There's a mighty 'all inside where they used t' store barrels o' ale. That's were th' curate comes to show us our letters. It smells sumthin' arful in there."

"You already attend?"

"Yes, miss, I knows me As and Bs, and me numbers. I'm goin' to be a clerk when I'm grown."

He sounded so confident that Minna prayed that he would succeed. This place was the only bright spot in the lives of these children, and the earl, *her* earl, had founded the orphanage. Her heart flowed over with love as she saw this side of the man she loved. Somehow she wished Mr. Gordon had shown her something unpleasant about Roarke. That way it would have been easier to forget him.

"Look, they're dolin' out the bread." The urchin launched himself into the sea of children. Soon a line had formed, and the serving girls distributed loaves and wedges of cheese.

Stepping closer, Minna couldn't take her eyes off the earl. He looked almost happy as he laughed at the children milling around him, their shouts and shrieks deafening. His eyes twinkled behind his spectacles as he studied the children closely, one in particular, a blond ten-year-old who was talking to him and gesticulating wildly with his loaf of bread. The earl nodded, and the boy grinned. Then the urchin dashed off, disappearing into a doorway farther down the block. Minna noticed that Roarke furtively wiped one of his eyes.

The earl scanned the crowd, and Minna's breath clogged in her throat. What if he recognized her? She drew back into the portal, but his roving gaze had stopped, burning into her. She didn't know if he could see her, but she sensed that he had. Holding her breath, she wondered what he would do next. She ought to leave before he came after her.

He took a few steps forward, but the crowd hampered his movements. She drew a sigh of relief. If he caught up with her, he would not hold back his anger. He would probably accuse her of further underhanded plans.

Before the crowds had dispersed, Minna decided to leave. She took a long look at him, imprinting on her memory the sun-streaked blond hair that glinted like gold in the sunlight, the hard jaw that said he brooked no nonsense, those arrogant, yet sensitive lips that had kissed her senseless. Something melted inside of her, filling her with a warm glow, and suddenly she couldn't stop the tears from flooding her eyes.

She hurried away from the crowd; she ran past all the staring almost-corpses that lined the walls of the hovels.

Her heart had been touched deeply as she witnessed the depths of her beloved's compassion. The loss of Roarke's son must have triggered his generosity. Roarke seemed to enjoy the company of these unfortunate children. Perhaps they reminded him of what he'd lost. She loved him more for it.

Someone came up behind her and wrenched her arm hard. She whirled around and stared into the earl's angry eyes.

"What are you doing here? Spying on me?"

She pulled away from him. "Yes, I was spying on you."

He crossed his arms over his chest. "And may I ask why?" His eyes smoldered with anger, and she felt a twinge of fear.

"Your cousin claims that I don't know everything about you. I was curious to discover the truth to that statement."

He started to say something, but anger prevented him from finishing his sentence. His face had paled, and a muscle worked in his jaw. "By God, woman." He was reaching for her, and she was afraid that he would strike her. "Why won't you leave well alone?"

"How did you recognize me in the crowd?" she asked.

"I know only one person with hair like yours, and it's the hair I least want to see. Please get out of my sight!"

"Roarke," Zach Gordon called out, and Minna was relieved to see him. "Watch your temper."

The earl turned around, ready to fight with anyone who interfered with him.

"Zach? What the deuce—?" he began, but didn't have time to complete the question as two burly men, the two lackeys from Gordon's coach, came up from behind and pulled the earl's arms behind him. He didn't have a chance against these stalwart men. Even though he struggled viciously, the lackeys managed to bind his wrists together.

"Good!" shouted Zach Gordon. "Bring him here."

Minna could not comprehend what was happening, and the gaunt denizens of Seven Dials could only stare with incredulous eyes. They shouted catcalls and moved closer to the fighting men.

"Let go of me!" the earl snarled as the two footmen dragged him to the coach.

"They are my men, Roarke. They don't take orders from you," Zach said.

Roarke struggled like a fiend, but the two husky servants were too much for him. He glared at Minna, his eyes cold with hatred.

"Is this your idea?"

Zach laughed, waving his crutch. "No, don't blame Miss Seager for anything. Entirely my plan. When I realized that reasoning would bring us nowhere, I decided that force was the only way."

Roarke's face darkened with fury, and Minna shrank against the carriage. She had no idea why Mr. Gordon wanted to abduct his cousin.

"What is this all about?" Roarke shouted as he rolled onto the seat inside the carriage.

Zach Gordon held out his hand to Minna, and she hesitated before taking it, but she had no choice. She sat as far away from Roarke on the seat as possible.

"Why, you two must be tied in holy wedlock. There's no other way about it, and since you're too stubborn for your own good, coz, I have taken matters into my own hands. I will not accept any more argument from you, and Miss Seager, believe me, this is the best solution for everyone."

"Marriage?" Minna asked with a faint voice. "I can't marry the earl!"

206

Chapter Seventeen

"It looks as if both of you are too obstinate for comfort," Zach said cheerfully. "Well, you'll soon be in a more positive frame of mind. Trust me."

"Where are you taking us?" Roarke demanded to know as the coach jostled along the London streets.

"Home, of course." Zach smiled angelically. "Then you two shall spend some time together and discuss your differences. Smooth them out as it were."

"You devil!" Roarke spat. "You cork-brained wretch."

"I've heard worse insults."

Minna's mind reeled, and she contemplated jumping out of the carriage. This was a turn of events she had never anticipated. She gave Roarke a worried sideways glance and her chest ached with unshed tears. It was so obvious that he didn't want to be anywhere close to her. He looked uncomfortable with his hands tied, and he repeatedly lost his balance on the seat as the coach swayed at the street corners. Bracing the heels of his boots into the floor, he glared at his cousin who whistled a tune as if nothing was wrong with the world.

Minna decided she would run away as soon as the carriage came to a standstill.

The coach crossed Swallow Street and turned into Conduit that would take them back to Berkley Square. Suddenly, Zach Gordon leaned out the window, and stared ahead.

"You love-sick dog," the earl chided. "The fair Aurora is not at home, so why bother?"

"You're wrong; she is. Lady Herrington returned yesterday," Zach said with a profound sigh. "Ahh, the fair Aurora. Was there ever a lovelier morning?"

Minna wondered what they were talking about. An urgency came into Gordon's face, and his hands gripped the edge of the window. "My God, look at that! Aurora just came out and is climbing into her traveling coach. The fair liar told me in her note that she would depart next week. The dragon is with her, and they're leaving." He pounded the roof with his crutch, and the coach came to a halt. The coachman opened the hatch, and Gordon said, "Go after that carriage, and don't lose sight of it!"

Minna had no idea what was going on, but her curiosity was piqued. She looked through her window, then realized that this was the perfect time to escape. But when she tried to step over Mr. Gordon's injured leg, he laughed softly.

"You're my prisoner Miss Seager, until this situation with my cousin can be sorted out to everyone's satisfaction." He barred her path not only with his leg but with his crutch. "Please return to your seat. If you cooperate I won't have to tie your hands."

"Damned blockhead," the earl swore under his breath. "You can't order people around like this. You might find yourself in prison for abduction."

That threat didn't do anything to ruffle Zach Gordon. He only laughed. "When this is all over, both of you will be grateful to me."

"I have business to take care of," the earl said as

208

the carriage gained speed. "You can't kidnap me like this." He tried to sit up straight, but his bound arms prevented him from any comfort. "I thought we were going home."

"We were, but due to Aurora's departure, the plans seem to have changed." The pace increased even further, and after half an hour the coach jostled into Southwark on the other side of the river. Zach Gordon hung out the window staring after the mysterious Aurora's coach.

"They are without doubt traveling to Berkland Park. I'll see Aurora there." He slapped Roarke on the thigh. "Yes, we're going home, Cousin, not to Berkley Square but to Sun Hollow. After my mission has been completed, you're free to go wherever you want, or stay with me. Perhaps it's about time you go back to your own heap of stones and bury Thomas's ghost."

Roarke groaned. "When I get rid of this rope around my wrists, I'll be aiming for your neck."

"Precisely. I won't be there; I must find a way to communicate with the fair Aurora. Therefore, your anger is a waste of energy." He rubbed his chin thoughtfully. "No, I think you ought to go home to The Towers. One day you'll have to face the ghost, and this week is as good a time as any. But first, Sun Hollow."

"You drop your plans at a moment's notice just to spy on Aurora Bishop?" Roarke taunted.

Zach nodded sagely. "Of course. I didn't plan to travel into Kent, but to be near her, to watch her is balm to my bruised heart." He patted the small white patch on his brow. "And to my wound."

Roarke snorted, and Minna wished she knew what they were talking about. She felt small and dejected in her corner of the carriage. One part of her was happy to be in close proximity to the earl, and the other wanted desperately to flee. When she looked at him she remembered their bliss together, but more strongly, she recalled her betrayal. If that treachery hadn't happened, where would they have been today? She hurriedly shook off that thought.

"Ahh, to breathe country air again," sighed Zach after they had traveled an hour in silence. He was leaning out the window again, staring after a coach that Minna couldn't see. "I wish I could share this moment of serenity with Aurora."

"Serenity? Only you feel that way, Zach." The earl pulled his brows into an angry frown, and he exuded an ever mounting wrath. "You just wait."

"Come now, don't be so glum," continued Zach. "We'll stop at an inn soon and have a meal. Miss Seager can spoon-feed you. I'm sure she'll be happy to oblige."

Minna glared at Zach, and the earl glared at her. His hatred hurt her almost like a physical blow. Her cheeks burning, she lowered her gaze in humiliation. "I don't think it's a good idea. If you don't let me go, I shall summon the law in the next village."

Zach seemed to evaluate that threat for a moment. "Very well, then you shall spoon-feed him when we get to Sun Hollow. You'll be locked up, and no one will hear you there except the servants."

"I'll cut your throat for that comment, Zach," the earl said menacingly. "Locked up? That's no way to treat a lady—however treacherous she is."

"I know, but under the circumstances I have no choice." Zach laughed, and Minna glowered at him, debating whether she ought to try her hand at manslaughter.

"Like I said before, one day you'll thank me for this." Zach looked out once more. "Aurora is surely

210

heading for Berkland Park. Lady Herrington thinks she can fool me, but I knew the exact moment she returned to London. Spies, you know."

"Spare us your romantic drivel," Roarke said with a snort. "Why would you want to marry a lady who's attached to Lady Herrington? With a dragon like that, you'll be beleaguered for the rest of your life."

Their conversation slowed and was replaced by sullen glares. As the evening sun slanted over the South counties, the coach pulled into a long private drive from a country lane somewhere in Kent, then stopped in front of a mansion.

Minna had never seen anything so beautiful as the old Jacobean structure built of mellow sandstone. Zach Gordon lived like a king in his own apple orchard surrounded by a stone wall. Profuse clematis grew on trellises by the front entrance, and myrtle grew on the slope on both sides of the house.

"How enchanting," she whispered.

"It is lovely, isn't it?" Zach said and eased his stiff leg out of the coach door. "But my cousin prefers the darkened rooms of his townhouse in foul-smelling London. He's spellbound by his studies."

"I must send a message to London," Minna said. "My staff will be worrying about me." She climbed down after him, and he pointed out distant parts that had a bluish-green veil of gathering twilight.

"The orchards of Kent." Zach looked at her kindly. "I'll see to it that your staff gets the message, Miss Seager. Meanwhile, you'll have to be my prisoner." He looked from her to Roarke who had struggled out of the carriage and was leaning against it.

"If I'm not wholly off the mark, you two need to

211

sit down and really discuss your differences. And since you're not willing to do that in a civilized manner, I've decided you shall share a room until the time you have reconciled." He snapped his fingers, and one of the lackeys stepped down from the coach. He came toward Minna with a rope, and she realized that he was about to tie her as he'd tied Roarke.

"No!" she said, trying to slink around the burly footman, but his cohort, who was even larger, caught her and held her arms behind her until the other man had tied her wrists. The knot was rather loose, but Minna was helpless.

"You simply can't do this to a lady," Roarke shouted, and struggled to get free from the cord binding his hands together.

"Ah! You do care about Miss Seager, as much is evident in your protest. Such thoughtfulness does you credit, coz. Come now. The faster you two cooperate, the sooner you'll be free."

"By God, Zach, *think*. Your tricks will make matters worse," Roarke said irritably.

"They couldn't be worse," Minna commented as the lackeys led her into the dim hallway.

The house had a deserted look, and she realized that Zach Gordon was the only occupant of Sun Hollow except a handful of servants. As if he'd read her thoughts, Zach said, "Mother is visiting friends up north, otherwise I would have been hard pressed to know where to put you. She would not have allowed prisoners here. But the servants are loyal to me; they won't say a word about this."

Roarke replied acidly, "They've seen it all before, or worse debacles, where you're concerned. This little oddity won't lift many eyebrows."

Minna wondered if it meant that Zach was a

trickster of great proportions, but she didn't say anything. The hall had a checkered marble floor, and a curving mahogany staircase. The plaster ceilings looked as if they needed a fresh coat of paint, and the gold brocade panels looked slightly tarnished. She had a glimpse of a drawing room decorated in goldleaf and turquoise brocade. The high ceiling supported enormous chandeliers, and over the doors plaster cartouches framed old portraits. The house looked elegant, but dusty and neglected, as if the housekeeper had left months ago without hiring a successor.

"I shall put you upstairs, in one of the guest chambers so that you can't escape out the window—if by the odd chance you get such a foolish idea." He climbed up the stairs, and the prisoners followed. "But remember, guards outside the door will hear any escape attempt."

"I'm so angry that any efforts to placate me won't work, Zach. This time I won't forgive you."

Minna agreed, but she was too tired and upset to speak. She wouldn't hesitate to pummel the man who so flippantly played with their lives.

"I know, I know," Zach said lightly, but his smile looked somewhat strained, Minna thought, as he held open the door to a guest room at the back of the house. He motioned for the footmen to untie Minna's bonds, and she drew a sigh of relief.

She rubbed her wrists as the key turned in the lock behind them. She stared at Roarke. *What was going through his mind?* she wondered. He looked extremely angry.

"At least Zach made sure we have comfortable chairs—and a bed," he said acidly. He refused to look at her as he mentioned the word *bed* and silence stretched between them.

213

Minna blushed as she viewed the high fourposter with its soft, inviting down cover. She could sleep a night and a day, but knowing that Roarke was in the room with her prevented her from relaxing. She couldn't think of anything but him, yet such was the chasm between them that he could have been on the moon and not so close that she could touch him if she reached out.

"I hope he won't let us starve," she said in a flat effort of humor.

Roarke didn't laugh. He went over to the window and stared outside. "My cousin always had hare-brained schemes."

Minna wished he would turn around and look at her, but he didn't. In fact, his stiff back told its own story. He rejected her, just like he had before. She didn't know what to do, but now she had her chance to explain.

"I don't know where to start, how to place the words," she said lamely. "There are some things I need to clarify."

He turned, his face twisted in a scowl. "I don't want to hear any more lies from you. In fact, I'm tired of the very sound of your voice." He walked panther-like across the floor to tower over her. His eyes were as cold as a winter's day. "If you're silent for a moment, I might figure out a way to escape."

She opened her mouth to protest, but he shook his head in such anger that she wouldn't dream of speaking.

"Please, be silent, Miss Smith . . . or Seager, whichever it is." The last words he said with such contempt that Minna's anger rose.

He could speak about her with scorn to others, but what right did he have to mock her? His father had married her mother to get his hands on

214

Meadow Hill. It was as simple as that. His heritage was no nobler than hers.

"I'm sure the truth about my identity made you uncomfortable, but you have no right to order me about. I'm not your servant." She crossed her arms over her chest, and met his gaze squarely.

Anger seethed between them. With a roar, he swung away from her, and sank down onto a chair. "When I get my hands on that scoundrel, I'll—"

"Don't waste your breath," she said icily. "If you think you're the only one who finds this situation intolerable, you're mistaken. I don't want to be here, not with you. I have business in London."

He glared at her from under a bar of eyebrows that bristled with ire. "I curse the day I laid eyes on you, Miss Smith."

"A bit melodramatic, don't you think? You can't change what's already happened."

He laughed harshly. "But why do I have to be reminded of it? I'd rather forget that sick interlude of my life, and concentrate on better things."

"The fact is, you can't forget any more than I can," Minna said, her voice breaking at the poignant memories.

He turned away until all she could see was his angry back. She longed to hug him, to soothe away the pain from his face and the hatred in his eyes. But nothing that she said or did would change his feelings. She stepped up to him quietly, and untied the cord around his wrists.

"If you can find a way to get us out of this, you'll never have to see me again. That's a promise."

Chapter Eighteen

The earl went immediately to the door and banged on it. A loud cough told them that guards were posted outside. Swearing under his breath, he tried the windows, but other than jumping twenty feet to the ground, there was no other way to escape.

"It looks like we're in Mr. Gordon's power for the time being," Minna said. Seeing the anger in Roarke's eyes, she wished that this farce was finished. It pained her unspeakably to see his hatred.

Her shoulders felt too heavy to carry, even her head seemed to weigh a hundred pounds. She slumped on the edge of the mattress. "I honestly didn't want to hurt you," she said, but her voice was barely more than a whisper.

"You had ample opportunity to back out of the infamous scheme with Mr. Wylie," he blurted out, and pushed a hand through his hair. "You deliberately sought to destroy me. For *weeks* you knew about the scheme and didn't say a word. You watched my humiliation without lifting a finger to help."

"I still love you," she said. Every word was an effort to pronounce.

"You don't know the meaning of the word," he roared. With two steps he stood in front of her and gripped her shoulders. Shaking her, he looked at her with such anger that she thought he would like to kill her right then and there.

"I d-didn't know a-about the i-inheritance," she said as her teeth rattled with the shaking. "I was as shocked as you were. Mr. Wylie tricked me; I didn't want to learn the truth about my origin, honestly. But I know I won't be able to rest until I find out more about my past. I wish you could tell me something about my real parents."

With a groan, he let go of her. She sagged on the bed, then pulled her legs up and dragged a pillow under her head. She shielded her face with her arm so that he couldn't see her tears.

"You can't demand anything from me, Minerva. But one thing I can tell you; Portia Harding was not a cold, calculating female like you. She was generous and kind, not grasping like you."

"She gave me to the first person who wanted to adopt me," Minna said, and the thought hurt like nothing else.

Roarke swore and began pacing the floor. "You can't soften me with your woes."

"I only want to know something about her. Is that so odd?"

With his back toward her, Roarke sat heavily on a chair that faced the window. "I have no desire to talk to you, Minerva."

Anger sprang to life, a searing flame in Minna's chest. She sat up and flung the pillow at him. It connected with his head, and a cloud of dust dispersed from the down-filled shell. "You idiot! How can we solve anything if we don't talk?"

"We don't need to solve anything," he rejoined acidly, and hurled the pillow back at her. "There's nothing to talk about. In fact, I wish I were far, far away from you."

"Ha! You can't escape your problems, so you'd better solve them."

"Don't tell me what to do! I don't want to talk."

Minna refused to listen. "You've told me very little about your life. Tell me all about Thomas, tell me about your childhood, your years before you came to London."

He turned tired eyes on her. "What for? I don't plan to discuss any of those things with you. You violated my trust once, so why should I tell you intimate details now? For all I know, you'll turn against me again."

He was right, of course. Minna pummeled the pillow in frustration.

"I consider you a stranger, Minerva, my enemy, in fact."

Yes, how could he trust her after her betrayal? she wondered. She had for one wild moment hoped that the gap could be bridged between them.

"Your cousin certainly has a lot of gall," she said. "What does he wish to accomplish with this?"

Roarke laughed hollowly. "Our marriage. He's serious about that."

Minna's eyes widened. "That's ridiculous. I thought he was joking."

"No, it's true. He has spent days trying to convince me that it's the only solution to my problems."

Minna couldn't believe her ears. "Why?"

Roarke's eyes glowed maliciously as he stared at her. "I want your inheritance, and somehow I shall have it. My horses need your land; it's as simple as that, Miss Wayland Seager." He rose slowly. "Perhaps Zach's idea isn't so bad after all. I can spend a lifetime punishing you for the pain you've inflicted."

Minna raised her chin. "So you intend to spend a lifetime nursing your wounds. Poor, poor Roarke. An idle fellow can certainly make such a woeful plan his mission in life." She took a deep trembling breath. "Unfortunately, it takes two people to consent to marriage."

Something very cold came over his face, and he looked as if hewn out of marble. "Well, your consent can obviously be bought. If Mr. Wylie was successful in his business with you, why shouldn't I be?"

All blood drained from her head, and fear skittered through her. "What do you mean?"

"It's simple. You marry me, I get the acres. I get full control over all your possessions. If you refuse, I'll make sure your reputation will be destroyed. I have some power in London, and if I hint that it's terribly *outré* to be seen in your creations, your patrons will flee so fast you won't have time to catch your breath." He smiled coldly. "Your reputation hangs on a gossamer thread, my dear."

Minna drew her breath sharply. "You wouldn't dare!"

"Dare?" He studied his boot. "What is there to be afraid of? Not you, surely. Who are you but a common upstart anyway?"

"You can't threaten me." Minna sprang from the bed. "I've worked for that shop with honest toil, from dawn 'til night. You don't know what it means to have real sweat on your brow. Peasants on your farms work to put food on your table, and you do nothing."

She was so angry that she wound her hand around the bedhanging and yanked until it came off. It crumpled to the floor, and dust tickled her nose. She longed to tear his hair out, but the look he gave her deterred such rash action.

"To maintain The Towers is no sinecure," he said scathingly. He rose and walked very slowly toward her. "In fact, I've pulled it from the brink of ruin."

She cringed under his icy stare.

He continued, "Your shop was built with money from that scoundrel Wylie."

"I didn't know his true character then," she shouted, beside herself with anger and misery. She tugged at the other bedhanging, and it came off.

He sneered. "You want me to believe that? I don't believe a word you tell me!" His voice rose until it gusted in her face. "For all I know, you crept into his bed to get your shop financed. That's the most logical explanation." His lips twisted contemptuously. "You came willingly enough to my bed."

She fleetingly remembered that dreary night on the bridge five years ago, but if she told him about that, he would laugh in her face.

"You use your beauty to further your goals," he continued, this time in an icy whisper.

She shoved her hands into his chest. "Just like you, then. If you were so wild in your youth to

220

father an illegitimate child, you've probably slept in every lady's feather bed in town, and then some."

His hands came up to slowly cradle her neck. She thought he would strangle her, but he only shook her head until she grew dizzy.

"At least I didn't lead the ladies to believe that I loved them. They got what they wanted."

She pushed hard against him. "Let go of me!"

He laughed, continuing to hold her head in a steely grip. "You led me to believe that you loved me. So, if that's the truth, then marry me. You can go on loving me all you want, and I get the acres."

She stared at him mutely. His deep blue-green eyes that she'd seen soft with love, were wintry and forbidding.

"No . . ." she whispered, her tongue dry as paper. He flung her away from him, and she landed on the bed. He braced one boot against the mattress, digging it into her thigh, and propped his arm on his knee. "What you said before was just a lie, about loving me, I mean."

"No," she cried. "It was not a lie."

His lips parted in a deadly smile. "So marry me. I'm thinking that Zach's idea wasn't so stupid after all. It will truly solve all my problems, and it is a fitting revenge for the pain you've caused me. Besides, it'll make me free of match-making mamas in town."

"I will never marry you!" she said, and scrambled away from him. Taking refuge behind the bedpost, she stared at him. The man was insane.

He shrugged and advanced toward her very slowly. "Tomorrow we'll return to London, and I shall put about a vile rumor that'll finish your career as a modiste."

She hated him at that moment; she'd never felt such darkness in her heart. "You wouldn't do that."

"Wouldn't I?" He laughed. "I would revel in it. Perhaps it would relieve some of the pain that you've caused me."

She could barely breathe as misery engulfed her. "If you marry me, you'll lose the opportunity to wed someone you truly love."

He held out his hands in a gesture to stop her from speaking. "Desist!" he spat. "*You* should talk about love? There is no love, other than the kind that we so wrongfully name love. It's nothing but a way to have power—control—over another person. The stronger usurps the weaker in a relationship. Some saints might have known the meaning of selfless love, but I've seen none of that in my life."

"Roarke, your father married my mother, Portia, to get his hands on her wealth. Now you're planning to do the same. Is that what you want, to walk the same path of greed?"

His eyes flickered momentarily. "Leave my father out of this."

"Do you want a life of misery for a few paltry acres?" she went on. "Why should you have it your way? Because you're wealthy and you have a title? People of my class have always struggled to survive, and to bow and scrape for the likes of you." She moved away from the bed, and he moved after her.

"You don't need the land," he said, "and I do." He crossed his arms over his chest. "Ever since I inherited the title, I've worked hard to save the old estate of Whitecliffe, and finally I have success within my grasp. I'm proud to be of a line that stretches as far back as the days of Richard III. I won't be the earl that failed to nurture Whitecliffe." He snorted. "You're not the only one who supports workers, you know. Your seamstresses would disappear in a vast holding like the Whitecliffe Towers."

"You have whipped me into size, my lord," she said with a mocking curtsy. "Very well, if your holdings are so vast, you don't need my heritage."

He gave her a faint smile. "Let me explain. Since we're wedged between marshes and rocks at The Towers, the fertile acres of Meadow Hill farther inland are vital for my cattle. It's the only land that is convenient for my stock. I might buy elsewhere but I don't have the funds at this time to buy anything."

Silence hung dense in the room. They stared at each other warily, and Roarke gave Minna the impression of a dangerous predator. It was one facet of him that had attracted her from the start of their relationship, but now she had to witness the negative side of that aspect.

"Well, what's your choice, Minerva? If you don't marry me, you'll ultimately get lost and forgotten on the teeming streets of London. As my wife, you'll never go hungry again."

"But I'll be the loneliest person in London."

"You said you cared what happened to the seamstresses who work for you."

She nodded. A cold shiver was creeping through her body, and she fought an urge to cry.

"Well, I'll pay off your debts to Mr. Wylie, and

223

business can go on as usual. As my wife, you cannot continue living at the shop, but you're certainly allowed to direct the business through your partner."

Minna stood perfectly still. It was as if she could literally see her world tumbling about her. No more cozy evenings in front of the fire with Ellie, no more fittings, no more imperious customers. Just then she realized how much she had come to love her work.

Whichever way she turned, she was trapped. She could of course give him the acres, but the thought was repulsive. She could sell the land to someone else, but her spite didn't reach that far. She wished no harm to befall him. "I could lease the acres to you for the time it takes you to gather enough funds to buy them."

He stared at her uncertainly, gauging her sincerity. Then he shrugged. "Very magnanimous of you, but you seem to have forgotten to read the fine print of the will. Aloisius made a stipulation that upon his death, the Harding lease on the acres would forever be forfeited. So much did Aloisius hate the Hardings that he made sure I would not get the use of the land. Yet, since you couldn't be found, the solicitors discovered a way for me to rent the acres. The revenue has been put in a special account for you."

"Why the stipulation? Was it because of what your father did to my mother, or me?"

Roarke laughed dryly. "No, it was a gambling debt. Aloisius could not pay my father, so he had to give Father free use of the land until his death." He crossed his arms over his chest. "So you see, you have no choice."

"You have won," she whispered between stiff lips. "I shall never forgive you for this."

Love was a word he had carefully circumvented.

Chapter Nineteen

Two hours later, when Minna thought she would scream with frustration, a knock sounded on the door.

"Are you friends now?" came Zach's cheerful voice as he turned the key and came inside.

Roarke pressed himself against the wall by the door, and as his cousin hobbled inside, he grabbed the younger man by the arm, then dealt him a resounding blow to the jaw.

Zach staggered back and lost his balance. Sitting on the floor, he rubbed his sore chin. "Roarke, you jingle-brain, what kind of welcome is that?"

"It may get worse," Roarke threatened. "You deserve a sound thrashing."

Zach glanced from Minna to Roarke appraisingly. "I take it you've solved your differences."

"Of all underhanded dealings —" Minna began angrily, "this is by far the worst day of my life, and you're at fault."

Zach held up his hands in a disarming gesture. "You've solved your problems then?" he asked with a grin.

"You can say that." Roarke laughed mirthlessly

226

and moved toward the door opening, but found it blocked by the two faithful footmen. "Zach, call off your henchmen, I'm leaving."

Zach got up and brushed the dust off his knees. "Wait a minute. I take it you've decided to marry?"

Minna's mind was preoccupied with various torturous ways to kill the grinning man. She seethed inside, and it was this man's fault that she was stuck in this intolerable situation. She grabbed the pillow and started beating him over the head with it.

He waved his arms to fend her off and was overcome by a bout of sneezing as dust clouded around him. "Stop it, d'you hear?" He pulled the pillow from her hands, and tossed it across the room. Then he rose with the help of the footmen who also retrieved his fallen crutches.

Wiping his face and smoothing down his ruffled hair, Zach continued, "I take it that wedding arrangements are called for."

"You put Roarke up to tricking me into marriage."

Zach's face creased in serious thought, but a wicked light leaped into his eyes. "A simple flash of inspiration, nothing else. You have to admit it was brilliant."

He hopped over to the door, and slapped Roarke in the back. "You did it! The land will be yours." Zach gave Minna a not-so-kind glance. "Just remember that she deserves it for her betrayal."

Roarke's shoulders slumped momentarily, but Minna could read no remorse in his face as he gave her a fleeting glance. "Yes." Without another word, he headed out the door.

"Minerva, my sweet. Don't worry about the arrangements. I'll take care of everything. 'Twill be a wedding to remember," Zach said. "By the way, I sent a letter to the shop in London that explained that you won't be back for a while. You can write to

227

your partner later. Now rest for a while. Tomorrow I'll drive you to The Towers, your new home."

Minna could not rest. She spent the remainder of the night pacing the floor of her room. However much she racked her brain, she couldn't come up with a solution that would free her from Roarke. He wanted the Meadow Hill acres, and he would marry her to get them. One thing she couldn't understand was the reason why he would consider throwing his life away on a loveless marriage when he might meet some other lady to love. He would forget her betrayal in time, wouldn't he? She remembered his vow that he would never marry and beget children, but in time his attitude might change.

Wringing her hands in distress, she viewed the gently rolling Kentish landscape spreading below her. The mauve light of dawn gave it a lovely, mystical air. Yet the serene surroundings did nothing to soothe her agitated mind. She wished she didn't love the earl so much that every breath hurt, and every thought of him pierced her with pain.

Later in the day she and Zach drove toward Roarke's estate. Minna looked out the window as the coach moved onto the private road that led to Whitecliffe Towers. Two square ragstone towers with battlements flanked the guardhouse entrance to the Whitecliffe estate. A crumbling wall went around the main castle that had once been a Norman stronghold, but a more modern estate had been erected by the old ruins of the keep. The crumbling remains were covered with ivy and climbing roses.

The straight graceful lines that predominated the architecture of the past century were evident in the gray stone walls of the Whitecliffe mansion. The simplicity of the style made the building blend in with the ancient parts to perfection. Magnificent gardens surrounded The Towers, which sat on a small hill overlooking a stretch of bog, and farther distant the dunes of the North Sea estuary of Herne Bay.

Minna marveled at the richness of the roses that grew everywhere.

The main entrance with its twin Doric columns and painted double doors was surrounded by roses, and more of the same flowered in the tubs lining the flagstones leading to the door. When the horses drew to a halt, total silence—except for the song of birds, and the drone of insects—reigned. Minna drew a deep breath of air that was fragrant with the scent of flowers and sunshine. If Paradise existed, this must surely be it. She wished she had come at a happier time. She sensed she could learn to love the old place.

There was no sign of the earl. For all Minna knew he'd returned to London. Zach Gordon stepped outside and held the door for her. "Lovely old heap, isn't it?" When Minna didn't reply, he continued, "It's a pity that Roarke doesn't want to spend much time here. Too many sad memories."

Minna gave him a curious glance. He meant Thomas, of course. She got down without accepting any help from the man who had lured her into this trap.

He didn't seem to mind her snub. Not much ruffled the feathers of this bird, she thought angrily.

He pointed across the fields. "That's Tulsiter bog. It was named after a man who lived there two hundred years ago, and who was said to have awesome magical powers. A sorcerer I believe." He pointed in the opposite direction. "Over there is nothing but sand pits and gravel beds. We are rather close to the sea as you can see." He chuckled. "On a clear day, you can see straight across to Foulness Point from the top of the tower."

"Everything is a joke to you, isn't it, Mr. Gordon?"

"Nothing wrong with humor, is there?" He pointed out another landmark, a tall cliff covered with furze. "That's Tower Rock. Beyond it lies Sun Hollow."

"The land looks fertile enough from here," Minna commented, viewing the green acres that stretched inland.

He shook his head. "The cultivated park around the estate is rich enough, but you have to travel farther into the country to find the famed farmland of Kent." He looked at her speculatively. "You've never been to Meadow Hill, your birthplace?" He pointed west toward the rolling hills. "Beyond that incline is the mansion. No one lives there now. Past the formal park and Meadow Hill, is the fertile land that Roarke uses for his bloods."

Minna didn't answer. A profound sadness weighed her down, and she couldn't begin to unravel the cause. By right of birth, she should have lived here, not all over England in mean cottages with the Smiths. Then she might have met Roarke under different circumstances and their love might not have died before its time. Still, she didn't regret her life with her adoptive parents, not for one moment.

"Since we're here, let's go inside. I'm famished," said Zach.

He held out his arm to her, but she ignored it. He shrugged and moved toward the house. Alone with her thoughts, Minna dragged behind. "This is about all I can take," she said to herself. How could the shop that had given her so much pleasure in the past five years, ultimately be the cause of her current predicament?

Perhaps she ought to ignore her misgivings and join Mr. Gordon in a repast. Her stomach reminded her that a meal was long overdue. Yet, she hesitated

230

to go inside. It hurt her pride to know that she wasn't welcome in Roarke's lovely old house, but what could she expect? Besides a traitress she was still the poor girl from the East End who had lost her parents, the humble curate and his wife. Portia Harding of these parts would forever remain a stranger.

Minna couldn't get used to the thought of being an heiress to land that perhaps supported scores of peasants. She didn't know how many farmers worked on her land. She had no idea of the size of her inheritance, and she wasn't sure that she wanted to know. Aloisius Wayland Seager was a stranger to her, and would always be.

But even if she wasn't interested in her newfound riches, she was curious about the woman who had been her mother, Portia Harding. That lady had lived in the area most of her life, and Minna wondered if she was the person who'd had such a passion for roses. She would never know unless someone enlightened her, and who would?

Just as she was about to go inside, she noticed a tiny gnarled man dressed in gray from head to toe. He was almost invisible against the gray wall. He looked up from the hole he was digging, and Minna was struck by his clear, penetrating gaze. It somehow didn't fit the old bent body. His smile charmed her, and he pulled off his greasy cap. "Good-day, ma'am," he greeted. "I be plantin' some new roses where the blight got the others."

Something about him struck her forcefully. She didn't know if it was the eyes or the youthful, lilting voice. She found that she couldn't speak.

"I've waited for you," he said. "This sad place needs you. It was about time you arrived." Then he went back to digging.

Minna shook her head, and debated whether to be

annoyed with his comment, but she felt no anger. The diminutive man intrigued her. How did he know she was about to become the Countess of White-cliffe? "What's your name?"

"Joe Tulsiter. Worked here all me life, as my father before me. I'm helpin' with the roses, but I'm really a horse man." He went back to his chore. "They like me; they talk to me. I always had a good hand wi' horses."

"And with roses," Minna said and entered the house.

The hallway was cool and shadowy, paneled in dark mahogany. Old portraits hung on the walls, and dry flower arrangements filled the silver urns on the small tables around the walls. No living roses here. Strange. The old flagstones rang under her step, and she slowed down as if afraid of awakening people, or rousing some long ago souls that might be listening for the sound of her steps.

She went through an open door at one end of the hall. By the stiff arrangement of carved giltwood and brocade furniture, the majestic paintings on the wall, and the massive chandeliers, she deduced that she had entered the formal drawing room. She admired the sculptured plaster ceiling whose lozenge pattern mirrored that of the blue-gray-gold carpet.

Over the mantelpiece hung a portrait of a lady. Minna gasped as she recognized her own pale hair and the same gray eyes. This must be Portia Harding. She was drawn toward the painting, but a reluctance to face her past overcame her as she moved closer. The portrait loomed over her as she stood below it.

Swallowing to ease her dry throat, she studied it. Portia Harding had been a statuesque lady of ample curves. Portia's face—somewhat like her own—had a sweetness of expression, an innocence that the artist had captured in the fleeting smile. The gray eyes held a sadness, though, and there was a stiffness to Portia's shoulders that belied the guilelessness of her smile. This had not been a happy woman.

"Your hair is just the same color," someone said behind her. "It's a pity you aren't more like her."

Minna whirled around. Roarke was leaning against the doorframe. She searched for a softening in his expression, but he returned her gaze coldly.

"Perhaps Portia used her female charms to lure my father into her bed, and not the other way around as you seem to believe. Father wasn't easily led, but perhaps he fell for her."

Minna felt a faint affinity with the woman in the portrait, and she resented Roarke's cold calculation. "Of course you would say that. No, your father fell for Meadow Hill—not for Portia. Next you'll have it put about that she gave me away by choice."

He only snorted in response.

"I don't care what you think of me, Roarke, not any more. I'm tired of this charade. The moment our vows are sealed, I'm returning to London. You can go out and graze the Meadow Hill acres with your horses. That ought to satisfy your greed—though grass might give you a bellyache. I hope it does."

She made as if to slide past him, but he gripped her arm.

"Aaao," she cried, and shied away from him.

"When you're my wife, *I* decide where you go, and what you do. That's the law."

Anger choked her, and she could only fume in silence. Every word hurt her as if lined with prickly thorns. They stared at each other for an unbearable minute.

"I thought you didn't care what becomes of me after the ceremony," Minna said with a rivulet of fear. "You'll have your land." She had a fleeting vision of a prison room in the old tower where she would be locked up for the rest of her life.

He was looking down at her with those cold blue-green eyes, and she shivered. "What are you going to do with me? Beat me like your father beat my mother?"

Even though he'd never told her about his father's relationship with Portia, she knew that she'd hit a nerve. She wished she knew more about Roarke's past.

He dropped his hand abruptly, and Minna saw that his grip had made imprints on her arm. She rubbed the sore spots.

"I can tell that I'm not the only one who'll be unhappy in this marriage. Greed never brought happiness." She paused, gauging his expression. It was stony. "I'd prefer it if we'd exclude all fanfare at the wedding."

He laughed. "Well, if that's your wish, then we'll make sure that the ceremony will be accompanied by all possible pomp."

Minna's anger flared. "Why increase the pain?"

"Pain? Surely 'twill be a day of celebration, for me at least." He laughed coldly and crossed his arms over his chest.

"Your vindictiveness is unforgivable." Without waiting for his reply, she hurried outside.

Roarke thought the walls would come crashing in around him. These days since that night in the gazebo, he'd barely been able to control his anger—not to mention his misery. He reeled from it like it had been a physical blow, and he wondered if anyone had ever loved as deeply as he loved Minerva. Even now, even after the humiliation of her trickery, he longed to pull her into his arms and kiss her. Every part of

234

him yearned for the feel of her against him, the fragrance of her hair, her graceful arms wrapped around his neck. Still, he couldn't stem the icy flow of anger that left no room for pity. He wanted her to suffer, yet a part of him recognized that he would ultimately be the one who hurt the most.

She had been strong enough to jilt him in the end, so why should he show himself weaker, more forgiving? Never. Where she showed iron strength, he would show more. He pounded his fist into the wall so that the paintings rattled and porcelain plates tinkled. She shouldn't get off scot-free; after all, she didn't know the full measure of his pain. Blowing on his bruised knuckles, he slumped in a chair. He quieted the voice inside that said revenge would only bring him more sadness.

But that voice could not be silenced. It whispered, "Roarke, beware. Filled with hatred and revenge you won't find the secret of life."

He jerked his head up, but no one was in the room. Where had that slightly familiar voice come from? He heard a movement by the door, and he turned toward it. His old groom, Joe Tulsiter stood on the threshold, twirling his hat. A gentle smile spread across his face.

" 'Tis time, my lord. Starlight is foalin' in the stables."

"Very well, I'm coming." Roarke rose to follow the tiny man. "By the way, did you hear anyone speaking as you came in?"

Joe shook his head. "Only myself."

The betrothal announcement in *The Times* swept a wildfire of gossip throughout London. Besides Davina Shield and Lady Barton, people that Minna didn't recognize came to ogle her at Davina's townhouse where she was staying pending her marriage to the earl. It wouldn't do for the future Countess of Whitecliffe to live over a modiste shop, nor was it proper that she stay at the mansion in Berkley Square. Minna felt sick with misery, and she debated if it was worth the pain of getting out of bed every morning.

The fact that she was Portia Harding's daughter by an earlier marriage did nothing to quell the tidal wave of tattle; it increased it.

"I knew you were gently bred," Davina crowed when she heard the latest *on dits,* "but how deliciously wicked it is that you're marrying your stepbrother."

Minna tried to smile, but she couldn't force her lips to do it. "Merely a business arrangement, Davina. I'd rather not marry Whitecliffe."

"Not marry him! That's the silliest announcement I've ever heard. First of all, you'll be good for Roarke. Second, you'll be a countess; you'll have properties in town and in the country. You'll never have to lift a finger, to sew another stitch again."

"But I *like* to sew! I don't know what I'll do with so much free time. I'll wither away and die."

"Nonsense." Davina nudged Minna with her elbow. "What with a virile man like Roarke, you'll be occupied with the nursery in no time."

Minna blushed to the roots of her hair. "I don't think so. We're—"

"You mark my words, Roarke looks at you as if he could eat you alive."

Minna refrained from informing her friend that Roarke's expression stemmed from anger, not from lust.

The wedding ceremony was to take place at St. George's in Hanover Square, one month—on the exact day—of the incident in the gazebo. Minna had spent time in London preparing the staff at the shop for her departure from the fashion arena. Ellie had personally helped sew the wedding gown, an elaborate cream satin confection with a ruffled bodice and straight skirt that lengthened into a long train.

"Blind me, but you're such a lucky person, Minna. First the shop, now this. I knew I did well to throw my lot in with yours," Ellie said.

Listlessly, Minna studied her reflection in the pierglass in her former office. "You're now the head of this shop, Ellie, and I'm glad you are. My concern has been the employees, and I know you'll treat them fairly." Tears burned her eyes. "I really don't want to leave. I've been so happy here."

Ellie hugged her tightly. "Balderdash! You'll be happy with the earl." She brushed away damp strands of hair from Minna's face. "Why, you once told me you loved the man."

Minna wanted to say *I do* but she couldn't begin to explain the complexities of her relationship with Roarke. "I've never been more surprised when I found out that I had noble parents. My father was the son of a viscount, fancy that." She blew her nose and dried her tears. "But I didn't want everything to end like this. Whatever shall I do with my life?"

"There, there," Ellie crooned and gave her another hug. "Don't despair, Minna. You must always help me to plan for the future of the shop. We can do that much together, now that no financial cloud hangs over it."

Minna wiped her eyes. "What do you mean?"

"Why, the earl paid off the last debt to Mr. Wylie. I got a receipt in the mail. We don't owe a penny, Minna."

"I had so many plans for that day," Minna said in a small voice, "but I never thought it would come."

"Like I said, I'll need your help with the plan-

237

ning," Ellie said, and brushed back Minna's hair. "Now, take off this gown before you get tear stains on it."

Minna obeyed and viewed the trousseau that the earl had ordered for his bride. At least he wasn't stingy, and it made her feel slightly better that he'd cared to secure the future of her employees even as she left the firm. Even though she hadn't seen him these last weeks since their meeting in the drawing room at The Towers, she could feel his invisible power closing around her. He was separating her from her past silently but forcefully. His choice of fabrics and designs would convert her into a fashionable countess on the outside. On the inside, she was still the unsophisticated person who had grown up in humble cottages, and ultimately survived in London's hell's acre. She was still the woman who had struggled to build everything that was around her, and bereft of it, what would become of her? What was her identity?

Longing to moan out loud in frustration, she restrained herself at the last moment. She stuffed her handkerchief into her reticule on the desk and continued to try on the rest of the trousseau. She feared the day when this shop would be gone from her life.

For a hostile future awaited her in Kent.

Chapter Twenty

The ceremony at St. George's passed in a painful blur, and Minna struggled to keep her composure. There was no love, there was *nothing* but a cool disdain in Roarke's face as he joined her at the altar. She felt that she was selling her life, but the gossips said she'd grasped the opportunity of a lifetime. It was such gall — a seamstress (though of noble lineage) marrying an earl, the whispered rumors said. It simply wasn't done. Minna could feel the haughty stares at her back, the icy rejection of the guests' averted faces at the reception afterward. They were there, not to congratulate the couple, but to sneer. They were there to give her a cold shoulder, to enjoy the scandal. Minna squeezed her eyes shut, trying to remember the reason why she was marrying the earl. Her shop was safe, her friends were safe from ruin. She never doubted that he would have fulfilled his threat to destroy her business if she had denied him. Anger seethed in the depths of his eyes every time he looked at her.

Tables groaned under the sumptuous buffet of turtle soup, lobster patties, salmon in aspic, turbot, jellied tongues, paté, coldcuts, cheeses and caviar, and a huge arrangement of flowers and exotic fruits as a centerpiece. The delicious smell of food brought the guests crowding to the tables.

Minna couldn't eat anything. Her mouth was dry with sadness and defeat, and she viewed the parade of gaily dressed couples—some ladies that had been her customers—passing her without as much as a glance. She wished the nightmare would be over.

Suddenly she felt someone staring at her, and she stiffened in defense. She could accept no more veiled insults. She turned her head slowly and saw a man she'd met once before, Melchior Harding, an older version of Roarke. His hair was the same blond color, but his face had none of Roarke's magnetism. When the man bowed, she noticed that his hair had thinned and that it was laced with gray. His tight waistcoat—or perhaps corset—pushed his protruding paunch into something less, and the cravat at his neck was tied faultlessly.

He smiled kindly. "I'm delighted to meet you, Lady Whitecliffe. Let me present myself, since no one else has. I'm Melchior Harding."

"We met at Mrs. Shield's once. You're Roarke's cousin," she filled in and accepted his kiss on her hand.

"How right you are." His pale blue eyes shifted to a spot above her, then drifted to the culinary feast. "They told me you were lovely, but words didn't come close. By Jove, you're an ethereal angel, and no mistake." His gaze darted to her face, then away as if he was afflicted by acute shyness. "Roarke always was a lucky fellow. He's like a cat, always lands on his feet."

Minna blushed, not knowing how to respond. He stopped a lackey with a tray and purloined two glasses of champagne. "You look peaked, though. A glass of this will put you into the spirit of things."

Despite his drifting gaze, he'd noticed her uneasiness, Minna thought.

"I'm surprised that you deign to address me. You must've heard about my past in *trade*," she said and sipped her champagne.

He pursed his lips thoughtfully, then said, "Since I am a Harding, I know more than most. I know about your real identity, Lady Whitecliffe. Dear Portia's daughter, and heiress to the most important land of Meadow Hill. No wonder my cousin was in a hurry to wed you." He cleared his throat in embarrassment. "I didn't mean to—"

"Never mind," Minna said, choking back the misery rising in her throat. "Do you live here?"

"Yes, I spend part of my time in London, but I have a small estate not far from Whitecliffe." He gave a shallow laugh. "Inherited it from my mother's side of the family. Not much more than a dignified cottage, really." He gulped down his champagne then gave a subtle burp. "In fact, if you're going down to The Towers for the rest of the summer, you must ride over and visit me."

I don't know how to ride, Minna thought. "Yes, that'll be pleasant," she said.

"Roarke has dashed fine bloods in his stables. Wouldn't mind some half as good. Once I had a great stable but compared to the Arabians that Roarke has bred—" He stiffened and glanced over her shoulder.

Another presence made itself known at her side. Her gaze darted to her husband's cold face. "Roarke—"

"I see that you've met Cousin Melchior. Mel, it was good of you to come to the wedding."

"I wouldn't have missed it." Melchior studied Roarke with narrowed eyes. "I thought you said you would never marry."

241

"Reality has a way of intruding into our dreams."

"Well, it's about time you set up your nursery. It's no good brooding in that old gloomy castle. Fill it with children." He winked at Minna, and she blushed.

Roarke folded his hands behind his back. "You haven't taken your own advice, coz. I hear no patter of small feet at Linkwood Cottage."

Melchior Harding rubbed his jaw. He sent Roarke a none too kind glance, Minna noticed. "I have to find a wife first, but they call me a fortune hunter in these parts." He turned toward Minna. "Y'see, I'm rather a church mouse, and half of London knows it."

Roarke's voice lowered to a growl. "You're family, Mel. I've offered—"

"We shouldn't speak of such a vulgar subject as myself in the company of your lovely bride. By Jove, you're a lucky man." He bowed formally. "I wish you much happiness. Now I shall remove myself to the culinary feast which has been beckoning me this last half hour."

Minna sensed the tension between the two men, but it didn't rival the one surging between her and her husband as she looked into his shadowy eyes.

She longed to lighten the mood, if only to forget her own pain. "He's nice, isn't he?" she asked, forcing a smile to her lips.

"Mel has his quirks like everyone else, but he's a decent enough sort, I suppose." Roarke sounded cold and aloof.

"You don't like him," she said tentatively.

He shrugged. "I don't dislike him. There were some bad feelings when Grandfather died without giving Mel a penny. Everything went to me. I tried to pay off Mel's debts—which he has many—but he wouldn't hear of it. Then there's the rivalry of the stables — I don't want to discuss it."

Roarke's hand closed around her arm, and she stifled the urge to flee. He had full control over her life now; she had to obey. She wished she could find a way to wipe the coldness from his face. How she wished there was a way . . .

"I want you to meet the rest of the family," he said with grim determination.

"Even though they don't want to meet me?"

"They are here, aren't they? Sooner or later, you'll have to be introduced."

"A tedious chore for you, isn't it?" she said under her breath as he pulled her across the room. His grip hurt, and her humiliation was complete when a dowager with a beaded turban snubbed her greeting. The rest of the day continued in a blur, and the only part Minna remembered when the reception was over was the kindness of Melchior Harding. Roarke had treated her as if she were a prize horse that had to be admired by everyone. He felt no pride in her, but he savored his victory over her. Just as she loathed Roarke for the pain that he'd inflicted, as much did she ache with her unrequited love for him. She couldn't forget the nights they had shared in perfect harmony.

As Roarke sat silent and cold beside her in the carriage that would take them to Whitecliffe Towers, she wondered if she would ever recapture that enchantment.

Roarke sighed imperceptibly. He was well aware of his wife's despair, and he wondered if he'd gone too far by forcing her to marry him. It had been cruel to threaten to ruin her business, but at the time, he'd been too angry, too frustrated to think clearly. His revenge had put balm on his anger, but now all he felt was bone-deep tiredness. This time the gap between them would surely be too wide to span. Had his revenge been too harsh? Perhaps, but without it, he would have lost her. He couldn't bear the thought of never seeing her again. Yet, was it worth the pain of feeling this chasm between them like a wound in his heart? She was sitting so close that he could smell her perfume; he could touch her, talk to her, but in spirit, she was far away.

By God he loved her, that had never changed, but he could never trust her again. The thought made his anger rise, and the bitterness of her betrayal returned. If her love had been real, she would never have fulfilled her part of the bargain with Mr. Wylie. She would have called it off.

Duplicity always drove him wild with anger, and the fact that she'd used him made him disgusted. Wylie's daughter had forced him to take care of Thomas, something he'd regretted at the time. There was no proof that Thomas had been his — until the boy grew blind — but he'd come to love him. The child had given him a purpose for living, a purpose for struggling to get The Towers out from under the burden of debt. He'd managed rather well considering, and then Thomas died. The boy's death had crumbled his granite confidence as easily as the wind disintegrated a seed puff. Her voice interrupted his reverie.

"What will happen next? Am I to be incarcerated at The Towers?"

He forced out a hollow laugh. "I'm not an ogre, Minerva."

Her gaze burned into him in the semi-darkness of the coach. "I thought differently."

"Your taunts will take you nowhere, milady wife."

Silence bristled between them. "So what am I supposed to do with my days now that you've taken the life I liked away from me?"

"For one, The Towers needs a woman's touch. It's been neglected for too long."

He threw a sideways glance at her, noticing the slump of her shoulders. Evidently, decorating a house was not one of her interests. He could think of nothing else to say; whatever he suggested she would reject out of hand.

The less he saw of her, the better, he thought with a guilty shrug. She stretched, rotating a slender foot as if it was stiff. The sight of her fragile ankle brought that familiar rush of desire that so often overcame him in her presence. His senses swam with the subtle fragrance of her perfume, and he was acutely aware of her movements as she shifted on her seat. She leaned back against the squabs and closed her eyes. Her face was a lovely, pale oval against the maroon velvet of the upholstery. He stifled an urge to lean closer and touch her jaw, to draw her closer. Instead he stiffened and moved aside an inch or two. She looked too pale in the faltering sunlight. An orange shaft of light touched her hair, changing it into a fiery halo. Her features held an ethereal transparency that made her look vulnerable, and a stab of guilt went through him. He abruptly averted his face. His staring at her might arouse his pity, and he didn't want to weaken. She had fallen asleep, her head tilting awkwardly to the side. Her slumber was contagious, and he leaned back, relaxing his tight control. Tomorrow would be another day.

An hour later Roarke awakened. One leg was numb, and his neck had stiffened painfully as his head tilted toward his chest. He pulled himself up gently, swearing at the ache of his tight muscles. As he moved, the soft weight on his shoulder shifted. A faint moan came from Minerva's lips as she snuggled closer to his side. Her hair spilled over his chest, and he noticed that her skirts had hitched up, revealing more than her tantalizing ankle. A slim leg invited his caress. Without thinking, he reached out and cupped her knee.

Sleep still lay like cottony warmth in his mind, and he tried to hold back that floating sensation between sleep and full awareness when nothing mattered much. *She* was there with him; that was all that mattered. In the warm fuzziness of his contentment, he reached out and caressed her hair. It was soft as a kitten's fur, and her earlobe was softer still. She repeated her moan, moving her head restlessly as he explored the rounded outline of her ear. A warm, honeyed desire invaded his being, and he held his breath at the power of that surge. Never had a woman tantalized him as much as this yielding softness, almost childlike frailty that was Minerva—Lady Whitecliffe. Her earlobe was so soft, so damned soft . . .

He gripped her head, and she stiffened with sudden awareness. Unable to stem the flow of desire swelling every nerve in his body, he tilted her face to his and kissed her deeply. The onslaught of his tongue in her mouth forced aside any protest on her part, and filled him with a savage heat. He wondered if the same storm of desire whirled in her blood; he was only vaguely aware of the helpless pounding of her fists against his chest. He crushed her closer, unable to relinquish the heady sweetness of her mouth. The silken softness, the hot thrust of her tongue against his, made him almost faint with desire.

Somehow she managed to tear herself away from him. Her eyes blazed with anger; he could faintly see the eye whites as if she held her eyes wide open. *Shock,* something whispered in his mind, but he refused to listen.

246

"Stop it, Roarke," she wailed as he gripped her shoulders to pull her back against him. "What are you doing?"

To silence another protest, he covered her mouth with his, and tunneled his fingers through her hair. He didn't want the coachman to halt the carriage and inquire if something was amiss. He wanted their bumpy travel to go on until he'd slaked his thirst for her, killed that desire that she'd inspired in him weeks ago, and that still burned as bright as that first time he'd kissed her. *God,* he thought, melting, igniting at the feel of her, *what shall I do to free myself of this enchanted bond?*

She felt insubstantial in his arms, elusive, and he yearned to snare her with his own longing. If she longed as much for him . . .

He dragged his hand over her satiny wedding dress, cupping one small breast. She fought him, but her strength was nothing pitted against his.

"I don't want you," she moaned as she managed to free herself momentarily from his punishing grip.

His lips tingled at the memory of hers.

"I don't want you," she repeated. Still, her breathing was erratic, and her voice faltered on the last words. Sensing her imminent surrender, he gathered her back into his arms, dragging her reluctant hand along his body to cradle the hardness that was the source of his sweet agony. She tried to jerk her hand away, but he held it there, at that provocative place that inflamed his desire beyond endurance.

He sensed her rising anger, her unwillingness to give him an inch of herself. As he came fully awake, his desire mingled with the need to chasten her—part of his revenge. Even if she had a stone-cold heart, he knew that under everything lurked that wantonness that he'd met before, and trigger-

247

ing her desire would be another victory for him, and — punishment — for her.

He pulled her rich velvet cloak from her shoulders, then ripped the bodice down as far as it would go and untied her stays. Her pearly white skin fascinated him, and he wished he could see her breasts. He moved his head toward the dark outline of her areola and sucked on her nipple until it grew turgid.

"Don't," she whispered, trying frantically to get away. "Why . . ." Then moaning, "Yes . . . oh, yes."

Resolutely, he lifted her onto his lap and held her pinned against him as his mouth rested against her breast. He pulled up her skirts, finding no obstructions except a froth of petticoats, garters, and silk stockings. She trembled in his arms as he dragged his hand along the inside of her thigh, and tickled the bare skin between the top of her stockings and the joining of her thighs. She drew her breath sharply as his hand moved up, touching her hot, naked flesh.

He could have died with pleasure at the intimate feel of her against his hand. The warmth, the wetness that spoke its own language. *She wanted him.* When he explored that most secret place, she grew languid in his arms, and moaned softly against his neck.

"Darling," she whispered.

He thought he would burst with pleasure. He'd never understand this wild excitement she could provoke with just a soft moan.

The coach crunched through a pothole, and she jostled against his lap. His passion heightened to a burning fever, and he half rose from the seat, lifting her onto the opposite bench. She didn't fight him, but she whimpered as he dragged her dress up to her waist, and parted her thighs.

"Don't humiliate me," she said, her voice rising to a cry. "I don't want . . ." she added, but raised her arms toward him as he pulled down his trousers. There was no way he could resist the wildfire forcing him to the center of her heat.

He touched the silky triangle at her thighs, knowing true surrender in her quivering flesh. *What was this?* he wondered in a haze as he lowered himself on top of her and yanked her hips up toward him. *Love?*

Minna cried out with exquisite pleasure as he pushed into her, filling her, fulfilling her aching yearning. He pulled out, and she wanted to cry because she missed him already. What was this torture, this dependence, this *need* that went beyond their differences, that circumvented his hatred? She couldn't think as he lifted her up against him, and pounded into her with wild abandon. Her every thought, her very self drowned as a churning wave of ecstasy swept her along on a long journey that ended in another wave . . . and another, one that also took him to the shore of fulfillment. Slowly, ever so slowly, she drifted back to reality. She didn't want to, but the wave that had rolled out had to roll back.

Harsh reality returned as her body returned to normal, and she fought against her desire to curl into a ball and hide in the corner of the bumping carriage. The hard edge of a trunk dug into her shoulder, and her legs felt sticky with spent passion.

He was breathing deeply, self-consciously against her shoulder, then stiffened perceptibly. The gossamer thin yet effective wall between them could not be denied. He raised himself up and a rush of cool air from the open window brushed over her bare flesh. She struggled to sit up and pulled her wedding dress down over her legs, realizing that now she truly was Roarke Harding's wife. No way back, not now.

"Why?" she whispered breathlessly. "I thought—"

"Don't!" he said coldly. "I consummated the marriage to make it legal; it has nothing to do with the rest of the farce that is our life together."

"You're cruel and selfish," she chided, sweeping back her hair and pulling the cloak over her shoulders. She laced up her stays as far as she could reach and tried to repair the damaged bodice. "You refused to hear my wishes."

He snorted and buttoned his trousers. "I know your wishes in the matter. Your lips say one thing and your body something else." He laughed, a low throaty sound that grated on her nerves. "It spoke quite adequately."

"How dare you!" She rose, but the coach lurched, and tilted to one side. Gripping one of the straps hanging by the door, she steadied herself, then sat down. "You make a mockery of our marriage."

"Just remember that our union is based on profitable business, nothing more, nothing less. Tonight I've sealed the bargain, and you're now mine—forevermore."

Anger made her stutter. "I—I detest you and your cold, calculating heart." She threw a basket at him and its contents of gloves and scarves spread over him.

"Shout all you want, Minerva. Nothing has changed, but at least I've slaked my thirst for your body. Mind you, this will never happen again."

Humiliated, Minna struggled to mend her ruined bodice. "Thank God for that!"

Chapter Twenty-one

When they arrived at The Towers, a line of servants waited for them on the front steps. Welcoming lights gleamed in every room on the bottom floor. Minna had difficulty composing herself after her confrontation with the earl. She swallowed convulsively and straightened her hair. It was useless since all the pins were gone. Nevertheless, she tied the cloak primly at her neck and pressed her bonnet over her head, arranging the ice-blue ribbons into a bow under her chin.

Roarke's eyes were unreadable as he held her begloved hand so that she could climb down. Gravel crunched under her shoes, and her knees trembled.

"This is your new mistress, Minerva, the Countess of Whitecliffe," Roarke introduced her in a toneless voice.

Minna smiled at the curtsying maids and bowing footmen, and nodded at the housekeeper, Mrs. Clemson. Kitson, the butler had followed them from London and would make sure to teach those "uncouth country bumpkins"—as Minna had heard him call the servants of The Towers—to run the earl's household smoothly. The servants had a healthier, rosier complexion than their pale counterparts in London, she noticed. There were too many of them to remember all their names, but she would learn in time.

"Mrs. Clemson," Roarke said, "you must show Her Ladyship to her room."

The rotund housekeeper, dressed in black bombazine and round spectacles, nodded primly. "It'll be my pleasure, milord."

Minna's smile stiffened as Roarke turned on his heel and left her. The servants seemed to melt away, all except Mrs. Clemson.

"I'm sure you'd like to freshen up, milady. We've aired the suite of rooms adjoining the master bedroom." The housekeeper moved ahead of Minerva up the curving staircase. The hallway ceiling soared a dizzying twenty feet, and at the top of the stairs, Minna got a view of the sea in the fan-shaped window above the front entrance. The interior of the house had graceful grandeur, and the furniture had been chosen to compliment the architecture's simple lines. She saw a blur of honey-colored wood, slender turned chair legs, airy Chippendale designs, panels covered in cream watered silk, sculptured plaster ceilings, flashes of lime-green and red and blue in carpets and upholstery as she hurried after Mrs. Clemson. The parquet floors shone with much polishing. Even though the house was well cared for, it had the atmosphere of emptiness, an abode without personality. No one lived here except the ghosts, and the servants in their nooks tucked away from view. Minna sensed a great sadness in the house.

"Did some countess in the distant past decorate these rooms?"

"Oh, no milady. The last countess chose the furniture."

"His lordship's stepmother then?"

"Yes, milady," Mrs. Clemson said and opened two wide doors with her pudgy hands. "Here we are. I

252

hope the rooms will be to your satisfaction."

Minna walked into a high-ceilinged bedchamber decorated in pale rose and gold. Ornate mirrors, paintings of flowers and fruits adorned the walls. The fourposter bed had an old crocheted cover of intricate lace design and a soaring canopy of rose silk. "Very feminine," she commented.

The housekeeper had clasped her hands in front of her. She stared at Minna without expression. "Anything else, milady? There's tea if you like."

"Yes, please bring some." Minna didn't know what prompted her to ask so soon after her arrival, but she couldn't quell the urge: "Did you know Lady Portia Harding?"

Mrs. Clemson's eyebrows shot up. "The last countess? Yes, milady, a very kind lady to us all. She knew a lot about healing, and helped the farmers through some bad times." The housekeeper licked her lips as if in a quandary about something. Perhaps she didn't like to gossip, Minna thought, but it was the only way to discover anything about her past. Roarke had been close-mouthed about the subject.

"When Lord Whitecliffe died, Lady Whitecliffe moved back to Meadow Hill. She never liked it here."

Minna caressed the smooth surface of an inlaid table. "I . . . I understand she looked a lot like me."

Mrs. Clemson's eyebrows rose once more. "That's a fact. The current Lord Whitecliffe hung his step-mother's portrait here when she died. I believe he missed her sorely." The crackle of bombazine filled the silent room as if the housekeeper was anxious to leave. "Anything else, milady?"

"No. Please have the footmen bring up the trunks. My personal maid, Rosie, will be arriving later with the rest of my luggage."

Lonely and frustrated, Minna watched the door closing after the housekeeper. Mrs. Clemson seemed friendly enough, but Minna sensed that she wouldn't commit herself to further gossip.

When Rosie arrived, Minna was fast asleep. She'd slept through dinner and through the night. When she awakened the next morning, she was pleasantly surprised to find a bath waiting for her in the adjoining dressing room. Her days as the Countess of Whitecliffe had just started, and it was clear that Rosie would pamper her to the level of her new status.

She dressed in a simple mint-green muslin gown with a pleated yoke, high lace collar, and a flared skirt that had darker bands around the hem. Worrying about her new role, she went in search of the dining room. She was still Minna Smith, modiste, and former seamstress from the dark side of London. Managing her shop had given her confidence and the experience to deal with all types of people, yet this was a position too far removed from the life to which she was accustomed. It would take time to get used to her new status in life. Still, this was her heritage; she had every right to be here.

A footman took her to the dining room that was located toward the back of the house, through a short corridor hung with a myriad of hunting prints. The dining room was decorated in pale green and cream, and furnished with an elaborate mahogany sideboard, table and chairs.

The earl was already eating, and at his side sat the infamous Zachary Gordon.

"You!" Minna blurted out as the footman left the room. "How dare you set your foot in this house after what you did?"

Zach shrugged. "None too pleased to see me, I take it." Laughter sparkled in his eyes. "Well, I must find a way to make amends. I came over here to convince Roarke that my solution—marriage—was the best of two worlds, yours and his. You must admit that the ceremony was first class. Everyone turned out when the most inveterate bachelor of London got legshackled. I worked my fingers to the bone to get it all organized."

Minna sat down, fuming. She could feel her husband's eyes on her, but she refused to look at him. "If I had my way, I would have you taken outside and shot," she said in an undertone.

Zach made round eyes, but he didn't appear afraid. "Oh, my," he muttered. "I suddenly shrunk two inches."

The butler entered with a silver pot and proceeded to fill Minna's cup with coffee. The conversation lulled as long as the servant remained in the room, but when he left, Zach said, "By Jove, you know how to hold a grudge, Lady Whitecliffe."

Her cheeks burned with anger. "You all but ruined my life! You're the one to blame for this parody of a marriage. You made Roarke realize that the land—"

"That's enough!" Roarke lifted his hand to control her outburst. "It's too late to rail at Zach," he said softly. The iciness of his voice forced her to look at him. His face had paled with anger, and she quite lost her voice.

"I can't believe that you approve of Mr. Gordon's involvement in our lives." Minna gulped down her coffee, scalding her tongue. The pain forced tears to her eyes. Wretched man, she thought and flung her napkin on the table. Her thoughts in wild turmoil, she clenched her hands in her lap.

"I won't argue this early in the day," came Roarke's dismissing voice. "You don't have half the loyalty that my cousin has."

"Why should I be loyal to the likes of you and your cousin? After getting to know Mr. Gordon, I understand that you applaud trickery of all sorts, Roarke.

255

Just another trait of your character, one I don't like very much." She rose and pushed her chair back. "I, however, won't accept Mr. Gordon's presence until he apologizes." Without another word, she left the room. Biting back her misery, she held her chin high and went into the hallway.

Oh, dear, why had this happened? What should she do next? She didn't have the faintest idea. Clenching her teeth to subdue the wave of tears that tried to burst forth, she walked hesitantly toward the drawing room. There she paused for a moment on the threshold, but spying the open French doors, she crossed the room and went outside into the warm morning sunshine.

Birds chattered around her, and a soft wind caressed the leaves of the roses lining the terrace. Joe Tulsiter was digging more holes in the borders, and he saluted her with a smile.

She slowly walked down the brick path that led to a fountain surrounded by clipped hedges and flower beds. Away from view of the house, she sat down on a bench in the lee of a hedge. Only then did she give in to her sorrow. Tears flowed down her cheeks, and she wiped them off with an angry twist of her hand. Ever since the ceremony that had linked her to Roarke, her sadness had built, and now it seemed to built even more. She dried her eyes on a handkerchief, gulping, but the flow continued. Embarrassed that someone might find her in this unraveled state, she dashed a glance toward the path, but only a sparrow hopped across the bricks.

She cried for what she'd lost, Ellie, her other friends in London, her employees, her shop. Her very identity had been absorbed by the ogre that called himself the Earl of Whitecliffe. He had spoken of a fitting revenge against her, but now it was time he tasted some of that bitter fruit himself. He had treated her as if she was lower than the lowest scullery maid; in fact, he probably treated his servants better than her. He had taken everything that mattered to her, and he'd stolen her land.

If only she knew something about him that would help her shape a fitting revenge. He had the upper hand in everything.

She'd been prepared to plead with him, to convince him that she still loved him, but she couldn't deal with his hostility any longer. Never again would she wear her heart on her sleeve.

She was startled as a man's voice broke into her reverie. Looking up, the sun blinded her, but she recognized Roarke's cousin, Melchior Harding.

"Sorry to disturb you, m'dear, but I'm on my way into the house to see Roarke, and I saw you sitting here."

She wiped her nose furtively, wondering if he'd noticed her swollen eyes and red nose. Tears always wreaked havoc with her face.

"I see that y'have a cold. Here, take my handkerchief. It's much larger than that scrap of lace in your hand." He handed her a pristine linen square, and she accepted gratefully.

"How did you get here?" she mumbled into the fabric, then blew her nose.

"I tied my mare at the edge of the copse on the other side of the bog that connects this property with my cottage. I have some matters to discuss with your husband, but first I longed to hear the tinkle of the fountain, and I found you. By jingo, this is a peaceful spot." He smiled at her. "I'm pleased that you discovered this place so rapidly. I predict that you'll spend hours sewing to the sound of this waterfall."

Minna couldn't stop a smile from spreading on her face. "You do seem to know a lot about Whitecliffe Towers." She made room on the seat. "Please talk to me for a while. I'd like to know everything about the history of this house, and whatever else you care to tell me."

"I've spent many a day at this estate," he explained. "It was rather lively during Roarke's — and my grandparents' time. They liked to invite guests for hunting parties in the autumn and balls in the summer. Ever since they died, The Towers has been a mausoleum. Roarke's father didn't get along with his neighbors. The first earl of Whitecliffe built the mansion among the old ruins of the keep, but it burned down in the last century. Roarke's great-grandfather built the current home. Life was quiet, except for when Thomas lived here."

"Roarke's son."

Harding quieted for a moment, staring at her intently. "I take it Roarke hasn't told you how much that boy meant to him."

"I know how much Thomas changed his life."

He clucked his tongue. "I don't think any explanation can do justice to the depth of love Roarke felt for that boy. Not that he confides much of anything to anyone. A close-mouthed fellow by all accounts. I thought Roarke would lose his mind when Thomas died; I think it happened too soon after Roarke realized that he was going blind like his father before him. Two heavy blows for the poor fellow. I believe that deep down, Roarke's a sensitive man, but he's trying not to show it."

"You feel pity for him, don't you, Mr. Harding?"

Melchior pursed his lips. "I suppose Roarke's life isn't easy, but he's managing splendidly. I admire him for that." He rose. "I've something to discuss with him."

"You don't sound as if you hold a grudge toward him. It seems that you have ample reason to resent his work with the horses."

Melchior heaved a deep sigh. "I do resent it, but I'd like to work out a compromise with Roarke. All he tries to do is buy me off." Melchior swatted irritably at a fly. "Money won't help my failing horse breeding business, and I wish Roarke could see that. Anyhow, he sees that it's his fault that my stables are losing prestige. His bringing Aladdin here gave the death knell to my business. We must come to an understanding soon." Melchior's face had darkened with discomfort, and Minna wished she could help him. She sensed that he had a kind heart if not a very forceful personality. Roarke might ride roughshod over his cousin's feelings. Minna decided she would do what she could to help the hapless fellow.

"Where is he?" Melchior asked.

"He was in the breakfast parlor with Zach Gordon twenty minutes ago."

Melchior bent over her hand. "As I said at the reception, Roarke is fortunate to have found you."

Minna's heart lightened at those words, and she felt that she could face whatever the rest of the day had in store for her. If she avoided her new husband, she could almost believe that she was on an extended holiday in the country. Almost.

Longing to get away from the oppressive atmosphere of The Towers, she returned to the house and ordered the carriage in half an hour. After changing into a riding habit, bonnet, and parasol, she waited in the hallway.

At first she only heard the sound of the wind soughing in the trees outside, but suddenly she was jolted by Roarke's raised voice. It was coming from his study, and she stifled an urge to flee.

As her heartbeat escalated with distress, she heard another, slightly softer male voice. It must be Melchior, she thought; he had business with Roarke. But why are they yelling? She couldn't discern the words, but clearly they were arguing. Just before the carriage arrived, the voices calmed down and Minna drew a sigh of relief. Putting a steadying hand to her heart, she viewed the closed door of the study uneasily.

She took a step back in shock as it burst open a moment later and crashed against the wall. Roarke stormed out of the room, his face dark with anger. His hair was mussed as if he'd been pulling his hand through it repeatedly, and the sight endeared him to Minna, until she saw that he'd jumped into the carriage that was waiting for her.

"What's the meaning—?" she began and climbed in after him. "I ordered the conveyance for myself—"

The coach started with a jolt, and she fell against the seat. "I'm taking a drive," she said as she had righted herself and her tilting bonnet. "And I resent your intrusion."

"So what?"

"I take it you don't care."

Roarke polished his spectacles diligently, then put them on. He gave her a long scrutinizing look that betrayed no emotion except anger, and she cringed in her corner.

"Where are you going?" she demanded. "I'm sure our paths are not identical." She gave him an icy stare, but he only shrugged. He looked achingly attractive in a black riding coat over buff corduroy breeches and topboots.

"They are, or what would you call this?"

"*I* ordered the carriage," she replied, ruffled.

A cold smile curled the corners of his mouth. "Then my lady wife, you'll oblige me with a detour to the stables, because that's where I'm going. Then I hope I won't have to see you again today or tonight."

She fumed in silence. If only he would rant and rave at her instead of treating her to this cold indifference. At least then she could defend herself, but this stiff anger unnerved her.

She twisted her gloves in her hands, wondering how to break the tension. If only he'd taken another carriage, and another road; if only she'd left ten minutes earlier. Now she had to endure his icy disapproval for God knows how long.

"Why were you shouting at Melchior Harding?" she asked at last.

He gave her a probing glance. "Mel and I don't see eye to eye on a number of things." He didn't elaborate, and she didn't want to pry.

"I like him," she said.

Roarke snorted, and she wondered what kind of feelings he had for his cousin. "I'm not surprised."

She dropped the subject and stared out the window. A heavy misery sat in her chest, and she doubted that it would ever go away. The path led over a wooded hill, skirted Tulsiter Bog, then traversed a gentle valley. On the other side it climbed another hill, and before she knew what was happening, the carriage had turned up a winding private drive. *Meadow Hill.* Her heartbeat escalated at the thought of seeing her birthplace.

Huge elms lined the drive, and shrubs and hedges looked unkempt and hostile. The coach came to a halt before an old sandstone mansion with a slate roof and many chimney pots. Her parents had walked the paths of the overgrown garden, and they had laughed in the rooms behind the mullioned windows. Or had they been fighting? Minna wished she knew more about the people who had been her parents. She cast a glance at Roarke, but the void of emotion on his face told her that he had no interest in the mansion.

"The grounds look neglected," she commented.

"It's too costly to have staff in both places. Old

Joe Tulsiter comes here once in a while to clear away the brush."

She had an urge to step down and explore, but the carriage continued past the buildings and turned onto a path that led through a thicket. She decided to return another day and go inside the house.

As the woods opened into another valley, she saw the land that Aloisius Seager had bequeathed to her. About fifteen horses grazed the rich grassland. She realized that the animals were Roarke's Arabians, and even from a distance she recognized the symmetry of their lines and their shining coats. No wonder Roarke had wanted these acres, she thought.

The carriage came to a halt at the stables which were built in a square around a courtyard. Grooms were sweeping the yard and cleaning out the boxes. Two horses swiveled their heads toward them, ears pricked with curiosity. Velvet eyes scrutinized them as they stepped out of the coach, and one whinnied a greeting to Roarke.

His face lit up, and Minna realized that the affection he had given her in the past, was now given to the horses. She watched him croon to the black stallion and rub him between the ears. Over the half-door of the box, the Arabian nuzzled Roarke's arm, trying to stick his nose into Roarke's pocket. With a laugh that made Minna ache inside with longing, Roarke pulled out a carrot and gave it to the animal.

"He always had a knack with horses," someone said at Minna's side. Startled, she glanced at the tiny man beside her, and recognized Joe Tulsiter.

Like the first time she'd met him, something about him captivated her attention. It wasn't the unprepossessing exterior, in fact, he looked disgraceful in a tattered tweed jacket and a grimy cap. His hair needed a trim, and stubble bristled on his chin. But her breath caught in her throat as she looked into his eyes. The clarity and kindness of those light blue eyes made her want to lay her head on his shoulder and cry.

"He's a right idiot, that husband of yours," he said familiarly as if he wasn't the lowliest of stable grooms. Minna couldn't find it in herself to reprimand him. "But he'll come to his senses, when he recovers from his hurt."

"You know much about him," Minna replied dryly, and wiped a tear from her eye surreptitiously.

"I've known the man since he was a wee babe. He has yet to accept his life the way it is, but when he does, he'll be strong. He already is, but not *inside*."

Minna stared at the small shriveled man who had such insight. His gnarled hands and leathery skin spoke of a lifetime of hard labor.

"I can tell that you're fond of his lordship."

"Without him, this part of the world wouldn't be the same."

Minna pondered those words, marveling at such devotion. He moved toward the box with the stallion, and Minna followed him. When Roarke saw her coming, he frowned and went away. She watched as Joe spoke with the animal who kept nodding his majestic head as if he understood every word. Joe went into the box and the stallion seemed to give a humble bow. He neighed fondly as Joe scrambled on his knees under a cot on the floor.

In a flash of insight, Minna realized that this was Joe Tulsiter's home, a cot, a threadbare blanket, a stool with a rusty oil lamp on it. A brindled cat was curled up on the lumpy pillow. "You live here?" she asked incredulously even though she knew the answer.

Joe got up carrying a basket of shriveled apples. He gave one to the horse then set the basket outside. "Aye, as good a home as any. Aladdin keeps me company." Minna glanced at the stallion who bent his head so that Joe could rub his ears.

He certainly was a strange man, but she sensed a power that seemed to increase every time she saw him. The animals evidently felt it too.

"Surely you could live better up at the estate."

His teeth flashed in a smile and a thousand wrinkles formed around his eyes. "I like to live among the humble beings."

Before Minna could ask him to explain further, another carriage pulled up, and Zach Gordon hobbled out. For the first time his crutches were gone, and he was leaning on a cane.

"He took the bullet meant for the master," said Joe, and Minna whipped around to stare at him.

"Bullet?"

"Aye, Mr. Gordon got that broken leg when he fell off Aladdin six weeks ago. He's a mighty fine rider, if a trifle foolhardy. One day he decided to try Aladdin — never rode him before." He gestured toward the horse. "One of the finest Arabians that I've ever seen." The old man shook his head and clucked his tongue. "That day almost ended in disaster. The lad was almost killed. Someone tried to shoot Aladdin from under him — thought he were the earl, no doubt. Gordon wore the master's old riding coat. Aladdin got a shallow gash in his rump, and today is the first day he's out since the assault. We don't want to endanger his life again."

Minna gasped. "Someone wants his lordship dead?"

Joe peered at her from under the frayed bill of his cap. "Well . . . perhaps only the horse. There are many around here who resent the presence of the stallion."

Melchior, Minna thought. *"Who? Roarke doesn't have enemies, or does he?"*

The old man held up his leathery hand as if testing the wind. "He's his own worst enemy, but that won't kill him."

Minna's eyes widened at the cryptic reply, and as she turned to look at Zach Gordon who had survived so miraculously, the old man disappeared.

When she asked another question she got no answer. He was gone without as much as a sound. Who did he suspect? She glanced around the yard, but there was no sign of the strange old man. A gust of wind eddied around her, and she had an eerie sensation of being watched from the shadows of the stables.

Roarke had told her nothing about Zach Gordon's accident, nor had he mentioned enemies who plotted his stallion's — or his — demise. Now he took great pains to ignore her completely. If someone wanted to see the earl dead, was that person stalking them at this very moment? Icy fear crawled through her at the thought, and she glanced furtively around the yard. It was a normal, sunny summer day, but she couldn't see where the shadows lengthened between the buildings, nor could she see through walls. The sun had taken on a positively evil glare. She took an urgent step closer to the man she loved.

Chapter Twenty-two

Two weeks had passed since her talk with Joe Tulsiter at the stables. Minna couldn't shake her misgivings, but when she returned to The Towers after a walk one morning, she had the pleasant surprise of finding Davina Shield in the drawing room. With her was Lady Edna Barton, whose country residence was situated not far from The Towers. Davina rose as Minna entered and opened her arms for an embrace. Minna accepted meekly, almost choking on the cloud of perfume that ensconced her friend.

"Dear Minerva! How do you like it here? Are the servants behaving? You look ravishing, doesn't she, Edna? Is Roarke kind to you? Wedded bliss with him must be—"

"Davina, let's talk about that later," Minna said dampeningly. "I'm pleased that you found the time to pay me a visit."

"London is desolate without you," Davina said and sat back down. "I don't know where to find a new modiste. They are all so *dull*. It's dreadful."

"Ellie Nichols is excellent, so why search further?"

"She's not *you,* though. I hope you'll help her plan for the next season. However, I hear she's doing very well considering that you left."

Minna sat down beside Davina after shaking Lady Barton's reluctant hand. The old baroness had not accepted Minna's new status, but Minna didn't care. She averted her gaze from the older woman's disapproving face. Under the circumstances, why did Lady Barton deign to visit?

"I for one sorely miss you, Minna," Davina continued.

"I thought you had all the attention you need from Leverett Epcott," Minna said with an innocent smile.

Davina blushed. Minna had never seen her friend blush before, so she knew she had touched a tender spot.

"In fact, that's one reason I've come down here. I'm staying with Edna, the poor dear, to think things through. Eve has asked for my hand in marriage."

Minna exclaimed in delight. "I knew he would make you happy!"

Starry-eyed, Davina sighed. "To think that I always considered him less important than the lowest servant of my household. He's so very *loving,* you know."

"I knew you two would suit one another. Anyone with such depth of devotion as Eve has for you must make the perfect husband." A twinge of unease ran through her as she thought about her own parody of a marriage. Roarke didn't know the meaning of the word devotion.

Davina's blue gaze probed her soul. "You sound wistful, dearest friend. Is there something the matter?"

Minna longed to unburden herself to Davina who had known Roarke all her life. Perhaps Davina could help her understand the man she had married. But she checked her tongue as she met Lady Barton's cool glance. No friend in that quarter. Not yet anyway. She'd better keep quiet until she could talk to Davina alone.

She turned to Lady Barton. "Sometimes it's lonely in the country, milady. I would appreciate female company once in a while. All the men talk about around here is horses. I can't say that I'm bitten by the fever."

"My nephew, Melchior Harding, is certainly the most knowledgeable on the subject in these parts," Lady Barton said with a sniff. "My husband, while he was alive, was quite the connoisseur of horseflesh."

"Melchior has been most kind to me; he has promised to teach me horseback riding."

"Had my sister been alive, she wouldn't have allowed Roarke to get in the way of Melchior's horse breeding business," Lady Barton went on as if she hadn't heard Minna. Her face took on a mournful look, and Minna murmured some expressions of sympathy. "Melchior always was a dear boy," the old lady added with a trembling sigh. "I wish Roarke wouldn't try to take over Mel's stables."

Minna wished she could assure Lady Barton that he had no plans to ruin Melchior, but she didn't know his plans. She didn't know a whole lot about Roarke. The thought gave her an uneasy feeling.

"I hear Mel's an excellent shot," Davina said with some asperity, and Minna gave her a curious glance. Did her friend allude to the shooting that had caused Zach Gordon to break his leg?

"He enjoys the hunt, yes," Lady Barton said noncommittally. "Always brings home his prey."

Narrow-shouldered and long of nose, Lady Barton reminded Minna of a predatory bird. Her sharp eyes missed nothing, and the plume in her bonnet nodded in a most indignant fashion.

"It's a disgrace how your young husband has let this estate go to seed," Lady Barton continued. "It was different during his grandfather's time, lavish balls and routs all summer long. Champagne flowed in rivers—not that I hold with drinking large quantities of strong wine, but the entertainment wasn't as parsimonious as it is today."

Due to lavish balls the estate hovered on the brink of ruin for years, Minna thought uncharitably, but she kept silent.

"I daresay dear Melchior would do a sight better here," Lady Barton continued.

"Melchior is a dreamer," Davina interrupted. "In Roarke's shoes he would bring the Whitecliffes to complete ruination," she argued with an angry frown etched between her eyebrows. "No one has worked as hard as Roarke since he inherited the title."

Lady Barton gave Davina a poisonous glance. "If you say so. You always were his champion."

"I know Roarke, and you do too, Edna. Don't let your jealousy over his inheritance cloud your judgment."

Silence descended in the room, and Minna ordered a tray of refreshments from Kitson, the butler. The ladies consumed sherry and iced cakes in stiff silence, and Minna noticed that Lady Barton ate and drank considerably more than her share.

Between nibbles of cake, Lady Barton said, "Now that you live so close, Miss Sm—Lady Whitecliffe, perhaps you would consider designing a few gowns for me." She tilted up her nose. "I would need them rather quickly, and I know you don't mind *working* hard hours."

Minna couldn't believe her ears. "I suggest you find another modiste. I'm no longer in that line of work," she said coldly. She trembled with anger at the lady's condescending tone, and knew that many members of the gentry shared Lady Barton's opinion that she was nothing but an upstart.

"Really Edna, that was uncalled for!" Davina patted her lips with her napkin. "Now that you've become mistress of such a grand estate, Minna, you must arrange a ball to meet the neighboring gentry. It could be quite jolly."

"I don't know . . . Roarke—"

"If the prospect daunts you, I'd be delighted to help," Davina said.

Minna touched Davina's hand impulsively. "That would be delightful. Would you mind staying here for a few days?"

Davina's face lit up. "I'll be back tomorrow—with my luggage." She stood. "Come, Edna. If you behave, we'll send you an invitation to the ball."

Two red spots glowed on Lady Barton's cheeks. "Well! I've never—!" Her chin held high, her hands lifting her black skirts delicately, Lady Barton swept past Minna with a look that said that Minna would never amount to more than her former seamstress.

Minna received Davina's maternal hug gratefully. She realized that her friend wanted to protect her, and to introduce her to society. "Thank you," she whispered. "I look forward to tomorrow."

For Minna, the rest of the day passed in a blur of activities. She had acquainted herself with every aspect of running a large household; this morning she was inspecting the linen storage. Mrs. Clemson was a tireless teacher, and a kind one. Minna shared neither lunch nor dinner with Roarke and Zach. She heard their voices once in the dining room but she had no desire to join them. Roarke's cold attitude toward her deepened her misery, and she rejected the very thought of him. His coldness intimidated her like nothing else.

That night as she went up to her bedchamber, she couldn't help but notice his lamp burning in the study. She halted where she could get a good view of him as he bent over the books spread on his desk. Every day there seemed to accumulate more material concerning his studies on religion and philosophy. Big packages arrived from London, and some from Oxford. She longed to talk to him about it, but during the current distance between them she couldn't think of a way to bridge the gap.

Every day that passed made it more difficult to take a step toward reconciliation. Deeply hurt by his hatred, she recoiled at the idea of pleading with him, but at the same time, the part that loved him deeply whispered that she ought to approach him, work on his resistance. Tonight he looked especially attractive in the mellow light from the oil lamp, his hair in wild disarray, his spectacles making him look curiously defenseless. She yearned to hold him, to smooth away the frown from his forehead.

As if he'd read her thoughts, he looked up and stared straight at her. He must have noticed her movements even though he might have difficulty seeing her in the dark hallway. His expression unreadable, he continued to stare at her with unseeing eyes. With a pang of misgiving, she realized that he failed to see her. How far had his blindness gone?

With a wave of pity, she watched in silence. She could take a step over the threshold, hold out her hand toward him, but instead, she climbed the curving stairs.

Roarke sensed her presence, feeling her sadness penetrating his cold armor. Anguish tightened his throat, and he wished he'd gone after her. He hated himself for his weakness. After all, she had betrayed him and their love, but a part of him had forgiven her that transgression. Time was softening the edges of his anger. There was no denying that he still loved her. Perhaps he always would. Still, he detested her for what she'd done to their blossoming love. He could perhaps forgive, but not forget. If she could betray him once, she could betray him twice.

He studied the dense script in front of him, feeling a tiredness so deep he thought he would never be able to pull himself out of it. He'd read hundreds of books, without getting any wiser. Raking his hands through his hair, he wondered if reading about the world's religions and philosophies was a waste of time. He'd learned nothing that he could put into practice. Tall, lofty words, vague promises, and the certainty of condemnation in this life and salvation afterward, were what most of the books preached.

Nothing he'd read had lifted his spirits, and to top off his despair, his eyes were playing more tricks with him. Without really noticing it at first, he now realized that his vision had narrowed considerably — especially in one eye. It was a treacherous process. Blindness was sneaking up on him like a thief in the night. He found it harder and harder to concentrate on the text of the pages on his desk, and just this morning he'd walked into a tree he could have sworn wasn't there.

With an angry sweep of his arm, he pushed a towering stack of moldy books to the floor. None of them had explained why some people went blind, and why children died before reaching maturity. Nothing explained the unfairness of the poverty and misery of the less fortunate, nor could he find an answer to the treachery of people he had trusted. No one knew why the sun rose every morning, or why he had the strength to get up and face another day of struggle. Still, every day he got up to dress and have breakfast. Life went on and he followed, like a leaf swept along on a turbulent river. He had no choice, but where would he find the strength to live day after day without the answer he was seeking?

The thought frightened him, and he leaned back in

his chair, his hands clasped behind his head. Another disturbing thought entered his mind; today when he'd been riding Aladdin in a lonely part of the woods, he'd understood there was a chance that someone wanted him dead. He'd pushed away that suspicion successfully in London, but here, the threat hung unseen and unheard over him.

Zach insisted that Melchior was behind the scheme, but Roarke refused to believe the accusation. Mel had everything to gain from his death, but he was too lazy and too easygoing to plan an assassination. *Yet the devil sneaked Tokayer into Aladdin's stall to mate them despite my warning. Surely that was as far as Mel's trickery had gone,* Roarke thought. *If Tokayer dies at foaling time he'll perhaps blame me, but I'll handle that when the time comes.* No, Mel might be bankrupt, but he wasn't a murderer. Still, Roarke couldn't shake the premonition that he was in danger, more here at The Towers than in London.

His skin prickled at the back of his neck as if he was being watched. He turned slowly and peered at the dark shadows of the bay window behind him. He failed to see anything except what appeared like a sudden movement.

The windows were open. Must be the drapes, he thought. They moved in the breeze, and a branch rasped against a pane somewhere close by. Stiffening in defense, he rose to investigate the drapes, and found only air. His imagination was running away with him, he mused with a sigh of relief, but the palms of his hands were damp, and the skin of his neck felt tight.

Dashing a hand across his eyes, he leaned over the windowsill and looked outside. He cursed his weak eyesight as the familiar grounds were nothing but a dark blur. The moon moved from behind a bank of clouds momentarily, and he thought he saw a shadow shift across the lawn. He blinked, the clouds covered the moon, and all was dark. With a slam, he closed the window.

Even though peace reigned in his study, he couldn't shake the feeling that the sword of Damocles was hanging over his head—in more ways than one.

Chapter Twenty-three

Minna heard Roarke undressing in the adjoining bedchamber and she pictured him taking off his various articles of clothing. Shirt would lift from his hard-muscled chest, breeches would slide over lean hips and taut buttocks, boots would cease to hold strong feet and calves. . . . Her reverie made her strangely tingling all over, and she longed to see the real man, not the phantom image beneath her eyelids. Her heart trembled at the thought of walking into his room without knocking. What would he do? Order her away in a stern voice? Highly likely, she thought, wondering if the daring effort would be worth the humiliation of his rejection.

At that moment she realized an impromptu seduction would be the perfect revenge for his unkind behavior since the wedding. He'd sworn he would never touch her again, and if she could make him surrender, well, then she'd be avenged. Besides, she might show him that he wasn't as invulnerable as he pretended to be.

The fact still remained — she loved him. If only she could penetrate his armor, perhaps they could find a way to solve their problems.

As she vacillated, his boots thumped against the floor as he discarded them. Her heartbeat escalated at the thought of surprising him in his bedchamber. He would not expect her to be that bold. Surprise would be in her favor. Still, the idea frightened her; she felt weak-kneed at the very thought of his disapproving frown.

Before she lost her courage, she slid out of her bed and pulled on a filmy dressing-gown. The lace barely covered her shoulders and breasts, and she knew the froth of lace along the front edge and sleeves was flattering.

Through the door she heard him mutter something, and she listened for a reply from Harris, but none came. Roarke was alone.

Taking a deep breath, she opened the door and stepped inside. She steeled herself for his icy welcome, but he was too intent on removing a pin from his neckcloth to pay any attention to her.

"Harris, is that you? I asked you to retire early, but now I'm glad you didn't. I can't get this blasted pin out — it's stuck around something."

Minna didn't reply, only stepped up to him and examined the tangled neckcloth.

He jerked aside as he recognized her. "What the deuce! What are you doing here, Minerva?"

"Do you want me to help you or not?" Her insides melted as he gave her a long measuring stare.

"I didn't invite you here," he said in a dismissing tone.

"I don't need an invitation to my own home," she countered.

They glared at each other, then Roarke shrugged. "If you insist," he said with a sigh.

"Come here, let me take a look." She beckoned him back toward the lighted oil lamp on his dresser. As he stood before her, stiff and suspicious, she deftly inserted her fingers between the shirt and the neck-cloth.

"The pin head got entangled in a loop of thread," she explained as she located the problem.

"What are you doing here?" he demanded.

"I couldn't sleep," she said glibly and pulled out the pin.

He moved back a step and untied the neckcloth. His flesh invited her touch in the opening of his shirt, but his rigid stance told her to stay away from him. "And now you plan to keep me from my sleep?"

His virile scent made her senses swim, and she remembered other times when she'd stood this close to him. He'd folded his arms around her and held her tightly . . . but tonight he stood unyielding—a human fortress—at arm's length. So as not to let her intimidation show, she took a step toward him, so close that she could touch him once more. With a provocative smile, she put her palm against his bare chest and pressed it against his heart. His heartbeat thundered, and she realized he was as acutely aware of her as she was of him.

"I thought we could keep each other company," she whispered.

He seemed to hesitate. "What are you playing at?" His frown softened, and his angry gaze flickered to the floor. "What has gotten into your conniving mind now? I don't want any more intimacy between us. I told you as much on our wedding night."

She moved her shoulder and the lace of her wrap glided off, coming to rest against her elbow. She knew that her summer nightgown was almost transparent, a merest whisper of fabric separating him from her naked flesh. "Do come to me, Roarke. Let's end the antagonism. We have to spend our lives together, after all."

"Who says?" He snorted, then pulled his shirt over

his head. His skin looked smooth and taut over his broad chest, and his shoulders spoke of strength and determination. A fever entered her blood as he revealed himself to her, and she wished he would crush her against him and take her to his bed.

"We are married, aren't we?"

"On paper, yes. But once you've acclimatized yourself to your new position in life you may live in London; or you may live here or at Meadow Hill. Just make sure that our paths don't cross. We might even succeed in never seeing each other again." He pointed toward the door. "Now leave."

She held her breath, for the next few moments were crucial. Their eyes fought, and she thought she would collapse on the floor if the tension tightened any further between them.

Her bare feet felt cold against the old parquet, and her legs trembled. She had come this far, and she would not back down now. She remembered everything she'd lost in London, and decided that she wasn't going to become a victim again. She would stand up for herself.

And she would not lose Roarke. She wouldn't, she kept telling herself as she moved slowly toward him, letting the wrap glide to the floor behind her. Embarrassed by her brazen seduction, she nevertheless held her head high, daring him to defy her.

"I want to put an end to the stupid feud between us," she said softly, "a glorious end. Let's burn the bad memories in the fire of our passion."

"You're a shameless hussy." He snorted and backed away until his legs were pressed against the bed. He could go no further without pushing her aside first. Would he shove her away? She stepped closer.

"I want you, Roarke, more than any man I've ever met. I love you."

His frown made his eyebrows gather threateningly

over his eyes. "What new game is this?" He put his hands on her bare shoulders and turned her around. "Look, there's the door. Go back to your room. I told you we would never touch intimately again."

She closed her eyes momentarily and took a deep breath to steady her composure, then faced him. "You want me, Roarke. Your desire is like a hot wave washing over me." Though she'd lost much of her self-confidence, she stepped closer. If he rejected her again, her resolve might crumble. Gulping, she continued, "You can't fool me. Arousal darkens your eyes."

He laughed mirthlessly. "You've lost your mind, Minerva." He sat down on his bed to remove his stockings. "Just go; don't make an issue out of this." His rebuff wounded her, but she couldn't allow herself to admit defeat.

She moved up to him and by pushing him down on the bed, she took him by surprise. Before he could stop her, she was straddling his hips. The barrier of his breeches was still between them, but Minna was well aware of the rigid shape of him between her legs. She had not been mistaken; he did desire her most acutely. Dragging the palms of her hands over his chest and down over the sensitive part of his stomach, she prayed that his resistance would be broken for good.

He glowered, but color rose in his cheeks, and his breath was growing ragged. A pulse beat rapidly in his throat.

"Get off of me," he demanded. "Now."

"It's my wifely right to spend the nights with you," she explained while working to undo the buttons of his waistband. "I'm demanding my right."

"I don't want you. I don't want another child."

She made herself sound brave. "You should have thought of that the other times you bedded me."

He groaned as she slipped her hand into the opening of his breeches and wiggled her derrière until it straddled his thighs.

"You should know that I regret my weakness in the past," he muttered. "I regret it bitterly."

"Liar," she chided. She didn't tell him that since their wild lovemaking in the gazebo she hadn't had her monthly curse. She took the most sensitive part of him into her hand and caressed him.

Passion glittered in his eyes, passion and anger. Taut as a whipcord he suddenly sat up and gripped her shoulders. Before she realized what had happened, he'd tilted her over on her back against the mattress and ripped the nightdress from her body.

"Be careful!" she admonished, but it was too late. Naked to his fevered gaze, she watched as he pulled off his breeches. In his hurry, he snagged his toe in the hem and fell over her.

Naked flesh met naked flesh and at that moment the nagging ache, the echoing loneliness in her heart was dismissed. Only he possessed her mind and her heart, just as he possessed her body. Arching over her like some animal of sleek muscular symmetry, he licked her nipples until they tightened with yearning. While massaging one breast, he parted her legs with his knee and entered her with one swift stroke.

Sweet, dulcet torture moved in waves through her, and she knew she had won him for the moment. He buried his face in the hollow between her shoulder and her head as he moved within her. She had imagined he would make it a slow, exquisite torture, but as she began to settle into the hurried rhythm, he got up and tipped her over onto her stomach. She cried out in protest, but he lifted up her hips and entered her again.

His breath quickened as he moved faster and faster. She'd never felt such deep spiraling pleasure. It was as

280

if he caressed every part of her insides, drawing a long, mind-shattering response from her. She struggled to touch him, but he was out of her reach. All she could feel was his warm grip on her hips, and his hot shaft inside her. His gasps of pleasure echoed her own.

An intense wave brought her into the oblivion of ecstasy. Then his grip hardened on her and he groaned as he came to a shattering release.

His breathing still ragged, he collapsed on top of her and her face was buried in his pillow. It smelled of him, and she didn't want to move, not even for a second.

In the stillness afterward, he rolled aside and she moved closer to him, fitting her body to his. Light from the oil lamp filtered through the open bedhangings, and she could see that he was staring at her from under hooded eyelids.

"Now go," he said hoarsely. "You came for what you wanted, and in my weakness I couldn't resist the temptation."

She chuckled, and drew her fingertip along the indentation in the middle of his chest. "I'm glad you couldn't."

"I'm sure you are," he snapped. "This is just a new way of torturing me, isn't it?"

Minna propped herself on her elbow and her hair spilled over his chest. "It certainly was new to me, but I didn't invent it," she teased.

"Oh, go! Just leave." He flung his arm in an exasperated gesture over his face, and she slid out of the bed. She had won this round of battle, and she sensed it would be unwise to goad him further. She slipped on her wrap and tied the sash at her waist.

"I wish I could spend the night in your bed," she whispered.

"Go back to your own before I throw you out." He

was reclining lazily against the pillows and she knew she had nothing to fear from that threat.

Glowing with the aftermath of pleasure, she kissed her fingertips and sent the kiss to him. "I want to do this again. You're always welcome in my bed."

"I've married a trollop," he spat.

"There are worse things," she commented and left. She closed the door and rubbed her hands together. Victory had been hers this night! If his ardor was any indication, soon she would hone away his resistance and they would be back to where they started. Yet, a persistent doubt remained in her heart when she remembered the furious look in his eyes. He would fight her at every turn.

Chapter Twenty-four

The next morning, Roarke slept late. He woke up refreshed and, for a moment, felt at peace. Rain spattered against the windows, and wind whipped through the trees. For a time, the seconds just after awakening, he wallowed in a pool of weightlessness. He wished he could remain in that state for the rest of the day, but he knew that when he moved the slightest, even his toes, the spell would be broken. Thoughts rushed into his mind, ruining the peace.

Memories of the previous night brought anger and humiliation. As he recalled the wild lovemaking, heat crept up his face. He'd made a total fool of himself at the sight of Minerva's fine silvery hair, rose-crested breasts and full-lipped mouth. He groaned in agony. His own weakness stared him in the face, torturing him with the truth. He had succumbed to her wiles! It hadn't taken more than one of her wicked smiles and the sheen of the creamy skin of her shoulder. The memory of her lithe body ate at his insides and he felt his groin tighten in anticipation. Had she been here, he wouldn't have been able to resist another intimate embrace. Damn, but he loved the feel of her silky hair, the softness of her skin, the rapturous look on her face as she convulsed in a climax. She had bewitched him, and he wasn't sure if he would ever be free of her. The thought left him cold.

Feeling trapped, he punched the pillow. He hated himself for his weakness, and her power over him. He'd lost the battle, and she might very well use the same weapon again. Best stay well away from her from now on, he thought, or he might forget that she was capable of betrayal. Damn the lying witch!

A knock came on the door, and Harris, the valet entered. Roarke was already out of bed, pacing the floor as he thought of ways to get back at Minerva.

"My lord, there are visitors downstairs, Mrs. Shield, and a young friend of hers, Miss Aurora Bishop."

Roarke whistled and stopped his pacing. "Does my cousin know about Miss Aurora's presence?"

The rotund and balding valet nodded. "Yes, my lord, Mr. Gordon is sitting next to her on the sofa." His eyes twinkled. "Very close."

"You never miss a detail, do you, Harris?" Roarke viewed the valet who had been in his employ since his Oxford days. Harris's black straight hair was parted in the middle and smoothed down with pomade, and his small mustache had perfect symmetry.

"It's my duty to have an eye for detail, my lord."

Roarke bathed himself thoroughly in a copper hip-bath, dried himself, then let Harris dress him in a crisp, starched shirt. "Since you're an observant man, Harris, did you see anyone in the park last night? I thought I heard movement in the darkness."

"No . . ." Harris hesitated, "I think Mr. Melchior was the last to leave. He spent time at the stables at Meadow Hill before coming here to collect his coach I believe. It was dark when he returned to Linkwood Cottage."

"I wonder . . ." Roarke began. "No one else? No visitors in the house?"

The valet shook his head. "After her ladyship went upstairs the house was quiet."

It hadn't been quiet in his bedchamber, Roarke thought with a grimace. He put on his glasses and brushed his hair. He tied the white neckcloth under the stiff shirtpoints. "If you see Mr. Melchior today, please send him to me in the study."

Harris bowed and held out the tailcoat. "It'll be my pleasure."

After finishing dressing, Roarke went downstairs. He heard Davina's penetrating voice and Minerva's softer one. His heart made a jump, and he was pulled toward the open door of the drawing room. He stopped short of the door, before anyone was aware of his presence. Devil take the lying hussy.

As sunlight flooded the room with light, he saw Minerva before she saw him, and the sight of her took his breath away. She reminded him of something pure and untouchable, the statue of an angel, but alive. Her hair was a light halo of curls and her skin was pale to the point of transparency. The slender curve of her neck invited the caress of his lips, and he had to fight an urge to call out her name. As always she spoke with graceful gestures and smiles.

She looked perfect this morning, but when he took another step closer, he noticed the dark smudges under her eyes. They spoke of disturbed sleep, and he realized that their lovemaking had taken its toll. The thought gave him a surge of satisfaction. He hoped she'd had a sleepless night.

But when she smiled her glorious smile, he could almost forget her treachery. Nothing but kindness and innocence shone in her eyes as they rested on Davina who was sitting beyond his vision.

In a flash he realized that he was needlessly torturing himself by having the woman he desired, the woman he'd married in a fit of rage, living under his

285

roof. Either he must find a way to forgive her, or he would perish by the sole merit of her presence under his roof. The thought made him icy all over. He ought to make her leave this very morning . . .

"Whitecliffe?" Davina called out as he coughed.

As if coming out of a trance, he broke his fixation on his wife, and entered the drawing room.

"How are you?" Davina continued, her face serious with concern.

"I'm afraid I stayed up very late last night," he said apologetically. He kissed his aunt's hand, then bowed over Miss Aurora's fingertips. The young woman looked enchanting with her midnight-black hair clustered into curls around her ears. Innocent violet eyes met his, and Roarke knew why his cousin had fallen in love with this lovely woman. An air of shyness and mystery enveloped her.

Sitting beside her, Zach certainly looked besotted, and Aurora gazed at him with love in her eyes, Roarke noticed. "I'm delighted you could come for a visit," he said to her. "Zach is in seventh heaven by the look of him."

"You haven't kissed your wife good-morning," Zach pointed out and gave Roarke a gentle shove.

"Ah, how thoughtless of me! I must keep up the image of doting husband," he murmured as he bent over his wife. He noticed as she raised her guard, and it made his anger boil. She smelled elusively of violets, and her cheek looked as smooth as a peach as he touched his lips to the roundness. The feel of her soft skin made his senses swim, and he longed to fall to his knees and bury his face in her bosom. He yearned to hold her, to speak to her, to confide his thoughts to her, to whisper words of love, to kiss every inch of her skin. How could such loveliness hide such a deceitful heart? He recoiled from her, as she smiled.

He straightened with difficulty, noticing the blush

on her face. His heart made a somersault, and he couldn't find his voice.

God, but he loved this woman! The truth stared him painfully in the face.

"Good-morning, Roarke," she whispered, and he noticed the wildly beating pulse in her throat. Desire, and something else—something hauntingly beautiful, simmered for a moment between them, and Roarke took an abrupt step back. If he didn't watch himself—

"Don't be a bore, Roarke," Davina interrupted his thoughts. "Come here and sit for a while. You aren't so busy that you can't spend half an hour with your aunt." She patted the sofa beside her. "Minna invited me to stay here for a few days. No objections I hope?"

"Of course you're welcome to stay as long as you like." Roarke sat down, and met Zach's amused glance. If this was a conspiracy against him. . . . That rascal, wait 'til he saw Zach alone.

"Davina suggested that we have a small gathering for the local gentry," Minna said. "You don't mind, Roarke?"

He refused to look at her lest he would reveal his turmoil. He shook his head, and studied the tip of his boot. "No."

"They'll all love Minna," Davina said. "And you, Roarke, you'll be heaped with compliments about your lovely wife."

For a moment he looked up, meeting Minna's eyes. She looked tense and miserable, as if she was holding her breath while waiting for his response. A cynical reply hovered on his lips, but he couldn't utter any angry words this morning.

He shrugged and turned to Aurora Bishop. "I hear from Zach that Lady Herrington is keeping you under strict supervision. I'm surprised she's let you out with Mrs. Shield."

Aurora blushed. "Well . . . I . . . she's prostrate with a sick headache, so I sneaked out of the house. Mrs. Shield saw me from her carriage and asked me to join her. But if my aunt finds out that I've been here, well then—"

"She won't find out," Zach said with conviction. "We must find a way for you to attend the ball." He clutched her hand. "Say that you'll come."

Aurora lowered her gaze. "I don't know. It all depends how it could be arranged. I'm sure my aunt won't accept an invitation."

"Drat that dragon guardian of yours," Zach spat, and started pacing the floor. "If only I knew what she has against me."

"It's not you," Aurora began. "It's me. She thinks that my father spoiled me dreadfully, but my father hardly knew that I existed. He was immersed in work from morning to night."

"Well, he was a well-respected scientist. No wonder he didn't have time for a young daughter." A dangerous light shone in Zach's eyes. "I think your father might have approved of me." He clasped his beloved's hand. "You can't live like a prisoner all your life. We must prevail somehow."

Prisoner, Minna thought. *That's what I am since I married Roarke.* Soon he would make her lead her own life, but before that time she must find a way to convince him that he loved her so much that he couldn't bear to part with her. They belonged together. That fact had been confirmed last night. In her hands lay the responsibility to convince him of that.

She pleated the striped gold-and-white fabric of her gown in agitation. If she looked up she would have to meet his glance, yet if she avoided him, he would patch the wall between them that had cracked last night. She tried to tell herself that he'd only married her for the Meadow Hill acres, but she recognized that flare of desire that had ignited between them as soon as he touched her. Perhaps he was powerless to deny it; she certainly was. At least he wasn't indifferent in his feelings toward her, but did he respect her? Respect was more important than desire, and *that* he might never give her. He certainly didn't trust her. Tears brought a tightness to her throat. Damn Mr. Wylie for forcing her to break Roarke's heart, and then propel her into a life that was wholly alien to her. The title of countess sat uncomfortably on her shoulders . . .

"It's about time you start to entertain, Roarke. The neighbors will be curious to hear what you've accomplished with Aladdin," Davina said, breaking into Minna's thoughts. "He'll be the champion of the decade."

"Too early to tell, but he shows great promise." He rose, towering over Minna. She met his icy stare defiantly.

"I'll leave you to your plans," he said, then leaned forward and murmured for her ears alone, "but don't include me."

As he left, she looked up but refused to stare at his retreating back. The sun went behind clouds and the day seemed gloomy after his departure. He had shown no indication of weakening after their night of lovemaking. Had it meant so little to him? She didn't know how she would get through another day of his cold disapproval.

"Idleness breeds discontent," Davina said. "Let's get to work."

On the following night Minna debated whether to visit Roarke in his bedchamber again, and she decided to try. With her heart pounding with fright, she turned the doorknob to his room and found that he'd locked the door. Mortified, she returned to her bed. His gesture hurt more than anything he could have said to her face. She didn't try again, and he didn't visit her. Sleep eluded her, and she worried about the future.

Roarke had heard the soft click of the doorknob as he lay in bed wide awake. He should have told her to move out of the house earlier, but when he'd met her that morning, the issue had flown out of his mind. Since Davina was visiting, Minerva must stay for the time being. She wasn't going to trap him again, however, no matter how daringly seductive were the gowns she wore, or how many alluring smiles she sent in his direction. He sighed, and tried to quiet the nagging longing in his heart. He thumped his fist against his chest. "Damn traitor!" he swore and rolled over on his side.

As the day of the ball drew close, Minna caught Davina's excitement. If Davina lacked certain tact, she made up for it in exuberance. She ordered the servants around until they glared resentfully, and she taught Minna every aspect of planning an elegant gathering.

Minna simply didn't have time to brood about her relationship with Roarke, and when the great day arrived, she felt that she'd accomplished something important, made another step toward accepting her new role as the wife of an earl. It didn't matter that Davina had done most of the work, with Mrs. Clemson and her staff of maids. Minna had gained new self-confidence.

The Towers shone from top to bottom with much scrubbing and polishing. Oil lamps lighted the windows and the prisms of the chandeliers reflected the light of hundreds of candles. Every vase in the house had been filled with red, pink, and pale yellow roses. They sent out a fragrance resembling dew and sunshine, making Minna slightly giddy. She waited anxiously by the stairs in the hallway for the guests to arrive. They were already fifteen minutes late. What if the guests had decided at the last minute not to attend?

Dressed in a rose silk dress of her own design, lavishly trimmed with Honiton lace around the shoulders and at the deep flounce around the hem, she knew it complimented her. Roarke, standing beside her, had a forbidding air, but looked splendid in black evening clothes — white satin waistcoat, knee breeches, black tailcoat, and faultless linen. She was more aware of his presence beside her than of anything, or anyone, else.

"Where are they?" she asked, agitating her fan in front of her face. "Perhaps they decided I — a wench from the dark side of London — wasn't worth the courtesy."

"Nonsense," Davina said. She wore a pink striped satin evening gown and pink roses in her hair. "You've every right to be in this position, Minna. Why, your father was one of the highest ranking peers of Kent." She clasped Minna's hand reassuringly. "Don't despair."

"Nevertheless, I'm Minna Smith, seamstress," Minna whispered, "and no one will let me forget that."

She felt Davina giving Roarke an entreating glance over her shoulder, and she wished she hadn't shown her fears.

Roarke said nothing. What would he be prepared

to say in her defense? She gave him a sideways glance, but he ignored her. Since the night of their lovemaking, he'd avoided her at all costs. It hurt to know that she was equal to the Meadow Hill acres, nothing more, nothing less. Why, oh why, did she feel so deeply about the man who had wounded her feelings? She wished she could turn off her tormenting love, and shut him out. If only she could create a life here at The Towers that didn't include him, but every day was a reminder of everything that stood between them. After this ball, she would return to London. Roarke would be pleased to see her go.

"The first guests are arriving!" Davina exclaimed, as the crunch of carriage wheels reached their ears.

"I'll be blowed!" the earl exclaimed. "Lady Herrington decided to accept the invitation, after all. Miss Aurora must indeed be happy tonight."

Footmen held the front doors wide to let Lady Herrington and her niece inside. Aurora looked ravishing in a pale gold gown of simple empire style sparsely adorned with two plain velvet bows on each sleeve, and one among her ringlets.

"Why, I've just left my sickbed," the old lady Herrington, dressed all in black, said. "Aurora literally badgered me into this."

"You must take your opportunities to dance while you still have legs, Lady Herrington," Davina said with a sweet smile. "Aurora, you look as fresh as a rosebud."

Through her quizzing glass Lady Herrington looked askance at Roarke, then at Minna. "Your wife is nothing like I thought," she said. "What I've heard is that she was a modiste in London. Not exactly a genteel occupation, but I must admit she doesn't look like a dressmaker." She failed to shake Minna's hand, and something snapped in Minna's chest.

"An honest occupation nonetheless. There's nothing genteel about idleness."

The old lady gasped, but Aurora's eyes smiled. Roarke took Minna's elbow in an oddly comforting gesture, and she fought back a hot wave of tears. If Davina hadn't pushed her into this. . . . "I wish nothing more than to be a success in my new home," she whispered, too late realizing that she'd voiced her thought. Roarke gave her a curious glance.

More guests welled inside, people she'd never met. She was grateful that none of her customers from London had been invited. Still, she found it difficult to keep the smile on her face when all she wanted to do was to hide somewhere from the disapproving, and outright icy stares.

"Keep your chin up," Roarke murmured in her ear. "If you let them intimidate you, you've lost everything. They'll come around eventually."

His encouragement helped to steady her, and she gave him a searching glance. Why had he bothered to reassure her? His eyes were hooded as he returned her gaze, but she could read nothing but aloof detachment in his expression.

A buffet dinner was served under a tent erected on the terrace, and the guests could eat at small tables set among the roses in the garden. Lanterns cast a soft light across the park.

An orchestra tuned their instruments in the large ballroom that had not been used since Roarke's grandfather's time. The guests gathered around the walls to watch as Roarke and Minna took to the gleaming parquet floor to open the ball with a waltz.

Roarke bowed coolly and pulled her into his arms. Minna felt as if touched by fire as he put one hand on her waist and gripped her fingers with the other. He swept her over the floor, and she followed, adjusting herself to his rhythm.

"You dance well—" she whispered.

"Flattery won't take you anywhere," he said with a smile that didn't reach his eyes.

"I don't stumble like I used to," she continued. "Do you remember the first night we met?" All she could think of was the intensity of his blue-green eyes, his strong grip on her fingers. She longed to melt against him, to hug him, to peel away every garment that lay between them and feel his naked skin against hers. But fifteen inches of air separated them, and Roarke's hostility.

"I'd rather not recall the most unfortunate day of my life." He gave another smile for the benefit of their guests. The fifteen inches of air might as well be a whole ocean, she thought unhappily. If only she could find a way to breach the rift between them. The dance seemed to last forever, and her cheeks grew hotter every minute. She was acutely aware of his male fragrance, and the powerful shape of his jaw so close to her that she could have touched it.

"I've been thinking," he said, breaking into her thoughts. "Davina will be leaving tomorrow. Since our marriage is nothing but a parody, perhaps we should keep separate households after this ball."

Minna gasped as her world, her hopes crumbled around her. She didn't trust her voice to speak.

"There's the townhouse in London, and then there's Meadow Hill. Since it originally belonged to the Wayland Seagers, perhaps you wouldn't mind living where your ancestors once lived. What do you say, Minerva?"

Anger rose like bile in her throat. "Tell the real reason for wanting me out of the way! You're ashamed of me, a former *dressmaker*, mistress of The Towers. You're a snob, Roarke, you can't bear the thought of my presence under your roof."

"That's not the reason, and you know it! You told

a string of lies without as much as batting an eyelash; you betrayed our love—the most sacred thing two people can experience together." He sucked in a deep breath. "You didn't even *hesitate* once. You're a cold and cruel woman, Minerva, and I can't forgive that."

"You don't know how deeply I examined my conscience. I had no other choice but to comply with Mr. Wylie."

His hand tightened around her waist, and he whirled faster. Soon the floor was a mass of spinning couples. Roarke's animosity had made Minna lose her rhythm, and she grew dizzy. Repeatedly, she collided with shoulders and elbows of their neighbors. After someone trod heavily on her toes, she tore away from Roarke and fled outside into the warm summer night. She leaned against the wall in the shadow of a pillar and searched her reticule for a handkerchief. Pressing it against her mouth she subdued her tears. The depth of her humiliation forced her to consider escaping from the estate this minute and never return.

A voice came from below the balustrade and the rosebushes.

"O, how this spring of love resembleth
The uncertain glory of an April day."

Startled, Minna stared at the old face that emerged like a full moon out of the greenery. She recognized Joe Tulsiter, the stable groom cum gardener, as he tipped his grimy cap. "Brought in more roses from Meadow Hill, my lady, but I see that I'm late," he said and disappeared into the night after handing her one dewy flower.

"What a strange man. He knows Shakespeare," she said aloud and wiped her eyes.

"He knows a lot more than Shakespeare."

Gasping, Minna whirled around and watched as

Roarke strode across the terrace toward her. He gripped her arms hard and swung her toward him. "Why did you dash off like that?"

Minna tore herself free. "Why should I dance with my enemy? I don't have to listen to your ravings."

He laughed hollowly. "Would you rather that I smile and tell you lies every time I see you?"

"I'd rather not speak to you—"

Anger hummed in the air between them.

His jaw hardened. "Minerva, think about my offer. At Meadow Hill you can live as you please. Once my venture with the stables is successful, I shall give you a generous allowance, and you can redecorate the house to your heart's desire."

"In other words, it'll be my luxurious prison." Minna's fingers knotted around her handkerchief, and misery fought with wrath inside her.

He shrugged, taking one step closer to her. "Call it what you will."

She thought for a moment that he'd been drawn to her, but it was the large, full-blown rose in her hand that beckoned him.

"Where would you rather live? What would you rather do?" he asked and inhaled the fragrance of the flower. "It doesn't matter to me what you choose to do."

"If I had my wish, I would like to return to London and work in my shop. Nothing keeps me here, and I'd rather go back to my past where I have real friends."

He took her shoulders in a hard grip and shook her. "You *cannot* be a shopwoman any longer! Just think what ridicule you would attract to the White-cliffe name."

"Ha! You don't care about honor! Your grandfather would surely turn in his grave if he knew that you married a shopwoman for her land. It doesn't matter what my roots are; I know only one life, the one I created for myself in London."

His grip tightened. "Foolish woman. Have you learned nothing?"

"Learned?" she spat. "I've learned that I don't want to be like you and your friends who think of nothing but material wealth. The likes of you constantly compare yourselves to each other to see how you measure up in riches." She wrenched away from him. "That's no life! That's bondage." She took a deep breath. "And now you're dictating my life, as if your own isn't enough."

He stood very still, his lips drawn into a tight line. Moonlight flooded the park, and Minna thought he looked tantalizingly handsome in the silver haze. She wanted to stroke his hair and beg that they start over, but this aloof man was not the same person who had made love to her in Davina's gazebo. If he'd spoken to her of love, of sharing his love with her and creating a family, her response would have been different. "We have nothing in common," she said coolly. "Get away from me!"

"Stubborn woman! If you're so against moving to Meadow Hill, then stay here." He rubbed his jaw. "In fact, if *I* move there, I'll be closer to the stables."

His words fueled her anger further. Anything that he suggested that would separate them seemed wrong. Now the possibility of him leaving loomed over her. The thought of not seeing him every day was unbearable.

She stepped closer to him, feeling the heat from his body. "You're a coward, Roarke. You don't dare to admit that you still love me, and you refuse the love I would so willingly give. I despise you!" She started to move away, but he caught her arm.

"Damn you, Minerva! What do you want? My heart on a platter, my innards ground into the dirt?

Won't you be satisfied until you've torn me completely apart?"

"Let go of me!" She tried to twist aside, but he pulled her up close, so close she could feel his warm breath on her face.

"What do you want?" he repeated. "My body? Like that other night when you gave yourself to me like a whore? Is that all?"

Minna was so angry that a crimson mist swam in her mind! "You're not man enough to admit your feelings, to admit that there's still hope for us."

He didn't reply, but neither did he loosen his grip. She continued, "By choosing to marry me, you followed your greed. I predict that you'll never change. You'll always go where profit beckons."

His hands encircled her waist and he hauled her very close so that only an inch separated their mouths. "You think you know everything, don't you, dear lady wife? But you really don't know me; you don't know a damn thing." Before she could protest he crushed her mouth with his own, robbing her of her breath. His tongue possessed her in a kiss that she could only describe as savagely hungry. It filled a profound need in her as he embraced her hard, lifting her inches off the ground. Sobbing deep in her throat, she wound her arms around his neck and clung to him, offering every ounce of sweetness she could muster in her response. It wasn't a struggle for her. Love poured out of her heart, and this was what she'd longed for since that time when she'd visited him in his bedroom. Not that this was the kiss of a tenderly loving man, it was a dizzying assault on all of her senses by a desperate man.

As the pressure of his mouth finally eased, she drew a ragged breath. If he set her down, she would surely collapse on the ground.

"The . . . guests will be . . . wondering where we

298

are," she said, her voice robbed of its strength.

"So let them," he growled. "I'm not a coward, Minerva. The fact that I kissed you won't change my opinion of you. You're still a liar and a trollop, and I treated you accordingly."

"Why, you!" She raised her hand to slap him, but he gripped her wrist and swung her arm aside.

Their wills fought each other for a long moment and the surge of their longing heightened between them. Minna could barely breathe as she gazed into his deep eyes. What went through his mind? Did he have the same intensity of feeling for her as she had for him? She wished she could read his thoughts. "At least I dare to say that I love you," she whispered.

"Cheap words."

Roarke memorized every detail of her face, the light halo of curls silvered by the moon, the cupid bow of her lips that bewitched him as always, the long lashes that cast a shadow on her pale skin. Soon he wouldn't be able to see her at all, and this was the way he wanted to remember her, her eyes flashing, every inch of her alive with emotion.

"God, woman, what are you doing to me!" He kissed her again, gentler this time, savoring the silky texture of her mouth and remembering the imprint of her soft lips. Like sweet wine. . . . He groaned and molded her closer. "I hate you," he whispered, but the words held no conviction. This was a night of magic, and he ought to give in to his urgent need to make love to her. Here, somewhere, hidden in the garden. Morning might only bring more misery. As he lifted her up into his arms to carry her down the steps and into the park, he heard voices by the doors.

"I thought I saw him go outside," a lady said, and Roarke recognized Lady Barton's voice. "Isn't that him there?"

Roarke sighed and set Minna down. She wobbled

and he placed an arm around her waist to support her. He turned toward the guests that had come out on the terrace.

"Mel, Lady Barton, I'm glad you could join us," he said with icy politeness.

"We're a bit late, alas," said Melchior Harding. "I had a spot of trouble with one of my horses."

Roarke frowned. "Nothing serious I hope?"

Lady Barton snorted. "Don't play the innocent with us, Roarke. Tokayer has a fever, perhaps inflammation of the lungs; she got ill after your stable groom rode her into a sweat, and I'm sure you were behind some nefarious scheme to put an end to the competition. Melchior sat up all night with that mare."

"I've never competed with Mel concerning the horses, you should know better than that, Edna. In fact, I'd hoped that we could put an end to our hostilities, but as things stand I'd say it's impossible." He took Minna's hand and led her toward the house. "Let's return to the ballroom."

Lady Barton muttered behind him, and Roarke felt a chill along his back. Did Mel really believe he had something to do with the illness of his champion mare? Damn the man! Roarke angled a glance at him, but Mel didn't look at him in return. Mel's shoulders slumped, and his face was creased with worry and pale with fatigue.

"You ought to stay with Tokayer at a time like this, Mel."

"Joe Tulsiter has visited Linkwood Cottage several times. He'll cure Tokayer if anyone can. If he fails, then—" Mel broke off, and Minerva loosened her hand from Roarke's grip.

"Don't worry, Melchior. It's good to get away from your vigil for a few hours." She slipped her arm through his, and Roarke felt a poisonous stab of jealousy.

Mel gave her a grateful smile and patted her hand. "My whole future hangs on this filly. If she dies, it'll be the end of my business."

Roarke gave Minerva a glare, then surrendered to his host duties. He offered Lady Barton his arm, which she refused. She joined Davina, and Roarke heard her complain anew of poor Mel's predicament.

Minerva sat next to Mel on a sofa and made sure that the lackeys served him a plate of delicacies and a glass of wine. Wondering if his wife had sided with his competition, Roarke watched them from the shadows of a bay window. He couldn't bear to see her warm smile, and the gentle pressure of her hand on Mel's arm. Still, he couldn't take his eyes off her. A longing so deep to hold her in his arms came over him that he couldn't move. Was it possible to love anyone as much as he loved Minerva without going demented? He was pulled between the desire to confess his love and carry her off to his bed for the night, and the knowledge that she had betrayed him.

How would he find a way to trust her? There was also the worry of procreation; what if she would carry his child, what if she already was carrying their child? The thought made him cold all over—yet, something had softened inside him since he met her. He rarely thought of Thomas's death now, and perhaps he could live with the fear of another child born with the strain that brought blindness. Guilt was his greatest problem at this point. Could he go through marriage and all it entailed knowing that he carried on the flaw of the Harding family? Still, the doctors had said that not every child would be tainted. Perhaps none. At that thought a surge of hope flowed through him.

As if she'd read his thoughts, Minerva suddenly

301

looked up, straight into his eyes. Warmth and yearning simmered between them, a flash of understanding. He read a promise in her eyes, and he turned abruptly away.

Even if they could resume their intimacy and live as man and wife, how could he ever trust her? No, better stay away from her, reevaluate the situation, but it would be the most difficult test he'd ever faced. However hard he tried to deny it, he still loved her madly. No reasoning could change his feelings, and he hated himself for his weakness.

Chapter Twenty-five

Minna noticed the jealousy in her husband's eyes, and it made her spirits rise. She still had the power to touch his feelings, so perhaps all was not lost.

She spent an hour with Melchior, trying to reassure him before he returned home to his sick mare. The guests were enjoying the ball; that much was clear from their laughter and lively participation in the dancing.

She rose to go in search of Roarke who had disappeared into the garden, but as she crossed the room, Aurora Bishop stopped her with an urgent, "Lady Whitecliffe."

"What's the matter?" Minna viewed the pale face beside her.

"I wanted someone to know about my plans. It's an awfully big step." She choked on the last word, and Minna pulled her aside. "What are you trying to tell me?"

Aurora's eyes were large pools of fear, but excitement colored her voice as she spoke. "I've decided to run away with Zach. My aunt will never allow us to marry, so we're heading south—tonight. We're going to France where we'll marry as soon as I am of age, which will be in three months." She clutched Minna's

303

hand. "I wanted you to know. There'll be an uproar of course, but I don't care. I love Zach."

Minna smiled grimly, remembering the day when he'd locked her up with Roarke at Sun Hollow. "He's a jackanapes."

Aurora nodded. "That's what I love about him. You never know what he'll do next." She paused. "I understand that you're angry with him, but he only wants what's best for his cousin, and you. He told me that you'll be the one to pull Roarke back to his old self; you'll give him happiness."

"Hmm, Zach is mighty sure of himself, isn't he?"

"Please forgive him this once. I'm sure he acted in everyone's best interest when he abducted you from London. He asked me in no uncertain terms to deliver his deepest apologies. He's waiting for me outside."

Minna studied the earnest face before her. "Very well, I forgive him. For your sake." She squeezed Aurora's hand. "Now hurry before you change your mind. I won't say a word to Lady Herrington until you've reached the coast safely."

Aurora's glorious smile touched her, and she realized that the young woman was deeply in love. Aurora kissed her cheek and hurried into the darkness in a flutter of petticoats.

"Be happy," Minna said, but only the wind heard her.

She had no more opportunity to search for Roarke as the guests slowly started to leave. As soon as she had a moment to herself, she went to Roarke's study and knocked. No answer; he wasn't there. Loneliness filled her. If Mel and Lady Barton hadn't arrived, perhaps she would have found a way to Roarke's heart . . .

As she returned to the foyer, a scream rent the air.

"That sounded like Lady Herrington," Minna said to Kitson, remembering Aurora's plan.

"Yes, my lady. I saw Miss Bishop and Mr. Gordon leave earlier."

"Please keep that information to yourself, Kitson."

Lady Herrington had swooned at the edge of the dance floor. The music had silenced and the remaining guests had clustered around the prostrate woman. They parted for Minna, who knelt beside the older lady.

"Send one of the lackeys after Rosie and my hartshorn bottle," she said to Kitson who was kneeling on the other side of Lady Herrington.

Rosie arrived within two minutes with the desired article, and soon Lady Herrington revived. "Wha— where am I?" she asked.

"At The Towers, Lady Herrington," Minna explained and placed a pillow that someone offered under the old lady's head.

"Where's Aurora?" The lady sat up with some difficulty. "Do you hear me? Where's my niece?"

"I don't know," Minna said. "Last time I saw her, she was dancing with your neighbor."

Lady Herrington's eyes bored into her. "You're lying! I know she's gone off with that scoundrel, Mr. Gordon."

To avoid telling another falsehood, Minna pinched her lips shut. She looked up and saw that Roarke had returned. She sent him a helpless glance, and he stared at her suspiciously. Another lie? he seemed to ask.

"Where's Mr. Gordon? Find him if he's here," Lady Herrington demanded as Roarke helped her to her feet. He carried her to a giltwood sofa along the wall and set her down against a heap of pillows.

"Calm yourself, Lady Herrington. Your niece probably went out for a breath of air."

"*Where* is that cousin of yours, Whitecliffe? Is he with her?"

The ladies fluttered around her, and Davina, who'd returned to the ballroom, took control of the situation. She pushed Roarke and Minna toward the door. "Find them."

As Minna was in no hurry to go outside, she noticed that Davina looked disheveled and very happy. Leverett Epcott standing by the door, looked equally happy.

"Don't dawdle," Roarke said between clenched teeth.

"They are gone," Minna said as the night engulfed them. "On their way to France. Aurora told me herself. They mean to get married once she's of age."

"Damned thoughtless!" Roarke swore. "Why did they have to be in such a hurry?"

"Perhaps they realized it might be their only chance for happiness. God only knows what husband Lady Herrington had in mind for her charge."

Roarke rubbed his jaw. "It looks like I'll have to ride after them. The old dragon will demand that of me once she discovers that the couple has fled." He sent her a cautious glance. "Why didn't you tell me earlier?"

Sensing another battle, Minna squared her shoulders. "I had other worries. Besides, they asked me not to alert Lady Herrington."

He dragged his hand through his hair. "You could have told me."

"You don't really mean to stop them, do you? Find an excuse."

"No, I'm not going after them. However much I disapprove of Zach's way of managing his life, I believe he deserves some happiness with the woman he loves."

"So do you," Minna said and stood on her toes to kiss him.

Roarke pulled away before she could touch him,

but he wasn't angry. "I'll take Lady Herrington home. Be back in an hour."

Minna filled with longing as she watched him return to the ballroom, head high, shoulders proud. Would they ever find a path of complete understanding together? She prayed they would, but doubt poisoned her hopes.

Chapter Twenty-six

Roarke rode back toward The Towers deep in thought. He hoped that Zach and Aurora had made it safely to the coast, and he wished them all the luck. Something that Lady Herrington had said preyed on his mind.

"I've always kept Aurora under my wing, making sure the filth of this world would not touch her," the old lady had said. "She would lie to me and try to leave the house when I wasn't watching. That's thanklessness for you, Lord Whitecliffe."

"Surely Aurora is a very well-bred lady," he'd replied. "She wouldn't do anything to besmirch her reputation — or yours. In my opinion, she's all kindness. By lying, she was perhaps trying to protect you."

"But she has brought shame to our house! Always sneaking away to meet that Gordon fellow when my back was turned." Lady Herrington had sniffed righteously and pulled her shawl closer over her shoulders. "I could never trust her."

When Lady Herrington had uttered those words, Roarke had realized she echoed his own feelings about Minerva.

As he rode along he compared his wife with Aurora and found that they were cut out of the same mold. Aurora was kind and thoughtful, and loving. So was Minerva. As if his perception had been adjusted to a different angle during his conversation with Lady Herrington, he could see now why Minerva had told the lies and connived him into loving her. She'd had no choice, just like Aurora had had no choice where Lady Herrington was concerned. Aurora had been a prisoner and knew that only falsehoods and evasions would keep her from evoking Lady Herrington's wrath. The fact was, under different circumstances, he was convinced that neither Aurora nor Minerva would resort to lying to get their way. Aurora, whose eyes shone with innocence, had been *forced* to lie—just as Mr. Wylie had forced Minerva into her desperate tactics.

She had done it to protect the people that depended on her. For once he could see the situation wholly through her eyes, and it dawned on him that her feelings toward him were true, not just some means to an end. His heartbeat escalated at the thought. All he'd been able to see so far was her deceit; he'd been unable to understand her struggle to save everything she'd worked for, and that she hadn't been out to ruin him.

He shook his head in wonder. She'd told him, but he'd failed to listen. Now he had to rise above his mistrust and anger, and start anew. Hadn't she tried her damndest to fill her new role at The Towers? She had courage and verve. What a fool he'd been!

He galloped back to The Towers, yearning to speak with her. When he arrived, he discovered that she hadn't slept in her bed. He awakened Kitson, only to discover that she'd ordered the carriage after the ball, and left without divulging her destination.

"Damn! Where did she go?"

Kitson scratched his head. "I don't know, my

lord, but I believe she'll return. She didn't take any luggage."

The sun stood high in the sky as Minna wended her way through the tall weeds at Meadow Hill. She felt dull and slow for the lack of sleep, and a headache pulsed above her eyes. She worried about Roarke's reaction to her sudden move, but aside from that she felt physically unwell. This morning she'd been so queasy that she couldn't eat her breakfast, and Rosie had given her a thorough scrutiny. Minna knew what it meant. It was perhaps too early to tell, but she might be in the family way. The thought both exhilarated and frightened her. What would Roarke say if her suspicion turned out to be true?

Sighing, she shielded her eyes against the sun and looked at the old building where she had been born. She wouldn't mind giving birth to a child of her own. The thought filled her with elation, and her spirits rose. In fact, a child, or children, would give her something to build her future on now that her shop was gone. She'd never thought about her life in those terms before. Minna Smith, mother. She smiled and skipped along the path to the front door. Every day she got more used to her new life, and she saw the possibilities rather than the obstacles. She would make a home for herself here, and she was beginning today after spending an uneasy night under the musty covers of the massive bed in the master bedroom.

Joe Tulsiter had evidently been here and cleared a path around the house as if he'd known that she was moving in.

The air in the rooms was musty, and very still. She opened the windows and flung back the shutters to let the sun inside. The floors had been swept recently, but dust lay thick on every flat surface, and the Holland covers were gray with grime. It had been a long time since anyone cared for this house, Minna thought and went in search of an apron and a broom. A practical task to concentrate on would make her mind stop revolving around Roarke constantly.

She whistled a tune, relieved that she could drop her role of countess for the entire morning. At The Towers everyone expected her to act in a certain way, and in fear of doing something wrong, she hardly dared to start any tasks. Here she was again Minna Smith, her own person.

After pulling off her tight-fitting riding jacket and covering herself with a voluminous apron and mobcap, she opened the back door in the kitchen and threw out a set of very dusty chairs. First of all she would scrub the walls, she thought and viewed the dirty plaster, and then the grooms could white-wash them. The oak shelving looked sturdy, and the pantry was spacious.

She glanced at the watch on the lapel of her jacket. Noon already. Where was Rosie? She should have been back long ago. A twinge of uneasiness went through her as she wondered what Roarke would say when he discovered that she'd left without a word. She dismissed the thought with a sniff.

Sighing, she pushed a stray tendril of hair back under the mobcap and began sweeping the floor. Dust whirled in clouds around her and she sneezed. She had to take a break and go outside. Just as she emerged, she thought she saw a movement at the edge of the woods. She stared at the spot, but everything was quiet. Probably a deer, she thought.

She returned to the house after admiring a cluster of lilies growing close to the wall. Another hour went by in a flurry of dust, and she returned to the front of the house and looked toward the drive. What had delayed Rosie?

She admired the spacious front parlors that had ornate plaster moldings and faultless parquet floors. The deep embrasures gave the house a cozy look, and she had already fallen in love with the old building. She couldn't wait to restore it to its former splendor.

When she returned to the kitchen, she noticed a shadow filling the doorway. She gasped, clasping a hand to her chest.

"Sorry I frightened you," said Melchior Harding pleasantly. "I was out riding and noticed that the door was open, so I came to investigate."

"How's your mare?" she asked as her heartbeat quieted down.

"Almost fully recovered. Joe Tulsiter gave her a thorough examination. She's in foal, as much is clear." He rubbed his hands together. "I'm so excited about that."

"Glad to hear it. By the way, did you see Rosie on the road this morning?"

He shook his head. "No . . . but Roarke rode over to Linkwood Cottage very early this morning. I thought he came by the stables to check on Tokayer, but strangely enough, he asked for you. Why, I wonder?"

"I didn't tell him I had moved to Meadow Hill." Minna dusted off a chair and offered it to him. "I wish I could serve a cup of tea, but there's nothing here." As he shook his head, she added, "If I may be as bold as to ask, what is your quarrel with Roarke?"

"Oh, it's the same old thing. The stables, the inheritance. Grandfather left me nothing, and Roarke wants to give me alms. I won't take them. What

Grandfather didn't plan to give me freely, I won't take second hand. Roarke is trying to ease my path, but he has to use the funds on The Towers. We've argued over it forever it seems, but I don't hold a grudge. I admit I'm worried about the stables, though."

He smiled, and Minna's heart lurched. He looked a lot like her husband, or the way Roarke would look in fifteen years.

"The horses are close to my heart. I've always wanted a foal from Tokayer."

"I can understand that, yet Roarke said it was dangerous."

Silence spread in the room, and Minna sensed that Melchior tried to hide something as he refused to look at her. Finally he spoke, "Roarke has always been fair to me, but perhaps where his horses are concerned—especially Aladdin—he's terribly jealous. He doesn't want me to have any part of that horse."

Minna furrowed her brow in thought. "You mean he doesn't want Aladdin to sire any foals?"

Melchior nodded miserably. "Not with Tokayer, no. Perhaps you could convince him there's no harm done—"

Minna shook her head. "He won't listen to me. He never has."

Melchior shrugged. "We'd better drop the subject."

Minna wiped the dirty silver surface of a wall mirror. "You never married?" she asked.

"Lady Barton put me off women with her harping ways, but if I'd met someone like you ten years ago, I might have considered wedlock. No, I'm too comfortable as it is." He rose, towering over her. "I must go." He gave a chuckle. "By Jove, that mobcap looks very fetching on you, m'dear."

He dusted some cobwebs away from the lace around her face, and Minna sneezed.

"What are you doing with my wife?" came Roarke's angry voice from the hallway that connected the kitchen with the rest of the house.

Melchior's hand hesitated in midair, then he dropped it to his side. "Oh, there you are, coz." He gestured toward Minna. "This lady was worried about you."

"I can see that," Roarke said icily. "So much so that she courts another as soon as my back is turned."

"Don't be ridiculous, Roarke," Minna said coolly. "Melchior came to investigate the open door, thinking that thieves had broken in."

The storm died from Roarke's eyes. He slumped on the chair that Melchior had vacated. "I'm indebted to you, coz." He sighed. "I had to spend hours trying to calm Lady Herrington last night. At least Zach and Aurora got away."

"I take it you didn't go after them," Mel said.

"No, I hope they arrived safely in France. If not, they soon will. There's nothing that Lady Herrington can do about it. She was hysterical, and the doctor didn't attend until late." He gave a huge yawn. "The more I think about it, the more I realize that Zach did the right thing to elope. Lady Herrington would never have let Aurora out of her clutches."

"Yes . . . Zach always had good judgment. He always takes an opportunity that comes along," Mel said, vacillating in the middle of the room. He turned the hat in his hands. "You might as well know, coz. Tokayer is well, and the foal is well."

Roarke's face darkened. "I'm relieved to hear it, yet you're taking an awful risk with that mare. I don't like it one bit!"

Mel was about to say something, but he changed his mind. "Right you are. Goodbye." He gave a lopsided smile, and Minna waved as he left the house.

Roarke looked up at her with an air of apprehension. "I thought you and he—"

"Sshh, I don't care to hear it. Mel is a good man, and I don't want to be a bone of contention between you." Tense, she watched him, wondering what he would do next. He didn't seem at all angry with her.

Roarke stood abruptly and lifted the broom from her hand. "You're not a bone. And now my lady *maid,* let's go outside before my nose gets clogged with all this dust. I need to talk to you."

Minna let him pull her outside, and laughter bubbled over her lips. She sensed a new lightness in him. "I thought you would be angry with me for moving here so abruptly."

He hoisted her up and swung her around. "So, you're happy to see me? You really worried about what I would think?"

"I'm happy now. To tell you the truth, I worried dreadfully."

"I'm glad to hear it." He set her down, then viewed his dusty coat. "Now look what you've done."

"You lifted me up, and got dusty, and . . . I'd like you to do it again."

Her heart fluttered madly as the charming wickedness she hadn't seen for so long returned to his eyes. "You don't have to ask me twice," he said, and encircled her derrière and lifted her high above him. She braced her hands against his shoulders and met his smiling gaze.

"Welcome home to Dusty Cottage," she said as he slid her along his tall frame until she stood on her toes, breathless with expectation.

"I love this old house," he whispered.

"So do I. I felt at home the moment I stepped across the threshold. It's as if it has a life of its own, a soul."

"And The Towers doesn't?"

"There's a formality about your castle that daunts the most reckless spirit."

He sighed. "Yes . . . this was my home until I had to shoulder the burden of the Whitecliffe earldom." He wet his fingertip and rubbed her jaw. "You have a smudge of dirt here."

Unable to take her eyes off his dear face, she lifted her mouth to his. "Kiss me."

With a groan, he complied with her request, and as passion leaped wildly in her stomach, she had a sudden urge to cry. She'd hoped for this when he had nothing but anger to give her.

The sound of a distant rifle shot echoed among the hills, pulling her from her concentration on him.

"What was that?" she asked.

Roarke listened, and another shot followed farther away. "Perhaps Lord Eccelston next door is shooting pigeons. He frequently does."

"Hideous pastime," said Minna, who hated hunting of every kind.

"Come," he demanded and took her hand. He brought her to a clearing not far from the edge of the wood. A quiet stream flowed between grassy banks, and butterflies fluttered among the wild daisies and bluebells.

"I used to fish here when I was a boy," he explained and pulled her down on a soft green spot where sunlight reached between the tall lime trees.

She held out her arms to him, and he sank down on her, pressing her into the ground. "I'm so relieved to see you happy again."

He looked deeply into her eyes. "That's what I want to talk about. I've come to the conclusion that I've been a fool where you're concerned."

When she tried to speak, he placed a finger over her mouth.

"Shh, Minerva, let me finish. I couldn't see your side of the story, the enormous struggle you had to survive after your parents died. All I could see was my own hurt, your betrayal of our love. You *did* betray, but you had no other choice. Your shop and your people were the only things you had, and you'd put every ounce of yourself into it."

She nodded, unable to stop tears from gathering in her eyes.

"You couldn't lose it, could you, Minna? Not for all the gold in the world, and not for me."

"No . . . but I seriously thought about letting the shop go, but then I knew I couldn't abandon my workers. They were my family." She stroked back the burnished hair from his eyes. "Like I hope we'll be someday."

"I pray that you won't lie to me again, Minerva."

"Never. *Never!*" She choked on the word, and he brushed away a tear from the corner of her eye.

"I feel I've risen above my resentment. Let's start over. In due time, we'll forget all about Mr. Wylie and his tricks."

"Yes. I'm eternally sorry for the pain I caused you, I really am." When he smiled, the heavy burden of guilt fell from her shoulders. "I love you," she whispered.

If there were any sharp twigs or pebbles digging into her back, she didn't notice. She only saw the curve of his lips, the light in his eyes, and the smile, that special smile that had always endeared him to her.

His tongue moved leisurely along the moist walls of her mouth, and she gave herself up to the melting, sinking feeling in her stomach. "Oh . . ." she whispered, "I need you so much."

He unbuttoned her simple blouse and pulled it down over her shoulders. "I need you too, darling."

She stiffened momentarily. "More than you needed Thomas?"

He looked solemnly into her eyes. "Yes, more than that. I felt responsible for him; I loved him desperately. He needed me, no one ever did before or since—until you came into my life."

"It's different, isn't it?" she asked, curling her fingers through his crisp waves.

He nodded, then began a slow seduction of her senses. It began with the skin on her shoulders, moved down to cover her breasts, and she wondered if she would ever feel such exquisite torture again at his touch. She had anticipated this since he'd kissed her on the terrace on the previous night, and now when it was happening, she couldn't get enough.

A slight roughness on his jaw raked over the tender skin on her stomach, and she could not remember how he'd removed her clothing. He nibbled a trail down to where her body joined with her thighs, and her whole world swirled in a golden confusion as he nuzzled the secret place of her womanhood. A rich pleasure like wine flowed in her blood, heightening every perception, bringing her toward the tightening spiral of ecstasy.

She moaned and dug her fingertips into the smooth muscles of his shoulders. Everywhere she touched there was naked flesh, not a chaste waistcoat, nor a stiff shirt. She had yearned for this to happen, she'd longed for his embrace.

"Roarke," she whispered, "please, don't delay."

He stopped his exploration of her body and

looked at her. "Why be in a hurry to leave paradise?"

His tongue made a moist trail on the inside of her thigh, and she lifted her hips toward him, to get closer, to offer herself to him.

Her every nerve caught the excitement, and his hands molding the curves of her body, fueled her desire until she was filled with such sweetness that she could neither think nor speak.

He moved up over her, pressing her into the grass. Gazing lovingly into her eyes, he parted her thighs and sank himself deeply into her. He covered her face with kisses, and she wound her fingers through his hair and kissed his hard jaw, his ear, the strong column of his throat. His scent intoxicated her, like it always had. This was the very essence of him, and she felt as if it melded with hers until they became one body that was slowly and relentlessly cresting the wave of ecstasy.

He moved faster, a sudden urgency filling him and it bore her along the wave that pushed her into a sea of rapture. With a cry, she wound her legs around his hips, locking him within her as he spilled his seed into her. He collapsed on top of her and there was wetness in his eyes.

Her heart overflowing with love, she kissed him where his shoulder met the throat, and caressed the springy hair at the nape of his neck.

He propped himself on his elbows and looked deeply into her eyes. "I suppose this was our real wedding day — or 'night.' For once we aren't arguing."

Sunlight gilded his hair and lent a golden sheen to his face.

"Yes," she said, "but I became yours when you made love to me that first time in Davina's gazebo."

His brow creased. "I'd rather not think about

that period of my life. I'd rather we start over."

"Yes . . . that would be for the best." A light veil fell over their happiness, it seemed, and Minna held him tight. Their newfound happiness was still too fragile to be set to the test. "At least this is a start," she said more to herself than to him.

"Yes, and a lovely beginning." He blew gently into her ear. "You always had a way of burrowing under my skin and haunting me." He raised himself slowly and rolled aside. Picking some grass from her hair, he said, "In a way, I'm glad for Mr. Wylie's revenge. He made our paths cross. Without you I wouldn't have found this depth of satisfaction. Portia would have been delighted that I found a way to your door."

"Tell me more about my mother."

Roarke pulled her up and brushed grass from her backside. "Though I can hardly take my eyes off you, I'd say we'd better get dressed. You never know who might decide to take a ride through the woods."

She laughed and curved her arms around his neck. "How shocking if we were discovered! There would be no end of gossip—about the earl and the *trollop* he married."

"Don't talk like that," he admonished. They embraced tightly and Minna felt the beginnings of desire awaken again. But she released him and bent to retrieve her petticoats, her batiste blouse, and her green riding skirt. Dust fell out of the folds of the thick material. They dressed in silence, then Roarke took her hand and led her down to the stream. Minna sat down on a tussock and dangled her grimy feet in the water.

Roarke folded his legs cross-wise beside her and stared into the blue-brown water. "I relish one special memory of your mother, Minna. I must have been about ten years old, and my father had heard about some prank I pulled at Eton. I can't even remember what it was, but it probably involved this arithmetic teacher that hated me as much as I hated him. Anyway, Father meted out the punishment of ten blows with a strap on my backside. Portia never dared to stand up to him, and he got more vicious with age. Father was blind at that time, so he ordered one of the grooms to take me out to the stables and deliver my punishment. Portia bribed the groom to pretend to beat me; then she took me to her rooms and let me rest there until Father had calmed down." Roarke smiled at Minna. "Your mother had the softest of hearts. I don't think she ever forgave herself for marrying my father, still, she treated me with love and respect." He looked into the distance. "Without her, I don't know what would have become of me. She kept me on a straight path. I didn't know your father, but Portia always mentioned him with love. She didn't love Father. He was wicked, and he never accepted his blindness."

Minna pulled out a long piece of grass and wound it around her index finger. "I've noticed that your eyesight has worsened this summer." She paused and stared at him intently. It mattered to their future what he would tell her.

"It seems to be getting worse faster than it used to. Sometimes I'm very angry, sometimes resigned. There's nothing I can do; there isn't any cure. I've tried some herbal concoctions that Joe Tulsiter's mother made while she was alive, but they didn't help. The pressure in the eyeball destroys the part where the optic nerve meets the eye. The vision loss is gradual."

He leaned over and touched her cheek. "I'm glad I had the chance to see your beauty. I will always remember you young and attractive, even when you turn eighty."

Minna laughed when she felt like crying. He looked at her through the brightness of tears.

"I'll always remember this day." His voice was choked with emotion and he buried his face against her shoulder. She wished she could take his pain into herself, but this was his lonely struggle. She stroked his hair.

"I'm sorry," he said after a painful moment that seemed to stretch into eternity. Minna would always remember it as his "taking farewell" moment, the time when he'd bared his secret pain to her.

"I've had thirty years of seeing the beauty of this world. Some people never see it."

Tears gathered in her eyes, and she wiped them away surreptitiously. "Seeing is something I've always taken for granted," she whispered.

He caressed away her tangled hair from her face. "You shall see for me."

Laughing and sobbing at the same time, she hugged him. "You can count on me." She could picture herself grow old and contented beside him.

"Portia would have been pleased," he repeated. "I'm sure she worried about your future, but knowing Father, he probably forbid her to contact you. She never mentioned you once."

Minna thought about the woman who had so patiently acted as her mother. "Portia's loss was another woman's gain. The woman whom I called Mother truly loved me. She was a lady of few words, but when she was happy, she used to call me her greatest blessing."

"That's a compliment if I ever heard one."

"Roarke, am I right to surmise that you've completely forgiven me?" She tensed as she waited for his answer.

He smiled and patted her cheek. "Yes . . . as long as you don't lie to me again, I shall forget the sorry business of the past."

Just as she gathered her thoughts to broach the subject of the Meadow Hill acres, voices could be heard at the outskirts of the woods.

"Lord Whitecliffe? Looord Whiiitecliiiffe?" came a chorus of voices. They sounded like the servants at The Towers.

"What's the matter now?" Roarke muttered with a frown. He rose and brushed off his trousers, righted his neckcloth, and strode toward the sound.

Minna jumped up and followed while stuffing her loose hair into the mobcap.

One of the footmen came running through the brush. "We've been looking everywhere for you, my lord." He stopped in front of them and brushed perspiration from his forehead.

"What has happened?"

Minna found herself holding her breath as the servant continued, "Joe Tulsiter sent a message from the stables. Aladdin has been shot. He's dead."

Chapter Twenty-seven

The noble animal lay lifeless in the paddock, a pool of blood slowly forming around him.

Minna's heart constricted at the sight, and Roarke fell to his knees by the still head and touched the gleaming mane. "Blast it all! By all that is vile—" he swore and drove his fist into the ground.

His sorrow tore at Minna, and she touched his shoulder gently. He slumped, and she could hear a string of oaths as he stared at the noble head of the Arabian.

"Damn!" He stood, his eyes closed as he fought for composure. Clenching his hands into fists, he turned to Joe Tulsiter and said through stiff lips, "You might as well bury him. Then I want to speak with everyone who was on the premises when this happened."

Minna watched his eyes clouding with sorrow. She felt utterly helpless against this new problem that would have far-reaching effects on their lives.

"Were any strangers here this afternoon?" she asked Joe.

He pushed his cap back and looked at her with

calm eyes. "Only Mr. Melchior. He wanted to discuss Tokayer's recovery."

Roarke's head jerked up. "Mel? Why didn't he tell me he was going here when we met? When did he leave the stables?"

"About an hour ago. He took the shortcut through the woods to Linkwood Cottage."

Roarke rubbed his jaw. He looked ashen, and his eyes began to seethe with suppressed anger. "It looks like I don't know my cousin very well. Zach always warned me about him."

Minna inhaled deeply and gripped his arm. "You don't suspect Melchior of shooting your stallion?" she said under her breath.

"Who else? I trust my staff. I've never had any reason to complain." He turned to Joe Tulsiter who hadn't moved an inch. "Who's responsible for this, Joe?"

The old man's face didn't change expression. "I don't know. At the time of the shooting, I was sound asleep. The lads said the shots came from the woods, and they went in search of the hunter immediately. On foot, they were too slow to catch him."

"One thing's for sure. A hunter wouldn't mistake a black stallion for a deer. Someone deliberately chose to end Aladdin's life with a well-placed shot."

"It wasn't Melchior," Minna said, worrying about Roarke's next move. If he went in search of his cousin and blamed him for the shooting, there was no telling what Melchior would do.

Roarke gave her a furious glare. "Why are you so sure about that? What reason do you have to protect him? You don't know anything about him."

"No," she said, her bottom lip trembling. "But he's not a violent, scheming man. He's kindhearted." She grasped Roarke's arm harder as if to imprint that fact on him, but he shook it off.

325

"Mel is good-natured and easy-going. That's the character he chooses to portray, but perhaps he hides a sly, secretive side underneath."

Minna couldn't believe she heard him speak those words. Anger swelled in her. "You're wrong! How can you speak with such lack of trust for your own cousin?"

Roarke gave her a molten glare and pushed her aside. "I would be quiet if I were you."

"Or I will have a taste of your wrath?" she chided, her anger getting the better of her.

Roarke muttered something and strode toward the stables. The day had turned gloomy and overcast, and in the distance, heavy rain clouds were creeping across the sky.

Minna felt a sudden chill through the material of her riding habit. Hanging her head, she went after him, but she knew he wouldn't listen to her. It was as if the earlier part of the day had been nothing but a dream. While Roarke questioned the stable hands, Joe offered to drive her back to The Towers and she accepted gratefully.

Roarke didn't return from the stables until late in the evening. Rain poured endlessly from a black sky, and a strong wind beat the rain against the windows.

A flare of hope entered Minna's heart as she heard Roarke's voice in the foyer. She put aside her embroidery and went into the hallway to greet him. They exchanged a long, searching look.

"It could only have been Mel. He was seen riding through the woods just after the shots," he said and headed toward the study.

"I don't believe it." Minna waited for him to reply, but he said nothing as he closed the door behind him. She turned on her heel and stalked in the opposite direction. She could have sworn that Mel-

326

chior was genuinely fond of Roarke. Could she have been so totally wrong? She'd always prided herself on being a good judge of character.

Her conviction of Mel's innocence was driving a new shaft between her and Roarke. An hour later she realized that she had to go to him, try to bridge this new gap. Bone-weary, she walked to his study and knocked on the door.

No answer came, and she peered inside. He was asleep with his left cheek leaning against an open book. Everywhere she looked there were papers and books. It had been some time since she'd entered his favorite room, but the stacks and stacks of literature appalled her. Viewing them and their metaphysical titles, she began to worry about Roarke's frame of mind. This spoke of desperation. Only once had he discussed matters of life and death with her, when they had been close, before Mr. Wylie's revelation. She hadn't known Roarke's depth of desperation, and now she wondered if he was involved in some sort of mad race with time.

She wanted to touch him, caress an unruly wave away from his forehead, but she couldn't bring herself to reach out. She knew the race involved his eyesight. Sometimes he walked into obstacles that were in plain sight. Perhaps there was more to his search.

Her heart constricted with understanding. This man wanted to do so much, see so much, and there wasn't much time left. I'll suggest reading aloud, she thought, but it would be an inadequate offer in this momentous task he'd set before him. The meaning of life.

She climbed gingerly among the litter of books, realizing that he must have shoved them to the floor in anger. He rarely let the servants clean this room, as he didn't want them to move his material. *Had he come any closer to the truth?* she wondered.

He looked exhausted, the lines between his nose and mouth deep with disappointment. Even in his rest, he had an air of desolation. He had loved that horse very much, and now all his dreams had crumbled.

She couldn't bear to awaken him. Perhaps his pain would be less tomorrow. She closed the door quietly behind her.

Roarke's neck ached as he tried to right his head. He groaned and rotated his stiff shoulders. Darkness lay heavy in the room except for the oil lamp that gave a weak glow across the table. Kitson must have entered and lighted it, Roarke thought, and massaged his wrists.

Sadness sat leaden in his chest at the thought of his dead stallion. By God, whoever had perpetrated the crime would not get away, he thought, and saw a fleeting image of Mel in his mind. If Mel had done this, he deserved the worst. "Even if it's illegal, I'll call him out. And the duel will be to death."

Roarke heaved a deep sigh. Where in the world would he find another stallion like Aladdin? He would have to make another exhausting trip to the Arab countries, or perhaps one less tedious trip to Ireland. He'd heard about a champion at a stable outside Dublin that shared Aladdin's noble ancestry. The problem was money. Where would he find the funds to sink into another Arabian? His plans for owning a stable of champion racehorses had been overturned before it started.

He pulled on his spectacles and glanced down at the page in front of him. It was a book of quotations, and he read:

* * *

328

"In the still eye of chaos
Above the riot of the storm
Within the silence of Silence
Lies the soul."

Soul! He laughed out loud and hurled the book across the room. No matter how hard he tried to find what these lofty words described, he felt that he was getting further away from the solution every day. His head had been filled with hundreds of different theories from the religious to the mystical, from the lives of saints to the dark side of black magic. Nothing spoke to him. Nothing gave him the spark that said, "explore me, I'm what you're looking for."

He couldn't remember a time when he'd felt more uninspired, *defeated*. His head weighed at least one hundred pounds, and his limbs were leaden weights that he had to move around all day. He glanced at the ormolu clock on his desk, noticing that it was almost dawn. If he went to bed upstairs, he would have to drag himself out later. He might as well sleep down here on the sofa with a blanket over him.

He felt sick as he thought about Minna. He'd lashed out at her, and now he would have to find a way to explain why his suspicions probably were true. Why had she taken Melchior's side so readily? Roarke was too tired to be plagued by jealousy, and he understood that Minna's interest in Mel was only platonic. Still, why did she stubbornly refuse to consider Mel's guilt? *Does she know something I don't?* Roarke sighed. Their intimacy earlier had seemed to smooth the way to complete trust, so why had she chosen to doubt him?

He stretched out on the sofa and went back to

sleep. All he wanted was a modicum of peace, but that seemed impossible to attain.

Minna's stomach churned as she crawled out of bed. She'd slept badly, worrying about Roarke and his problems. Now it looked like she had one of her own. This was the fifth day in a row that she'd been unbearably queasy. Only a glass of milk would assuage the awful nausea.

She barely had time to run into her privacy closet and retch. The bout took all strength from her, and her body was covered with cold sweat. There was no doubt in her mind that she was in the family way. She'd never been sick like this before.

Rosie entered with a breakfast tray and Minna had to rush back to the closet at the smell of buttered toast. Rosie gave her one of her lopsided grimaces that was her brand of smile.

"There's no doubt about it, you're going to have a child," she said quietly and poured the tea. "The master will be pleased."

I'm not so sure about that, Minna thought grimly and massaged her aching stomach. She would put off celebrating until she learned his views on this new turn of events. Even though she didn't want to admit it, she already knew what his opinion would be. He would be horrified. This was the time to brace herself if she didn't want his negativism to break her.

"Please help me dress, Rosie," she said and sat down at her dressing table. She sipped her tea as Rosie started brushing her hair. "Have you heard from Ellie?"

"No, my lady, but I heard from Mrs. Collins. Ellie hasn't lost any customers even if the summer months have been slow."

330

"She'll be busy in time for the small season when everyone returns to London." Minna felt a stab of longing for her old friend, but there was always Davina. However, Davina spent more time at Leverett Epcott's estate, Briarpatch, than at The Towers. Before long there would be an announcement of their nuptials, Minna thought with a smile. She was glad she'd told Eve about Davina's secret spot, and it was clear that they were busy exploring that spot, and others.

She gazed out the window while Rosie's brush strokes soothed her. The summer had seemed like an endless sunny day, although rain interrupted the serenity at even intervals. She had discovered that she enjoyed the countryside with its myriad of birds, insects, and lush vegetation. Every day she was learning something new, and she was becoming more and more accustomed to her new life and its responsibilities. She hadn't thought she would enjoy her new role as much as she did. If only she could breach this new gap with Roarke . . .

After her stomach had settled, she went downstairs in search of her husband. She found him sleeping peacefully on the sofa in the study, his jaw darkened with stubble, and his eyes ringed with dark circles of exhaustion.

Smiling, she touched his brow, brushing aside his tangled hair.

"Darling?" she said. "Wake up. We have a lot to discuss."

"Wh—er—what?" he asked with a yawn. When he recognized her, he stiffened. "What's wrong?" he asked. "What has happened?"

"Nothing is wrong. Whatever gave you that idea?"

With a groan, he unfolded his long limbs, evidently cramped after sleeping on the hard horsehair

331

sofa. "Ahh," he said after gaining his feet and stretching his arms over his head. "I slept terribly."

"It was late when you came back home," she said, stepping closer to him. "Aren't you going to kiss me good-morning?" She went so close that their bodies touched and lifted her face to his.

He joined his lips to hers reluctantly. "What are you doing here?"

"What kind of greeting is that? I'm your wife." She sat stiffly on the edge of the sofa.

"I know that you don't like the idea that Mel might be the person who shot Aladdin. But with the stallion gone, his mare is the finest blood in these parts."

"I still don't think Melchior had anything to do with the shooting. He's not a violent man." She raised her chin a notch, and they exchanged a wary glance. "Is this to stand between us as husband and wife?"

"If my wife believes the innocence of a cold-blooded killer, and I don't, there's no possibility of sharing a carefree relationship."

Minna trembled inside with anger. "Since you're constantly pushing me away, then you won't accept a family life together. Is that so?"

"If Mel is innocent, let's discuss this again later. I know that Mel appears to be a charming fellow. But you don't know the whole of it. He's desperate. He went behind my back once despite my explicit warnings. He 'wed' Tokayer to Aladdin without my knowing about it, and now Tokayer might die at the time of foaling." He pulled his hand through his hair. "She almost did once before, and we knew it would be extremely dangerous to try again. I'm angry with him for taking such mad risks. How do I know he wouldn't try something else behind my back—like killing Aladdin?"

332

"What he did surely wasn't a crime?" Minna clenched her fists. "Never mind Mel at this point. I'm awfully tired of waiting for you to make up your mind about whether you love me or not, Roarke. My patience is worn out. We have to start living like a normal family. Perhaps you might learn to love the child that I carry, but I doubt it."

Oh, God! She could have bitten her tongue off. In the heat of the moment, the secret had slipped from her grip. She had planned to give him the truth gently.

He reeled back as if receiving a heavy blow. "Child?"

She nodded miserably and read the apprehension on his face. "I'm fairly sure about it, but I haven't seen the doctor yet."

He slapped his hand to his forehead in a gesture of hopelessness. "What have I done?" he shouted, "I've been crazy to let this madness go on."

"Madness? I thought it was called love." A wave of misery engulfed Minna, and she couldn't face his horrified expression any longer. She fled without another word.

"Wait!" he called after her, but she didn't stop. "Minerva!"

Half an hour later she saw Roarke riding away from the house on an old hunter called Cobble. She wiped her tears, but they had given her no relief.

Roarke liked the bone-jarring gait of the old nag. It reminded him that he was alive, and not the automaton that he felt like inside. He likened himself to a bottle that, over time, had been filled to the brim with useless knowledge and pain. There was room for no more.

This new turn of events had made the bottle overflow, and he had no idea how to deal with it. One part of him spoke of the wonder of a new life coming into the world, another side of him admonished himself for recklessness and foolishness. Why bring another flawed being to this world? What would such an act accomplish? Was it the desire for his wife that had made him act continuously in a selfish manner, or was it a deeper need—a need for affection, love—that he tried to satisfy?

Once a fool, always a fool, he thought as the horse jumped over a crumbling stone wall and onto the forest path. Under the green canopy of the trees, he might find enough peace to think clearly.

He halted the hunter in a clearing and let him loose to graze. The old horse never ran off, and if he did, he wouldn't go far.

Roarke sat down on a moss-covered stump to think. If only he could sort through the morass of issues that clamored for his attention, he might come to make peace with Minerva and himself.

He heard nothing besides birdsong and the buzz of insects as he examined the various problems in his mind. Only when a branch snapped did he look up. A stranger in tattered clothes stood at the edge of the clearing leveling a rifle at his head. Roarke stared with horror at the muzzle pointing toward him.

Just as the weapon exploded, Roarke threw himself on the ground and rolled aside. A burning pain tore through his flesh. He lost his breath, and his chest felt as if it had burst. Then oblivion swallowed him.

Chapter Twenty-eight

Minna went about her day supervising the cleaning of The Towers. Too upset to do anything practical herself, she wandered from room to room in the old house, looking at nothing. Why had she told Roarke that she was in the family way? What if she wasn't? She had been so angry that the words had slipped out of her by themselves. Anguish tore at her, and she glanced for the fiftieth time toward the drive. Where was he? The hunter had not arrived at the stables. It was already noon, and Roarke couldn't have spent the entire morning riding. Perhaps he'd left her for good.

Finally, she couldn't stand the suspense any longer. She went downstairs to speak with Kitson. "Please have the carriage brought up as soon as possible."

As she pulled a straw bonnet adorned with a blue ostrich feather on her head, she wished she'd had time to learn to ride. With the carriage she could only travel up and down the lanes crisscrossing the area to Birchington. She dared not think of the possibility that she might not find him.

She had only gotten as far as the end of the

drive when two riders approached at furious speed. She recognized Melchior Harding, and the other man looked like a steward of some sort. Perhaps he was from Linkwood Cottage.

The men pulled in their reins as they came up to the carriage, and Minna leaned out the window. An icy premonition came over her as she noticed Melchior's serious face. "What's wrong?" she demanded.

"We were riding through the woods and came upon Cobble in a clearing." Melchior took a deep breath. "Steel yourself, Lady Whitecliffe. We found Roarke sprawled on the ground with a bullet hole through his side. He's unconscious and feverish."

The world swam in front of Minna's eyes. "Can we get to him with the carriage?"

"There's a path close by, but we'd better get some men and fashion a stretcher." He turned to his servant and issued orders. "Have Kitson send for the doctor," he shouted at the back of the retreating servant. "Come with me, Minerva. I'll show you the way."

Minna's hands trembled as she clutched the frame of the window. The carriage could not move fast enough for her, but the horses were advancing at break-neck speed and the coach jolted over potholes and bumps. Let him be alive, she prayed over and over.

Melchior was riding ahead to show the coachman where to turn, and before long bushes and branches scraped the sides of the carriage. As soon as the horses came to a halt, she flung the door wide and jumped down. Running, she asked, "Where is he?"

Melchior slid out of the saddle and led her through the undergrowth to the clearing. She

336

sobbed with anxiety as she saw Roarke on the ground. Mel had draped a cloak over him to keep him warm.

"Easy now," Mel admonished when she flung herself down beside Roarke. She lifted her husband's head onto her lap and brushed his hair back. His skin had a gray, transparent hue, and she feared that the end was close. Cold sweat covered his face and trickled onto her hand. Fear tore at her insides, and she couldn't stop the tears welling in her eyes. *Please, Lord, don't take him away from me,* she begged silently.

Melchior lifted the cloak and examined the wound. All Minna could see was the tattered flesh on the far left side of Roarke's chest.

"He has bled heavily, but it has slowed to a trickle. I don't think his lung was pierced, but the ribs — He's struggling for breath — "

"Please don't say anything else, I can't bear it," Minna whispered, fearing she would faint as darkness lurked at the corners of her vision.

Mel gave her a kind smile. "Don't worry, m'dear. Roarke is strong as a horse. He'll survive."

Minna couldn't help but notice the flicker of doubt in his eyes before he turned his attention to the wound once more.

"I'm grateful that you found him when you did," she said. "He rode off early in the morning. You see, we quarreled."

"Roarke always was a proud and stubborn man. He isn't easy to reason with in the best of times." Melchior pulled the cloak up to his cousin's neck and tucked it around the sides of the still body.

"I know," she said. "Our marriage didn't start on a positive note. There's much anger between us — or there used to be. Roarke has difficulty trusting me after — "

"Don't worry," Melchior interrupted. "He loves you. I've seen it in his eyes every time he looks at you."

Melchior's words warmed her, but only for a moment. *"Where* are the servants? "If Roarke stays much longer on the damp ground he might get pneumonia."

"It isn't that cold, and the ground is dry, thank God. There they are at last!"

Heavy boots crushed the undergrowth and four servants emerged on the path among the trees, Melchior's steward among them. They were carrying a stretcher, and before long they had lifted Roarke onto it. Minna felt bereft as the warmth of his head left her lap. She followed the men to the carriage where she kept a close watch as they carefully arranged Roarke's tall body on one of the seats.

Melchior rode ahead to make sure that Roarke's bed had been prepared and heated with warming pans.

The journey back to The Towers was interminable, and Minna kept praying for Roarke's life. He looked even more transparent than before, and his lips had taken on a blue tinge. *Dear God, let him survive. Don't you see, I have to make peace with him, or I may never forgive myself.*

A weak sigh issued from Roarke's cold lips, and she touched his clammy cheek. A tear rolled down her face and dripped onto his forehead where she wiped it off.

The carriage came to a stop by the front entrance, and servants clustered around the stretcher. Mrs. Clemson stood by the door, winding her apron around her hands.

The doctor's gig arrived just as they carried Roarke up the stairs to his bedchamber. Minna gave orders for boiling water and bandages to be brought up, then followed the doctor.

An hour later, Doctor Arthur Gower washed his bloody hands and rolled down his sleeves. As he snapped his bag closed, he gave Minna a calculating glance. "I'd say you look exhausted, Lady Whitecliffe." He brushed his graying hair back, and shrugged on his black frock coat. "Come along, let me talk to you in private. There's nothing you can do at this moment."

Minna reluctantly tore her gaze from Roarke's pale face against the pillows and followed the physician into the corridor.

"Let's go into my sitting room," she invited and opened the door next to Roarke's bedchamber.

Shoulders straight, her hands clasped hard in front of her, she faced the older man. "Will he live?"

Doctor Gower's eyebrows rose, and his lips pursed in thought. "I'd say there's a good chance, if the fever doesn't develop into something worse, like pneumonia, or if gangrene doesn't settle into the wound. Two ribs broken, but they didn't puncture the lung, only tore the muscles and the flesh." The doctor shook his head in wonder. "All things considered, he was a fortunate man."

"Someone wants him dead. Did you know that his prize stallion, Aladdin, was shot yesterday?"

The doctor nodded. "As I go into every house, I hear all the gossip whether I want to or not. At present, everyone is discussing that poor horse." He gave her a close look. "If I may say so, Lady Whitecliffe, you don't look like you're in the healthiest of bloom. You're too thin. I would like to examine you."

Minna blushed. She might as well reveal her suspicion to the doctor. "I believe I'm pregnant."

Rosie entered with a tea tray, and she stayed while the doctor made the examination. "I believe you're right, Lady Whitecliffe. How many times have you missed your cycle?"

"Twice," she said and buttoned up her gown after he'd listened to her heart.

"Well, if the earl awakens you must tell him the good news," the doctor said briskly, and put his instruments into his bag. "It'll help him to recover faster."

A shiver of dread traveled up Minna's spine. "I will," she said, and lowered her eyes. She couldn't tell him that Roarke's reaction had triggered the ride that brought on the attack on his life.

"I wonder who wants him dead," she said.

"The constables will be waiting downstairs. You'd better speak to them."

Even though it was a warm summer day, Minna felt a bone-chilling cold. She heard angry voices downstairs, and now that Roarke was unable to execute his authority, it fell to her to deal with the problems.

The local constables, Midas Cogg and Joshua Blunt, of sturdy peasant stock from the village, waited to interrogate her downstairs. Evidently the magistrate, Squire Eustace Milton, had not seen fit to get involved. Cogg and Blunt had clapped Melchior in irons, and he glowered like an angry bear as he argued with them.

"What's going on here," Minna demanded, for a moment pushing aside her worries for the man upstairs.

"We're arrestin' Mr. Harding, my lady," said Cogg, his red side whiskers wobbling with indignation. "For the killin' o' the stallion, and the attempted murder of His Lordship."

"This is ridiculous! If Mr. Harding were guilty,

would he bother to save the earl's life like he did? He's innocent."

Mr. Cogg gave her a suspicious glare. "Such action would push suspicion away from himself, my lady. His Lordship seems to think that Mr. Hardin' killed Aladdin. We've been talkin' to all the stable lads at Meadow Hill, and the last person leavin' the stables wus this here Mr. Hardin'." The burly constable got a grip on Melchior's arm and pulled him toward the door. "He's goin' before the magistrate. That's the law."

Minna wrung her hands. There wasn't anything she could do to stop them at the moment, unless she could prove Melchior's innocence. She couldn't, but she didn't believe that he was guilty. He harbored no ill will toward his cousin, but it had been mighty convenient that he'd arrived at the scene of the shooting just in time to save Roarke from dying from loss of blood. No, she thought, if he'd wanted Roarke dead, he wouldn't have lifted a finger to save his life.

"Melchior," she said, putting a restraining hand on his arm. "I'll find a way to help you out of this dilemma." She didn't know how, but there must be a way.

Melchior gave her a wan smile. "Don't worry about me, Lady Whitecliffe."

She watched as they led him to the wagon outside, then she ran back upstairs. Roarke lay as she had left him, still and pale against the pillows. She chafed his cold hands, and tucked the blankets more tightly around him. Harris entered soft-footed, carrying two warming pans. His brow was creased with worry, and Minna realized how fond the servant was of his master. All the staff had shown a high degree of distress at Roarke's situation, and their solicitude warmed her heart. She

341

would have to remain strong through this ordeal.

Sinking down on the edge of the mattress, she bathed Roarke's forehead. She wished she could reach him, tell him how much she loved him.

Roarke swam in a red sea of warm water. Unearthly music — or was it voices — undulated through him as if he was without substance. He felt no pain, but the heat bothered him. He moved forward, finding it difficult in the extreme, as if the water was glutinous. Minerva, or someone that was a weak echo of his wife, moved naked toward him, but she got entangled in the arms of seaweed. He longed to reach her, but the water thickened even further, and the heat rose. When it grew unbearable, he was sucked up and out of it, to lie in the blinding sun of the desert. He recognized it as the land of the Arabian horses where he'd first seen Aladdin.

The stallion moved toward him in a cloud of dust, leaping, prancing, thundering straight over him where he lay immovable. The hooves made no imprint on his body, they stepped right through him, and then the horse was gone.

The sun burned, hurting his eyes, hurting every part of his naked body like needles. His skin blistered and burst.

He fought to get onto his knees and crawl for shelter, but he couldn't move. He struggled until the sun burned his flesh into something resembling a leather hide. The sun finally got a grip on his breathing and tried to burn it out of him, but he fought for the only thing that the heat hadn't already claimed. If only he had some water . . .

* * *

"He's very restless," Minna said, and Harris helped her to bathe Roarke's feverish body with cold water. "I . . ." she said, but could not continue as her voice broke. "Do you think he'll live through this attack?"

Harris looked at her with worry in his eyes. "He's a strong man . . ."

"But," Minna filled in, "the fever isn't going down, is it?"

The valet shook his head. "It's rising."

Worry drenched her, weakened her limbs. She inhaled deeply, searching for the strength to support her through this ordeal. She could not let Roarke die . . . She would not permit it!

Chapter Twenty-nine

For two days Roarke tossed and turned in his bed, his face flushed with high fever. Minna didn't stir from his side, and finally, when she couldn't keep her eyes open any longer, she stretched out on the bed beside him. Holding his hot, dry hand against her cheek, she prayed that it soon would be over. She couldn't bear to see her beloved suffer such agony—if he knew what was going on.

She drifted off to sleep, burrowing as close to him as she could. He was scorching, so terribly hot, yet shivering with chills. Dear God, please let him live . . . please.

Roarke felt himself sink deeper and deeper into a cooking pot of black, molten liquid. Creatures of fantastical shapes surrounded him in the swirling cauldron. The liquid sucked him into the middle and he was helpless against its force.

One part of him observed the hellish apparitions with cool detachment, another part could not help but scream with voiceless terror. It seemed there were two worlds, one light, airy world that only a hand, then two, anchored him to. The other world was a realm of extreme spectacles, like a theater where only plays of parody were shown. He knew it would soon be over. He would drown in that strange dream. Disappear. At that moment he fought harder than he ever had before.

The groan building in his chest would not come to his lips. He struggled, but a silent moan was all he could manage when in reality he wanted to cry out for help. Then he remembered the two hands, his two thin lines to the surface of sanity.

He held on to them in desperation, one soft yet strong, the other gnarled and warm. That old hand had uncommon strength, and life seemed to flow from it into him. Life, a cool, rich soothing stream flowed into his lungs. He would have likened it to chilled cream if someone had asked him how it felt and tasted. Fulfilling, it contained everything and created a subtle distance between him and the repulsive dreams of the black liquid. Ahh, so soothing. . . . Now he was conscious of aching eyelids, burning face. He forced the crusty eyelids apart.

Sunlight blinded him painfully, and he had to keep his eyes half shut to cut the glare. Through his eyelashes, he saw an old face. It was surrounded by an almost imperceptible glow, a light so pure that he couldn't describe it. In a flash, he recognized Joe Tulsiter. The old groom winked, his eyes glowing with humor. "Ye decided to live then," the old groom said.

Roarke blinked twice, and the gnarled hand melted from his grip. He looked toward the side of the bed, but no one was there. In his other hand he felt the gentle pressure of that soft grip, and he turned his head with difficulty.

"Minerva," he whispered, and watched as tears

345

overflowed her eyes. She looked disheveled and tired, but happiness shone through her distress.

"Thank God, the fever has broken. I thought you would die."

He noticed that he was bathed in perspiration, and that his body ached from head to toe, especially on the left side. A dull pain pounded behind his eyes, and he had to close his leaden eyelids.

"Where did Joe go?" he asked sleepily.

"Joe? He hasn't been here since yesterday when he came in to find out how you were feeling. I don't understand him. He was worried, yet wholly unconcerned."

Roarke stared at her in surprise. "I could have sworn he was here a minute ago. He held my hand."

"He did briefly yesterday," she explained. "That old man is uncommonly fond of you."

"I've known him all my life. He taught me to ride a long time ago. Though he's only a servant here, he's the truest friend I've ever had. Never told me a lie, nor praised me unduly." He found it difficult to speak. *He's the only man who understands what I need,* Roarke realized in a flash.

"I think the doctor has arrived," Minna said. "I'll go down and tell him that your fever has broken." She bent over him and kissed his lips lightly. "Life would have been unbearable without you."

Roarke didn't want to let go of her hand, but she slid away, and he hovered on the brink of sleep. "I love you," he croaked, but he heard the click of the door behind her retreating form. "I'm sorry for everything."

Just as he said those words something stilled in him and he experienced that weightlessness he sometimes felt at waking up in the morning.

Everything was quiet in him, and in the span of a breath he realized that everything around him was quiet as well. In that silent awareness he saw the truth of his existence. A gentle but forceful power sustained him and held up the world around him. He could only call it love, and it was within him and around him. Everywhere. It had always been underlying the chaos of everyday life. Always there, patient, silent. God, it was so simple that he had to laugh! All the books in the world would never have taught him that. Laughter bubbled out of him and a deep happiness filled him.

Just as subtly as the realization had come upon him, it faded, and he was back in his tormented mind. Yet some awareness had shifted inside him, perhaps the angle of his perception, and he knew the torment would not hound him as fiercely as before. A profound peace filled him and he drifted off to sleep, an innocent sleep he hadn't known since childhood.

When he awakened again, Doctor Gower was leaning over him, examining his bandages. "Awake at last. I was here yesterday, after your fever broke, then this morning. You've slept for thirty hours, Lord Whitecliffe."

Roarke stretched luxuriously but the sharp twinge in his side stopped him suddenly. "Whatever happened?"

"Do you remember being shot?" the doctor asked.

Weak and trembling, Roarke looked around the room and discovered that Minerva was standing by the bed, her face pale and drooping with fatigue.

"Yes . . ." Roarke directed his thoughts back in time and remembered the clearing.

347

"They have arrested Melchior for attempted murder," Minerva explained. She stared at him intently, evidently worrying about his reply.

Roarke shook his head against the pillow. "No, it wasn't Melchior. I saw a tall, burly man, probably a servant, or perhaps a poacher aiming his rifle at me. I threw myself on the ground, and rolled aside, but that devil got me anyway."

"You were lucky to have such quick reflexes, my lord. All you got was a flesh wound and a couple of cracked ribs. You'll be in pain for some time, but you'll be back to normal soon enough," the doctor said briskly.

"I'll send for the constables, and you can tell them about the stranger," Minna said.

"Yes. There's no reason for Mel to rot in the detention house at Birchington."

After the doctor had cleaned the wound and strapped clean bandages around his chest, Roarke slept the rest of the day. His sleep was profound and devoid of strange dreams. The next day he felt refreshed and demanded to get up.

"It's too early," Minna protested.

There was more bounce in her step and a new gleam in her eyes. Did his recovery mean that much to her? He dared not broach the subject fearing that he would blubber in front of her. His illness had brought his emotions to the surface, and he seemed to see and hear everything more keenly than before.

"A little fresh air would do wonders," he said and sat on the edge of the mattress. "Please," he begged when he noticed the mutinous set of her chin. "Just ten minutes. If I lie here any longer I will perish with boredom. Fetch Harris, my darling."

Minna obeyed with a sigh. She waited obediently in her rooms while Harris dressed him in trousers and a long robe of quilted wool. It was warm outside, but Roarke didn't complain about the heavy outfit, as long as he could get into the sunshine for a few minutes and breathe fresh air. There was nothing more depressing than a sickroom.

Happiness seeped through every nerve as he entered the terrace that bordered the garden below. Besides the beauty of the flowering roses, he enjoyed the pressure of Minerva's arm around his middle. He didn't have the strength to lift his left arm, but he cradled her close with the other.

As he sank down on an armchair that had been moved from the study, she asked in a voice tight with worry, "Do you recall why you rode off that morning when you were shot?"

He nodded. "I was such a fool." He grimaced at the memory. "Did you speak with the doctor?"

She nodded, and pulled up another chair close to his. "Yes . . . he confirmed my suspicion."

Roarke closed his eyes, letting the news sink in. He expected the raw anguish, the tormented questions to return inside him, but they didn't. Not even the thought of Thomas's death could trigger his sadness. Nothing could disturb the contentment that filled his heart. He looked up, and noticed Minerva had gone. That jolted him for a second, but then his attention was distracted to the old face peering at him over the marble balustrade.

"Good morn', my lord."

"Joe!" Roarke exclaimed, experiencing a sudden dryness of the mouth. "Thank you for visiting me and wishing me well." He wanted to deliver the burning question on his tongue, whether the old man had come to his sickbed and held his hand as he came out of the fever spell two days ago. He found that he couldn't speak.

The old man nodded, touching the brim of his grimy cap. "You were sayin'?"

"I—I thought I saw something . . . a light around you," Roarke said, fumbling for words. "I understood something important about my life right after you left. The answers to all mysteries lie inside myself . . . how do I find a way inside?" He couldn't believe he'd asked those words, yet the question made sense. He looked earnestly at the old man.

"Thirst forces the student of life to search for water. He who seeks will find. If you wish, you shall be taught how to embark on the journey of Truth, but you need someone to show you how."

"How?"

"A teacher finds his student when the student is ready," came the cryptic reply. "But mind you, the teacher is more likely to be a beggar than a king."

Taken aback, Roarke stared at the strange little man and saw uncommon strength and purpose in that weathered old body. Kindness and humor shone in those clear eyes. Joe winked. "I can show you. I'll be waitin'."

As Roarke inhaled deeply and pondered those words, the old man disappeared among the roses. Of all the surprises—who would have guessed that he would find the key to his search right on his own doorstep? A precious peace filled Roarke, and he couldn't recall when he'd ever felt better. His chin slowly descended toward his chest . . .

After leaving him alone for half an hour to think about the child growing in her womb, Minna returned. She found him asleep as she spread the blanket that she'd fetched upstairs. Not wanting to disturb him, yet longing to talk with him, she gently tucked the blanket around his legs. She sat down beside him studying that dear face that had been ravaged by fever. Yet a comforting stillness lay over him, and his forehead lacked creases of concern. She'd never seen him so peaceful.

As she looked at him, he awakened. He smiled, and she touched his face.

"Come here," he said, and she sank down onto the terrace beside his chair. He cradled her head with his hands and kissed her deeply. Sighing with pleasure, he looked into her eyes.

"Have you decided on any names yet? I would like to have a say in the matter."

She laughed, suddenly very light at heart. "Of course. I didn't dare to think about it until I knew how you felt about the child. The earls of Whitecliffe have many names. Come to think of it, I've never heard yours in its entirety."

"Roarke Dennison Maxwell Horatius Cromwell Harding."

"Ugh," Minna said with a grimace. "Though Maxwell is a possibility."

What if it's a girl?"

"Emma Portia Harding," Minna said without a doubt.

Roarke rubbed his chin. "Not exactly mesmerizing names, but —"

Minna touched his cheek. "So you truly accept this child?"

He kissed the tip of her nose. "Yes. My only concern is . . . well, I pray that he or she won't inherit the eye disease."

Minna nodded. "No." Her heart slowly filled with that conviction. It looked like their problems were over. If only they would discover who had shot Roarke and why, but that discussion would come later when he was stronger. She had sent a message to the constables in Birchington, and soon enough she would hear from them. "I love you," she whispered and touched his cheek.

"And I love you."

His eyes looked bluer than they ever had, she thought, and less green. Worry perhaps made them green. His smile had a deeper radiance that she hadn't been aware of before. Perhaps love gave her the same silly grin. She laughed and was about to kiss him when Kitson cleared his throat in the doorway.

"Lord Whitecliffe," he said, "the constables state that they have found the man who shot you. They have him down at the detention house."

Roarke frowned. "Do you know his identity?"

"No, my lord."

Roarke swore under his breath and tried to rise, but collapsed instantly in his chair. "Damn, I'm weak as a kitten! I wish I were strong enough to go down to Birchington and confront the fellow."

Minna rose without hesitation. "I'll go. I want to speak with Melchior and ask him to come for a visit. You must bury your differences with him. You must discuss Aladdin's death with him."

Roarke nodded. "That's true, but I don't want you to go down there alone. Who knows what rough customers you might run into."

"Nonsense. Kitson will accompany me."

Roarke said, "I still don't like the idea." He tried to stand once more, but Minna held him back.

"I'll return straight away. I won't be gone more than an hour at the most. Rosie can sit with you since Harris went to the village."

Roarke frowned at the sky. "It looks like rain. I'd better return upstairs."

Minna realized he was more tired than he cared to admit. She knew that as soon as his head touched the pillow, he would be asleep.

Kitson helped him upstairs, and Minna went to her bedchamber to fetch her bonnet and pelisse. Rosie was darning a petticoat by the window. She sounded as if she had a cold and she touched her nose repeatedly with her handkerchief. Then Minna noticed Rosie's red eyes.

"You're crying," she exclaimed. "What's wrong?"

Rosie's head lowered, and all Minna could see was the lace at the rim of her mobcap. "Tell me."

"The people at this place are afraid of me," Rosie said with a hiccup. "They hate me. Everyone hates me."

Minna went over to the window and touched her maid's shoulder. "They'll get used to you."

She felt the maid stiffen at her touch, and Minna demanded, "Look at me."

Rosie lifted her face, and dashed away the tears from her eyes. "I'm so foolish—"

Minna frowned, sensing that something was very wrong. Rosie, who never drank, now smelled strongly of sour wine. "You've been drinking!"

Rosie nodded, and her hands trembled around the fabric of the petticoat. "Are you going to send me away?" She made that special grimace that was her smile. "I don't blame you if you want to let me go, now that you're a countess."

Minna sighed. "No, I'm not planning to do that, but you must not carry your problems alone. I'll speak to the servants." She turned as if to leave and Rosie clutched her arm. Then as if remembering that she had stepped over the boundaries, she jerked away as if burned.

"Sorry, my lady. You've always been good and fair to me."

Minna smiled. "Don't be silly, Rosie. You're behaving as if I'm royalty." She took Rosie's hand and pulled her to her feet. "I'm going out for an hour or two and I want you to sit with His Lordship while I'm gone. First, wipe your tears. Everything will be fine here once I've had a word with Kitson."

Fiddling with her apron, Rosie bobbed a curtsy. "Thank you, ma'am. I'll bring my sewing if you don't mind."

Minna watched as Rosie entered Roarke's bedroom and closed the door behind her. That woman didn't have an easy life with her repulsive face.

Pulling on her gloves, she went downstairs. Kitson was waiting for her in the hallway, and the carriage was already by the front steps.

The village of Birchington, as every village, had its curious spectators at the police headquarters. Kitson could barely shoulder his way to the entrance of the house where the constables held the man who'd shot Roarke. Minna tried to protect herself from jostling elbows and clumsy feet, but she felt bruised once they were inside the building.

As her eyes adjusted to the gloom of the sparsely lit room, she found the interior drab and uninviting. Walls and ceiling were painted a uniform gray, and the heavy furniture looked scuffed and listless. On a chair in the middle of the room sat a big burly man in a brown wool coat. He had a fleshy, morose face, and he peered malevolently at Minna from under unkempt black eyebrows. Black stubble on his cheeks gave him a dangerous air. She shivered, grateful to discover that his hands were manacled.

"Is this the man?" she asked, knowing the answer already.

"Yes, my lady," said Constable Cogg briskly, rising from his desk. "This man is Hector Jones, a known miscreant from the town of Margate. I thought he'd be hanged for stealing, but I found out that he'd escaped—and now showing up on my doorstep."

"Caught him redhanded stealing a chicken this dawn," explained the younger constable, Mr. Blunt.

Mr. Cogg continued, "I told him we were sending him back to Margate and the hanging tree there, which made him angry. Tried to flee, in fact." Mr. Cogg pointed proudly to the bruise on the man's cheekbone. "I stopped him just in time." He went over to the prisoner and poked him in the shoulder. "The man knows he's going to hang, so he confessed to shooting at your husband. He figured he didn't want to hang alone."

"He didn't kill Roarke, though," Minna said thoughtfully. "I'm surprised he confessed."

Mr. Cogg kept poking the prisoner with a pudgy finger. "Vindictive fellow, he is. Like I said, he would like to take as many as he can into the grave with him." Mr. Cogg took a deep breath and puffed out his chest. "I know for a fact that Lady Edna Barton planned the shootin' that aimed to put an end to His Lordship."

Chapter Thirty

Minna gasped. "Edna? But why?"

"She's this very minute locked up in another room in this establishment," Cogg said. "You shall speak with her shortly, but first you must see Mr. Melchior Harding, who's at this very moment having tea with my lady wife upstairs."

Confused, Minna let Kitson lead her to a connecting door and up a flight of narrow stairs. Melchior looked right at home in the cozy parlor with its crocheted doilies and smothering atmosphere. The matron, Mrs. Cogg, presided regally over the tea tray as if she was spending the afternoon with a duke. Melchior rose with a smile as Minna and Kitson entered. He bent over Mrs. Cogg's hand and gallantly kissed her fat fingers.

"You must come again soon," she said in a quavering voice, her eyes widening. With a stiff nod at Minna and a murmured excuse, she left them alone in the room.

"I see you've moved up in the world," Minna said teasingly.

"Much more comfortable up here than down in the cellar," Melchior said with a laugh. "The lady served a most excellent tea."

"We're here to take you home. I'm sorry you

had to go through all this." She watched as his face fell into folds of sadness.

"I had no idea that Edna was that unhinged. I knew she had lofty aspirations for me. She sort of adopted me since she had no children of her own. I was her dear, *dear* sister's boy," he explained, mimicking Lady Barton's whine. He sighed, smoothing his wilting neckcloth and rumpled clothes. "We might as well get going."

"Yes, let's leave. I'm relieved they found the man she hired. A dangerous man by all accounts."

Melchior scratched his head. "I would like to see Aunt Edna a last time before they take her to the prison at Margate to await trial." With an air of sadness, he pointed toward the door.

Minna went downstairs experiencing mixed feelings about seeing the woman who had never accepted her as the Countess of Whitecliffe. Come to think of it, Lady Barton had barely accepted her as a modiste. And she evidently hated Roarke.

Mr. Cogg was waiting for her, and to her relief they had removed Hector Jones. The younger constable entered, pushing Lady Barton ahead of him.

"Don't touch me!" the old lady shrieked as the lawman took her elbow and propelled her to the chair that Mr. Jones had vacated. Lady Barton gave Minna a contemptuous stare as she sat down.

"Have you come to gloat?"

Minna shook her head. "No one was more surprised than me to hear that you were involved in this," she said angrily. "I would like to slap you for causing me such worry! My husband almost died because of you."

"I wish he had," Lady Barton said. "He should not be the Earl of Whitecliffe. Melchior is older and should rightfully have been the earl."

"That branch of the family was not meant to inherit the title. Roarke's father was the eldest and inherited the title; he was older than Melchior's father." Minna's voice trembled with wrath, and she clenched her hands into fists at her side. "Therefore it's pure logic and English law that Roarke is the earl, no coincidence as you seem to believe."

Lady Barton's eyes did not soften, nor did her stiff posture. "Melchior started breeding horses, and when Roarke saw that, he had to compete and try to oust his cousin from his eminent position on the turf. It has always been like that— Melchior gets a brilliant idea, then Roarke has to monopolize it."

"Aunt Edna," Melchior admonished. "It wasn't like that at all. Roarke and I discussed horses long before we got started in the business."

Lady Barton snorted. "But he had to travel the world to make sure he got the showiest piece of horseflesh in the south counties."

"*You* were behind the shooting of Aladdin," Minna exclaimed. "It was Mr. Jones that shot him, wasn't it?"

Lady Barton pursed her lips in contempt. "I wish the man had been as successful when he aimed his rifle at Roarke's head."

"Aunt Edna!" Melchior pulled his hands through his hair in a gesture of distraction. He stood beside his aunt and looked down into her face. "How could you do this?"

The old lady tossed her head. "And *who* would have ended your horse breeding business? Roarke. I did it to protect your interests."

Melchior threw up his arms. "You've got it all wrong! Tokayer is my mare, and the foal she carries will set my affairs to rights. I know I'll have a champion in any foal of Aladdin even though Roarke tried to stop me at every turn." Perspiration gleamed on his forehead, and misery darkened his eyes. "How could you meddle, Aunt Edna?"

"So it's true what Roarke told me—that you bred Tokayer with Aladdin despite his express warnings?" Minna inserted.

"Yes . . . he's sure Tokayer will die in foaling—some blarney about Tokayer's—er, shape. She had a dangerous delivery of a dead foal a year ago. Roarke maintained it was too risky to breed her again and refused to give me access to Aladdin." He lowered his eyes. "I'm afraid I *stole* the opportunity one night. That's why Roarke has been so angry with me. He didn't want me to risk Tokayer's life, but Joe Tulsiter says the horse'll be fine when the time comes."

He returned his attention to Lady Barton. "So you see, Aunt Edna, I'm quite capable of managing my own business."

Lady Barton's face crumpled, and her proud bearing sagged. "I was only trying to help you. I've loved you as my own."

Minna and Melchior exchanged weary glances. "Totally misguided, I'm afraid," Melchior said.

"I believe it's time to leave," Minna said. "We have nothing else to say here."

"She's out of her mind," Melchior whispered under his breath as they walked toward the door.

"I would do it again," Lady Barton cried after them. "Why should Roarke have everything, the lovely Towers, the land, Meadow Hill, and you Melchior—you only having a ramshackle thatched cottage? Tell me that?" she shrieked.

Melchior turned around at the door. "Because Roarke was the legitimate heir to all that, it's as simple as that." He put his hat on his head, and pulled Minna into the protective circle of his arm.

Lady Barton's shouts of rage followed them as they pushed through the crowd outside. Fleeing into the coach with Kitson, they drew a collective sigh of relief as the coach pulled away from the mob.

"What will happen to her now?" Minna wondered aloud.

"She'll be tried as an accomplice to attempted murder, perhaps more than that. I don't know." Melchior looked mournful in his corner of the coach, and Minna placed her hand over his. "I shall have to talk with my solicitors, find her good counsel."

"I'm sorry you had to go through this, but it's over now. Roarke wants to speak to you once he awakens."

Melchior's face brightened. "I'm glad! I hope his anger is gone." He looked at his watch. "I could do with a pint of something to strengthen myself."

"Let's have tea in the village before we return home," Minna said.

They entered the old cross-timbered inn with its steep thatched roof at the outskirts of the village. Small mullioned windows let very little light into the taproom that had been partitioned into smaller, private areas. Minna chose the table closest to the window and sat down on the long wooden bench. Kitson ordered tea for her and beer for Melchior, then he went outside to wait in the carriage.

"Well," Melchior said and wiped his brow. "I've never lived through a more trying time. A pint won't be amiss."

"I'm sorry you had to take the blame for the

shooting. The constables were too hasty in their judgment. Do you know how they caught Mr. Jones?"

"He was stealing a chicken from a farmer whose brother saw Jones in the forest right after he shot Roarke. Almost at the same spot. He even heard the shots."

"We're lucky that Mr. Jones wasn't a careful man," Minna said. Now that the suspense was over, a profound tiredness weighed her down. "I knew all along that you weren't guilty."

Melchior smiled wearily. "Thank you for your vote of confidence. I feel I gained a friend as Roarke gained a wife. By jingo, he's a lucky beggar. You look very happy."

Minna blushed and fiddled with her gloves. She was loath to discuss her love for Roarke until she was sure she would keep it. She still had seeds of doubt concerning his feelings, yet knew in her heart that he returned her love. Their trust was new and fragile, and she worried that something would happen to shatter their brittle love — like what had happened before.

"He wants to apologize to you," she said.

Melchior scratched his head. "While I was in prison, I pondered the possibility of having Tokayer bred — next year — with another champion I know of in Berkshire. Roarke could have the foal of Aladdin. That way we could start over. It was a pity about the stallion."

"Yes, Roarke took it hard." Minna stopped talking as a young serving wench, dressed in a coarse black dress, mobcap, and a white apron came forward with a tray. She served the tea, and Minna drank gratefully.

While she was served a second cup, several farmers entered to slake their thirst at the tables closest to the counter where the ale barrels were stored. They grew loud and jolly after a few drinks, and Melchior said, "Perhaps we ought to leave now. This isn't exactly a place for ladies."

"I'm enjoying my outing," Minna said, realizing how isolated she was at The Towers. She had a sudden twinge of longing for the bustling city, and as soon as Roarke was stronger, she would ask him to take her to London for a visit. She sorely missed Ellie's cheerful chatter.

"Well, perhaps we ought to go. Roarke'll be eager to see you, Melchior." She rose, and he followed suit. Just as they approached the door, a gentleman entered. He stood silhouetted against the glaring sunlight in the doorway, and Minna thought she recognized him. He took his hat off slowly, and gave her a wary stare. As he stepped into the taproom, she gasped.

"Mr. Wylie, what are you doing here?"

"I came to pay you a visit, Lady Whitecliffe." He looked pale and haggard as if he hadn't slept for days.

"Why? I have nothing to say to you. Our business dealings are over," she replied coldly.

He twirled his hat in his hand, staring suspiciously at Melchior. He started to say something, but his mouth closed on the first word. "Let's go outside," he said with some urgency. "I have something to tell you."

Minna stiffened, feeling a prickling sensation at the base of her neck. Her heartbeat escalating, she followed him outside.

"What's the matter?" she asked, dreading his next words.

His face fell into a study of defeat, and his shoulders slumped. "I'm looking for my daughter, Isobel."

Minna gasped, and clapped her hand to her heart. "But your daughter is dead! You told me so yourself."

Melchior had taken her arm as if to steady her, and she was grateful for his presence.

"Well . . ." began Mr. Wylie, "Isobel was dead to me, but only in her mind. She didn't kill herself, but she damned well tried!" he moaned as the last of his defenses crumbled. "After she gave away Thomas to the earl, she made an attempt to end her life by throwing herself in front of a carriage. She grew more and more unstable mentally and I had to put her into a nursing home. After the suicide attempt, there was no reasoning with her, and she lost her beauty—in fact, she looked hideous. Her face was mangled—"

"Rosie!" Minna gasped. "You're describing my maid, Rosie Long!"

Chapter Thirty-one

Rosie watched the sleeping man, remembering the summer many years ago when she'd been so happy with him. She'd thought she'd reached the gateway to heaven in his arms and that it would go on forever—in marriage. A long time had passed since then, and she'd changed a lot inside, growing more and more bitter as if a poisonous growth of hatred was eating away at her. Let him sleep a bit longer, she thought. Soon enough he would have eternal sleep. *I can decide when the right moment comes,* she thought, and reveled in the feeling of being in control. Distractedly she fingered the dagger under her apron.

She remembered the first time he'd kissed her. They had walked along the churning sea, away from the bustle of Brighton, away from the noise until they and the seagulls were the only ones left in the world. He'd found a sandy hollow between two rocky outcrops, and he'd pulled her down and kissed her like no other man had kissed her before. She would always remember that sweet invasion of her mouth, and his hard hands on her body. Yet he'd stopped before the deep, hungry yearning inside her had been satisfied. It had left her longing for more. He'd said he didn't want to take advantage of her. Bah, as if love was taking advantage!

After that, she took for granted that it was only a matter of time before he would propose. She waited patiently for him to mention the day when he would go up to London and approach Father. Thurlow Wylie was a powerful man in the city, and she didn't see any obstacles to taking her place among the gentry. She'd gone to the best schools, and she wore the loveliest gowns that money could buy. Her father had pampered her from the moment she was born. Why shouldn't she reach the social pinnacles? She had scorned the man Father had chosen for her, his young partner, a pimply stoop-backed young man with shrewd eyes and clammy hands. Oh, how she'd loathed him!

He was a fool. I couldn't abide that man. Rosie squirmed in her chair uncomfortably. Perhaps she should have married him, after all. She hated the thought that her father had been right all those years ago. She threw a glance at the man in the bed and hated him as well, so such so that bile rose in her throat.

"I'll get even. After all these years, this is the day of my triumph," she said to herself. "I've waited for this."

He had seduced her with his blue eyes and clever hands. His wicked smile had made her stomach somersault with pleasure; and it still did, but now with hatred.

The day when Thomas was conceived had been glorious, a golden day at the end of the summer. The sweetness of their embrace had a tinge of bitterness at its core. He'd never mentioned the word marriage, but when he held her in his arms in that sandy hollow for the last time, she had been unable to deny him the pleasure of her body. In fact, she had eagerly urged him on—begged him. Perhaps afterward, he would propose. After he'd deeply satisfied her—and himself—he told her that his father expected him in London. Their summer was over, and he hadn't proposed. He hadn't said he loved her.

She'd cried for days and endless nights, and terror had gripped her when she realized she was carrying his child. What a fool she'd been! To believe that yielding her body to him would produce a marriage proposal was the dream of a naive girl.

Then she discovered that the gentry would never marry *trade,* and her father was at the heart of trade, no matter how wealthy and influential he'd been over the years. No matter how long she lived, she would always be beneath the nobility. She swore under her breath as she relived past humiliation. He would pay! She'd waited patiently for the perfect moment, and it had been handed to her today. She was glad that the man who'd shot the earl hadn't killed him. It was her prerogative to kill him. After all, he'd killed her those many years ago. And he'd killed Thomas.

She'd sent the boy to his father to get the life she'd dreamed of for herself, through him. She'd pinned all her hopes on the boy, believing that perhaps one day she would gain the gloss of aristocracy. It wasn't too much to ask for, was it? Not after she'd carried the son of an earl.

Roarke Harding had killed her child, of that she was sure. Her father said a fever had taken the boy, but she knew better. . . . Roarke had been unable to keep the constant reminder of her around him.

She stared at him, his pale face on the pillow, a small smile on his lips, and she longed to take a mallet to that face and destroy it. After all, he was responsible for her disfigurement. If he'd done the honorable thing and married her, she would never have thrown herself under that carriage.

Ever since she gave birth to Thomas, she'd been obsessed with revenge. The thoughts of ruining the earl had traveled in ever tightening circles until the grooves in her mind were so deep she couldn't get out of them. She'd bribed the matron at the nursing home not to notify her father until the end of the summer, when her mission would be accomplished.

And it would be. Today. She had to kill him, or never find peace again. Somewhere in the recesses of her mind she knew her goal was wrong, but she could do nothing to change it. He would have to die, or she would burst, explode from inside. She already felt as if her head was expanding with pain.

Fumbling among the folds of her apron, she pulled out the hunting knife and tested its blade. Caressing the smooth wooden handle, she knew it would do its job swiftly and efficiently. Ever since she'd left the asylum, she'd planned for this day. And now it was here. She got up and walked slowly toward the bed. In dismay, she realized that he was awakening. She had to act fast.

Roarke stirred from a deep slumber and stretched with contentment, feeling slightly better. The sapping weakness that had weighed his limbs since the shooting was still there, but not quite as debilitating. It seemed as if his every cell had been revitalized by his sleep, and his blood sang in his veins.

He longed for Minerva, wondering how her mission at Birchington had turned out. Today he would embrace her and tell her how much he loved her. He longed for her kiss, he longed for much more than that, in fact. A sure sign he was getting better.

He pushed himself up against the pillows, halting as a twinge of pain speared his side. From the corner of his eye, he saw a movement. He'd thought he was alone in the bedroom. He turned his head and watched the woman coming toward him, Rosie, Minna's repulsive abigail.

The woman looked sickly pale and beads of sweat ran down her face. He noticed in alarm that she was trembling, and as her hand emerged from the folds of her gown, he saw the deadly glitter of a blade.

Minna's skin seemed to tighten with worry as she watched Mr. Wylie on the opposite seat of the coach. He'd been silent all the way from the village, but his face held a ghostly green pallor that spoke of his agitation. His knuckles looked white around the knob of his cane.

Minna gave a prayer that the carriage would travel faster, but the fastest pace was not fast enough. Melchior held her hand in a firm grip, and she wished he could stop this nightmare, but like her, he was helpless until they arrived back at The Towers.

"Rosie has been working for me all summer," Minna said to Mr. Wylie. "Why didn't you try to find her before this?"

"I had no idea that she'd escaped from the asylum. It seems that the generous allowance I sent to Isobel went to bribe the matron. You see, it's a small and rather exclusive nursing home, and the matron—who's also the owner of the old house—has absolute power."

"Isobel is dangerous. She's played the part of grateful maid for so long that I would never believe your slander against her—if it weren't for the evidence of her mangled face." Her anger was rising slowly as she watched the old man who'd ruined her life once, and—through Rosie—would ruin it again.

"I can't forget the day she got that face," Wylie said, brushing his hand across his eyes. "She was demented after Thomas died. She kept saying that he was her last chance."

"Chance to what?" asked Melchior.

Wylie sighed. "She had dreams above her station in life. Always wanted to become part of the gentry. I'm afraid I'm partly to blame. I spoiled her terribly."

"It's too late for regrets now," Minna said coldly. "Let's pray that she hasn't attacked Roarke in his sleep."

At last, the carriage turned up the long drive. She could barely sit still for the anguish of not knowing what had happened at The Towers. Rosie would have had plenty of time to execute her revenge.

Rosie lunged, her arm lifted above her head, the blade glistening in the sunlight. In any other circumstance Roarke would have kicked out against her arm and disarmed her, but at this moment his legs were trapped under the cover. Besides, he still hadn't regained his strength. Just as the knife made the downward turn from her hand, he rolled over. The blade cut through his pillow with a ripping sound. He heard her harsh breathing right next to his ear.

In a split second he lifted his head and cracked it backward, hitting her face. She screamed in pain, but as he dashed a glance over his shoulder, he noticed that she was standing again, the knife back in her hand. Blood streamed down over her mouth from her nose, and feathers from his ruined pillow danced crazily in the air around them.

"Why?" he grated between stiff lips, as he gathered the strength in his legs to push away to the other side of the wide bed. "Why are you doing this?"

A keening noise came from her mouth, and she made another attack, this time slicing through his nightshirt close to his waist.

The sheets were tangled around his legs, and he couldn't get leverage enough against the soft mattress to gain the opposite side of the bed. His wound ached as he made a lunge for her hand that still held the weapon, but she was faster. His fingers brushed against the sharp blade as she pulled it out and up over him. A sharp pain sliced through his hand, but he didn't care. Knowing that he was trapped in the bed, he fought desperately to get away. As she struggled to maintain her balance, blood dripped from her chin onto him. He yanked a pillow from the bed and pushed it at her head. She hacked at it with her knife, then ripped it from his grip in fury.

With both her hands, she lifted the hunting knife above his chest, but before she could sink it into his flesh, he launched himself from the bed and went for her throat. He felt the coldness of the blade rip the side of his nightshirt, shaving the very hairs off his skin. Even as the old wound in his side burst into flames of pain, his hands closed around her neck and squeezed. Her mobcap shielded her hideous face from view, and she bucked and fought, lying half on the mattress, half off.

Dots of blackness entered his vision, and he felt faint with weakness. He couldn't let go . . . if he did he might fall into oblivion and then she would finish him off. His hands were losing strength, and he trembled all over, his skin growing clammy with perspiration.

Her movements had stilled somewhat but she was tough. He tried to squeeze that sturdy neck harder. Only a few more seconds . . . a few more. His body screamed with pain, and he knew he would faint at any moment with the sheer agony of the exertion. One, two, three, four, five . . . he counted the seconds, but she was still thrashing. Then all at once, his strength left him and he felt weaker than a baby. He slumped down on the disheveled bed, his consciousness coming and going with every breath.

She lay very still at first, but soon stretched her body and started coughing. Somewhere in his hazy mind, he knew when she got off the mattress, and he heard the faint scrape of metal against the floor as she retrieved the weapon.

Urgent signals from his mind told his body to move, to do something to protect himself, but every ounce of strength had drained from him. As he sensed her stretching up, up, arm lifting with a crackle of fabric, he raised his leaden arm to shield himself from the blow. Blackness hovered, closing in on him rapidly.

Minna rushed up the stairs closely followed by

Melchior. He was faster and passed her on the landing. "Hurry, please hurry," Minna muttered under her breath, although he was running as fast as he could along the corridor.

She heard a blood-curdling shriek coming from Roarke's bedroom, and Minna's heart almost stopped with fright. Her legs seemed to lose their substance as she stumbled along the interminable corridor.

Thank God for Melchior, she thought, watching as he wrenched the bedroom door open and plunged inside. Minna reached the threshold, and saw Roarke's lifeless body in a welter of bed-clothes. Blood was everywhere on the white sheets.

The crazed woman had turned on Melchior, the knife flashing evilly in her hand as she sliced it down at his arm. Melchior side-stepped neatly and kicked out, sending the knife flying through the room and clattering to the floor at Minna's feet.

She stared at it hypnotically, then lifted it and dropped it into a deep copper flower urn by the door.

Rosie sat down on the edge of the mattress sobbing, her hands hiding her face. Melchior jerked her upright and led her across the floor. He pushed her down into a chair at the other side of the room.

Minna's legs trembled so much she thought she wouldn't reach the bed without falling down. Sobbing, she stared at her lifeless husband, noting his pale face and blood-smeared shirt. She smoothed down his hair, and to her surprise, he stirred, moaning.

"He's alive," she cried and dipped a towel in the wash basin beside the bed. Placing that cool wet pad on his forehead, she watched him regain consciousness.

"Am I in heaven then?" he asked as his eyes focused on her. They were dark with pain.

"No . . . not yet," she said softly.

Rosie's wails rose higher as Mr. Wylie entered the room. Panting hard, he was leaning heavily on his stick. Minna threw him a cursory glance, then returned her attention to her husband.

"I was worried sick," she began, and searched his body for knife wounds. Besides the old wound that was bleeding again, she found only a shallow cut along the inside of the fingers of one hand.

"Why did Rosie attack me?"

Minna's gaze flew to his face. "You don't know? She didn't tell you?"

"No, she came at me with a knife. Thank God I had just awakened. I could protect myself, but it was touch and go. She almost got me in the end."

"Well, you're safe now." Minna took a deep breath. "She's not really Rosie Long; she's Isobel Wylie."

Roarke flinched as if she'd slapped him. "Isobel? But I thought she was dead."

"Mr. Wylie led us to believe that, but in truth, she lived at a private nursing home in Berkshire. It seems that Thomas's birth unhinged her. She got that disfigurement after she threw herself in front of a moving carriage." She gave him a searching glance. "How do you feel?"

"Weak, but glad to be alive. Phew, I'm glad you arrived in time, or our marriage would have ended before it even started."

"I feel somewhat guilty about this. After all, I hired her in the spring believing that she was a woman who'd fallen on hard times. I see now that she had this planned all along."

"But how could she know that you would get involved with me?" he asked, creasing his

373

brow.

"We must ask her that after I've sent one of the footmen to fetch the doctor."

Mr. Wylie stomped across the room and sat down in a chair across from Isobel. "What in the world induced you to attempt killing the earl?" he asked gruffly. "Don't you have enough misery on your plate?"

Isobel stubbornly refused to look at him. Melchior was holding a detaining hand on her shoulder. He looked murderous. "You could hang for this," he threatened.

"I don't care," Isobel said sullenly. "What do I have to live for?"

Minna joined the small group. "I could strangle you, Rosie—Isobel," she said angrily. "I trusted you implicitly."

Isobel looked up, her eyes filled with hatred. "I worked for you, yes, but do you think I liked it? If you must know, I hated brushing your hair." She spat toward Minna, who took a step back at the vicious outburst.

"I hired you when no one else would."

"Ha! I didn't need your money. I kept my father under surveillance for some time after I left the nursing home. I overheard your conversation in the courtyard at Clifford Street and I discovered Father's blackmail scheme. Then I realized that I could take advantage of that."

"Why didn't you come to me?" Mr. Wylie asked in a broken voice. "I could have helped. Besides, in your name I ruined Lord Whitecliffe—up to a point." He gave the earl a dark glance. "I've noticed that he's turned his difficulties to his advantage, and my hat is off to him. I admire such strength and determination."

"Nothing but his death could assuage the pain

in my heart," Isobel wailed. "Don't you see? He ruined my life."

Minna frowned, longing to slap her former maid who'd deceived her from the start. "No, Isobel, you ruined your own life."

Isobel gave her a venomous glance. "What do you know about life? You were the daughter of humble clergy, then learned a trade. Why should you—who's nothing more than me—marry nobility?"

"It wasn't the end of the world when you couldn't marry a nobleman, Isobel," Mr. Wylie said in a tired voice. "You could have had any number of wealthy, influential husbands if you hadn't been so stubborn. Anyway, Lady Whitecliffe is in reality the daughter of an aristocrat. In the time of her deepest disappointment and despair she worked harder. She accomplished with little money and in a short time what no idle nobleman could have accomplished in a lifetime."

Minna gave the old man a glance of grudging respect. At least the old man had understood her struggles and supported her when she needed him. And he'd conveniently forgotten that trip to the bridge that dark night long ago.

"What shall we do with her?" Melchior asked, staring at Minna. "She could be tried for attempted murder."

"No," said Roarke from the bed. He'd heaved himself up against the pillows, and Minna went to his side.

"Is that what you really want, Roarke?"

He nodded. "Isobel," he called out. "I was very young and arrogant when I met you in Brighton. It was the habit of young blades to have a mistress, and I thought you were lovely and desirable."

Mr. Wylie scowled at him and Isobel sobbed in her hands. "Let me continue," Roarke said. "I know that what I did to you was terrible, but at the time it never entered my mind to wed you. I'd never been taught to respect anyone but my peers. However, I learned from my mistake, and I know I can never repay you for your pain." His voice broke, and his throat worked convulsively. "I didn't deliberately set out to ruin your life."

Isobel was standing now, but Melchior was holding her back. "I hate you; and that will never change. You killed Thomas."

Roarke stared at her with disbelief. "You know better than that, Isobel! Thomas died of a fever. I would never have done anything to hurt that boy. He was the light of my life!" Roarke moved agitatedly as if to get up, but Minna restrained him. "Thomas was the best thing that ever happened to me. I was going blind and loneliness closed in around me when he came into my life. He taught me to laugh again."

Isobel stared uncertainly at him, and an appalling silence hung in the room. Minna held her breath, and everyone else seemed to do the same.

"I owe you a thank you for sending him to me, Isobel," Roarke said quietly.

Suddenly Isobel's shoulders sagged and she started to cry noisily. She slumped to the floor at Melchior's feet and beat her knotted fists against the Oriental carpet.

"What now?" Melchior asked, spreading his hands in a gesture of defeat.

"Let her cry," Roarke said tiredly. "Then it's for Mr. Wylie to decide what to do with his daughter. I won't press charges."

Minna quelled the protest on her tongue. Rosie-Isobel had betrayed her deeply, but she could tell that Roarke still felt guilt for the careless acts of his youth. Through Thomas he'd been linked to Isobel in a complex way, and perhaps long-ago memories colored his decision.

"I'm grateful for that," Mr. Wylie said weakly. He looked as if he'd aged ten years in one day. He walked to his crying daughter and placed a protective arm around her. "Do you understand now, Isobel? The earl truly cared for Thomas." He pulled out a handkerchief from his pocket and pressed it into her hand. "Let's put all this behind us and start anew. Forgive and forget is the only way out." He led Isobel toward the door, and she went without a struggle. She stopped before leaving the room and faced Minna.

After wiping her nose, she said, "I didn't mean to lash out at you. Your heart is full of compassion, and I envy you for that. I'm sure nobody else would have hired me." She bent her head, her gaze shifting away. "Goodbye."

Minna's heart twisted at the pathetic sight. Anger mingled with pity as she watched the broken woman leave, leaning heavily on her father.

"What a waste of life," Minna' said, and vowed silently to cherish every day as it was given to her.

Melchior retrieved the hunting knife from the urn and wrapped it in a towel. "Best get this out of sight." He made a move toward the door with the weapon, but Roarke halted him.

"I owe you an apology, coz," he said, "and a heartfelt thank you." He drew Minna down beside him on the mattress, and held her hand firmly. She wanted to snuggle up beside him, but not as long as Melchior was in the same room.

Melchior gave a lopsided smile. "Don't mention it. If you were in my shoes, you would have done the same thing." He came toward the bed with his hand outstretched. Roarke pulled him down and gave him a hug.

"I'm sorry you had to live through the pain of losing Aladdin, then the torture of your wound. It could have finished you off, you know," Melchior said as he stood once more.

"I'm as tough as a leather sole."

Melchior's color heightened in his already ruddy cheeks. "I can't tell you how ashamed I am for Aunt Edna. I knew she bore a grudge toward you because you were the Whitecliffe heir, but never in my wildest dreams did I think she would plan your demise."

Roarke frowned. "What are you talking about?" He stared from Minna to Melchior. "Did you know about this?" he asked Minna.

She nodded. "Lady Barton hired a ruffian to shoot you, a man from Margate called Hector Jones." She shuddered delicately. "Not exactly the kind of person I would like to meet on a dark country road." She caressed the smooth skin of Roarke's hand. "This will come as a shock, but he even confessed to shooting Aladdin. Edna's twisted belief was that you would ruin Melchior's livelihood with that horse."

"Of all the hare-brained—" Roarke began and tossed to his side. He groaned in pain, and Melchior helped him back up against the pillows.

"She misunderstood the whole operation," Melchior explained. His brow furrowed in thought. "Tokayer is in foal, I know that now. By Aladdin. I want you to have that foal."

Roarke gave him a long, penetrating stare. "Do you really mean this? What if she dies?"

"Joe Tulsiter says she'll do fine. Yes, you shall have that foal. I'll get more offspring from her—champions all. The important part is to get the business ventures to succeed, or else we'll eat bread made of tree bark before long."

Roarke smiled. "I accept most gratefully, and I suggest we combine our efforts from now on. If we work hard, our stables will be the best in England."

Melchior slapped Roarke's shoulder. "By Jove, I'll settle for that." He headed for the door whistling a shrill tune.

When he left Minna said, "Alone at last, darling. I want to kiss you before the doctor arrives."

Just as she bent down to fulfill her wish, a knock sounded on the door, and Kitson entered with a letter on a tray. He smiled reverently at Roarke. "I'm most pleased that you're feeling better, my lord."

"Thank you, Kitson. What do you have there?"

Kitson held out the tray and Roarke took the letter. As the butler left, Roarke read the missive rapidly.

"It's from that devil, Zach." Roarke handed her the note with a laugh. "He and Aurora are as happy as pigs in mud. Zach says they are eagerly awaiting the day when Aurora comes of age, and then the nuptials will take place. He wants to know if we'll be able to attend. Will we?"

Roarke pulled Minna down and held her against his good side. "What do you think, my lady wife? Will the doctor allow you to travel with my offspring in your belly?"

Minna pursed her lips in thought. "Hmm, I don't know if I've quite forgiven Zach for his high-handed ways, but I wish them all the happiness. Aurora is too dazzled by love to see anything but the devious charm of that scoundrel."

Roarke laughed. "We must give Zach credit for our marriage, though. If it weren't for him and his highhanded ways, we might still be sulking in London."

"We must not forget Davina," Minna said. "If it weren't for her and the birthday party in your honor, it would have been next to impossible to meet you."

"Yes," Roarke said with a laugh. "By the way, she sent us an invitation to *her* wedding in London next month. It arrived right after you left. She and Leverett Epcott aren't wasting a moment to tie the knot."

Minna traced the firm outline of his jaw. "That union has made Davina a happy woman. She helped me, and I'm glad I could have some small part of her happiness."

"What part?"

Minna laughed in delight. "I told Eve about her secret pleasure spot."

"You conniver! Where is it?"

"I'm not telling you!"

Without wasting another second, she kissed him deeply, savoring the smell and taste of him. In her heart she gave thanks to the powers above that he was still alive and kissing her back so hard her world began to tilt.

At last he whispered, "I love you, Minerva Smith Wayland Seager Harding, Lady Whitecliffe. I love you very much."

"And I love you, my dearest. I can't wait for the doctor to pronounce you well enough to sample the ardor of my love."

"To hell with the doctor," he said and pulled his hand down to her hips. "There's nothing wrong with the part of me that desires you most forcefully." He moved against her and winced. "Well perhaps . . ."

"You'll have a lifetime to prove just how much

you love me," Minna said teasingly.

He smiled, then gave a profound sigh. "My life has come full circle. I'm complete, with you I'm complete, and I have made peace with myself. It's the happiest day of my life." He kissed her hand thoughtfully. "You came into my life and brought a ray of light. It reminds me of some lines I came across in my studies:

In eternity without beginning, a ray of thy
beauty began to gleam, when Love sprang
into being, and cast flames over all nature."

He continued, "You brought love into my life, Minerva, and God illuminated my soul."

Minna wiped a tear from her eye. "It is indeed a happy day."

About the Author

Maria Greene sold her first book six years ago, and she has been writing full-time ever since, publishing Regency romances and Historicals set in such varied times as Georgian and Victorian England, and seventeenth century France.

She lives in the Finger Lakes Region of New York with her husband and two disobedient cats. She is currently working on her next Zebra romance.